MW01180540

Round Table Magician

A Paranormal Regency Romance

by Ann Tracy Marr

ISBN: 978-1-58749-631-8

Earthling Press ~ United States of America

~Dedication~

This book is for Katie and Martha. Like all good daughters, they read it again and again. Like all daughters, they complained, whined and groused their way through it, but they did it. And I couldn't have written it without them.

Chapter One

"Let me go!" Martha demanded.

She fought to detach the man's hold on her arm, dimly registering scarred boots and coarse material, dirt streaked and smelling of the sea. Her captor ignored her struggles, hauling her toward the rear doorway of the shop. Wielding his huge stomach like a lance, he shoved her maid into the shelf-covered wall. Baskets tilted, spilling ribbons. One straw container fell atop Daisy, obscuring her panicked face.

Martha lost her footing amidst slippery ribbons and tripped over the maid's extended leg. She thought her heart would stop beating when the hand clenched around her arm didn't shift.

"My lady," Daisy howled.

His cruel fingers dug tighter, twisting and tearing her sleeve at the seam. She squirmed, hitting at the man with her reticule, mostly missing and flailing herself instead. The panic of an unarmed squire facing a rogue dragon assailed her. Would her luck hold against this unkempt fiend? Or would he beat her—stab her?

In an instant, they were in the doorway to the back room, tangling with a curtain meant to shield the eye from the littered storeroom. He pulled at the cotton with a curse. The nails holding the material let go, bouncing off Martha, and the curtain draped around her shoulders. Sneezing, she tried to dive to the floor. Her attacker hauled her, curtain and all, into the room.

Dear Lord. Like the flash of deathbed memories, the scene branded into her mind. Two skirmishing groups made a melee of the shop. The first cadre was roughly dressed men, unshaven and evil. For some reason, they wore skirts. The second, a contingent of King's archers, wore the polished Badge of Arthur on their chests. Men were everywhere. Shields, cudgels, swords, bolts of cloth and scissors waved.

Frantic women darted among the battling males. Some escaped to the street; others shrank back from the warriors. Through the broken window, Martha could see the fight continuing on the street.

The lout slid his other hand around her neck and pulled her against his chest. He assaulted her senses. Pads of rolling, shifting fat enveloped her like a grossly overstuffed mattress. She was drowning in a pillow, suffocated by a stench of sweat, rotting fish, and something vile that gagged her even as his arm shifted to throttle her. A raspy curse growled in her ear. Her captor was nothing better than a rabid dog—or a dragon. She redoubled her escape efforts, sinking her elbows and heels into fat.

The cause of the dragon's curses appeared in the doorway.

Tall, dressed not in archer's green but in Bond Street's finest midnight Bath cloth, a man stalked through the now curtainless doorway. He held a sword, its honed tip above Martha's head, pointed at the ruffian. Black hair, humorless steel gray eyes, and dark coat proclaimed him Lucifer, as did the scent of battle emanating from his athletic figure. Martha, beleaguered as she was, decided that rather than the devil, he had better be the archangel Michael come to save her. Or St. George.

"Let her go," the man said. "Hiding behind a skirt won't save you, Marshall."

"Ain't gonna," the ruffian growled and swore again. "I'm goin' out the back and ye best not folla' me, not if ye wants this mort back in one piece." He jerked Martha. She clawed at the scaly arm where it pressed against her neck and dragged fingernails across the back of his filthy hand. How dare the dragon speak so to her avenger?

He roared and shook her like a rag. That broke the stalemate between the smelly beast and the dark angel. Martha caught a flash of blinding white from his perfectly tied cravat as the man leaped forward. The sword sang over her head and the arm imprisoning her fell away.

She dropped to her knees, gasping, barely aware that the dragon behind her had also fallen. Her hair lost its few remaining pins and cascaded in a dark tangle around her shoulders. Her new cottage bonnet was gone. Shocked, she huddled on the floor.

She had come to rest at the feet of the divine avenger. He knelt and laid the sword at his side. The shining tip dripped red and she flinched at the sight. Then relief at deliverance pushed away the scruples that would normally make bloodshed untenable. *The angel won,* she exulted as the sounds of battle diminished in the front room. *He killed that nasty dragon and saved me, just as a proper hero should.* She sighed approval. His attire no longer seemed devilish.

Pinching her chin in his fingers, the celestial being's voice rumbled like distant thunder. "No, my dear," he said, "don't think about Marshall. It is sufficient to know he is no longer a threat. Did he harm you? Are you injured?"

The dragon? She did not care about the dragon; the heavenly being held her attention. "No, not really," she responded. "There wasn't time before you came." No longer the cold of freezing rain, the seraph's eyes had the sheen of a lake glinting in the summer sun. "Thank Avalon you came. You arrived just when you should. Thank you."

He glanced over her shoulder into the shop, where the sounds of battle had faded into the booted cadence indicative of a military victory. Reminded she should still be on the edge of panic, Martha asked, "What is happening? Where did the dragons come from?"

"Not dragons," the angel responded, turning back to her, "smugglers; a repellant group of them. This one," he gesticulated, "was the look-out, Marshall. No kitten, don't peek. Marshall is not worthy of attention." He controlled her swiveling head, burying his hands in her hair. "We started out at the docks and ended up here. The smugglers are wilier than thought and slipped through the net set to capture them. If I had realized they would invade the shop, I would have..." His lips quirked. "Well, hindsight is clearer than the falcon's eye. Gaol will be full tonight."

"Is there any pretty silk?" she asked before she thought.

"Silk? You don't want to purchase smuggled goods," he said, cocking his head. "I imagine the archers would frown on that."

"But..." she trailed off. She wanted to say, "Distributing lengths of silk would quiet complaints about this dreadful happening," but it was not her concern.

While they spoke, the celestial being smoothed her hair into a respectable braid. He reached the curling ends and tied the three rich hanks into a neat knot. His handling her hair almost dissolved Martha. Who would have thought angels could be fierce one moment, slaying vile dragons or smugglers, and tender the next, playing maid. Her savior's touch did more to unsettle than his words soothed. It tingled. She instinctively shivered.

Lord Brinston misunderstood the chit's trembling, taking it for a sign of residual fear. Thinking what form that emotion would take in most of the ladies of his acquaintance, he knew his duty: placate the girl and get her to some smelling salts as soon as possible. Above all, he had to keep from laughing. Did she really think she could buy smuggled silk with a contingent of archers watching? To come up with that with Marshall on the floor behind her...*Either she's nicked in the nob or she's as fey as Coletta.*

Keeping his touch gentle, Brinston brushed wisps of dark hair from the girl's face. By Arthur, it was the softest he'd ever touched. Curls twined around his fingers like ivy up a signpost. *Enough,* he ordered his fingers to behave.

Dalliance in the face of death—what was he thinking of?
He'd better divert the chit from the horror of the past
minutes or she'd start screeching. Nothing was worse than
screeching women.

She stared up at him like a lamb missing its mother.

Merlin, he recognized this one now. Her brother had
shown him a miniature; there could be no mistake.
Dunsmore, that would be her last name. He couldn't recall
what Hurst called her—Margaret? Agatha? She'd been a babe
when he met Hurst at Eton, so she'd be about seventeen
now—a schoolgirl.

Saving the chit from the smuggler became personal;
his friend's sister needed him. *That puts paid to my
interrogating the spy immediately. Damn the lieutenant for his
ineptitude—puts me in charge of a girl I have no business being
near. If he fumbles one more time, I'll see he commands a unit in
the hinterlands. I'll have to escort this kitten back to her school.
Can't just leave her to get where she belongs.*

*And no one to chaperone. Wouldn't the gossips love to
hear about this. They'd have me seducing her in a pool of
Marshall's blood.*

"Daisy," she murmured and leaned into the warmth
of his chest. "She was pushed down." With the slightest
pause, Brinston lowered his head and brushed his lips across
her forehead, though he could not have said why he did such
a shocking thing.

*Praise the innocence of Perceval, hope she doesn't fall
apart on me now.*

"A moment, my dear. I will check on your Daisy," he
whispered. Positioning the girl at the door to the alley, facing
out, he motioned an archer to watch her and went out front
to talk to the subaltern. Lieutenant Collins bumbled the
entire operation. *No wonder Du Lac wanted me here. Can't do
the easiest pickup without me to hold their hands. To let them get
into town, near the ladies...Now, I'm saddled with the balmy
chit. Silk. She wants silk.* He shook his head at his half-hearted

grumbling and surveyed the scene.

The front of the shop was a shambles with three men staring sightlessly at the ceiling. On the street, archers still sorted out the malefactors. One man disdainfully stripped skirts off smugglers, tossing them into a pile in the gutter. Not a citizen in sight, not even the shop owner. *Only to be expected. Stores might as well close for the day. How are we going to smooth this over? The mayor's going to want someone's head.* Making a quick survey for the lost Daisy, he rushed through the business of cleaning up. He ordered the smugglers off to gaol, heavily guarded. The pile of skirts could be left. Someone would spirit it away.

"Collins," he barked, "Wake up, man. Fetch the bolts of silk the smugglers hid in that cave and offer them to the shop owner. He can sell the goods cheap—that will satisfy his complaints, and maybe some of the others that are going to fly over this mess. I'll take responsibility."

He had to get back to stave off hysterics.

Brinston made it back through the doorway in record time. By all that was holy, she was twisting her head, looking around like the curious kitten he had called her. If she wasn't careful, she would get an eyeful of Marshall's body—with a distinctly untidy slash in the forehead. Females could be the devil. Couldn't look at a corpse with composure. They screamed and carried on, even when death was unavoidable, like now. If this one took a good look at Marshall...

The archer scurried away at his approach. The man obviously didn't know what to do with the Dunsmore chit. Neither did he, not really. Clean her up and get her back to her school; let someone there comfort her.

No reasonable topic innocuous enough to divert hysterics popped into his head. "Ramsgate is pleasant," he said, wincing at the confounded drivel, but unable to stop. "I became familiar with the town when the Navy began embarking for Persia and the search for the Ark." Belatedly, he thought he could have introduced the weather as a conversational topic.

He dug in his pocket and produced a handkerchief to wipe her face. When one recalcitrant spot of grime defeated Brinston, he whispered, "With your permission." Then he licked the cloth and wiped again at the dirt. It came off skin as smooth as the bowl of the grail.

No, she wasn't his sister, not with those chocolate eyes. Or that soft as soap hair...She wasn't even whimpering. Just stared at him like he was Excalibur.

"About the silk," she said softly. "I don't want it, but it would placate the shopkeeper."

Alarmed at the tenderness he felt, Brinston nodded and lifted her by the elbows, careful to keep the plucky girl facing the alley so she didn't see the fallen smuggler. Saving her from Marshall had been a duty not to be shirked; now he could legitimately abandon her by finding a respectable lady to return her whence she belonged. Collins would need him to handle the mayor. Instead, he intended to see this valiant soul home.

Valiant soul? Gads, what's wrong with me? Going poetic. There isn't anything special about her; she's only Hurst's sister. Just a child. But she thought about the damage to the shop—what it would mean to the owner.

She didn't come to his chin, the feisty little kitten. Brinston smoothed his fingers over the reddened skin of her arm as if to wipe away the rising bruise. *Yes, she is valiant; look how she struggles to contain herself. Even my sister would be in hysterics after being hauled around by Marshall. This chit, young as she is, has the presence of a queen. She is shaken, but not stirred out of her composure.* Tugging at the curtain that clung to her back, he untangled the young lady.

"I think I should accompany you home, my dear," he rumbled. "Your Daisy has already disappeared. Most of the females had escaped when I came." He noted the red streaking her back. It would take magic to get all that blood off her. At least she hadn't noticed it.

"Keep your eyes closed, kitten," he ordered. The Dunsmore girl's eyes fluttered closed, but darted back and forth under the lids is if they would open any moment. Mumbling a few indistinct words, he made a curious gesture along her shoulder blades. A myriad of tiny lights sparked along her back. With each twinkle, flecks of blood and gore fell from the dress to the floor. Before she could blink, all of the blood had slid off the girl.

"Now, open your eyes," he commanded. Her lids flipped up and he chuckled at her docility. Thank Merlin, that didn't faze her. Better the smell of lilac than blood.

A breeze blew in their faces from the open door. Led by the hand, Martha Dunsmore picked her way through the filthy alley. Broken crates and barrels littered the way. Ale fumes lingered. A solitary wagon sat with a broken wheel, its driver nowhere in sight. "I wonder, are you always so obedient?" her angel asked. A smile reverberated through his words. "From the way you fought Marshall, I thought you had spirit."

Overcome by his proximity, Martha stared at her savior, thoughts twinkling in her head. He handled everything in such a masterful manner...and Avalon, he had kissed her forehead.

His eyes flickered like lightning. Just like lightning. Her skin sizzled.

"A moment," he murmured and deftly tucked the torn sleeve of her gown up. "Now you pass muster," he promised, and took her into the street, leaving behind the stale aroma of dust and ale. "Where do you live?"

She gave him the address of Miss Kilborn's school. Then Martha had to leap to keep up with the angel's long stride as he moved down the street. He didn't look in shop windows or gaze at the passers by, but swung his arms and legs with military precision in a ground-eating march.

My, he doesn't like to amble, does he, Martha thought. *He walks faster than my brother. It is those long legs. Men forget that ladies cannot go apace.* She skipped, jumped, and half-ran to keep up. With the brisk exercise, the shocking events in the shop were fading. She found her tongue.

"I can't believe what happened. I was looking for a present for Aunt Pemberton—there was a lovely pink Norwich shawl. And purple gloves. But those men barged in. They broke the door—and the window—one woman was pushed out the window. Her boots caught on the frame." Her angel put out a hand to check her while a dray lumbered over the cobblestone, then took her arm and crossed the street. "They threw bolts of material at each other."

She stumbled over the curb, missing the step because her gaze focused on her avenger. He glanced at her, a flickering of steely gray, but didn't answer. "That smuggler, Marshall. What did he do that the archers were after him?"

She blinked hard and tried again. "You said Marshall was the look-out. Was it a large group of smugglers? From what I could see, there were hundreds of men fighting." A puddle of mud had her tiptoeing in double time. "Though I daresay that is an exaggeration. Hundreds would not have left room in the shop for people to move."

"No, there were not hundreds," the man said dryly.

"Perhaps a score or fifteen of each, then. I think there were five or so smugglers in the shop, not counting that dreadful Marshall. It is silly, but I could have sworn they wore skirts. No–" A servant laden with packages to the eyebrows stepped into her path. Martha swerved in avoidance and hurried to catch up with the celestial Bath cloth. She nearly collided with the servant's mistress.

That woman, double chinned but dressed to the nines, stared at them and huffed, "Well, I never." Then her mouth opened in astonishment. "Why, are you in Ramsgate?" she asked rudely.

Giving a quick bow, he mumbled, "No you never will again, either," and whisked around the corner.

She seemed to recognize him, Martha thought. *Why*

wasn't he more polite? "I apologize," she began, but her angel had moved on. Shaking her head, she hurried around the corner. She had to catch up.

He was grumbling. "Would have to run into her. By Merlin, why couldn't it have been someone else?"

"Do you know that lady?" Again, he didn't reply. Thinking that angels could be as maddening as brothers, Martha went back to the absorbing topic of smugglers. "Did they do very bad? Or merely smuggle, as smugglers are wont to do?" He didn't even turn his head, so she explained. "The quest for the Ark is ended—I doubt they were spying. My brother told me that smugglers did a drop of selling information to...that pest, Napoleon." Her breath came in gasps.

Not losing a step, he pivoted his head. "What did your brother say?"

A knot of schoolboys blocked the walkway. Martha pursed her lips. Ah, they parted like the waters for the Lady of the Lake. "Hurst didn't say much," she tardily answered, "only that some smugglers...helped France against us."

He said something. It sounded like "Can't keep his trap shut." She put on a spurt of speed. If she were at his side, rather than tagging along half a step behind, she could hear better.

"I don't know any...smugglers personally," she gasped. Her breath was about gone. "Well, perhaps Marshall. But...they don't do a great deal of harm, do they? They only...bring brandy for gentlemen...and...silk..."

At least he looked at her. This angel was more enigmatic than those in the holy book. *Vera would say he is the strong, silent type. But he definitely walks too fast.* The angel outpaced her. Martha gave up and slowed her step. Taking a deep breath, she continued, "Since the search is over, even if they sold information, it wouldn't count, would it? Not now. Or did these particular smugglers need catching for doing something more dreadful during the search? I know that

Napoleon was ruthless, trying to beat us to Mount -"

He stopped. Stopped walking, stopped swinging his arms. Unprepared, Martha nearly walked past him. "Your brother," he snapped. "He didn't perhaps tell you what happens to curious cats, did he?" His eyes shot sparks. Long, darting flames of sparking magic dust danced in his eyes. Then he started walking again and she couldn't see his eyes. For a miracle, he shortened his step.

Martha couldn't catch her breath, so she kept silent, as did the man. She hadn't been offended by his abrupt scold; it was rather comforting. Her brother tended to be curt also. But Hurst's eyes never looked so marvelously fierce.

By the time they arrived at their destination, Martha would have braved a thousand Marshalls to spend a minute more in her seraph's company, but his leave-taking was brusque.

"I'll not come in," he said at the steps. "Girls' schools don't like men cluttering up their halls. Good day, miss." He swung on his heel and strode away. Martha watched him sidestep a footman walking a leashed pug and then turn the corner. Standing on the steps, inhaling grimy smoke from the chimneys above her head, she neglected to examine her innermost feelings, but captured the unvoiced thought like a butterfly on clover. *Perfect.*

Thankfully, the stern proprietress of an Academy for Young Ladies, a mortal dragon known as Miss Kilborn, didn't witness her charge's bedraggled return from a shopping expedition. The repercussions of so dire an event would have been more traumatic than the smugglers' battle at the shop. After verifying that Daisy had made a safe return, Martha closeted herself in her room, soothed by her roommate, Vera Jackson. They analyzed the ordeal, although smugglers were the farthest thing from Martha's mind.

"Vera," she said, "I have changed my mind. Heroes such as you find in novels are real." She was remembering an angel, dressed in vengeance and Bath cloth.

"Pooh," was the wide-eyed reply. "You don't mean that. You scoff at my books."

"Oh, but I can, and I do. The man who saved me was so..." Martha couldn't find words and fingered the bruise that ringed her arm where the smuggler had handled her. "He had a sapphire pin in his cravat. I forgot to thank him for saving me. Or did I?"

"It was most romantic, I must admit," Vera said. "But why call him an angel? He sounds more like St. George."

"He is more special than St. George."

"Who is he?"

Martha sighed. "He never gave his name. But he walked me all the way back. Vera, his eyes...they looked so cold at first, like the mist on a winter's morn, but then they turned silver. His manners were gentlemanly and he took the greatest care of my sensibilities. It is by his doing that my hair was knotted—he tidied it and put it in a braid." A shiver ran down her back. "He is very good with a sword also," she said inadequately.

"You will most likely never see him again," Vera reminded her. Both girls sighed.

* * *

The exclusive club was quiet. Sir Hurst Dunsmore sat by the fire, hiding behind a newspaper. He was thinking about his sister, Martha. Next year she would be at Camelot for her first season; he had resorted to writing lists of things to do for the momentous event.

Only a year before she came out. Sir Hurst wanted to be ready.

Trying to remember the name of the outstanding orchestra Mrs. Denby had hired, he was startled when Brinston dropped into the chair opposite, juggling a bottle. The newspaper fell and a grin split Hurst's face when he recognized one of his closest friends.

"Well. If it isn't Richard, the Most Honorable Knight Shipley," he said dryly. "Thought you had disappeared into Merlin's cave. Where've you been—on a quest? I looked for you in the Great Hall and later at the Heraldic ball. Thought sure you said you'd be there. Missed quite a gala—Caro and Byron had a dustup on the dance floor and the queen flapped her hands at them like chickens in her vegetables. I haven't laughed so hard since Perth fell out of the saddle."

Lord Brinston smiled. "My apologies, I was out of town." He scratched his stomach. "Forgive the vulgarity, Hurst, but Lady Pewett served marzipan. Must have had cinnamon in it; I've got welts all over. But that isn't my title, you knothead."

"It is now."

"Great Merlin. You mean the Council dumped another knighthood on my head?"

Hurst nodded. "Yes, the third, isn't it? For your services during the time of the quest."

"As if that mattered." Brinston sighed. "Searching for the Ark of the Covenant was one of the most witless things the Council of the Round Table has ordered. England's knights didn't need such an all-encompassing quest thrown at them."

"It spurred Napoleon and France on. Don't think those bloody jousts would have happened if he hadn't been determined to conquer every land he thought might hold the ark."

"As long as he stays on St. Helena. I have my hands full without him agitating."

Hurst filled his teacup from his friend's bottle. *Good old Brin.* With his vast estates, endless investments, and matchless manners, the man's calendar frequently exploded. One couldn't be offended if he bogged down with something, even welts. Hurst asked, "You hale enough for a whirl? Could use your support. There's a new den on King Street that promises excellent sport. Perth wants to lose his fortune there."

Brinston shrugged. "Think I can come. Appears the Council will leave me alone. I was in Ramsgate; Du Lac was certain Collins would flub and begged me to be on the scene to wipe up after him. He was right. It got a bit nasty." He leaned over and poured more brandy into Hurst's cup. "Drink up; you're not going to find my tale as amusing as Caro Lamb."

Hurst enjoyed his chum's dramatic story of smugglers evading a military ambush. There could be no surprise the marquess was in the thick of the action; Brinston had served the Council of the Round Table for years and had all the fun. Look at his first quest: he'd organized the climbing boys of London into one organization with trustworthy men to oversee them. The unscrupulous sweeps who formerly held sway over the business had tried to kill Brin. He was, after all, dismantling a lucrative trade for them. The sweeps earned the money; the climbing boys did the work for no reward other than beatings and neglect. No more.

It was just like him—Hurst had never known his friend to shy from danger. Not only was he daring, Brin was whip smart and honorable. Wasn't fair he could spin a spell...Well, wouldn't do to get into that.

Brinston could paint the Sistine Chapel with words; Collins making a mull of the maneuvers put Hurst into whoops. "Fifteen of the ugliest females ever to grace the earth; that's what the men thought of the masquerading smugglers. They clomped into Ramsgate, boots under their skirts of all things, and the archers never thought a thing of it. Thank God Collins's subordinate was awake. He got a snoutful of the tale and hied off after the group with ten men who'd been posted to watch a warehouse. He took a chance, deserting his watch, but it paid off."

Through his chuckles, the thought hit Hurst. Why was Brinston relating this tale when he was normally so reticent about his activities?

"The archers caught up with the smugglers on the high street of Ramsgate, in front of a lady's emporium," Brinston continued. "You know the sort of place—a couple of counters—ribbons and lace. The lieutenant, after his genius deducing the smugglers' plan, made the mistake of challenging the 'women' right there in the presence of the citizenry. The gang headed into the shop in their skirts." He shrugged his disgust. "They had nowhere else to go."

His laughter fading, Hurst began to worry. Brin had warned he would not like the tale. The setting being Ramsgate, he had a suspicion... He interrupted. "My sister is at Ramsgate—Martha. You know what she looks like; I showed you her miniature." Brinston nodded and stared at the floor.

Silence fell as Hurst digested the tale, then he raised sharp eyes to his friend. "Finish," he demanded. "I had better know the worst."

"It isn't quite that bad," Brinston said. "She was in the shop of course, and one of the gang hauled her into the back room. Evidently, he thought your sister would make a dandy hostage. I intervened before Martha suffered more than slight bruising and saw her back to school. Never guessed that I removed the bastard's blood from her with a spell." His mouth tilted. "Your sister has as much pluck as you ever did. Called them dragons." He raised a hand as Hurst opened his mouth.

"Allow me to finish. Your sister was not hurt, but I did spend considerable time with her alone. And Sir Belvedere's lady saw us on the street. You know how she embroiders her gossip. She'll say we had an assignation. If that tale becomes common knowledge, Martha will be compromised. People are perfectly capable of saying I took advantage."

Then Brinston said the unthinkable. "I am prepared to offer marriage, though it's a damn shame your intrepid sister should be forced into a marriage that might not be to her liking."

"I would have no objection to you as a brother-in-law," Hurst said, knitting his brows. "You're one of my closest friends. How could I object? I agree, your reputation could make it look bad. However, Martha shouldn't be pushed into wedlock at the point of Lady Belvedere's tongue. She's just leaving school, for God's sake."

"Martha deserves a season and the chance to be the reigning toast before she chooses a husband." Brinston slammed the empty bottle on the table.

Hurst finished his brandy with a flourish. "I know your opinion of arranged marriages."

"Those appalling alliances should be banned." Brinston's chin elevated. "They are the ones that turn out licentious. Having witnessed my parents together, I believe common attraction the only valid basis for wedlock. Couples should have a minimum length of acquaintance of at least six months before they wed. Takes that long to know each other."

He stood and bowed as if to Almack's doyennes. "But you don't need to hear my rant again. I've said it often enough. There are situations where my convictions cannot hold. This may well be one." He took a deep breath. "At this time, I ask your formal permission to wed Martha if it becomes necessary."

"You ask my permission because you must?"

Lord Brinston said, "Never would I be unwilling. That would be to insult a lady who is the equal of any man in the land. In looks, manner, and spirit Martha is wholly delightful. No, if we wed, it will be entirely to my liking."

Deep inside, a little voice started chattering. No, it would not be to his liking, not at all, but sometimes there wasn't anything less to do. Not if one considered himself a true gentle knight.

* * *

"Stay back, Vera," Martha cautioned. "Miss Kilborn is in the hall." The girls shrank into the shadows of the service stair, hoping the white of their night robes would not give them away.

"The bowl is heavy." Vera's voice was the tiniest thrumming thread.

"Don't drop it. That would ruin a scrumptious prank. At least, it will be if the Killer ever retires." Quietly, a door closed. "There. Give her a few minutes." Martha muffled a giggle with the hand not occupied holding a bowl of wet, bland smelling porridge.

"Come. That's long enough."

Two ghostly figures, one with dark curling hair loose over her shoulders, the other sporting a tidy chestnut braid, drifted along the hall. Two serving bowls tilted, their contents piled three inches deep at the edge of the door on the practical brown Axminster carpet. Fingers patted the substantial pile, then the figures flitted, white threads glimmering in the pale moonlight, to fade at a door at the end of the hall.

Vera and Martha tiptoed into the room they shared, giggling at the prank and hoping for the most dramatic conclusion to it. "Bless Ardeth for making the porridge," Vera said, scrubbing her hands with a cloth. "Miss Kilborn deserves some measure of humiliation for her tyranny. It's lucky the hallways were rebuilt. If they had not been done so, the door would open the other way and our brilliant prank would be useless." She sighed and picked under her fingernails. "How do you think them up?"

Taking her turn at the wash stand, Martha grinned. "I see possibilities," she intoned mysteriously. "Gypsies foretell the future; I sense mischief gathering in the air."

"What a lame excuse. Rather, you have your mother's imp in you."

Martha looked up, startled. "What do you mean?"

"You told me yourself. Your mother was fond of pranks and you are much like her."

"I'd forgotten," Martha said faintly. Dear Lady, she had almost revealed her deepest secret to Vera, who couldn't keep a secret to save a life. She settled for an innocuous, "Yes, I inherited an impish nature from my mother."

Vera threw her arms around her for a quick hug, smearing a bit of porridge on Martha's back. "I believe it is your most endearing trait. And none of your pranks hurt anyone. Most people get nasty—like Deborah Gaddings when she cut off Sara's braid. I am glad you come home with me tomorrow. We can create mischief at the manor to our heart's content."

"With my brother in Dorset, home would be dull as can be." Martha spread her fingers; porridge stuck them together like webbed feet. "Uncle Pemberton is immersed in his history and Aunt is so unimaginative. She never thinks clever things." When Vera looked askance, Martha clarified her comment. "Oh, I don't mean that Aunt is so very bad, only..." She sighed. "I wish living with them was more exciting." She scrubbed globs of porridge off her hands.

"My mother is tolerant of adventures," Vera promised. "I ache to get on a horse. The whole area is amenable to riding. We almost never take the carriage."

"I haven't been on a horse since I started school."

"You will like the Manor of the Ashes, even if your seraph isn't there. I doubt Papa knows anyone remotely resembling *him,*" Vera said out of the blue, attacking her fingernails with a small stick, "Oddly enough, your meeting that man sounds like a novel. I'm the one who adores reading them, and you are living a romance. I don't envy you—it sounds vastly uncomfortable."

Martha's lip wobbled, she shook her head so hard. "Man? Romance? Nonsense. Vera. That was weeks ago. And I don't even know his name; how could he be my love?"

"You have to meet your love somehow. A grand affair

with your angel would suit you. For me, an all-encompassing passion would be disquieting. I prefer comfort to excitement."

"I can do without such excitement. Though his coat could only have been made in London. It fit without a wrinkle." Martha made a *moue*. "I don't wish to wed the gentle knight, Vera, only meet him."

"From the way you speak, you are in love with him. At first sight, just like in my novels."

Startled chocolate eyes turned to her friend. "Oh, no. Not love at first sight. I would not dare. He was much too...too..."

"Perfect," Vera finished. "I told you."

Dark curls swept over the pillowcase as Martha scooted into bed. *If you knew, dear friend. It's not his perfection I find daunting, but the mastery of life I saw dancing in his eyes. He doesn't need me, even if I am descended from a puka.* Aloud she said, "Tomorrow is our last day in this dreadful place. Just think, even if Miss Kilborn figures out we piled the porridge against her door, she shan't be able to punish us." She smiled smugly.

Before they left school, she and Vera would slay the beast called Zillah Kilborn, the battle being waged with porridge arrows. Wouldn't Hurst be proud if he knew.

Chapter Two

On the chime of eight, a great thumping resounded through the hall. The downstairs maid jumped and stabbed the feather duster at a walnut table. "Oooh! Miss Kilborn's in a right bad temper this morning," she exclaimed, peeking up the stairs. She could not see the door she assumed the mistress pounded, but who else would dare?

The chatelaine stormed from the kitchen. "What is that racket?" The impertinent maid flourished her duster, guiding her superior up the stairs. Spying a group of girls milling in the upstairs hall, the chatelaine snapped, "What're you doing?"

"Coming to breakfast," Martha replied. She stood at the back of a chattering group. "We were almost to the stairs when Miss Kilborn began pounding on her door."

The chatelaine eyed Martha. "It's your fault, whatever the matter is. Bless the Lord you're leaving today," she muttered. "Well," she boomed. "Miss Kilborn, what's the matter?" Her voice slammed over the chorus of girls.

"I am locked..." the remainder of the sentence drowned in the foam of girlish voices.

"I'm frightened! I want my mama!" One little girl wailed and another, deciding it was a good idea, followed suit.

"Mama! Mama!"

Miss Kilborn shouted, "Get this door open!"

It took the handy man ten minutes to come up from the kitchen to view the situation, another ten minutes to find a chisel and hammer, and five minutes of slow hammering to break the dense pile of dried porridge into pieces and dust all over the carpet. He managed to gouge the door twice.

Finally, the portal scraped opened, a dread sight being

revealed. Miss Kilborn in her starchiest black bombazine, quizzing glass swinging from a thin black ribbon, stood revealed. Gray hair pulled back from her forehead into a knob so tight her crow's feet stretched.

At the fearsome sight, sound deadened. "Miss Dunsmore."

"Yes, Miss Kilborn. Did you wish something?" Martha's voice was sweet, modulated, and respectful of her teacher.

"Nothing," Miss Kilborn surrendered with a sigh. "Thank goodness the girl is leaving," she mouthed to the chatelaine.

* * *

The journey from Ramsgate to the Jackson estate took one convivial hour with a brief stop in Braintree for a snack of pickled cucumber sandwiches. Miss Agnes Bridewell, Martha and Vera's chaperone, didn't dampen the fun, only kept it in bounds tolerable to her ears. Martha felt comfortable following Vera's lead, treating 'Bridey' as a valued confidante.

Bouncing on the carriage seat, Vera looked ready to burst. "Bridey, it's around the curve. Watch Martha's face when she sees."

"Just keep your eyes on the right," Miss Bridewell said. As the carriage rounded the curve in the road, a vista opened. Green meadows sparkled and in the distance, a house peeked through a well-kept wood. Two tall slender turrets marked the ends.

"Vera, you never told me your home was so beautiful." Inhaling the fresh scent of grass and sunshine, Martha hung out the carriage window, admiring the myriad of mirrored windows pictured through the trees. "I have been imagining any old place. You fooled me."

Vera's lighter head popped out the window, crowding her friend in the limited area. "Did you think I live in a cottage? Ooh, look—there is Bryce Irvine on his new horse. Papa wrote how splendid the steed is. You will like him, Martha. Everybody does."

The girls watched the stallion prance along the far edge of an open green, a man straight and easy in the saddle. The thoroughbred showed excellent conformation, leaping a low hedge with its midnight tail streaming behind. Pulling into a graceful circle in front of the manor, the rider turned his head and saluted.

Martha drew back from the window, leaving room for Vera to waggle her arm at the distant figure. As she returned to her seat, Miss Bridewell straightened her chip straw. "It's time to stop playing hoyden, girls," she chided. "When we arrive at the house, I would appreciate ladylike behavior, not the crazed hooliganism you have exhibited in the carriage."

"Crazed hooligan; I like that description." Martha grinned at the prim lady on the opposite seat.

Vera pulled her spencer down where it had ridden up. "Bridey, I don't know any longer how to be a hooligan. You know Papa sent me to Miss Kilborn for that tendency to be stamped out. It worked. I am now the model of a proper young lady. I can flirt with the best."

"But my brother sent *me* to Miss Kilborn to turn me into a hooligan." Martha's reticule fell to the floor with a plop. "That is an improvement over the gremlin I was." She reached for the reticule. "Did it work, Vera?"

"Oh, yes, you are just as I was before I became improved —crazed and so much fun to be with. I hope you don't think I am too dull."

"Never!"

Miss Bridewell quieted the laughter. "Lady, hooligan, or gremlin, we are almost at the door."

"Vera, who is Mr. Irvine?" Martha asked.

"Mr. Bryce Irvine." Vera sighed. "He works for Papa with Round Table business. He is connected to Sir Hertford in some way, but hasn't a fortune. That's why he works for

Papa. He is the nicest man, and so handsome." She sighed less happily. "But...not handsome."

"And not to be flirted with, ladies." Miss Bridewell's tone was firm as a pincushion. "He has no interest in you—as you know, Vera—and his work is important."

Martha's eyes opened wide. "Miss Bridewell, I promise to be good. Can't we flirt, only a little?"

"Flirting never came to any good for a lady. You would do better to improve your minds with sermons and embroidery." Miss Bridewell's voice was so dry and her expression so comical that the carriage drew to a stop amid a gale of laughter.

The ladies debarked at the front door of the gracious manor house with Irvine's aid. Martha's knees had stiffened, but she managed to retain some measure of grace, clinging to the man's hand for a moment. Feet moored on the gravel, she scrutinized Vera's Mr. Irvine.

He was handsome, just as Vera said. Of slim build and respectable height, he had brown hair cut in a strict Brutus and a square jaw. A thin scar on his cheek added interest—did it come from a joust? Then he turned his head. Oh dear, his face did not match. Whereas the one side cut cleanly, with only the scar to mar a visage to gladden any maid's heart, the other side slipped. The cheekbone was not as prominent and the jaw sagged. No wonder Vera said he was handsome...but not.

"It appears I am the advance guard," Irvine said, bowing to each in turn. "Welcome, Miss Dunsmore. I trust you had a pleasant journey. Miss Bridewell. It is good to see you, Miss Vera."

They moved into the house. In the hall, Robert and Amelia Jackson embraced their daughter and welcomed her friend to the Manor of the Ashes. "Your presence adds to our family, my dear," Mr. Jackson said. Vera bore a remarkable resemblance to her sire in the form of her snub nose and generously curved mouth.

Mrs. Jackson added, "Vera has written so fondly of you. The two of you will rule in solitary splendor for now, Mr. Jackson and I your willing slaves. I so looked forward to having you." Vera's mother seemed a warm-hearted woman, not high in style and comfortably plump. Her most obvious characteristic was the humor with which she viewed the world. Affection brought her arms around each of the girls' waists, enveloping them in a cloud of lavender scent. "You come in good time. We will be merry later with a house full of guests."

"Guests, Mama? Pray, who has been invited?"

As Mr. Jackson disappeared down the hall, Mrs. Jackson said. "Janice will be here at the end of the month, bringing a group of her friends. Why, nearly every bedchamber will be taken."

"How delightful." Martha minded her manners.

"I consulted with Mrs. Pemberton and Sir Hurst whilst I was in town," Mrs. Jackson said, crinkling tiny lines at the corner of her eyes. "Your brother and aunt give permission for you to join in the activities of the party. Young ladies of seventeen, in my estimation, are more than ready to enjoy parties and need a bit of experience to smooth their Camelot introductions. Since you will be presented next spring, it will stand you in good stead. I will keep an eye on you." Over Vera's excited squeal, she continued, "You may begin this evening. Robert has a guest, Lord Brinston. But he will be leaving tomorrow, sadly enough." She wagged her head. "I enjoy his visits."

The girls were rapt with joy. To be out of the schoolroom—and with a noble to meet!

In the salon, they found seats arranged around Mrs. Jackson's worktable. Lavender lingered in the air, mixed with the yeasty smell of starched canvas. "Please say you find nothing amiss in my stitching." Vera's mother took up a tambour frame. "It is one of the joys of my life, Martha. This piece is for the footstool in Robert's...Oh, dear. Where is my needle?" She began patting the seat around her. "Dalton!" she called.

The butler opened the door. "Madame?" he inquired.

"My needle, now I have lost my needle." Mrs. Jackson looked pathetic. "What if someone should sit on it?"

"We shall find it, Madame." Under his direction, a footman and maid filed into the room and began searching every tabletop, seat, and around the floor. Through the doorway, others could be seen doing the same in the hall.

Five minutes later, a maid entered, curtseying. "Found it, Madame. Was in a candle, stuck straight in."

Mrs. Jackson looked perplexed. "How did I do that?"

Mr. Jackson wandered in, holding a parchment close beneath his nose. A squint testified to the lengthy periods he spent reading and lessened any similarity his eyes may have borne to his daughter's wide blue gaze. "My dear," he began, never lifting his eyes from the paper. "Would you agree to move dinner back a few minutes? Brin and I want to go over some papers before we eat. I want to be sure we finish with them. Most disturbing numbers..." He looked up. "Ah, it will be so pleasant to have these young ladies at table with us, don't you think, Amelia?" His nose dropped back to the paper and he drifted from the salon.

Vera rolled her eyes.

* * *

At dinner, the gentlemen grouped around one side of the round table, the ladies opposite, rather than intermingled, as was the custom. Unsettled, Martha kept peeking.

It was him. The Marquess of Brinston, with a crispness that bespoke Camelot, with dark hair and gray eyes like ice in water, was her celestial being of the smugglers' battle. He wore the green of fir trees and an emerald nestled in his cravat.

They met in the dining room, Mr. Jackson having

delayed the gentlemen in his study. Watching the door, Martha thought she might have seen the slightest hesitation in Lord Brinston's step when he spied her. Then again, with Mr. Jackson pausing to allow Mrs. Jackson to give him a fond kiss, he may just have been avoiding Irvine's feet. When he greeted Martha, Lord Brinston was polite. No hint of prior acquaintance flickered in his face. Her dark angel might have been greeting any lady in the kingdom, rather than the one he had saved from disaster and converted into his undying admirer with a kiss on the forehead.

Martha, on the other hand, raised an impulsive hand toward his sleeve, only to draw it back. How to explain her acquaintance with the marquess to Vera's parents? What did one *do* in this situation? She doubted her own feelings; Martha felt...oh, she didn't know how she felt. Ecstatic, hurt, confused and giddy, all at the same time.

She felt an overpowering urge to flirt, but did not dare. Now she peeked at him across a vast expanse of polished round table.

Mr. Jackson had thrown off his earlier distraction and was in a jolly mood. "This fish is tasty, my dear." He smacked his lips as he swallowed another bite of trout. "Did you send one of the lads to the stream this morning?"

"Yes, it was Jordan's turn." Mrs. Jackson beamed as she answered her husband's question. "He took less than an hour to hook a whopping number of fish so you could have your trout for dinner." She turned to Martha. "He insists on the freshest fish, my dear. It is a blessing we are so close to the coast. Trout comes from our own stream, but we have to send a groom to Ramsgate when we desire other." She shook her fork at her husband. "Most inconvenient, but Robert is adamant."

Vera leaned forward. "Papa says it's well to allow the servants to fish; every soul is improved by the contemplation of a line and running water."

Hadn't he recognized her? Toying with her fork,

Martha supposed the ache in her stomach presaged hunger. It couldn't be from thinking of the gentle knight. Lord Brinston. Her avenging angel. Her heart gave a queer little thump and the ache in her stomach intensified. She peeked again. He looked so fine—her memory from Ramsgate was accurate. The rich Celtic red of the walls suited him.

Her thoughts went in circles, chasing their tails like puppies. Hadn't he recognized her?

Bryce Irvine dragged a bite of fish through the sauce on his plate. "I should take up a pole myself and test whether I may prove a better angler than Jordan." He looked at Mr. Jackson, "We have a few more days until anything arrives from the Council, do we not?"

Jackson nodded. "The Ship is bringing it down for us. Till then you are free." The men fell to discussing where the best waters were; at the water hole past the bridge or the sheltered stretch of the stream farther up, where the water ran free and clear over stone but was shaded by willows.

The marquess was versed in the manly art of fishing, Martha noted. One could tell by his comments.

Miss Bridewell told Vera and Martha about Camelot; she and Mrs. Jackson had been in London with Janice, Vera's older sister. That young lady had enjoyed her season. Indeed, Janice was a considerable success. "I am so pleased for her," Miss Bridewell said. "She and Mr. Lacey look to be developing a sincere attachment."

Mrs. Jackson nodded and added in a low voice so the gentlemen should not overhear, "I could wish she had interested Lord Brinston. My dears, there is a man to dream of. All the ladies yearn for a glance from him. He holds himself aloof, dancing only once with any lady at the balls and showing none any particular attention. He is not as handsome as his younger brother, Squire Michael, whose profile belongs on a coin, but Brinston is a true gentle knight. And kind, which you do not find often in society. Thanks to him, we were invited to dinner at Uther House, which you know increased Janice's standing at court. Connections are so important at Camelot."

Careful not to be seen watching him, Martha's eyes wandered past her angel to the painting over the sideboard. Two hunting dogs, pointing as if just sighting their quarry, frozen forever in a golden field. It was well enough for a painting, but she wished something prettier hung there. Perhaps a dark St. George...

Mrs. Jackson noted where her eyes had traveled. "Oh, I am glad you reminded me, Martha." She beckoned to the butler. "Dalton, tomorrow the painting changes. Let's see, what shall we have?" She tapped a dimpled finger against her chin. "Yes. The landscape from the burgundy bedroom, please. Its soft tones will be much more pleasing to the ladies."

"Can't we have Cador's Pride, Amelia?" Mr. Jackson asked.

"No my dear, you may not have one of your horses. We shall be entertaining and I would be mortified to have Janice's friends stared at by a horse while they dine. Quite puts one off their meal. As if I set the table in a stable."

Lord Brinston smiled. "I doubt any gentleman will notice the decorations on the wall. The feminine decoration at the table is all-engrossing." His silvery eyes flirted with Mrs. Jackson, who actually blushed.

Vera leaned close to whisper, "Mama and Papa never agree on what art to hang in here, so they rotate the paintings. Papa likes still life's, horses, and dogs; Mama favors Constable's landscapes." Martha nodded, tasting dust instead of glazed carrots.

* * *

Five hundred good families in the kingdom. Why did she have to be visiting this one? Brinston's eye wandered down the table. It was a trick he had learned from his father;

keep one eye planted on the person seated next to you, and deliberately cross the other and look elsewhere. Thank Avalon for that Shipley trait. Not many were able to cross just one eye. Whenever he did it, he marveled that no one noticed. Jackson, for all his powers of observation, didn't.

His right eye confirmed his earlier glances. She was lovelier than she seemed in Ramsgate. Perhaps not surprising—her hair wasn't tumbled; her face wasn't frozen in horror. She didn't look like a child. Only seventeen, but older. In a way.

Not tasting the contents of his plate, Brinston reflected that the meeting had to happen sometime, but he hadn't thought it would come here. Rather, it should have been at Camelot, at the crush of a ball, where he had the safety of numbers. In the park. On Bond Street. Or at Kay House. Anywhere but under the sharp eye of Robert Jackson.

Gads, she looked as tasty as one of Elaine Kay's lobster patties. Definitely not a schoolgirl.

Movement caught his crossed eye. The tray tilted. The footman who held it was not paying attention. Miss Dunsmore would be bathed in a fountain of wine when the full tray of glasses tipped.

Red wine on that white gown. On those white shoulders. With no time to consider what he did, Brinston did what came naturally. He muttered and under the table waved his hand. The faintest shimmer of magic arced from his fingertips and flickered around his feet.

The tray tipped. The glasses fell up, sloshing good burgundy over the footman's livery. The servant's panicked cry drew attention, but the butler whisked the sputtering man out of the room and a quick mopping did not disturb the meal.

Brinston took care to give no hint that he had met the chit before, but he didn't take the time to wonder why he needed a buffer against Martha. His focus was on behaving normally in front of Jackson.

That and chastising himself for not keeping sufficient control of himself. The servants might suspect and that would never do.

* * *

The gentlemen turned their conversation to the paddocks of Newmarket. Martha, Vera, Agnes Bridewell, and Amelia Jackson held a discussion of the excursions available in the neighborhood. In the next days, the girls could choose between visiting the village, with its shops and picturesque inn that served cakes and lemonade, visiting neighbors, most especially the vicar and his family, and taking a picnic to the local ruins.

Miss Bridewell offered to review wardrobes with the girls. "Your gowns may not suffice for evenings. It would be better to be forewarned of a lack." With a glance to Mrs. Jackson she added, "I would be pleased to accompany the girls to Mrs. Tweed."

Mrs. Jackson sighed dramatically. "Agnes, you are a diamond to rival all diamonds to take on this onerous chore." A dimple flashed as she explained to Martha, "You see, my dear, although most ladies delight in all aspects of the wardrobe, it bores me silly. Miss Bridewell, on the other hand, enjoys choosing patterns, materials, and trims. I concede her superior enthusiasm. Mrs. Tweed is gratified. A wizard of a seamstress, she would bar me from her door if she dared."

"Oh, Mama!"

Ignoring Vera's faint protest, Mrs. Jackson continued. "She scolds me so; I hardly dare raise my eyes from the ground." The lady's lips twitched. "So many things are ever so much more important than wearing a stunning bonnet."

"Your superior sense of management saves you from doom, does it not?" Miss Bridewell laughed. "How else could Mr. Jackson tolerate your failure to make the best of your looks?"

Mrs. Jackson, patting the flawless bloom of her cheeks, directed the change of courses with an airy wave the butler had no difficulty interpreting. "Robert would not notice if I sprouted a wart upon my chin, Agnes, as you know. He is equally oblivious to the deficiencies of my household management." Noting her daughter's chagrin, Mrs. Jackson changed the subject.

"When our guests arrive, excursions will be planned at which you will be in attendance. It would not be good manners to disappear all the time." She leaned forward to whisper to Martha, "Wear a bonnet that is becoming."

Bemused by the teasing and achingly conscious of the gentle knight around the curve of the table, Martha colored as Miss Bridewell said, "We haven't the remains of a monastery or grand castle for you to clamber over, only a tumbled down medieval pottery that once flourished past the mill."

"It's an appealing ride, Martha," Vera promised. "Papa will not make me take a groom there if you come with me. It is almost on our land."

Vera's mother was gentle but insistent. "If you wish for a picnic luncheon, it would be as well to take a groom, my dear. I have lost too many forks and baskets from you abandoning them at the ruins. How embarrassing it was to have to crate the supplies that time we took the Herringbone family picnicking. Not a basket was available." Mrs. Jackson turned to Martha. "Vera went out every day that week, the weather was so fine. Six baskets she lost for us."

"Mr. Irvine found five in the ruins, Mama," Vera returned.

"But two belonged to the vicar and one basket had sheltered a vixen's pups and was fit for naught but the stables. Remember, Vera. Take a groom so the basket comes back."

Martha's stomach sank toward her toes as Lord Brinston ignored her. The male conversation had reverted to fishing. Mr. Jackson queried his wife, "My dear, did you remember to order that reel from London that I saw in the Gentlemen's Quarterly? Irvine should use that. I daresay it may give him the edge over Jordan at the river."

Mrs. Jackson rose, indicating the girls should leave the table. "Yes, my love," she responded, "it came the other day. But I don't recall...My lamentable management fails me again." A mischievous smile lingered on her lips. "Dalton was to have given the reel to Jordan to put on a pole, so it may no longer be perfectly new."

They left the men to their after-dinner drinks. Taking their favorite seats by the fireplace in the drawing room, Mrs. Jackson and Miss Bridewell occupied themselves with deciphering a confused embroidery design. The girls were left to themselves. Dragging Martha off to the corner, where three chairs had been arranged for conversation, Vera plopped into a chair. Looking at the elder ladies, Martha decided she had best not mention angels. They might overhear.

"So, what do you think of Mr. Irvine?" Vera asked.

"He is very gentlemanly," Martha replied. "And it is apparent he likes sauces."

Vera stifled a giggle. "I am impressed with your powers of observation. He has Cook's undying admiration; Mrs. Forge is always dreaming up new sauces for his enjoyment. It's not fair though—he ingests the heaviest as liberally as tonight and never bulges at the waist."

Picking up a portfolio of etchings from the table, Martha flipped through them, feeling the textured edge of the paper. They were uninspiring. "The sauce was good. He can't be blamed for enjoying it. How did he get the scar? Was he in a joust?" she asked, concentrating on her mental confusion about angels. Lord Brinston had enjoyed the sauce also.

Her distracted mind flew back with a jolt when her friend dissolved into laughter. "Vera," Martha exclaimed, setting down the portfolio.

"A-a j-joust," Vera gasped through her mirth. "Ho—ow ro-mantic." At last, she dragged a handkerchief from her sleeve to wipe her eyes. A smile still tugging at her dimples, she said. "Mr. Irvine wasn't in a joust." It almost, but not quite, set her off into gales again.

Martha assumed her version of the patience of Job. She crossed her arms, tapped her toe, and with Vera's infectious laughter rolling, her lips quirked. "Then how did he get the scar?"

"Last year in London Mr. Irvine stayed with us. Janice had a friend visiting." Vera crescendoed a series of chuckles, but sobered when she saw Martha's irritation. "Oh, all right. I am sorry, but it is just too funny to recall."

"It may be funny, but I haven't heard the story."

"Come and sit. I will tell all." Vera pulled Martha down onto the chair next to her. It was an uncommonly comfortable chair; Martha sank back.

"As I said, we were in London," Vera began. "Before the season began, Papa was busy. He went to the Knight's Council offices every day, but he left Mr. Irvine at home most of the time. We had a house on Pendragon Square. Janice's friend, Miss Ortonwell, came from the country to stay. Her parents were delayed by something or other and she couldn't go to their townhouse alone. Mr. Irvine liked her and decided to cut some roses to perfume her bedchamber."

"What is so funny about that?"

"I was in the conservatory when he did it. He didn't have the gardening shears, but a pair from the estate office. They didn't cut. He sawed away at the stems of Mama's favorite red roses but didn't do well at all. So he leaned over and bit one."

"Bit...a stem?"

"He scratched his cheek badly. That is the scar."

"How...repelling."

"I didn't know then, I found out later, he had already cut close to six dozen flowers and sneaked them into Miss Ortonwell's room, crammed every which way into all the vases he could find. The funniest thing is Miss Ortonwell didn't appreciate his decorating. She suffers from rose fever. She and Janice exchanged rooms for a week."

Martha didn't find the anecdote amusing. She was saved from comment by a call from Mrs. Jackson. During two hours spent in the drawing room, Martha stewed about Irvine's strange manner of courtship and her angel. Angels were more interesting; for every moment spent mulling Irvine's scar, she spent a minute on dark-haired beings.

When it was clear the gentlemen were not coming to the drawing room, the girls were released from the salon. Martha, disappointed at the missed opportunity to see her divine protector, nonetheless drew Vera upstairs. "Vera," she hissed. "It's him."

"Him?"

"My angel. He's he." A perplexed face said that Vera had not understood. Whirling the girl into her bedchamber, Martha crowed, "The marquess is my angel. Lord Brinston is the man who saved me from the smuggler. Oh, my friend, tell me, what do I do now?"

"What do you want to do?"

"Talk to him. It came to me the moment I saw him. I have not been able to forget him. I think him perfect." She plopped in a chair. "He, on the other hand, did not show by so much as a blink of his eyes that he recognized me. Oh, Vera, how do I catch his attention?"

"There is nothing you can do. If Lord Brinston wishes to pursue the acquaintance, he will make it clear." At Martha's violent motion, Vera repeated, "There is *nothing* you can do."

It chafed, but Vera was right. There was no way a lady could properly approach an angel. It was up to the gentleman to make the first move.

"There is always hope."

"Yes," Vera said obediently. The two regarded each other. Suddenly, Vera grabbed Martha and waltzed around the room. "Free at last. No more Killer and no more schoolroom."

"There will be scores of gentlemen for you to flirt with. We may join all the activities."

"And be together."

"With Camelot to look forward to; and I may talk to my angel. Vera, stop rolling your eyes."

The next morning, Lord Brinston departed the Manor of the Ashes.

Chapter Three

A week later, the friends ambled the path to the stables, arguing as to their destination. "The village store has just received from London an enthralling box of buttons," Vera hinted. She delighted at all times in clothing and its assembly.

"We can rummage the store later," Martha responded. "I want to see that ruin you were telling me of. I can't believe, after all the interest you generated in me with tales of that place, that I have not seen it yet. Perhaps the ghost of a potter will turn our hair white with fear."

"But we neglected to get a picnic."

"Pooh, we can do that another day." Martha kicked a small stone into the cropped grass with a sturdy riding boot. "I am not the least hungry. Not after those delicious scones."

In the stable yard, Hutchins, the head groom, bent over the magnificent stallion Bryce Irvine favored. The man lowered the hoof he had been inspecting as the girls tripped up, swatted at a fly and brushed grizzled gray hair from his forehead. "New shoes for ye, Master Beastslayer." The groom scratched his head, looking worried. "Mornin', misses."

"Is there a problem?" Vera put on her best mistress of the manor air.

"Beastslayer needs shoeing, Miss Vera," Hutchins said. "But all the lads bein' taken up with a sick mare, there's none to take this gent to the smithy." He scratched his head again. "If only Eddie'd been more careful, he would'na broke his leg and I would'na be short a man. I don't rightly know what's to do. P'raps Ben can be spared in a while." His forehead puckered.

"We shall deliver the horse to the smithy," Martha

decreed. "Vera, you may do your shopping. I shall see the ruins another day."

Hutchins was grateful for the assistance and the girls were tickled at the thought of being responsible for the noble stallion. Vera trailed Beastslayer's reins and the girls held their mounts to a walk, conscious of the black's hooves. A light breeze blew the scent of leaves, softening the sun's warmth. Vera reminisced as they went.

"See that tree, the oak with the branches that hang over the path?" she pointed. "I climbed it with my apron full with berries. When Janice came along, I pelted her. How she howled. She was dotted all over."

"Vera, I have the most delicious idea."

"What have you come up with?" Martha whispered. Vera began to smile and nod. "Oh, yes, we must do it. Mr. Irvine is so good-natured he won't be offended."

"Are you certain? I don't wish to offend."

"Martha, don't be tedious. It's a bit of fun and won't harm Mr. Irvine."

By the time the village came into view, the scheme bloomed. The young ladies walked their horses to the blacksmith's shop; Beastslayer, belying his ferocious name, trailed them. "Mr. Baker...?" Vera caroled into the smithy. A squat, muscled man appeared in the doorway, wiping his hands on a spanking new blacksmith's apron.

"Well, Miss Jackson. Heard you was back. Welcome." His voice, as powerful as his arms, boomed across the street.

"Thank you, it is good to be back, Mr. Baker. May I introduce my friend, Martha Dunsmore?" Vera, with the help of the smith, slid from her horse.

As he moved to assist Martha, the blacksmith smiled. "Welcome to ye also, Miss Dunsmore. Do ye ladies have business with me?"

Vera twinkled. "Yes, you are to shoe Beastslayer. Hutchins says he needs all four hooves re-shod. Mr. Baker, we have the best idea."

In the end, the smith reluctantly agreed to shoe the horse as Martha and Vera asked, all for the price of a dozen blackberry scones straight from the manor ovens.

"Mrs. Forge makes the best scones. Papa says her baking would have won England's eminence over Napoleon, if only she were pitted in a cooking joust against his chef." Vera swung in a circle. "She has a soft spot for Mr. Baker; it will be easy to coax her to bake." She circled again.

Martha grabbed Vera's arms and stilled her. "Tomorrow, when Mr. Irvine rides Beastslayer, he will be so surprised."

* * *

The next day, two muslin-clad figures strolled the raked gravel at the front of the Manor of the Ashes. They made a fetching picture, one in palest green with bits of white lace, the other in white edged in blue. Delicate bonnets framed their faces and once in a while, one or the other would give a little skip of exuberance. Altogether, they looked what they were, two graceful young ladies on the brink of womanhood.

What also showed was their anticipation.

"He should be here any moment. Hutchins said he went to the south meadow to check the bridge, so he should pass the front of the house on his way to the stables." Vera prodded the gravel with the tip of her parasol. "After the rain last night, Martha, the ground is a bit damp; just right." They turned, startled at the sound of carriage wheels and horses.

"Who is it?" Martha asked.

"Oh," Vera, spying a face, grimaced with dismay, "my sister Janice. Now our fun will be cut in half."

Sweating horses and a black traveling carriage, both dusty and mud spattered, crowded the drive. Men dismounted. The door of the carriage opened. As the steps were let down, one gentleman, tossing his bay's reins at a groom, turned with a flourish and raised his hand to the lace-edged glove that emerged. Following that glove, a vision of Camelotian fashion minced down the step, spoiling the pretty picture with a scowl.

"Vera! What are you doing out here?" she demanded in a preemptory tone.

"Greetings to you, Janice." Vera turned mulish. Martha, warned by her friend's voice, stayed in the background. Ignoring Martha's presence and turning a cold shoulder to Vera's grumpiness, Janice Jackson drifted toward the group of London belles and beaus now milling on the drive.

"Can't believe I left London for this."

"I am tho glad to be quit of that carriage."

"Isn't the façade pretty?"

"Gads. What a ride."

"Mayhap your father will agree to hold a ball."

"...lovely *mise en scène*."

"Miss Jackson, I am your eternal servant for the invite to your charming home."

"My ruffle is sadly wilted."

"Take the horse, man. Don't footsy around..."

"Nonsense. You look as fresh as if you just stepped off Bond Street."

"I am so glad you came with us."

"My jewel box; I left it on the seat."

"...counting the boxes."

Martha and Vera exchanged glances. Vera rolled her eyes. "My sister Janice and her London friends. Papa calls them the Banshee Brigade."

"Banshee?"

"Because they raise such a fuss over everything. Mama dotes on them. Papa complains that they are indistinguishable one from the other—all equally shrill. I thought they were not coming till the morrow."

They watched the confusion of four ladies and four

gentlemen, all talking at once. The ladies wore the latest in traveling costume as if they had just stepped from the pages of *La Belle Assemblée*. The gentlemen were in standard men's wear, albeit embellished with modish fancies. Here a chain laden with half a dozen fobs, there a cravat intricately tied. Parasols, kerchiefs, and whips flourished.

Then, past the whinnying of the standing cattle, the girls saw what they had been waiting for. "There he is. Mr. Irvine," Martha whispered. Vera nodded enthusiastically.

Mr. Jackson's assistant rode the proud Beastslayer at a walk around the carriage and horses. The black stallion lifted his hooves onto the grass verge, turning his nose toward the newly arrived cattle in inquiry. At the last moment, a restive chestnut forced the black into a circular flowerbed to the left of the group. Cleared of the remains of tulips and with an herbaceous grouping in the center, the dirt had been turned, but not planted.

Janice noticed the rider and lit up like a beacon. "Mr. Irvine," she cried, tripping toward him, raising burgundy and gray ruffled skirts above the ground. Her court, loath to be abandoned, followed her. "Oh, Mr. Irvine. It is so good to meet you again." She appeared ready to grasp his boot.

"Miss Jackson, you are a vision to parched eyes." Irvine swept his hat in an arc, bowing from the great height the stallion lent him. "You bring a touch of Camelot with you this visit."

Janice simpered. "You know most everyone, Mr. Irvine. May I present Charlotte and Maria Wentworth? You met them at Christmas, did you not?

"Miss Honoria Silvester you have not had the pleasure of, I am sure." As Janice introduced Miss Silvester, Irvine froze atop Beastslayer. The wispy ends of the lady's stylish coat fluttered on the breeze and she dipped a graceful curtsey, smiling. Her proud nose twitched in acknowledgement of his homage.

Janice breezed through the introductions. "Of the

gentlemen, your old friend Mr. Dom Lacey, and over beyond the ladies you see Sir George Colby, Squire Michael Shipley, and Mr. Peter Silvester, Honoria's dear brother." Irvine bowed to the gentlemen, but his eyes kept returning to Honoria.

"Goodness, he seems bowled over, does he not?" Martha murmured. Vera remained silent and Martha glanced at her friend. "What is it?" Vera shook her head, but did not speak. Her eyes flickered between her sister and the horseman.

Irvine replaced his hat. "I will return Beastslayer to the stables, Miss Jackson, and join you after I have removed the dirt of my ride." He bowed again, flashing another glance at Honoria Silvester, and wheeled the black the only direction he could for all the people, through the empty flowerbed.

A Banshee pointed, drooping her shawl on the ground. "Look! Thuch funny horthe printth." she lisped.

"Mr. Irvine," Janice trilled. "Whatever have you been doing?"

"Heart-shaped horse prints."

Irvine twisted in the saddle and looked down. Each of Beastslayer's steps had imprinted a heart shape in the loose dirt of the bed.

"Heart horseshoes, Irvine?" One of the men boomed out. "Gone courting, what?"

"Courting *what?*"

"There are those who love their horses more than ladies, we all know," Honoria choked, "but I do believe this is the extreme." She resorted to the handkerchief a gentleman thrust in her hand to wipe tears of laughter from her cheeks.

"Wait till the Four Horse Club hears of this."

"I declare I have never seen the like." As he stared at the prints in the freshly turned earth, Irvine's face reddened.

"Brummell. Won't he turn up his nose."

"Why shoe his horse in such a ridiculous manner?" The embarrassed rider straightened in the saddle. His hands clenched the reins and Beastslayer shied in response. The laughter of the London crowd took on a hurtful edge. His face now white, Irvine snapped the black away from the drive.

Martha and Vera, aghast at the unfortunate direction their prank had turned, shrank back.

One of the men did not jeer as the others did. Classically handsome, with curly dark hair and the profile of a statue, Martha's heart thumped when she saw him—he looked startlingly like Lord Brinston. The little ache that never left bumped into her lungs when her heart thumped. She had to pause to catch her breath.

The hateful laughter and taunts escalated. Mr. Irvine, that estimable man, withdrew, urging Beastslayer toward the stables, but the crowd continued to mock him. To escape the distressing scene, the girls raced through the rose garden.

"That did not go as I expected, Martha," Vera said.

"I am sorry for Mr. Irvine," the dark haired girl responded. "How shall we atone for that unfortunate prank?" Martha sat on the grass, her skirt tangling. Soft blades scraped her ankle. "I must find some manner of making it up to him. I will put my mind to it." And something would come to mind. Pranks were as much a part of her as her toes, but whenever they inadvertently caused harm, Martha suffered agonies of regret. Firmly tamping the urge to cry, she glanced at her friend. "What's wrong?"

"My sister," Vera bit the words out, "has been flirting with Mr. Irvine for the longest time. Janice can be unpleasant, and if she loses his admiration, she is bound to be unbearable. She has done it before. When Mr. Merryweller danced twice with another lady, Janice spent a week in the boughs. I stayed with the Brooms two days to escape her cattiness."

Martha slapped her skirt. "I was afraid *you* had lost your heart to him."

"Me? Mr. Irvine? Never! Though why I should not, I do not know. If you may fall in love with Lord Brinston, so may I care for Mr. Irvine. I vow I should prefer to fall in love with Squire Michael. He is quite the handsomest man. Seriously, Martha, watch out for Janice. She is the cattiest cat."

"I fear Mr. Irvine more. What if he takes revenge for the prank?"

"We will find a way to make it up, I am sure. It is too bad that Vera brought Sir George. He was here before. If you listen to my sister, he is of the highest nobility, but I dislike the man. He is as you would imagine a country squire, loud, smells of horses, and hasn't two words of proper conversation. Supposedly, he is highly regarded at court for his knowledge of horses, if for no other reason. Sir George was knighted a few years ago."

"What was his quest?"

"Something to do with breeding the ideal hunting dog."

Martha gave her a disbelieving look. "What of the others?"

"I don't know them all. The Misses Wentworth have been; they are of the silliest."

"And Squire Michael?"

Vera put her nose in the air. "He is a younger son of the Duke of Haverhorn, my dear," she drawled.

"I knew from the title that he must be from a noble family, but a *duke.* That's impressive," Martha said. "We have come up in the world."

* * *

Spirits restored, the girls skipped across the lawn. They met up with Miss Bridewell, her arms full of flowers. Each step she took caused a flower or two to slip to the ground. "Bridey," Vera danced around the older woman. "Is that a bouquet from your latest admirer?"

Miss Bridewell laughed. "Of course, Vera, Mr. Broom

denuded his garden just for me."

"The vicar as conquest? What does Mrs. Broom say?" Vera teased. Martha listened, wondering if she would ever become accustomed to the Jackson's lighthearted chatter.

"Mrs. Broom encourages his *tendre,* my dear," Miss Bridewell said, "and will gladly continue to do so as long as I arrange the altar flowers for your mother."

"Why should Mama stop arranging the flowers? She always has done so."

Miss Bridewell's eye fell on Vera, biting her lip. "Mrs. Jackson has enough chores on her platter. I wish to ease her way by taking over those tasks less to her liking. These flowers are not destined for the church, but for the adornment of the hall. Mr. Broom insisted. I believe he desires to impress the London visitors when they arrive tomorrow."

"Oh, they have come today, just a few minutes ago."

"Vera," Martha interrupted her friend. "Miss Bridewell is leaving a trail for her swain." She looked at the older woman to check that her teasing was acceptable. "Do you suppose he will appear this night, picking up the discarded stems and singing outside your window?"

Miss Bridewell laughed and tilted her armful of blooms, cascading more flowers to the ground. "A delightful thought. Mrs. Broom can play the music room pianoforte in accompaniment. If we open the windows, the vicar should be able to hear the notes well enough to follow."

In charity with each other, the three made their way to the house, the girls retrieving wayward flowers and piling them back into Miss Bridewell's arms, teasing that her admirer would lose his way and never be seen at the manor again.

* * *

In contrast to Agnes Bridewell, Amelia Jackson bustled into the hall, her plump arms prosaically filled with clothing. "This is for the church bin," she told Dalton, tumbling the pile onto the broad table and smothering the silver tray and red box that already reposed there. "Millie is bringing a basket to pack it all in. If you would have Holt take it over, my mind will be at ease. How I forgot that the poor boxes are sorted this week is a mystery to me. And to have Janice arrive early. This must be done today, regardless of the confusion."

The butler straightened the top items of the stack. "Not to worry, Madame, I trust Vicar Broom to have left plenty of time to organize everything. He knows visitors were expected and will understand your preoccupation."

A maid ran into the hall, a large hamper banging against her legs. "Here is the basket you wanted, Madame. Oh, Mr. Dalton, sir, Cook is ever so fussed. The pot is boiling over and she's ascared to lift it off. She asked you to come right away." She set the basket in front of the table, made a distracted curtsey and rushed to the back hall. Moans drifted from the kitchen on the aroma of herbed, crispy-skinned chicken roasting.

Hand to her forehead in dismay, the lady of the house determined she would stay out of Cook's way. Mrs. Forge was having a bad day from the sound of it. No wonder, with so many extra mouths to feed with no warning. The planned menu had been overturned to allow for the expanded company. With scant hours to prepare so much extra food, the kitchen was abustle.

Nevertheless, I dare not forget those clothes, she thought. *I fear the chore shall go right out of my head. What if Dalton should forget also? Vicar will be most displeased. He was so cross when I neglected to place flowers on the altar for services.*

I cannot bear this affliction of mine. Amelia paused on the stairs. *I did do the flowers last week. How could I have confused Thursday with Saturday? The poor things were all wilted; Mrs. Chapin threw them out the instant she saw them. So there was nothing on the altar. I believe Vicar Broom thought I had forgotten. Thank goodness Agnes has agreed to take over that charge.*

Making her way along the upstairs hall, she paused. "Holt!" she called. A footman turned from his task of placing candles in the sconces lining the hall. "I need a chore done. It has become something of an emergency."

Back at the well-polished hall table, Mrs. Jackson pushed the pile of clothing into the basket, where it made an untidy mound. "This goes to the church hall ever as promptly as you may get it there," the plump woman twinkled. "It's my fault it is late, so you take the consequences and must hurry. Since you will be so out of breath rushing there, please dawdle back. The candles can wait. If Janice complains, she can just go back to London." As the servant hefted the basket, Amelia swept away, pleased to have accomplished her assignment so handily.

Next, she had to check that each guest was settled in his or her room. Had Dalton switched the picture in the dining room? Avalon, if Janice saw that awful hunt scene...

* * *

"Dalton, where is the dispatch box?" Irvine asked an hour later.

"It was on the hall table, sir. I thought Mr. Jackson had taken it to his study."

"No, it ain't either place."

"It was there just a short time ago, Mr. Irvine."

"It must be found at once. Mr. Jackson wishes to review the report." A while later, four men assembled in the wide hall. The table's polished sheen reflected the silver salver that always reposed there, nothing more. None of the masculine faces looked happy.

Robert Jackson took the lead. "Let us recreate the events of the afternoon. That should tell us who had access to the box."

The butler was shaken out of his phlegmatic manner. "I should have spent the entire time in the hall. Ever since its arrival I should have been within sight of the dispatch box."

Jackson made an impatient gesture. "Who else entered the hall?"

"The s-servants have been about their duties," Dalton stuttered. "Miss Bridewell distributed these handsome arrangements of flowers." His hand waved, encompassing a regiment of vases spraying colorful blooms over tables around the hall. "Miss Vera and Miss Martha went to the drawing room. They played the pianoforte for some time. Then they retired upstairs, I believe to attempt new hair arrangements." He paused and thought. "Squire Michael and Mr. Lacey took guns out, just returning moments ago through the courtyard door. The Misses Wentworth, Miss Silvester and Miss Janice took the carriage to visit Mrs. Broom and have yet to return. The box was there after they all passed through the hall. I left for a mere five minutes when Cook needed assistance at the range."

"Who does that leave?" Irvine had been ticking off on his fingers as Dalton produced names. "Only Colby." He ricocheted his eyes between Michael and Mr. Jackson. "Do you think he would have taken the box?"

Jackson frowned. "You're forgetting my wife. Was Mrs. Jackson in the hall, Dalton?"

"Yes, sir, but she did not have an opportunity to mislay the dispatch box. She retired upstairs before I went to the kitchen."

"What did Mrs. Jackson do here?" Jackson sounded resigned.

"She brought a pile of clothing to be delivered to the church hall, sir. For the poor boxes."

"Where is the clothing now?"

The butler looked bewildered. "It must have gone."

Michael spoke for the first time. "Who would have taken it?"

"Holt is to go, sir. It was necessary to move a larger glass into Miss Wentworth's room so I have not yet given him direction to do so. After moving the glass, I set Tyler and Ben to finding chairs for two of the bedchambers. The maids were upstairs already, freshening up for the guests."

Time was spent checking for Holt, who was nowhere to be found. As Dalton hurried back to the tense group in the lofty hall, Martha and Vera, her arms full of unwieldy red box, entered the front door.

"Papa," Vera said breathlessly. "Isn't this yours?"

Mr. Jackson leapt forward. "My dear Vera, where did you get that?" he asked.

"At the church hall," Vera heaved, trying to catch her breath. Irvine leaned against the table and folded his arms. Michael nudged him, and they shared an intense glance. Irvine shook his head.

"In the study if you please, girls."

In Mr. Jackson's private room, two tired, hot young ladies sank into wing chairs fronting the desk. Bryce Irvine and Squire Michael buttressed bookshelves as Mr. Jackson placed himself in his leather chair, setting his hands flat atop the red leather box in front of him. "Now, my dears, I will hear your story of how you came upon my box."

Vera began. "We wanted to keep out of the confusion of Janice coming with all those people, so I took Martha to see the church, Papa. It is supposed to be a fine example of late Celtic stonework, though I don't know anything about it."

"We went to find Vicar Broom to tell us what is so superior about the church," Martha continued.

"He was in the hall. You should see the clothing he has collected. The poor boxes are generous this year."

"The first he saw us, the vicar asked if Mrs. Jackson had forgotten to gather clothing."

"We offered to help sort, since there was so much."

"One lady sent the most cunning knitted scarves.

There were ten of them, all different colors, were there not, Vera?"

"And then Holt came in, carrying a big basket from Mama. Vicar was ever so pleased."

"So we started to sort that too."

"Only the box was at the bottom of the basket. We brought it back straight away." Vera beamed at her father. "I knew you would be worried about it, Papa. Holt had left already, so we hurried to bring you your box."

"It must have been a tiring activity. Martha, you and Vera look winded. Thank you, I was indeed concerned." Mr. Jackson smiled and ushered the girls from the room. "Lemonade and a period of quiet should be just the ticket to restore you. Might want to check your hair before your mama sees you," he whispered to his daughter as she passed.

The door closed behind the girls, leaving four vastly relieved gentlemen in the study.

Chapter Four

"Oh my love, I am so sorry. How could I have lost your dispatch box?" Amelia wailed.

Her husband sped to her side. "Sweet, all's well that ends well. The girls found it right off and brought it back safely."

"But it is so distressing. I can't remember anything anymore. I put things in the strangest places, all without thinking." Nervous fingers toyed with the lid to a powder box. It rattled under the tremor of her hand, spilling powder on the table. The scent of lavender puffed.

With strong arms, Robert folded the distraught woman against his chest. "Didn't your friend say this often happens to ladies your age?"

"But Robert, because it happens to others doesn't mean I am happy with it. It is most distressing. I arranged flowers in the blue Canton vase. Did Dalton tell you we finally found it, both vase and flowers, on the stair to the attic. How can I do these things?" Her brow furrowed, Amelia blurted, "With Janice's premature arrival, it has been an upsetting day. I've been at sixes and sevens trying to prepare rooms, consult with Mrs. Forge, and see that tomorrow's plans fit with so many guests. I did my best to be organized and thought I did so well. But I lost it. What if Vera hadn't found your box?" Her eyes filled with tears.

Robert's reply was nonverbal, lengthy, and left her unsteady, though not with the worry her absentmindedness caused.

Some time later, having steadied Amelia's nerves, Robert dug a fresh pair of breeches out of a cupboard. "I have kept Bryce waiting, love," he said. "I'll be in my office if you need anything."

* * *

A false twilight chased shadows into the recesses of the bookshelves. Most of the curtains were drawn. One window stood open, daring the light to fade leather book covers. Flirting with fate, a beam of sunlight splashed over the brooding medallions of the blood-red figured rug, flowed over the crown of a hulking chair, and speared a red box sitting on the broad table before coming to rest on a section of books.

Facing the box and leaning back as if he feared contamination from the sun's warmth, Bryce Irvine shuffled papers. Where was his employer? They were to have met here more than an hour ago. He shrugged and gazed out the window. Working with Robert Jackson on the latest nonsense from the War Office palled; he much preferred to seek out the luscious Honoria for a bit of flirtation.

The daintiness of the lady left him bemused. Turning a wickedly sharp paper knife over and over in his fingers, Irvine let his thoughts dwell on her. He wanted her. Irvine wanted Honoria Silvester's money, her connections, her very being. He didn't think he even minded that there wasn't a brain to go along with Honoria's being. It would be enough to have her body between the sheets. The thought made him burn. Honoria. His dream.

Irvine would have been the first to admit his enchantment, if anyone had bothered to ask. No one did, of course. It simply was not done. He was glad no one asked. His feelings were too tender to be laid open to the amusement of the house.

The door opened and the scent of wax scurried into the shadows. Silvester poked his coifed mane in the room. His bushy eyebrows needed combing; the hairs went every which way. "I say, can I interrupt?" he asked. "Wanted to drop a word in your ear."

Conscious that this was the beloved brother of his more beloved Honoria, Irvine nodded. "Any time, old man. What can I do for you?"

"Ah, not what for me, Irvine, but for Honoria. Bless her heart, would do anything for the girl." Silvester wandered his way to a chair. "Mind, she don't know I'm here. Bit awkward, but have to say it. She's the light o' my life, ye know."

Irvine was impatient with incoherence. Surely the man had a point to make.

"Well, onward to the contest." The Brigade associate spouted a stream of words without looking up. "She ain't goin' to aim her arrow your way, you know, old man. Has her bow cocked at Colby. Loads of lovely money, a house in London, another in Brighton, as well as two estates buried in the country. Expensive tastes."

Silvester's coat buttons were brass, big, and heavily chased. Polishing one with his sleeve, he mumbled, "Likes the gowns and falderals, not to mention the jewels. Even likes the horses. Colby'll suit fine. Want to let you down easy, don't you know. Not her type, not dandy enough. Better if you backed off a bit, like Johnstone did, don't want you to throw a spanner in the works. Word to the wise. What ho."

With his speech said in the shortest possible time, Honoria's brother huffed at a recalcitrant spot on his middle button and wandered out the door, leaving it wide open. Irvine, not having moved a muscle since the opening fusillade, stared blankly at the dust motes dancing in the shaft of sunlight. Time passed and his eyes lowered to the papers stacked in front of him.

* * *

After dinner, the party gathered in the drawing room. "Shall we have some music?" Mrs. Jackson suggested, gathering Banshees with practiced ease. "Miss Silvester, I heard you at the pianoforte at the Morgan's in London and much enjoyed your Bach prelude. May I beg a repeat?" Looking toward her husband, her face softened. "Robert so enjoys a well-played piece."

Squire Michael strolled to the group. "I shall turn the pages for you, what?"

Honoria consented. With her possession of the instrument, Banshees congregated at that end of the room, away from Robert. *He hasn't the patience for them tonight,* Amelia thought. *I expect he's still worried about his report, poor darling.* She moved to her husband's side to support him with her presence, if nothing else. She kept an observant eye on the room.

A hum of twitters and rumbles accompanied the spirited rendition of a Bach prelude. Irvine lounged, watching the Brigade. Near him, Vera had folded her hands in her lap, quite the polished lady. *That school was a success,* Amelia thought. *No matter how she complained about the headmistress, Vera's behavior is faultless. And I like Martha. Just the sort of friend Vera should take up.* Straining her ear, she could just catch her daughter's conversation.

"Isn't that the same piece Miss Kilborn tried to drum into your head?" Vera asked.

Martha replied, "I believe it is. But it does sound different so much quicker, doesn't it?"

"I don't recall those crescendos either."

Amelia swallowed a smile as Honoria pulsed her hands over the keys. *How is it Vera is so much more sensible than Janice? Especially in her choice of companions.* Dismissing the children from her thoughts, Amelia turned her attention to the music. Honoria ended the piece and Banshees howled.

"Oh, thuch a melodic rendition."

"I have not been able to play that section. I must put the seat too far back."

"À merveille."

"Ain't that a pianoforte?"

"I could never match your exquisite timing."

"Never could understand why the other ladies sound so dreary compared to you."

"Handel never sounded so good."

"Stuuupid, you have to bring your left hand under, not over."

"A performance *par excellence.*"

"Almost as stirring as hearing the hounds bay."

"M'mother's always banging on one just like it."

"That was pleasurable," Mrs. Jackson spoke over the Brigade salvo. Inwardly she winced, but kept her smile as inviting as before. "Would anyone else care for an opportunity at the keys?"

The next piece was sung, leaving Robert with a slight frown between his eyes. The frown did not falter over a full hour of musical offerings. After Honoria Silvester skipped unevenly through 'Cherry Ripe', he cleared his throat. "Shall we hear from Vera, my dear?" he asked. "She used to soothe me with her etudes before she went to school. I would like to hear if she still can stretch her fingers on the keys."

Yes, Vera could still manage a pianoforte. After thinking for a moment, Amelia whispered in her daughter's ear. Following her suggestion, Vera played Beethoven's *Sonata quasi una fantasia.* Amelia relaxed and took a seat on the sofa with Agnes. The piece's chords and tempo would soothe Robert.

That intense piece rolled around the room, eventually silencing every comment and aside from the Brigade. Robert's forehead did indeed smooth. By the time Vera sensitively finished the piece, he was smiling and Amelia mentally promised Vera her favorite dishes for dinner.

But elder sisters have a way of denigrating younger—Janice tapped her toe and when the last chord sounded, she spoke disdainfully. "You never did understand the theory behind the music, Vera. I heard Mr. Walgraven play that piece at the Herringbone's musicale last May. He placed entirely opposite dynamics to you. *He* sounded divine. *À demi.*"

Mrs. Jackson folded her smiling lips into a line. Practiced hostess that she was, her first reaction was to canvass the party. Vera shrank an inch in embarrassment. Robert looked askance and merry Agnes scowled. Martha bridled.

The Banshee Brigade and its fearless leader, Janice, were oblivious to the nuances and settled to a game of charades. *Just wait, Janice,* Amelia thought. *Just wait until I get my hands on you.*

Later that night, alone in the sitting room of their suite, the master and lady of the house discussed the house party and the worrying behavior of their elder daughter. "I wish you would speak with her, my love." Robert ran the brush through his wife's hair. It was a calming ritual for both and badly needed at the moment.

"She is still feeling her power over the gentlemen, dear." Amelia relaxed her shoulders. "I spoke to her; we should see an improvement in her behavior."

"If only you hadn't invited that demned Brigade. They make my hair stand on end. Can't tell them apart, no matter how often I see them. The caterwauling over the pianoforte..."

"They liven up a dull party, Robbie. You have to admit no one has been yawning over tea."

"As if that is a reason for cutting up my peace. Besides worrying about the troop plans, I now fear for the furniture," he growled.

"Jakes was most promising about your chair. It may be done next week."

"The library isn't comfortable without it," Robert grumbled. "Are you sure I can't bar Bumbly—Howlby—Sourby—oh, what's his name, from my library?"

"No, dear," Amelia giggled again. "Sir George *Colby* is

a guest. You cannot lock him out of your room."

"Send him home," he moaned.

* * *

A single candle shone in another chamber. Despite the late hour, Martha and Vera lounged on the bed, chattering as only bosom bows can. The silk coverlet was mussed, pillows littered the mattress, and a stack of Mrs. Jackson's fashion periodicals fanned at their feet.

"Perhaps you can share my ball. My brother will open the ballroom at Dunsmore House. It's huge!" Martha flung her arms wide. "I can't imagine it full of people, but Hurst said it becomes so crowded one may hardly find room to dance."

"We must be presented at Court first. Those hoop skirts are so ridiculous."

"Squire Michael will ask you to waltz at Almack's. Even better, Sir George. Did you not hear he is a nabob? Catching him would put you in clover."

"Oh no, Sir George will be following my sister like a tantony pig." Vera tugged one of Martha's curls. "I don't believe I like Michael, even considering his looks. He is the handsomest man here, but so aloof. I prefer a more approachable gentleman. Don't you?"

"Don't lie; I can see how you yearn for attention for him." Martha shook her hair away from her friend's meddling fingers. "He is eligible. Isn't his father a duke?" She unknotted the curl and drew it across her lips. "Just think. You could be a duchess, Vera. Then I would come after you in precedence."

"He is not the eldest son. "Horrid to think of someone having to die," Vera's scolding voice sounded like Miss Kilborn. An impish smile belied her tone. "Fine, I will accept Michael. You had better attach his elder brother. You know who that is, don't you?" Martha shook her head. "Your

Lord Brinston. Marry him and *you* can be duchess without machinations."

"I didn't realize Michael and the marquess were brothers," Martha shrieked. "And you speak of him dying. Shame Vera! Shame. Why didn't you tell me before?" Vera giggled.

"I do believe you forgot that the younger sons of dukes are given the honorary title Squire."

"No, I just never connected them. Oh, Vera. No wonder they look so much alike." Martha's brain churned. "Your father keeps the *Knight's Register* in the library, doesn't he? We could look the family up."

Sliding off the bed, Vera said, "I am hungry. Let us raid the larder for something to eat."

"I will find the *Register*—you go to the kitchen and we shall meet back here. We can read about my angel and enjoy a meal." In turn, Martha slid off the bed and began searching for her slippers. "Get something sweet if you can."

* * *

As Martha crept down the hall of the Manor of the Ashes, silence coated the walls. The gentlemen would be hunting the next morning (or that morning, if the time had passed midnight) and retired early. The candle cast shadows distorted into fantastic shapes and faded light into the darkness.

The carpet runner insulated against the cold floor but a chill lingered in the air. Martha was uneasy. Step by step, the hair rose on her arms. The darkened hall was too quiet. No clock tocked, no mouse nibbled. In a forest, in a novel, such silence would herald the presence of a wicked magician. *No villains,* she thought. *There aren't any.* She glanced over her shoulder, half-expecting to see Marshall, the smuggler from the shop in Ramsgate, rushing at her.

The drop or so of puka blood handed down through

generations bubbled alarmingly in her veins. The story was her great-great-who could recall how many greats-grandfather had appeared before her as many times great-grandmother first as a coal black stallion, and then as a heartbreakingly handsome man. Before he broke her heart, the puka gifted the lady with a child, one who could shift between fairy and mortal worlds. But time and marriage had dulled the talent. Martha couldn't change her form—her Mama had been able to make her eyes appear different shades, but Martha couldn't even command her hair to straighten with a comb.

The only ability she could claim from her puka ancestry was the compulsion to plan pranks, no deterrence to evil. Certainly not the evil she sensed here. Black, billowing invisible clouds of animosity floated around her head.

A doorway loomed to the left. Inching her feet past the blackened space in the wall, she held her breath, imagining hands reaching.

There was no one there. She crept down the main staircase in the gloom, her new chenille robe fastened against all danger, conscious of the ominous sense that she was not alone. Some unseen looker-on lurked in the shadows. Not Marshall, but someone. She shook her shoulders to rid herself of the prickly chill of fear. Someone watched; no, it was her imagination.

There, in one of the niches. A great, hulking man lurked behind the marble bust of Arthur. No, it was a phantom curtain. Midnight velvet, if she recalled.

Martha's mind flitted, seeking to distract her from the eerie atmosphere. She missed her angel with a dreadful intensity—Vera couldn't understand, and to be truthful, neither did Martha. She only knew that when she lay in bed at night, sleep wouldn't come. Instead, silver eyes hovered, sparkling like dew. Oh, to have Lord Brinston return to the manor. Not that she would do more than bask in his presence. Aware that the elegant peer could not share her impetuous feelings, Martha merely wanted to see him and perhaps talk to him. Just once a day.

It had been so long since she had seen him, his features were a little blurred in her memory. But not his eyes...

Reaching the hall, she meandered in the direction of the library. Her hip bumped a half moon table. "Two doors; the drawing room, and then the library," she mumbled, skimming her hand along the wall. Ah. Finally, the library. She turned the handle. The door groaned, a tiny sound like a faraway person moaning in pain. Martha jumped.

Then she let out a small huff. *You managed to scare yourself out of your skin. A person in pain, indeed. If it was, and not just the door hinge needing the smallest bit of oil, Mrs. Jackson and Miss Bridewell too, for that matter, would be with him, dosing him with anything and everything from the stillroom to relieve his distress.*

Shadows ran across the noiseless walls, slid over mute picture frames and inky sconces. Finding the book listing England's knights and peers was more frightening an errand than she had believed. She looked around to orient herself.

The shadowed library was darker than the night with maroon velvet drapes pulled across the tall windows. Furniture, standing candelabra, plinths for statuary rose like sentinels out of the opacity of the air. The sense of being watched leapt again from the gloom. Martha almost lost her nerve, almost turned and scurried back up the stairs. A strength she hadn't known she possessed made her stand her ground.

Vera had shown her the layout of the shelves; the *Register* should be at the far end of the room near the black marble fireplace and the door to Mr. Jackson's private study. It was a marathon distance from the door with only a candle to light the mammoth dark. Martha turned that way, stubbing her toe against a table leg.

"Ouch. Too much furniture in this house," she grumbled as she slid the candlestick on the offending table and bent to rub her toe through the thin satin slipper. Abused digit eased, the girl stood and moved again toward the far wall, using more care to evade obstacles. Then a fragile glimmer of light flashed and Martha stopped.

"Who's there?"

The light disappeared. *Imagining things again. What is the matter with you?* Martha's own candle seemed brighter by contrast. Still, she could not peer into the gloom. *There is no one there. You are alone, just as you were in the hall and on the stairs.* Martha moved forward again, trying to remember the book's location.

Suddenly, a dark shape loomed and something hit her on the forehead hard. Martha reeled from the attack, her candle bouncing on the carpet and snuffing with a sizzle. The shape rushed past, tangled for a moment in the hem of her robe, and then the door crashed back on the wall. She was alone, sitting on the floor with a sore forehead and wet face. Footsteps echoed down the hall.

Wet face? She stuck out her tongue and tasted the wet. Sharp, sour and strong. Brandy!

Using the robe hem, she wiped brandy off her face before it could drip into her eyes. First, find the candle. Feeling on the carpet, her fingers located something smooth. Cool. A glass. That was what had hit her—a glass of brandy. She felt around more and found the candle. It was as wet as her forehead. Now to light it; there should be a flint on the mantelshelf. Martha crawled the first few feet, then rose. She teetered.

Scrabbling a hand along the mantel, she found the flint. Wiping the damp wick on her robe, she managed to light her candle. That done, Martha assessed the situation; a glass lay on the carpet and the odor of brandy was strong. The odor of brandy was stronger on her. Her hair dripped on her shoulders and her elegant azure chenille robe was streaked down the front. A darker streak from the candlewick was on the hem. Despite these woes and an overpowering feeling of fear, Martha gathered the wits she had marshaled and went into Mr. Jackson's study.

Besides, you stupid girl, how could you forget? Along with your propensity towards impishness, as Hurst says it, you have luck. Mama said it was 'the luck of the Irish', but Hurst calls it 'dumb luck'.

Nothing looked disturbed. Neat piles of paper lined the desk. Shelved books and ledgers, all tidy, rimmed the room. Martha shook her head and retreated, sending the call to her wits to help her back up the stairs, down the long hall to her room, where Vera waited with biscuits and a small pitcher of milk.

* * *

Damn the girl. What was she doing in the library this time of night? Planned it so carefully. Everyone abed. The house silent. How was I to tell she was going to come waltzing into the library? She almost nixed it. She'll have quite a tale tomorrow. By Accolon, if he guesses...

The brandy snifter was pretty clever. Inventive. And successful. It was a good omen, thwarting the girl that way. The plan will work.

Better get busy. She went up, but there's no saying that she won't decide to wake everyone.

The hiding place had been chosen after much thought. The rug pulled up with ease, exposing the wide floorboards of a quarter of the salon. In a neat row, one next to the other, the five pages were laid on the floor well away from where the edge of the rug belonged. *No time to read them now—later, later.*

Then the rug was unrolled back over the floor, the two chairs and an occasional table were repositioned. No one would find them there.

* * *

Next morning, the uproar was muted. Robert Jackson did not want to advertise the occurrence. He and Amelia had the breakfast room to themselves; the knights had eaten earlier and taken guns out after rabbits; the ladies were still abed. Satisfying their appetites, Mr. and Mrs. Jackson parted, she towards the solar, he to his office. It was then Robert created the uproar, yelling down the hall for the butler.

After a conference in the master's office with the door closed, Dalton in turn whispered to maids and footmen. The uproar spread with the noise of an osprey searching a stream. It was not as successful as the fish hawk's quest generally was.

Then the uproar died a covert spy's death—concealed, ignoble and unlamented. Thanks to Dalton's diplomacy, none of the servants picked up the ripples of disquiet. They moved about the manor, serene and purposeful in their work.

Perturbation was left to the master and his lady. Amelia fluttered around the solar table. Her dismay was palpable. "How could I lose your papers, my love? I haven't been in your study."

Robert took her hands and squeezed. "Now, you're not the only person who mislays things, my sweet. I never thought you lost my papers, not for a second."

"But I did manage to tuck your studs into the flowering crab in the conservatory. And the translation of Hoger somehow was in the kitchen with Cook's receipts..."

"Homer, my love, not Hoger. You were not near my study, so you could not have mislaid the document." Robert kissed his lady on the nose. "Please do not worry your pretty head with this matter. I shall find it." He left the room, a frown creasing his face after the door closed.

Amelia squared her shoulders and vowed never to lose so much as a hairpin again.

Later, when the knights tramped in from the fields, he spoke a quiet word to two. Changing in record time, they made their way downstairs.

In the study, Robert Jackson imbedded himself in his chair and spoke. The occurrence took only a moment to recount. Then, peering at the three men arrayed before him, he took the lead. "Let us recreate the events of the evening. That might tell us who could have had access to the box." He drummed his fingers on the desk and peered around as if a sheaf of thick buff vellum might have jumped out of the dispatch box and blown into a corner.

Dalton spoke first. "The household retired at eleven o'clock, sir. The staff settled as usual; I heard nothing. Cook reports someone took biscuits and milk during the night. That was most likely Miss Vera and her friend. Two glasses and a pitcher were brought from Miss Martha's room this morning, as well as a plate." He rocked on his heels.

"The gentlemen went up about eleven. I was last and followed Squire Michael and Lacey. I heard nothing either." Bryce Irvine placed his hands behind his back and stretched his neck.

Michael lounged against the wall. His pose was nonchalant; his voice was tense. "But someone was here. There is the spilled glass of brandy in the library, also a smudge of soot."

"What is missing, Mr. Jackson, if I may inquire?" Irvine turned to his employer.

"Plans for a rocket troop." The older man passed a hand over his chin. "Just revised. Wellington isn't interested, what with Boney away and the search for the Ark abandoned, but they may prove useful elsewhere. The only reason Wellington wished to have the troop in Persia was to get their horses. 'I do not want to set fire to any town, and I do not know any other use of the rockets', he said, so Lieutenant Colonel Fisher is trying to increase the efficiency of the troop. Make them more useful." He shook his head. "But the French don't know that. They might think Congreve's rockets are meant for them. Napoleon's abdication or not, they might not have left off all hope of a search."

"It is a measure of Boney's arrogance that he calls his defeat on the field an abdication. There are other dangers. China has been massing an army on their western border. They could be planning an assault on Mt. Ararat," Michael mused. "Could they have turned up an ancient manuscript that indicates the Ark of the Covenant was on Noah's Ark?"

Irvine said, "Scholars have surmised that Noah named his craft 'Ark' in honor of its purpose. If China should find the remains of the ship before we do, they would destroy it."

"That is unfounded speculation."

Silence spread like ink over the men, erased by a timid tap at the paneled door. "Papa," Vera's chestnut head poked in. "May we talk to you?"

At Mr. Jackson's somber welcome, Martha followed her friend into the study. The presence of the butler, assistant, and the highest-ranking male guest of the house demoralized both girls, but Martha was determined to tell her tale. The faint blue and green bump on her head testified to the woes of the night before.

"She smelled horridly like brandy, Papa." Vera finished the explanation of Martha's trial.

Mr. Jackson turned an intense eye on Martha. "This person threw a glass of brandy at you?"

She nodded. "It spoilt my chenille robe and gave me a headache."

"Did you see who it was?"

"Did he have anything in his hands?"

"Do you know where he went?"

"How big was he?"

"How did he get in the study?"

"Did you see anything around he may have been interested in?"

"Did he say anything?"

"Was there anyone else there?"

"Did he have any papers?" The rapid questions

answered, Vera and Martha retreated, confused but aware of the strategic seriousness of Martha's encounter with a brandy glass. The men remained in the study, mulling over the disaster and their lack of information or clues.

"This will not do, gentlemen," Jackson concluded.

* * *

"Have you turned up any hint?" Robert Jackson's low voice rumbled in his assistant's ear. "We cannot dilly dally over this affair, you know."

Irvine shook his head. "Not a whisper as to who could have been in your bookroom, sir."

"Blast. Nothing for it but to contact the Owl. Embarrassing, but can't let this slide." He forced his mind away from the absorbing mystery and concentrated on his duties as host. Tea was proceeding without a hitch. As he expected, Amelia had everything in hand. Except the Banshee Brigade, drat it. That one, what's her name, was making faces. Robert slid along the wall a few feet, far enough to overhear what the Banshee was saying.

"He's always around," Honoria hissed to Janice. "Can't you make him leave me alone?"

Dear Arthur, he thought, *either there's a scandal brewing or that Banshee needs a spanking.* With the report missing, he didn't need Banshees howling. He headed for his chair, knowing he always thought better off his feet. He could compose the note to the Owl in his head. Amelia would take care of entertaining the party.

* * *

At the edge of London stood Camelot. Likewise, at the edge of Camelot stood the House of the Round Table. Consulting a map made it clear that the House of the Round Table was a buffer zone between the court and the city. As befitted the illustrious neutral meeting place of sovereign and subject, the House was a magnificent sight. The façade and public rooms were sumptuous and rich.

The Round Table was the most palatial of all. The original table King Arthur used was in the center of the room with a mosaic tile floor. Dark with age, its weighty air was enhanced by hanging banners depicting coats of arms of the knights who had sat at around the table. No one sat at that table any longer—polished by centuries of arms brushing the wood, it gleamed with history, if not a fresh coat of varnish. Galahad's position, revered for healing sickness in those who graced it, was roped off.

As Britain unified into one kingdom, annexing Scotland, Wales, and Ireland, a new round table was crafted. Massive sections of oak, maple, and other indigenous woods fitted together, making a circular table that could seat upwards of three hundred knights. Seen from the doorways of the vast room, it was deceptively plain. Inlaid designs represented deeds of the Knights of the Round Table. Pellam's Dolorous Stroke, Gareth's defeat at the Castle Perilous of the four knights holding Lynette's sister hostage were interspersed with historic moments. A copy of the painting of Walter Raleigh on the Ark Royal done in ebony and oak and a fanciful interpretation of the tragic death of William Wallace on the spines of the serpent in Loch Ness were crowd favorites.

The House of the Round Table dripped history. Just one block away from the glory of England's rule stood a simple four-square building. The front entry was restrained and windowless, the inside hall starkly clad in black and white marble. Upstairs, where the casual visitor never stepped, austere barrenness gave way to extravagant luxuriousness. Only distantly related to the House, this building held as much power as any knight or king. It did not scream this fact to the world—that is why the world saw unostentatious plainness.

Lord Brinston strode through the outer office, ignoring the fine artwork and sidestepping the three assistants who clogged the center of the room. Leaning over a polished rosewood desk, he said, "Mr. Moneypenny, I need to see him."

The sleek-haired blonde swiveled his eyes from the letter he was copying. "Can't it wait, sir? He's due in a meeting in five minutes."

"I won't take long, my friend," Brinston promised.

Moneypenny signed his superior's name with a flourish. "All right," he grumbled. "But don't keep him, please. He's to meet with Mr. Ver Bek, who is suffering from gout and won't appreciate delays."

He was reading something. Brinston leaned against the closed door and waited. The overpowering impression of wealth and dynamism in front of him didn't impinge on his senses; he had been in this room many times and wasn't impressed. He hadn't ever been. Familiarity hadn't bred contempt either. Respect for the owner of the room was uppermost in Brinston's emotions.

Nine hundred square feet of inlaid hardwood. Four master's paintings balanced the gold and white stripe of a full drawing room of upholstered furniture. The paintings hung in embrasures surrounded by overflowing bookshelves. The counterpoint to the richness of pale European walnut was the desk; an endless expanse of dark ebony floated above four dark veined marble Grecian pillars.

The papers dropped. The man behind the desk beckoned. "Come in, my boy, come in."

"I wanted to let you know I am off to Robert Jackson's," Brinston said, shaking hands. "The Manor of the Ashes, outside Southminster."

"Oh? Something serious, or are you taking a holiday?" The man sat back in his chair.

"Potentially serious." Brinston leaned against the ebony of the desk.

"Do tell."

"It's the rocket troop plans. Someone's made off with them. Although Jackson could handle it himself, he's asked me to take care of it."

Command reverberated around the room with a single word. "Well?"

"It's nothing for you to worry about," A half smile lifted Brinston's lips. "The Owl is getting itchy."

"You plan to use your magic?"

"If necessary."

The man set piercing eyes on Lord Brinston and said, "Remember. No one is to learn of your abilities. If it becomes known you are a magician, your usefulness would be at an end. So would your peace, my boy."

Scowling, Brinston toyed with a crystal paperweight. "It chafes that Mordred's bad blood should haunt us. It's been centuries."

"It is the way of the world. Much of Arthur and Merlin's time may have been lost in the mist of the past, but the fear Mordred's deeds engendered is ground into man's psyche. You can't fight fate. Even the Lady of the Lake hides."

"Don't misunderstand me. I'm not urging that the Council of Mages reveal its existence. I appreciate the disaster that would be. But people are better educated than in Merlin's time. Superstition about things like mistletoe has lost its bite; why not fear of magic?"

"Mistletoe doesn't bring down rulers, Brin. When it was discovered that sorcery brought about the end of James' reign—that his daughter Mary made a pact with a wizard under the auspices of Elizabeth Villiers—it resurrected memories of Arthur. If and when people forget the chaos a callous magician can create, we can reveal our existence."

"That won't be in my lifetime."

"No, it won't. So take care, my boy."

Chapter Five

Martha peeked around a tree. The gentlemen had been so concerned about papers when Mr. Jackson and the others questioned her about the incident in the library. Important documents were missing? Was it her attacker who took them? She was going to solve this puzzle and she would bring Vera in to help once she figured out what was going on. After all, it was partly her fault. She should have trusted her luck and fought her attacker. If Martha had seen who had thrown the brandy glass, the dastardly plot could have been foiled. Mr. Jackson's papers would be safe.

Besides, she had to do something with all the energy she had bottled up. How was she to bear it if she never met her angel again? She pinched herself. Martha meant to hear if Mr. Jackson had anything important to add about the incident, not torture herself with memories of Lord Brinston. Thus, she skulked behind a tree at the edge of the stable yard in her dark blue riding habit. In case anyone was curious about her intentions, she could say she awaited Vera's appearance for a ride.

Mr. Jackson and Squire Michael left the stables, straightening their coats after a hard ride. "He should be here soon," the older man said. "I wish we could find that report before he arrives. The Council of the Round Table is not pleased."

Michael placed a reassuring hand on Mr. Jackson's shoulder. "Not to worry. There aren't so many here that we can't solve this with speed. Probably won't need his aid anyway." With Mr. Jackson still looking worried, they took the path that led to the house.

Martha pulled behind the tree. Eavesdropping left a

curdled taste in her mouth, much like nostrums or tonics. Despite the ignobility of spying on her host, it had been profitable. Tossing the train of her riding habit over her arm, the girl sped to the clearing in the copse where Vera applied charcoal to paper. Dropping to her knees, she blurted, "Vera, what kind of papers would be in your papa's red box?"

"Government information." Vera rubbed the charcoal absently across her nose. "They send him things to read. Why?"

"Well, something has gone missing." A handkerchief rubbed out the smudge across Vera's snub nose. "Whoever hit me in the library must have taken it. I have been mulling it over and am decided. We shall solve the mystery."

"Oh yes. Papa will be ever so grateful." The charcoal was dropped back in the small box and paper rolled up, smearing irretrievably a lopsided drawing of a wildflower and its hovering bee. "How shall we do it, Martha?"

* * *

Once they returned to the house, the girls split up. Vera intended to poke through the conservatory where many hidey-holes could hold a sheaf of papers. In the butler's pantry, Martha turned the pages of old newspapers. Not reading articles, the pages turned quickly. She was looking for papers. Missing papers, not old news. *A stack of discarded newsprint is a good hiding place,* Martha thought. *It is lucky I spoke to the butler. If he hadn't told me of their usage, I would be suspicious of the papers' condition.*

The foot-tall stack was the past several weeks' issues of the *Camelot Daily Herald.* Mr. Jackson had read them and torn out articles pertaining to certain governmental matters, Bryce Irvine had read them, removing snippets of business and political news. Mrs. Jackson had glanced through the society news with faint interest, as had Bridey. They ripped out paragraphs pertaining to their social acquaintances. The guests looked over one or two; Janice caught up on the society news she had been too busy to read while in town, Dom Lacey rifled the pages looking for the opening announcement of a museum devoted to snuff. Charlotte Wentworth pilfered jeweler's ads. Both Martha and Vera had turned pages looking for items of interest.

Then the staff laid hands on the sheets. The butler read the news with almost as careful an eye as Mr. Jackson. The cook searched for recipes containing the Indian spice Mrs. Jackson had mentioned. Two of the maids often checked the advertisements for new household cleaners that would make their chores effortless and one ambitious footman kept an eye open for a smart London household looking to hire a butler cheap.

The newspapers were a mess. There were no odd pieces of paper inserted in their pages. Pushing her lower lip out, Martha examined her hands. Filthy. After staring at the dirt for several moments, thinking, the amateur investigator washed her hands in the sink. In the absence of a towel, she dried them on her stockings.

She knew what to do next.

* * *

Squire Michael was most cautious that the girl did not see him spying on her.

Someone else was spying also. *Hope she isn't looking for the report. It'll make it hard on me. Have to move it to be sure. Hard to find time to do it. Much less the privacy so I don't get caught. I'll have to get up in the middle of the night.* The spy moved back behind the door as Michael slipped away. *Too many people in the house.*

I shouldn't have taken it. Didn't think it through. It was wrong. I know it was wrong. It'll brand me a traitor. I'll hang. I could put the document back in the dispatch box and no one would ever know it was I. That's what I should do. But...

The question is can I manage to sell the report. If I can, the money will help. Lord knows I need help. Don't think I can swing it without the money. No. Maybe I didn't think of all the ramifications, but I don't care. I have the report and I'm going to sell it. Woe to anyone who gets in my way. The shadowy figure watched Martha wash her hands.

* * *

Amelia Jackson bustled along the corridor. Reaching her younger daughter's door, she tapped lightly and opened it without waiting for acknowledgement.

"Girls," she said without ceremony. "I want you in your gowns and downstairs in a twinkling. Not for the world will I have you hold back dinner. He is here."

A quick explanation had Vera and Martha scrambling. They were the first in the drawing room, arriving before even Mrs. Jackson. As reward for their obedience, Vera and her friend missed not one eye blink of the Banshee Brigade's fawning, toad eating, and breathless adoration. Tucked against the wall in their accustomed chairs, they unobtrusively did the same.

The Marquess of Brinston accepted a bumper of brandy from Robert Jackson. "This preposterous dancing party is a good excuse for your presence, Brinston. At least it isn't a full blown ball," Jackson said. "Thank you for bringing Lady Coletta. Should throw a bit of dust into anyone's thoughts on your presence."

"Didn't mind coming at all, especially when she heard Silvester would be of the company," Brinston said. "Letta likes to keep an eye on him for some reason. She also has a fondness for Lacey. Brother of her *bien amie,* you know. My sister thinks he has redeeming features. Arthur knows why."

They looked over at the coffee-haired lady gowned in misty green. She was in conversation with Janice and Mr. Lacey, who was gesturing wildly. Lady Coletta looked content. Polished as any noble hostess, the ducal daughter added a note of constraint to the Banshee Brigade.

Brinston told his host the story. "They met up with her at Almack's one evening—the Brigade was in full cry after a young miss who had spirited away Charlotte Wentworth's beau.

"Peter Silvester was determined to spill punch on the unsuspecting innocent. Coletta's foot got in the way and the punch went over his own breeches and spotless silk stockings. A few short, sharp words later—you can guess what Letta said—Silvester withdrew in defeat. The Brigade has since studied respect for Lady Coletta. They accord her the awe offered Almack's patronesses."

Leaving his sister to her amusements, his slate-hard gaze surveyed the room, lingering on certain faces. Honoria, who had perked up upon hearing the title of the manor's newest guest, flirted at Brinston from across the room. He passed over her with little thought. "I have my suspicions as to the culprit," he said. "Only need the house party to continue a week or so to find the document." The tall, loosely knit figure pivoted at Mr. Jackson's side, showing an exquisitely cut blue coat, buff breeches, and gleaming boots. The sharp eyes rested upon one the marquess was determined not to be overly familiar with.

"The young ladies?" he drawled.

Jackson smiled fondly. "My daughter Vera and her friend, Martha Dunsmore. You met them last time you were here. Just sprung from the schoolroom and to be presented in the spring. Amelia is grooming them for company so they join the house party. Hope you don't mind."

"I recall. Dunsmore. Hmm, Hurst has been scarce these past months. Wonder what he's up to?" Brinston straightened his cuffs, careful to give no hint that he had prior acquaintance with Martha. He remembered her—had not been able to put her out of his mind, in truth.

It wasn't her fault, but Martha was his nightmare-in-waiting. Gossip hadn't caught them out, but that could change. It could change his life. Marriage. Gads, it was enough to make a man head for the Antipodes.

Brinston appraised her. Like a wife. A bloody wife. That thing she had on, was that appropriate for a schoolgirl? It looked fine. More than fine. She looked good enough to eat, nothing like a schoolgirl. Damnation. If he had to add temptress to the equation, he was sunk.

Rather get on with the business without distraction, Brinston grumbled to himself. *I hate distraction. Especially the kind that comes in muslin and tight corsets.* Nevertheless, Brinston headed for his nemesis.

Martha looked up as the eldest son of the Duke of Haverhorn approached with Vera's father. She appreciated the fine male figure even as her young heart turned over. Such a prime example of the court shone in the present company; the Banshee Brigade was but a flawed reflection of the glory now introduced to the house party. Her angel.

To think he is Martha's true love was Vera's thought.

Martha's mind was more confused. Paralyzed by her feelings, her heart pounded and her palms slipped. She wished nothing more than to throw herself in her dark seraph's arms, but his elegance intimidated. Tonight Lord Brinston seemed more exalted being than mortal man. Tall, cultured, and exceedingly interesting. To compare him to the angels seemed fitting. He was as unapproachable as Prince George. Further, Martha suspected that he had come about the missing document.

"My brother has mentioned Lord Brinston," Martha murmured. "I think they are friends."

"He spoke to everyone else first," Vera reminded her. "Don't bet he is going to glide you into a waltz at Almack's. Lord Brinston acts as if he doesn't remember you."

"Nooo, he is far above my touch." The dark-haired girl's voice held a tinge of wistfulness. It was impossible to reconcile her memory of the tender man who had saved her from the smuggler with this paragon of society. Martha's mind reeled and her heart thudded.

Then they were facing the object of their fascination. Mr. Jackson performed the introductions; Vera curtsied. Martha, struck dumb at the sheer presence of the marquess and recalling the feel of his arms around her, dipped when she should have swept. The ducal heir wore a glittering sapphire in his cravat. It looked like the jewel he had worn that fateful day in the shop.

Lord Brinston accepted the girls' polite but unintelligible murmurs at his introduction, then he turned the full force of his metallic eyes on Martha. "I miss seeing your brother in town, Miss Dunsmore. I trust all is well?"

"He's in Devon, my lord, working on an estate." She cleared her throat.

"Working? How unusual." The fashionable Camelotian drawl stabbed Martha and her cheeks dulled crimson. He hadn't been so supercilious in the back room of the shop.

"I don't know if it is unusual, my lord," Martha did her utmost to match his lofty drawl, "unless prudent management is something the nobility finds remarkable." No way was she going to chance another gaffe in front of this patronizing man. He would put her down for a provincial.

Brinston's eyes sharpened; Martha expected a scalding setdown. But he mildly replied, "Of course, now I recall. Hurst won an estate at cards. It must have needed a great deal of attention to bring it up to snuff to keep him from Camelot so long."

"My brother wrote of an uncomfortable house. I hope to see it next summer." This man was jumbling her mind. She kept seeing silver eyes bending over her in the shop and couldn't concentrate. "There was no staff to speak of."

"It was rundown?"

"He engaged someone to set the house to rights as he labored on the estate. He had to hire an entire complement of farm hands. Hurst is pleased with it."

"I see," Lord Brinston said, dismissing her by turning to Vera. "I understand you have your introduction next spring, Miss Jackson. I look forward to dancing with you at Almack's. A fresh comely face is always welcome at Camelot."

Of course, Vera simpered through the remainder of the conversation. Martha steamed. Was she not as pretty as Vera? Hadn't he kissed her? How dare her angel slight her.

Then Robert Jackson and Lord Brinston slipped off to the bookroom. Martha watched them leave. The urge to commit mayhem warred with her good sense.

* * *

They didn't have a great deal of time for a private talk, but then again, there wasn't much to be said. They discussed the theft, the thief, and the contents of the stolen papers.

"It's in code?"

Jackson thumped his fist on the chair arm. "I don't think it can be broken."

"Who devised it?" Lord Brinston asked, lounging back in his chair.

"A retired Wellington aide. The code is a mix of three languages; using a specialized vocabulary that combines individual words in those languages."

"Hmm?"

"Since its primary use is to transport military information, it was simple to convert terms. But it applies to numbers and terms. The gist of our plans is fairly clear."

"No one else knows this code?"

When Jackson shook his head, Brinston continued. "Not that it matters. Try hard enough and long enough, any code can be broken. It's not so much who took the plans, but the use they will be made of. Its only value to our thief is to sell it."

Jackson slammed his palm onto the desktop. "I know, I know," he growled. "I don't have to like it, though."

"I'd be surprised if you did. To answer your question—it's a simple matter to retrieve the plans. I, for one, am more worried about the motive for stealing it."

"I haven't a clue. Do you think you'll have to use magic?"

The silence felt heavy. Brinston kept steady eyes on his old friend until Jackson relented. "Okay, okay. Shouldn't have said it. I'll leave you to sort it out."

"To tangle the matter up, the Council insists that I apprehend the thief while in possession of the report." Brinston rose. "That bit of politics is what makes this mission tricky."

* * *

Sir George Colby demonstrated to Dom Lacey the hit that had taken his man down at the fight in Witlington. His arms milled and he tapped Lacey between the eyes. Mr. Lacey's pink complexion attained a color similar to that of his cravat pin, a russet ruby; he instinctively feinted back. Unfortunately, instinct made his response a trifle too authentic and Colby bumped his head on the tree, knocking askew the hair he had combed over the receding edge of his hairline.

Colby demonstrated remarkable agility rubbing his head with one hand and shaking his fist at Mr. Lacey with the other.

Charlotte Wentworth giggled as Peter Silvester swept her into an impromptu waltz around the sundial. He grinned. Tucked in the middle between a high forehead, large chin, and stocky neck, his thin mouth matched narrow foxy eyes and downward slanting nose. Blinded by feathers and lace swaying on the breeze, Silvester danced his graceful partner up against the sundial. Charlotte peremptorily sat on the stone and squealed. The curls at her temples bobbed.

Honoria Silvester, a Pomona green parasol twirling above her head, linked arms with Janice as they strolled a path in the rose garden. She had dressed to please Sir George in ivory with touches of gold and her nose elevated in a complacent manner. No one had ever dared to tell that fashionable lady that green silk sunshades do not flatter skin tones, especially when the sun strikes through them. Her dimpled cheeks appeared ill. Janice did not benefit from the green tint lent to her by Honoria's sunshade any more than Honoria—her dress took on the most dubious shade of puce.

"My dear, how can you bear to be near that strange looking man?" Honoria asked with a shuddering glance to the veranda.

"What man do you mean?" Janice was half-listening, her attention on Mr. Lacey.

Honoria adjusted the parasol. "Bryce Irvine, who else? His face does not look *right.*"

Janice looked her astonishment. "Mr. Irvine? There is nothing wrong with him." Having been around her father's assistant for years, she saw nothing unusual in his features.

"But," Honoria whispered, "his face is misshapen."

Janice, fluttering her fingers over the flowers, felt free to dismiss Irvine, but she could not allow this comment to pass. "Oh, I pay no heed to that. He is a well-enough companion," she said. Her blue eyes looked everywhere but at the veranda. It was a lesson how Janice contrived not to acknowledge Irvine. Too bad the man did not notice—his eye trained on the Goddess Honoria. That delicate lady shuddered.

In a shady nook, Squire Michael reclined his bamboo yellow inexpressibles on a garden bench, unaware he had managed to sit on a patch of moss. Those green baby plants persisted in growing, encouraged by the lack of sunlight. When he stood up, he was going to be sorry. He wafted a cut lily toward Maria Wentworth, who was perched on the other end of the bench, her face tilted towards him in an adoring posture. That proper lady sniffed the lemon-streaked bloom and sneezed as pollen drifted over her face.

Looking like a classical Greek statue come to life with his chiseled features and gloriously waving hair, Michael pulled out a handkerchief and flicked at her cheeks. He only succeeded in grinding the staining powder into Maria's skin.

The hubbub of mingled conversations floated. The Banshee Brigade had taken to the gardens for air.

Lord Brinston and Bryce Irvine stood on the veranda with Robert Jackson. Their conversation was less frivolous than any of the Banshee's.

"I oppose the Corn Laws." Irvine said, tapping his leg with a finger. "The effects have not been considered."

Brinston said, "Rumor is that the King is relieved the Round Table adjourned after the latest debate. His illness heightens His Majesty's distress that the knights remain polarized between the factions that think something—anything—must be done and those who fear to upset a delicate balance in trade, like you, Mr. Irvine. But the numbers are swinging; we will have the Laws enacted soon, be they good or bad."

"You oppose them also?" Irvine spoke rationally, but his eyes followed a certain parasol as it made its way around the garden.

"I am torn. It is more than time to begin righting the impossible conditions farmers face. Hearing some of the knock-kneed plans that have been tossed around, the Corn Laws are a reasonable idea. At least they can garner enough votes to pass. Once the deadlock is broken, the country can get on with trying to moderate them into something useful."

"You sound sour on the Laws, Brin," Jackson said. "Roads are so bad there is not enough grain in one part of the country, and plenty in another. The proposals will address that problem."

"Yes, a prohibition on exports should force better

distribution. I hope it does; I can see no other benefit."

Jackson shook his head. "The biggest benefit will be the attempt to keep farmers on even footing. They realized such high profits during the quest for the Ark that land changed hands at extravagant prices, and the loans and mortgages financing those sales were set on what have become impossible terms. Unless legislation addresses falling prices and the foreclosures those prices will demand, our agricultural system may fail."

Irvine's comment, "Well, you can't claim big landowners are getting their own way in this. Fewer than half the knights at the Table come from the nobility," made Jackson clench his fists. Not in the best of moods, resentment of his employee's dig at Brinston stung.

Robert Jackson was juggling a full platter. He deplored the guest list of the house party; his daughter's friends gave him the headache. Their incessant chatter and tendency to drift like sheep made it difficult to tell them apart. His report was missing; it must be found without delay. And now Irvine was harping at his noble guest. This was not the best time to pull such a stunt. Robert was close to losing his temper. Under Brinston's commanding eye, he took a deep breath and reminded himself of the little game he had devised.

Robert derived a measure of pleasure watching Irvine's bumbling attraction to that girl, whatever her name was. He hadn't a prayer of attaching her, but it was fun to watch him try. He looked to see where she had got to with that preposterous sun shade.

At the farthest reaches of the garden, the girls had ensconced themselves behind a small gazebo. Sunlight - dappled lattice screened them from view. Vera said, "Have you ever seen anyone enjoy scones as much as Mr. Baker?"

"One bite and it was gone; at least the blacksmith appreciated Mrs. Forge's baking." Martha abruptly changed the subject. "I am glad Lord Brinston is here, Vera. Now I have an opportunity to come to know him." She smoothed the nap of a flower petal with her fingertip.

"Silly," Vera hooked her arm in Martha's. "Never say you felt a lack, my dearest friend, not with Janice's friends here; particularly Squire Michael. Any lady would appreciate his presence."

"Lord Brinston is Galahad compared to the Banshee Brigade," the older girl stared at the ragged edge of leaf under the flower. "I cannot tell them apart. Like my brother's hunting dogs; they look and sound alike. But I cannot forget my champion. I don't quite understand it. I only met Lord Brinston the two times, at that dreadful shop and one evening here, yet his departure left a larger emptiness in my life than the absence of my brother. I would have said my brother was the most important person in the world..."

Martha shook off her contemplative mood. Hesitant to bring up the scheme that had come like a hiccup to her in the night, she was compelled to mention it. "Dare we try another prank, Vera? After the debacle of the horseshoes, I fear to suggest the brilliant idea I have had."

"I don't know. Mr. Irvine was furious. He might wring our necks if he catches us in mischief again." Irvine had determined their culpability regarding heart-shaped horseshoes and made it clear he did not appreciate the girls' ingenuity. His attitude was such that Vera and Martha had not dared to speak to him for a full day.

"Her delicate form and ethereal blonde hair, encased in seductive Camelotian fashion, brings out the ravening male beast in his heart. Thrice he has approached the lady, only to be rebuffed each time." Martha smiled, flashing an elusive dimple. "I thought a pricking would be the thing to deflate Sir George's attentions to Honoria. Make her notice him. Wouldn't that restore us to Mr. Irvine's favor?"

"Pricking? What did you have in mind?"

"You remember the apple pie bed—how Dalia couldn't get her foot in the sheets. Couldn't we do something similar?"

"You mean turn the sheet up on his bed?"

"No, we can do a bit better than that." She whispered, concluding, "Dalton must agree."

Vera waved a bit of fern. "Dalton was not pleased when Sir George dragged the chair from the library to the terrace. Imagine, the pomposity of reading his periodical outside and abandoning the furniture in a shower so as not to wet his hair. The least he could have done was call someone to drag it back in. The chair had to be sent to the village for repair; the wood grain was raised. Worse, it is Papa's favorite." Anything that made her father unhappy made Vera unhappy also. "Shall we ask now?"

Hand in hand, the two went to find the butler. Lightness passed over Dalton's unresponsive face when he heard the plot. "Neat stitches, Miss Vera?" he begged.

Agnes Bridewell floated in as he spoke. Looking quizzically between the conspirators, she chortled. "May I enter into the fun? I so enjoy a bit of entertainment."

"Oh, no, Bridey, much better you not," Vera gasped.

Martha took pity on the elder woman's crestfallen face. Slipping a hand around Miss Bridewell's elbow, she whispered, "You should not be aware of this prank until it happens, ma'am. That way, you can give us an alibi if we need."

"How will I know...?"

"You will not miss it. I promise." Martha said.

* * *

The Banshee Brigade was going for a walk. "Walking will be acceptable if we go slowly," Honoria tittered to Colby.

"Plenty of time for dalliance with the daisies."

"Can't we take carriageth?"

"It's too cold not to wear your coat, silly."

"Horse has the best stride I've ever seen, pon rep."

"Ooh, dust and pebbles."

"Elle nostalgie de la boue."

"It is only a mile."

"What say, rather take out guns after rabbits."

"Thould I tire, I would apprethiate a ride in a carriage."

"Dalton, we need wraps," Janice ordered. With a bow, the butler gave direction, and in a few moments, three footmen came down the stairs bearing coats, bonnets, and gloves in a rainbow of colors.

"I will assist you if you tire, my dear."

"Isn't there a better..."

"I vow the walk, gently taken, will do no more than bring roses to your damask cheek."

"No, you don't tie the ribbons that way, goose."

"A good gallop from the beast."

"You are tho kind, my lord."

"Batiste is much too light for the style."

"...a proper bow."

"You are so kind to little me."

"Jolly good sport I wager."

"With your athithtanth, I believe I may attempt the village."

Vera and Martha strolled into the hall, Miss Bridewell tucked between them. They paused to watch the chaos. Janice and Honoria jostled each other for prime position in front of the looking glass, donning bonnets and coats grand enough for the Camelot strut. Whatever one thought of the Camelotian belles, one must admit they dressed with the flair great expense imparted. Each lady's attire was distinctive. Martha would have admitted to a preference for Janice's lemon walking dress because of the color. Vera could hardly take envious eyes off Charlotte Wentworth's gay sprigged muslin. It had a starched ruff that ran around the bodice and ended behind the neck, framing the face. Vera could *see* herself wearing it.

The gentlemen posed in manly position, being assisted into greatcoats by footmen. Their attire was not found faultless by the girls. The coats had a preponderance of capes, shoulders were padded high, and cravats looked tortuously high and tight. Michael was the clear winner in the clothes department—his attire was the most restrained, though his shirt points cut into his cheeks.

Dalton himself held a murky green coat for Colby, ready for that gentleman to slide his arms into the sleeves.

"I wathn't pothitive thith wath the betht material."

"Bit rough over the hills for rabbits."

"Does the emporium in the village have watered silk ribbons?"

Honoria dimpled. "Sir George, how do you like my new bonnet?"

With the question, Dalton brought the coat up Colby's arms. With a jerk, Colby yelled "Blast!" and the coat pulled out of the butler's hands. His arms pulled back with the coat hanging from his elbows, He swung toward Dalton, but tripped over the hem. He staggered, arms held at his side.

"Sir George!" Honoria was shocked. "Really, if you don't like my bonnet, you can at least be polite about it. I am shocked."

"My arms won't go through the damned sleeves," Colby howled. The London gaggle surrounded him, chorusing questions and exclamations.

Martha and Vera, Miss Bridewell in hand, tiptoed back to the solar, closed the door and collapsed against it, giggling. Miss Bridewell beamed. "That was it, was it not? The plot."

In the hall, Colby's voice bellowed above the uproar. "Who sewed up my sleeves?"

A voice plaintively said, "I did not know you sewed, Sir George."

Irvine, in the shadows at the rear of the hall with a ledger, waiting for the crowd to disperse, smiled in satisfaction. He was quick to note Honoria Silvester's recoil at Colby's belligerent tone and hoped his rudeness would turn the delectable lady against that bluff man. That would give him the opening he needed to press his suit, be damned to her brother.

"Psst," hissed a voice from the conservatory.

He turned his head. "Mrs. Jackson," Irvine began and looked closer. "What's the matter, Madame? You look distraught."

She twisted her head. "How could I lose it," she moaned, "after I promised myself to be more careful. I wasn't going to lose anything again." She stamped her foot. "I will just have to find it myself."

"Mrs. Jackson," His voice soothed as he moved to her side. "Pray do not be disturbed. I understand your difficulty. Mr. Jackson has explained that this is a common occurrence for ladies at your delicate stage."

"I don't care," Amelia hissed back. "It's intolerable."

"Let Dalton help, please."

Her shoulders slumped. "He is good at finding things when I lose them." She had a glimmer of tears in her eyes. "Would you be so good? Tell him..." her voice lowered to an undertone, "I can't find my garnet necklace. I had it on an hour since."

A whisper later, Dalton clapped his hands and four trained servants appeared in the hall, sliding around the milling Londoners. Mrs. Jackson had been in the breakfast room, the garden, and the kitchens. Fifteen minutes later, the solicitous butler draped a sparkling garnet and gold pendant over her hand.

"Where was it?" she asked, resigned.

"In the potting shed, Madame, draped around a hoe."

* * *

In the solar, two girls danced a jig around one

woman. "Ahh, that was so satisfying." Martha opened the pianoforte and rattled through a Mozart sonata, missing notes due to her dancing feet.

"I love a good plot." Miss Bridewell hugged Vera. "Please, if there is another, may I..."

"Of course, Miss Bridewell. You are an excellent conspirator." That lady beamed as if the king had bestowed a knighthood upon her.

"Did you see Mr. Irvine?" Vera leaned on the pianoforte.

"Yes. He looked pleased."

"We must be out of his black books. Now we can be comfortable again."

"Yes, Vera," Martha replied obediently. "He surely has forgiven us the horseshoes."

Chapter Six

Pewter, ceramic and silver, the holders were a hodgepodge. The candles were beeswax, every one. White wax candles in a variety of bases. A circle of seven lit candles, not on a table but on the floor. Richard, the Most Honorable Knight Shipley, Marquess of Brinston, sixth of ten known magicians in the country and heir to the Duke of Haverhorn, knelt inside the circle. He cupped his fingers around a candle's flame, muttered a confusion of syllables, and blew gently. It flared up and died back. After a moment, Brinston shuffled on his knees to the next and did the same. Again the candle flared. The third candle did not flare when he blew on it. Its flame shone steadily, evenly.

The magician, if he felt emotion at this unexpected reaction from a common candle, repressed it. Instead, he moved to the next. And the next. The fifth candle blazed. Like a fire laid with pine, the flame darted, spitting sparks. Pulling his head back to avoid being burned, Brinston puffed again and again. The flame responded as if a pinecone had fallen in it; it sizzled and smoke coalesced. Brinston studied the sparks, studied the flame, studied the smoke. After a time, he moved to the next candle, which responded to his ministrations with a lethargic gleam.

The last candle stood in a chased silver holder. It looked no different from the other candles; its flame seemed in no way remarkable. Brinston cupped his fingers, spoke the same words, and leaned over to blow. Like lightening, the flame shot straight up. The magician rocked to avoid being punched in the nose.

The candle burned a steady yellow, the flame a foot above the wick. Brinston leaned in close, his eyes searching within its depths. He blew again. The flame did not waver, nor did it shrink. For a full five minutes, the bright glow of fire gleamed in his eyes. It illuminated his face and threw steady shadows into the corners of the room.

The magician blinked and moved past the seventh candle, back to the first. Taking up a silver snifter from the center of the circle, he began dousing the candles, one by one. Finally, he reverently capped the foot high flame of the last and bearing down, he forced it back into itself, into the candle. Then the snifter was over the wick and the flame was doused. For all its height and heat, the candle had not melted.

The rite was over. Lining the mantel with candles and tossing the snifter on a table, he moved into the next room, leaving ghostly gray smoke scenting the air.

In the bedchamber, Brinston hauled his shirt over his head and tossed it to his valet. The torso of a mere man, albeit sculpted with firm muscle, was revealed. The servant, accustomed to the view, did not so much as blink an eye until the marquess spoke.

"Most illuminating spell. Barnes, I have an assignment for you. One of those in residence, Martha Dunsmore, needs taming. You are going to help me cage her, the little minx."

"I beg pardon..." The valet's eyes flickered. Never had his employer asked anything remotely resembling this request.

Brinston's eyes twinkled. "Don't pull that face with me. I know what you're thinking. She is but a schoolgirl, not up to my weight. But Martha is looking to take a nasty fall and the two of us are going to see she stays upright. She fancies herself an investigator—Fenice's faith knows she will insert herself in the midst of this problem without understanding the gravity of it. I owe it to her brother, at the least, to keep her out of the muck. The less she learns, the safer she will be."

Falling into a study while he slid his shoes under the bed, Brinston stripped off the remainder of his attire.

Impertinent chit. But young, very young. She was a trooper fighting that smuggler; has bottom, this one.

Standing in the middle of the room in his natural glory, he found, to his embarrassment, that he had to turn away from the servant to hide an all too obvious interest in Martha.

If she were a schoolgirl, they had improved the breed. She was as compelling to him now as she had been facing that smuggler. That gown she had on; did Hurst know she wore her necklines so low?

As for his alert valet, Brinston could only try to keep Barnes in the dark. Thoughts revolving on the plucky Martha, Brinston gave his collaborator absentminded orders. "I wish you to be friendly with those servants likely to be aware of the lady's activities. When possible, be around to make sure she is safe, Barnes. I will do the same. Together, we should be able to head off any danger to the little darling."

The valet's mouth twitched even as his master's slipped. Lord Brinston's response to the lady was evident, no matter how he might try to hide it. "I take it you are not going to confide in Miss Dunsmore," he said.

"Lord, no. I'm not going to tell her a blessed thing. Not on any front. Oh, and Barnes, keep in mind—I don't want to retrieve the papers, not unless they are in the possession of the thief. The Council needs that proof. So, if you stumble across them, let them lay."

Barnes settled into a chair by the fire with a pile of mending. Brinston unlocked the tall standing cabinet on the wall opposite the fireplace, releasing a whiff of old spices: saffron, oregano, and perhaps a touch of sage. Taking up less than half the space inside the cabinet was a leather valise, battered as if it had been run over by a curricle.

A quiet word caused the luggage to glow. Brinston examined the surface, then satisfied at what he didn't see, he lifted it gingerly by the handles. No one had disturbed it.

The dilapidated valise, light as it was, looked like the

body was going to part ways with the handles. It held together as the magician extracted it from the cabinet by lifting it straight up, then out. Still glowing, Brinston carried it to the table, taking care not to bump it on anything. By the time he crossed the room, the glow had faded to a soft mistiness that emphasized every crack and scratch of the leather. Set on the table, it collapsed, folding upon itself. The light went out.

"Is it damaged?" Barnes asked, threading a needle.

"No," Brinston said, "If it were a man, I'd say it was cranky. It's magic degrades when it is kept from fresh air."

Barnes threw the magician a reproachful look. "And you're the one insists on speaking deferentially of magic, my lord."

Brinston bowed. "I apologize. Meant no disrespect. Being shut up in the cupboard isn't very good for it, but we can't be too careful. There's a thief here. I'd hate to have to track it down. Or if it were damaged. I'd feel terrible, just terrible." He passed his hands over the valise. It straightened, raising three inches. A few of the worst cracks smoothed out. "There. No harm done. We have a lot of work to do, Barnes. It's going to be a late night. If you object, you'd better tell me now."

The valet grunted. "No skin off my hide. I still say you are going about this wrong."

"What would you have me do?"

"It wouldn't hurt to trust the young lady."

Brinston flinched. "You mean I should reveal myself to Martha. I am not telling her *anything*. Certainly not about my magic."

A short silence buried the room in unseen mist, then Brinston spoke. "I don't agree with you, Barnes. Magic and marriage don't mix. Since I will have to wed someday—to provide an heir for the estate—I will be careful to choose a lady whom I can lock out of that part of my life. I can't see Martha as that candidate."

Silence.

He settled at the worktable Amelia Jackson had placed in his sitting room. "You and Coletta—you're worse than Coletta. Both of you nattering about Martha. I should think about marrying her," he said, his voice taking on a mimicking quality. "She'd make the perfect consort for a magician. It'd please the duke no end. About time you got shackled. Thank Merlin I don't have to follow your advice."

"I didn't say anything about marriage," Barnes said. Brinston laughed shortly, but the valet was unperturbed. "I didn't. I said you should trust her. She is puka."

Opening the valise, Brinston began pulling books and paper from it. When a stack of a dozen tomes was piled in front of him, he picked up a penknife. He whistled as he trimmed a quill. "Enough. Please. Let's get started on *important* matters."

"Try Hebrew," Barnes said. "We may be more comfortable in Latin and Greek, but the duke's book relies heavily on Hebrew."

"You think so?" Brinston frowned. He started to write. Not smoothly, as if he were penning a note to the duchess, but haltingly. This was no lighthearted bit of doggerel Brinston and Barnes were composing. Often, he would pause and think aloud, question his companion on a point, scratch a line out and replace it with another.

A great deal of effort produced a single sheet of paper. Barnes sewed three buttons on coats, hemmed a shirt, and began embroidering a monogram on a handkerchief.

Once a rough draft was composed, Brinston began replacing words. Barnes mumbled phrases in three languages, changing the inflection, searching for the perfect wording. A lively debate between the two amended the concept. Consulting books and the valet, and once in a while pulling at his ear and staring at nothing, Brinston at last completed the work and wrote out a fair copy. Arms stretching straight over his head to work the kinks out of his shoulder, he said, "Gads, this was harder than I thought. Take note, Barnes."

The valet stabbed his needle into the arm of the chair and listened intently. Brinston read aloud that which was written on the page. "Can you think of anything we missed?"

"Dozens of possibilities." Barnes smoothed the handkerchief, frowning. The valise slumped down until the handles rested atop the leather, flat as it could be.

"True," Brinston said. "No spell of this nature can be comprehensive. Pity I can't take more direct action. Considering how we cobbled this together, it feels remarkably solid. Still, I am uneasy about it."

"Seems to me the world keeps turning. What will be, will be."

"No, my friend, that will not do and you know so. You may be a fatalist, but there are a number of innocent people liable to be harmed; too many for me to trust to the fickleness of fate." Brinston began gathering papers together.

"You are trying to make all run in your harness again, my lord. It would take an army to make everything spic-and-span here. People aren't so easy to guide."

"Call me an idealist if you must; the tag does me no harm."

Barnes shook his head sadly. "It's what you always do. Never learned proper humility. Like your father, it has ever been your nature to protect. Not that it's a good thing."

"Where does that come from?"

Brinston gathered his pens and ink on the tray and Barnes picked his needle up. "Tell me, my lord, what does 'protect' mean?"

"No, you don't. I am not entering into a debate on semantics with you—I could not win."

"You win just about anything you put your mind to. And the spell is good."

Startled, Brinston said, "Thank you, I had no idea you had such faith in my abilities. If you think so, it must be as right as it can. Never known you to be wrong." Barnes nodded and packed away his sewing materials.

Reading again what he had written, the magician was disturbed by a soft knock at the door. Tensing, he relaxed when his sister Coletta slid in, moving with a whisper of sound on bare feet. Quick as a wink, Barnes pulled himself up to his full height. He looked a century younger.

"Have you written it?" she asked.

Brinston gave her a smugly masculine look. "Of course."

"Can I see?" She reached a hand out, turning a smiling face to the valet as she did so. "I've been trying to think how to compose it, but with the hordes of people involved, I keep getting tangled."

The paper was proffered. Coletta read, then threw Barnes an admiring look. "Very neat. I would not have thought to extend the protection in that manner. To prohibit anything from being used as a deadly weapon—it's highly economical." She peered at her brother. "Do you have sufficient power for this?"

"I must," Brinston replied. "It's too important, considering the mindset of our thief, not to. Think, Letta. If I protect against every malevolent thought, the spell will drain faster than a cup with a hole in it. People being what they are, I would be warding against the tweeny tripping a footman." His brows met in a frown. "But there are myriad ways to hurt a person: countless weapons that could be wielded. It is difficult to provide for all the ins and outs. I hope this will serve. By the way, this was very helpful." He handed her a book. "It's the one Father found on Kalymnos. Look at the page I marked."

Coletta opened the book and read. "Oh," she breathed. "I see what you mean. But this deals with people and animals—controlling them. Will it extend to inanimate objects?"

"Not the way it's written. That's what took so long. We had to revise. If either of us knew Hebrew better, I daresay it would have been quicker. And if we could guess all the ways our thief could come up with to harm someone—or *who* the target would be—I would feel more assured." He plucked the book from her hands and propelled her to the door. "It's late. Off with you. I have to set the spell and I don't need you mucking it up."

"I don't muck—" The door closed in Coletta's face.

Brinston turned to Barnes. "You're as bad as a dandy. Letta doesn't mind your wrinkles. She knows you've earned every one. Relax." The valet sagged. "And you talk to me of Martha Dunsmore."

Chapter Seven

The mustiness of damp dirt filled Martha's nostrils. Sitting in the lee of the hedge, she was reproducing the details of a cheery yellow primrose in watercolor. The plant was tucked under the bushes with a splash of sunlight streaking its petals. Without a spot to darken its yellow perfection, she was content to spend her time painting it. Vera should be along soon; she had promised to meet her after satisfying Mrs. Jackson's need for assistance in the stillroom.

"It will be a while before Mama allows Ben to angle for fish again," Vera had said. "Imagine not noticing a patch of nettles. Mama needs my help concocting her soothing balm—I should be no longer than an hour. Then we may take that walk to the ruined pottery you have been yearning after."

"I will take my paints out in the meantime. Look for me at the end of the garden."

A cooling breeze ruffled through the alley of the hedge. It was comfortable on the stone bench, shaded by trees and collecting a gentle waft of air. Martha dissolved the image of dazzling gray eyes that wished to form and concentrated on petals. No sense dreaming. There was nothing to hint that she was considered suitable; indeed, the opposite.

In the drawing room last night, he'd been cool, almost insultingly so. With an acquaintance that stretched perhaps four hours over three separate occasions, Lord Brinston seemed to disapprove of everything she said and did. What a pity.

A fountain tinkled a cheery note. The watercolor looked well enough, though Martha was not satisfied with her shading of the primrose. It was difficult to show the frilled coral fading into the yellow. Perhaps she should...

Gravel grated. At the other side of the hedge, low voices intruded on Martha's concentration. Someone was walking the garden path, crunching gravel as they paced.

"If we sell them, we would have ample funds for the next season."

"But it ith wrong. They do not belong to uth—wath it not thtealing to take them in the firtht plathe?" The nature of the conversation rooted Martha to the bench. The voices, conspiratorial in tone, rang a bell of warning to the inadvertent eavesdropper. Stealing?

"I don't care who they belong to. They are the answer to our dilemma. Whom does it harm if we sell them? No one cares. If Charles had not been so improvident at gambling, this would not be necessary. But I have been assured a goodly sum and we need the money."

"But Charlotte, what if we are found out? Would it not plathe uth in a deal of trouble?"

"Pray do not be a ninny, Maria. Would you prefer to retire to the country with our dear brother on a repairing lease? We have not a prayer of obtaining the funds..." Gravel shifted and obscured the remainder of the sentence.

Martha released the pent-up breath she had been unaware she was holding. Her fertile imagination filled in the gaps in Charlotte and Maria's conversation; they had taken Mr. Jackson's papers and planned to sell them.

Then the deliberate crunching of gravel heralded another approach. Her head came up just as Lord Brinston turned the corner of the path. Dressed for riding and tapping a riding crop in the palm of his hand, Brinson looked prime. He stopped politely and said, "Good morning."

"My lord," Martha replied, wishing she had worn a prettier dress. "It is a lovely day."

"Yes, yes it is. You paint?" He peered at the drawing she sheltered with her hand.

"Not that well."

"I see. You perhaps should squint at the page to see how best to proceed. My sister does that. She says taking her work out of focus helps show her what needs doing."

Unaccountably irritated, Martha didn't respond. She didn't need a lesson in watercolors. She already knew her work was lacking. Having it confirmed by this godlike man rankled. Brinston glanced at her face; his brief impersonal look irritated her further.

He rubbed the crop along his jaw line. "Ahh, enjoy the sunshine," he said and turned toward the house.

Martha mumbled, "Thank you," to the crisply pressed tail of his coat. She watched Lord Brinston stride away, swinging his crop, conscious that there had been no more to the exchange than any man would have offered to any female of his acquaintance. That was what irritated the most—the any part.

Vera was the next person to come tripping along the walk from the house. "Ready? I left Tom at the turn—he is going to come with us to carry the picnic basket." Martha jumped up, eager to get a glimpse of the famous medieval pottery and to tell Vera of the incriminating conversation she had inadvertently heard. As to Lord Brinston, the less said, the better.

They could ride to the site, but the distance through the woods was short and the day ideal for a lazy stroll. While they walked, Martha repeated almost verbatim the words she overheard. The Wentworth brother's character was shredded.

"Uncle Pemberton says gambling is the bane of the English aristocracy. I presume this is the sort of thing he means," Martha said. "Imagine losing so much money at the tables that your sisters could not remain in town. He should be ashamed."

Exclaiming at the rabbit family browsing in a bed of clover (each and every one froze into statues, then, when the human presence did not further threaten, they began hopping again, little mouths munching), Vera and Martha speculated on the various constructions to be placed on said conversation. Miss Jackson's prosaic sense was of great value. She pointed out that the Wentworth sisters could be contemplating selling items ranging from their jewels, consisting of necklaces in inexpensive garnets and tourmalines and two faultless strings of matched pearls, to something of their brother's—perhaps a phaeton. Not necessarily Mr. Jackson's papers.

Squealing at the fox that darted past (one had to conclude the poor creature was more scared than the ladies —its eyes popped and though its tail caught on a bramble and left a tuft of red fur waving, the fox careened out of sight), plans were laid to inspect the Wentworth's bedchambers. They were suspects and must be investigated.

For good measure, Dom Lacey's belongings would also be scrutinized for stolen papers. Secrecy was paramount—servants, guests, and family alike must be bamboozled. All had to be away from the corridors and bedrooms for sufficient time to allow for a thorough search of three large rooms.

Dabbling fingers in a tumbling brook, they discussed the meat of the matter. Search rooms they could, spy on conversations they had, but both lacked the essential knowledge to fit all together into a cohesive whole. At last, the budding detectives set their intellects to deducing *what* they were in search of.

"Papa works with the government. I don't know on what, other than that sometimes it is frightfully important." Vera's finger waved at a small fish. It darted away.

"This must be important; it doesn't matter what they are about. We know papers are missing. Wouldn't he be pleased if we could oblige your papa by finding them?"

The young ladies enjoyed their bucolic amble.

Footman Tom trailed beyond earshot, swinging a filled picnic basket. His enviable task was to escort the young ladies, eat ham, and ensure the picnic basket arrived back at

the Ashes. He whistled between the gap of his front teeth
—'twas amazing how that small space forced out the most
intricate sounds. Tom couldn't imagine a more pleasant day.
If he had moved just a bit closer, if he had heard the earnest
discussion, the poor man would have revised his opinion of
the excursion.

"Martha, you suspect every one of Janice's friends.
They can't all be guilty."

"We have to start somewhere. If we hear anything
suspicious, of course we have to investigate. Once we find a
person does not have the papers, we can clear their name."

"But could Janice, of all people, be friends with so
fundamentally evil a person? The Banshees are the silliest
cluster of fribbles." Martha did not bother to respond to the
corkbrained comment. What better way to confound
suspicion than by being thought ludicrous?

Walking arm in arm, Martha said, "I have been
meaning to ask you about your estate's name. Manor of the
Ashes, isn't it unusual?"

Vera grinned. "It is, but appropriate. It's a long story;
do you want to hear it now?" At Martha's determined "Yes,"
Vera began her tale. "The Manor of the Ashes is an ancient
estate, founded when King Arthur gave the lands to a knight
named de Escoville. It was built and flourished for about fifty
years and then it burnt, leaving a shell of stone walls. The de
Escovilles, now Scoville, rebuilt, making the house a bit
larger. Fifty years later, it burned again. They built again in
the style of the time, yet ever larger. Thereafter, the house
burnt every one hundred years." Vera brushed a ladybug off
her skirt.

The path narrowed and Martha fell behind Vera, who
raised her voice. "They kept trying. Sometime around 1500,
the Scoville family lost possession of the estate; Papa said they
drained their coffers. No one has heard of them in ages. The
Newton family took the estate over and the house burnt
seventy-five years later. They rebuilt using more wood than

stone or brick, so the next time it burnt, there was nothing left—no walls to speak of were standing. The Newton's gave up, let the land lie, and established themselves in Shropshire." She pushed aside a branch; Martha paused to avoid the whip of it bouncing back into place.

"Papa's family bought the land in 1678. They built a house and spent twenty years trying out name after name for it. Jackson's Manor and Jackstone were two of the most banal. Then the house burned. When they rebuilt, the mistress of the house named it Manor of the Ashes. It hasn't burned since."

The path widened again. Martha clutched Vera's sleeve. "What caused the fires? It wasn't wizards, was it?"

Comfortably abreast, Martha had no difficulty hearing her friend's suddenly hushed voice. "Of magical activity, there was no sign. Some of the fires, no one knows. Others were from various natural causes. Only once did the house burn for a peculiar reason."

"Do tell!"

"It was in the 1400's, when the Scoville family was still in possession of the estate. It was a clear summer day, not a cloud in the sky. They were on the front lawn of the Manor entertaining the principal families of the district. It is written in records all over the county how a bolt of lightning struck the roof and it commenced burning. It was to the ground by nightfall."

"The lightning came from a clear sky? They were brave to keep building after that," Martha commented. "Are you certain the burning is done? Or is that why your papa sent you to school—to keep you away from the fireplaces?"

Vera gave a mock reproachful look. "A barn burnt when lightning hit it. That was during a storm. Papa thinks the estate likes the name, so is mollified. There hasn't been a fire since forever."

The pottery was all Vera promised. A tumbled stone building with three walls gaped holes for long vanished windows and two wide doorways front and back. Ivy had grown to cover the golden stone; the ground had been cleared to keep delicate ankles from turning. Paths through the remaining rubble offered agreeable strolls under the trees that forested the area.

Vera ran to a large, nearly flat sheet of stone. "Here is our dining table," she announced.

Martha oohed and aahed. Overhead, cloudless blue peeked through mottled green. The sun dappled her face—not enough came through the trees to make the clearing overly warm yet the air was fresh, not dank. She felt a fathomless sense of time slowed, if not halted. It was a lover's tryst, without Martha's love to make it complete.

"Tom, put the basket here. We shan't need you again until we go," Vera directed. The footman swung the basket to the stone and extracted a packet, his portion of the picnic. Nodding politely, he ambled away.

Martha said, "I'm not hungry yet. Shall we explore?" The girls spent an hour wandering, occasionally spying Tom, but seeing no other humans. Animals abounded, however. Bank voles and wood mice scampered from their feet. Of the paths, some ended in the wood, some meandered around the tumbled stone of the building and took one past tiny treasures. Moss growing thick on a stone traced a fine design, violets flourished. After skipping the paths, Martha's attention diverted to the remains of the pottery itself.

Rough stone crumbled, pocked with moss and other plants. Chinks in the walls had built layers of rich humus over the centuries and ivy, violets, and other sturdy greenery had sunk root. The random result of years was an appealing sight.

Inside the roofless building was one featureless room. "We can dig in the dirt floor with a stick for medieval remains," Vera claimed. The young ladies, heedless of the constraints of propriety, cleanliness, and the exigencies of adulthood, could not resist.

"Oh, look what I found," Martha breathed.

Vera scooted around in the dirt. "Trust you to find something—you have all the luck."

"It looks like a coin."

"It's a button," Vera corrected. "See the nail in the middle?"

"Avalon, our buttons are superior to this."

"It's made of pottery. Papa told me they used to make some of wood also, but those have not lasted." Vera's digging was unproductive; she found stones and a penny piece but a few years old. "Vicar Broom found a jeweled button once—that raised the neighborhood's interest for a while. Papa stopped men from destroying the site looking for more."

At that moment, the tinkle of stone cascading in a miniature avalanche reached their ears. Both girls looked up, startled. Martha peeked out the gaping rear doorway of the building to see Squire Michael, dressed for riding. He was at the back of the clearing under an ancient spreading oak, rummaging in a pile of stone.

Vera joined Martha in the doorway. "Squire Michael, I did not know you were coming here today!" she exclaimed. The man jerked and whirled, scraping stone with his gleaming boot. Gold tassels swung. Martha grinned that they had so startled the handsome man.

He caught himself and emoted. "But, soft! What light through yonder window breaks? It is the east, and Juliet is the sun! Arise, fair sun, and kill the envious moon." His voice faltered and died under identical pairs of disbelieving eyes. Neither Martha nor Vera knew the tale of *Romeo and Juliet* in any great depth.

With a grimace, Michael lowered his voice to a tone less like a cracked dinner bell. "I heard from a little bird that enchanting ladies were come to this medieval dell. Wanted to see it and couldn't think of superior company to do it with." His voice smoothed and became a croon. "Was coming to find you when I got distracted by the glint of something bright." His boot scuffled in the stone, collecting scratches.

Someone's valet was going to be peeved later.

Vera preened, thrilled that he sought them out. It seemed one of her secret fantasies was coming true. She, Vera Jane Jackson, would steal a beau from her condescending sister. What better choice than the exceedingly handsome son of a duke? Rich even without his father's backing, if her guess of Janice's priorities in friends was correct. Broad shouldered and clothed in Bond Street's finest, the youngest son of the Duke of Haverhorn would be a feather in any girl's cap. Vera decided on the spot that she would like a whole headdress of feathers, Banshee Brigade or no.

She didn't think further, an unusual occurrence for the girl who usually kept her head. Worse, Vera exhibited the utmost lack of grace—no girl should be so foolish as to believe such an arrant flirt as Michael showed himself to be.

The arrant flirt continued on a sigh, "To explore the mysteries of the past with the beauties of today. O happy day."

Martha muttered under her breath, "I'll believe it when mice chase cats." She sniffed.

Who was this Juliet he babbled about? Why did Squire Michael not tell them when he arrived at the pottery? Wouldn't he have come from the manor along the same path and appeared at the front of the ruin, as she and Vera had? Martha eyed the gelding tethered to a bush. As he rode up (surely he would have taken the path and not forced that elegant horse through the woods, chancing damage to its velvety coat?), he would have seen the picnic basket and he would have seen them. They should have heard him arrive. How long had Michael been there anyway?

Mindful of missing documents, the mistrustful girl itched to check the pile of stone Michael had been overturning so industriously. Grudging of the interruption, she tagged along as he and Vera flirted their way around the ruins.

* * *

Returned to the house after a stultifying hour spent with the 'infantry', as Squire Michael regarded any lady just released from the schoolroom, the would-be Romeo reported to his superiors his blighted investigation of the medieval pottery. Robert Jackson's study was clouded with cigar smoke.

"They caught me searching the ruins." He plunked down on the settee. "Your daughter, Mr. Jackson, is a darling. Believed every word I said. Hope you understand if I have to pay her some few attentions in the coming days to keep her off the scent."

Jackson waved a hand. "You shan't pass the line." A steely look belied the airiness of his words.

"Oh, no, shouldn't think of it," he replied, appalled. "Sweet thing, Miss Vera. Have all respect for her."

"Did you find anything?" Irvine leaned against the mantel, puffing. "Aught we can go on?"

Michael shrugged. "Not a pebble out of place, I should imagine. Spent above three hours eying stone after stone pile. But Martha Dunsmore! I say, Mr. Jackson, are you sure she is a proper companion for your daughter? Suspicious, flinty-eyed gel."

He would speak no further of his burgeoning suspicions, but Michael was beginning to think Martha was not the innocent schoolgirl she portrayed. No mere girl could be so unresponsive to his practiced charm. In his experience, no lady could resist being likened to the immortal bard's Juliet. That dratted Martha had looked at him as if he belonged in Bedlam.

Brinston, knowing his brother, deduced what he was thinking. Martha was too observant and discriminating to have fallen for Michael's flattery. Despite this faint praise, the marquess could not help but think Martha was a problem. No wonder that smuggler grabbed her. *She attracts trouble,* he thought. *If I didn't know better, I could almost think she was cursed.*

Jackson laughed and ground his cigar out. "She exhibits much the same quickness of thought as her brother. See that Martha doesn't steal a march on you and find the plans. I would hate to have her enmeshed in anything dangerous."

The group broke up. It had been a long day, fruitless and frustrating. Brinston mounted the stairs, debating in his mind the avenues he could explore.

* * *

Barnes hastened along the corridor. His lordship would be interested in the tidbits he had gleaned at dinner. Vera's maid, Bess, was wide-eyed at the attention the lofty valet paid her. She was a pretty lass, not so countrified that Barnes found her disgusting, but Bess' mouth wasn't as tight as it should be. She chattered about her mistress and her friend through the soup and meat dishes.

The two young ladies were hot on the scent of the traitor.

In his lordship's rooms, Barnes busied himself gathering the necessary. If only the man would wear a nightshirt. It disturbed the valet's fine sensibilities that his employer entered his sheets with no cloth on his hide. He risked a chill, even lung fever, going to bed like that. The valet had a set, still in its packaging, that he hauled wherever his lordship went, but the stubborn man wouldn't wear them.

"Good silk, they are," Barnes grumbled. "Blue, nothing funny or silly about them. The piping's the same color as the material too."

Brinston entered, startling the busy servant. The satiny sheets which Barnes was about to turn back fluttered out of the valet's hands. "Oh, my lord, gave me quite a turn, you did." Barnes calmed the sheets, restoring neatness to the bed. "I was that busy, thinking."

"Talking to yourself again." The master began unbuttoning his waistcoat.

"Wasn't really talking to myself, was telling the bed to be comfortable. I have news to report—" Barnes came to a military salute. "Their maid is free with her tongue, my lord. The two ladies have decided to search for the missing document; the maid is to keep her eyes open for clues. They have no idea, from what Bess let fall, what they are getting themselves into.

"Worse yet, Miss Dunsmore has been through most of the public rooms, peeking into drawers and such like." Barnes pulled to remove the coat from his lordship's shoulders. Seeing Lord Brinston attired in a long velvet robe, the valet continued.

"Mr. Lacey has exhibited symptoms compelling the young ladies to investigate that gentleman. It seems they witnessed a suspicious departure from the manor. Again, Dalton was able to provide details. Mr. Lacey did indeed act odd."

"He always comports himself strangely," Brinston interrupted. "Can't help his idiocy; it runs in the family. His departure was to meet one Nehemiah Light, a tradesman interested in collecting snuffboxes. My sources think Light contemplates opening a museum devoted to the taking of snuff."

He poured water into the basin while Barnes tidied his clothes. "Lacey's grandfather was one of the preeminent collectors of the gold and silver boxes of his time. There would be a mint in snuff boxes floating around the Lacey house. He will bear tighter investigation, though, to be on the safe side."

Barnes cleared his throat, unsure how his employer was going to take the remainder of his report. "And, uh, my lord?" At Brinston's cocked brow, the valet continued. "Your brother seems suspicious to Miss Dunsmore. His behavior today at the medieval ruins was most unfortunate."

"Already divined that." Brinston lathered soap on a cloth. "Females have much too much curiosity. Never know when to leave things alone. Martha has about as much sense as a cat stepped on by a cow to place Michael in the shoes of a traitor. If Jackson would..." He paused and sighed. "The only way to stop that girl from poking her nose into this business is to magic her. Can't do that—it isn't ethical. You have done well; keep me informed, Barnes. Any iota of information may be helpful."

A deep silence fell between the two. Water trickled, then splashed. Brinston washed his face while the valet tidied the room, tucking his lordship's boots under his arm. Just before Barnes left the room, Brinston spoke again, his voice muffled in a linen towel. "There hasn't been any mention of the Owl, has there?"

"No my lord. I haven't heard your nickname at all."

Chapter Eight

The Banshee Brigade was reading a book.

Janice sat on the sofa in the blue salon with a shaft of sunlight from the open window peeking over her shoulder. Always conscious of her appearance, she pleated her white dimity skirt artfully on the velvet-covered seat. A handsome leatherbound book before her eyes, she prepared to read aloud. The Brigade disposed themselves around the room in varying attitudes of annoyance, forbearance, and fortitude.

For once they were silent, bowing to the avid desire one member exhibited to read the book in question. She had nagged, begged, cajoled, and urged until the Brigade bowed to her request to shut her up.

Maria, the instigator of the scene, perched on a hassock at Janice's feet. Alone of the group, Maria wanted to read the book, yearned to know the tale. She had heard of this book; it had been praised as being a tome the entire world should read for its sense.

Her father always said she had no sense. "She has more than she shows, my dear," her mother would mutter under her breath whenever Maria did something her father thought ninnyish, which was almost every day. "She merely wraps her sense in cotton wool to keep it fresh."

Charlotte has sense, Maria thought, as Janice cleared her throat, preparatory to beginning. If the one sister had all the sense, did the other have the sensibility? She didn't know, but Maria did not want it to be so. Whatever sensibility was, it did not sound useful. Her father would not appreciate it.

That was why Maria wanted to read the book—maybe it would teach her what sense was versus sensibility. When she was as sensible as Charlotte, her father would be pleased with her, and perhaps, just perhaps, he would allow her to determine her own fate, allow her to marry where she pleased.

"'The family of Dashwood had long been settled in Sussex. Their estate was large,'" Janice read aloud the first sentences. She was interrupted by Colby.

"I say, don't know any family of that name in Sussex," he boomed. "I'm acquainted with most everyone too, because my estate is there. Would have heard of them, at the very least, if their lands are of any size. Did you get that right, Janice?"

"It's a pretend family," Michael informed him. "This is a novel. It's not real."

"Oh," Sir George replied. "That's all right then."

Janice continued. "'Their estate was large, and their residence was at Norland Park, in the center of their property, where, for many generations, they had lived in so respectable a manner as to engage the general good opinion of their surrounding acquaintance. The late owner of this estate was a single man...'"

"Late owner!" Charlotte indignantly slapped a pillow. "Is this a story about the heir? You said this was a proper novel, Maria, not one of those purple tomes Mama wishes us to avoid. You led me to believe this book would be uplifting. Instead, we are treated to the gothic nonsense my parents deplore more than *Americans*. I know how these tales proceed; the heir arrives and is a rotter. He persecutes the daughter of the house and forces her to wed with him. How could you bring this rubbish to our attention?"

Lacey laid a hand on Charlotte's arm. "Wait and see, my dear, wait and see. We are hardly into the tale; perhaps it is not so purple. Must say, seems too dull to be wicked."

Janice glared at the interruption and sought to find her place on the page. "Here," she mumbled, and continued reading. "'...who lived to a very advanced age, and who for many years of his life, had a constant companion and chatelaine in his sister.'"

As Janice took a breath to continue, Lacey spoke over her head to Charlotte. "See, my girl? Nothing improper here. The man takes in his spinster sister. My own uncle did much the same thing and never did an inopportune thing in his life."

"Could not the man have hired a chatelaine?" interposed Honoria. "It sounds as if he used his sister as a drudge. I would never allow that to happen to me."

"Wouldn't dare try," her brother inserted. "You'd poison me first turn."

Maria let out a peep. "Pleathe, can we continue the thtory?"

Ignoring the Silvester siblings' glares, Janice read on. "'But her death, which happened ten years before his own...'"

"I told you," Honoria crowed. "He worked his poor sister to the bone and wore her out. Ladies are much too delicate to be used as servants, no matter how one justifies the situation."

"She should be useful to her relations since she did not marry," Silvester defended. "What else was she to do? Not like the sister could manage an estate of her own."

"So if I choose not to wed, you will make me a scullery maid in your household," Honoria turned on Peter. "I would poison you for such dastardly behavior, brother."

"No, no," he hastily said. "Never would dare to do that to you, sis. Fact is, wouldn't have you in my household for all the tea in China. Bad enough to live under the cat's paw with a wife, but with m'sister? Unthinkable."

Honoria exploded. "I have my own resources, brother dearest," she hissed, "and have no need to rely on your unsteady support. I would not live with you for all the tea in Britain."

Colby tried to take them over the fence lightly. "Can't imagine you not marrying, my dear Miss Silvester. Your beauty and grace would charm any man. Not for such as you the position of scullery maid. Chit in the book must have been a dowd."

Honoria batted her eyelashes at Sir George. "You are too kind, sir."

Raising her voice, Janice returned to the page in front of her. "'...her death, which happened ten years before his own, produced a great alteration in his home; for to supply her loss, he invited and received into his house the family of his nephew Mr. Henry Dashwood...'"

"No. Don't continue." Charlotte jumped from her chair. "I knew it, I just knew it! The nephew will be a villain and he will try to do unspeakable things to some poor lady. She will be frightened to death and unless a gentle knight comes to her rescue, she will be ruined. Please," she begged Silvester, "I do not wish to hear this story. I know not what has gotten into Maria, but my mother would disapprove. I wish to go into the garden, or play at cards, or even do my needlework. Anything rather than listen to that nasty story." Charlotte had worked herself into a fine state. "Please, Peter, take me from here."

Silvester knew his duty to his agitated lady. "Of course, my dear. Shall we walk the lane and admire the trees? Let the others stay and corrupt their morals, I shall protect you from opprobrium." The two exited the room, Silvester leaning toward hers, offering consolation for the trial she had undergone.

At the door, Charlotte turned to her sister. "Wait till I tell Mama," she threatened.

Those remaining of the Banshee Brigade stared at Maria. Janice closed the book with a snap. "That is quite enough, I believe," she said under her breath to the girl on the hassock. "How could you have introduced us to that unprincipled tale, Maria? Your sister is overset and I vow my ears are burning."

Colby added his mite. "Books are nonsense anyway. Haven't finished one since Eton, nor do I want to do so now.

Muddle my brain with pap." He turned to Honoria. "Too famous a day to stay cooped up. And in a blue room, what? Enough to make a man gouty. Would you favor me with a drive into the village? Can luncheon at the inn."

Honoria preened at the marked attention of that buff gentleman and off they went, giving stiff good days to the people remaining in the salon.

Janice looked at Lacey. "Your dulcet voice reads remarkable well," he intoned. "The depth of understanding and emotion you put into the reading moved me."

"Thank you," she said. "I tried my best to please."

"You did, as you please me in all things. Shall we discuss your amazing ability whilst we wander the garden? I should like to hear more about how you cultivated that lilting tone."

Squire Michael and Maria were left alone in the blue salon. She drooped on the hassock, forgetting to tuck her feet under her hem. Michael, true to the ravening nature of the male beast, enjoyed the view of a neatly turned ankle and tried to think what to say. He could find nothing to ease his beloved's distress. Michael knew deep in his soul that Maria meant no harm, but the book did seem unsuitable.

Knowing he had to say something, he blurted thoughts without editing. "Wonder why such a shocking book is in the library here. Jackson must have windmills in his head to leave the dissipated thing where you ladies can find it."

Her god's disapproval was the last straw to Maria's camel's back. She dissolved into tears. "I am thorry. I wanted to learn about thenthe. Oh, Michael, I am tho thorry." She picked up the book and threw it across the room. The leather binding gleamed through the sunbeam and landed on the floor four feet from her. The pages bent and the cover faced up, the spine sparkling with gilt letters.

Michael kicked the book as he hurried to comfort her. His toe cracked the spine down the middle and the words, the title of the horrid book, *Sense and Sensibility,* lost their sheen as gilt flaked along the crack.

* * *

Laughing. She was on the terrace, leaning against the wall by an open window, filled with hilarity. The legendary Guinevere could not have presented a prettier picture.

Brinston watched Martha, aware of her every breath. He couldn't help but smile at the infectious levity. He could see his brother Michael with his beloved through the window. That silly Maria must have done or said something to make Martha laugh so. But when she pulled a handkerchief from her sleeve and wiped her eyes, it shook him to his soul. Just so did the duchess leak tears when she was filled with mirth.

It was then he realized how much Martha resembled his adored mother. Brinston could almost feel his heart tightening. They were silken bonds, those bands clenching around his heart, not painful in the least. A man could get used to them, which was a good thing. They didn't feel like they were going to dissolve any time soon.

He heard the echo of his father's words. "I couldn't resist the way she laughed." It was always said with a chuckle and an underlying honesty that couldn't be doubted. It was why his father had married his mother. They were devoted to each other, but it all started with her laugh.

Everyone, including Brinston himself, joked at how much the son resembled the father. He stared at the sky, silently begging Merlin to have pity on him.

* * *

After lunch, Mr. Lacey descended the stairs. Making a lightening decision, Martha nudged her friend and whisked behind one of the matched pair of porcelain heraldic shields that flanked the library doors. Rolling her eyes, Vera followed suit. Tucking her skirts close, she slid next to the wall by the other shield. With the indulgent eyes of the butler upon them, they had no intention of eavesdropping, but neither had any desire to see the Banshee. Mr. Lacey wouldn't be able to see them hidden there.

"Dalton, has a horse been called? I must be going if I'm to return in time to dress for the evening." Lacey's voice echoed off the high ceiling.

"Yes, sir." The butler bowed, raising his voice to be heard over the clock's pealing of the hour. "One of Mr. Jackson's geldings, I believe, has been saddled and is at the door."

Lacey fiddled with his cravat in the mirror, tugging starched folds towards the grass green of his lapels. His jowled face lowered, adding a third chin. His neck, so short as to be nonexistent, was red where the high starched neckcloth rubbed the skin like a hemp noose.

Dalton, the consummate butler, held Lacey's beaver and gloves. He gave no hint that two sprites hid behind the massive shields mere feet away, straining shell-like ears to hear the conversation.

Lacey slid a glance around the apparently empty hall and laughed, a slight tremor tinting his voice. "Do wish I hadn't to go. But damn, this is the only way to pay the debt." He tugged a glove over his fingers, and began smoothing it up his hand with the merest brush of his fingertips. "Debt of honor, what ho." In his concentration, his lips smoothed out to their natural straight line, with tiny dimples at the corners.

The butler made no reply, eyes correctly lowered, but fascination glowed in them as he covertly watched two fingertips smooth a slight wrinkle in Lacey's glove.

He continued to mumble, intent on the precise fit. "Don't like the cut of his coat. Deuced mushroom. But if this'll burn the vowels, will do it, by God. Wonder what he wants them for?" He turned to the butler for his hat, placing it over his impeccably tousled hair. "Talley ho, man, and all that rot. Don't let the ivory turners sink their claws into you, Dalton. Makes one do the damnedest things." Lacey lifted his hand and left on his mysterious errand.

With the closing of the door, puckish sprites erupted around the butler. "My word, Dalton, Janice has deplorable taste in men. Are all her friends such loose fish?" Vera danced.

Martha peeked through the light to the left of the door. "His mannerisms are as peculiar as a Punch puppet's." Turning her head, she queried, "What is an ivory turner?"

Wise to the vagaries of romantic young ladies, Dalton did not answer and Vera could not, knowing no more than her friend the cant of the gaming table. Vera only knew those few phrases she had picked up in the stables like 'loose fish'. That had been applied to the stable boy who was hired and fired, all within two days, for currying Beastslayer with the head groom's hair comb.

"Where is Janice?" Vera asked, tired of idiotic men.

"In the gilt salon, Miss. She and her friends are to play cards."

Vera said with satisfaction, "Good. Mama won't expect us to join them. Martha, let's rummage for those fans I told you about. I believe I know where they are."

The butler turned away and Vera started up the stairs. Martha, with a mischievous glance, opened the glass fronting the clock and turned the minute hand back five minutes. Then she followed her friend up the stairs.

As Martha and Vera clattered up the attic stairs, a confrontation was taking place in the gilt salon. "I saw you," Janice hissed. "Making eyes at Honoria. It was a disgusting display. Papa should send you back to London." Yes, Janice was peeved. How could Bryce Irvine fail to be aware of that? She did never like to have an admirer turn away. If he kept his temper, if he didn't respond, Janice should eventually wear out her anger.

But Janice's rage was not ready to burn out.

She took the glass of lemonade, the one she had been

sipping before Irvine happened upon her, and threw it at him. Typical lady, her aim was wretched. The glass hit the floor at least five feet from him, shattered and sprayed lemonade in an arc across the Aubusson rug and the sculpted legs of Mrs. Jackson's prized Louis XIV furniture.

Providentially, none of the spray landed on Irvine. He looked at Janice, who had the grace to blush. They both knew their association had only been a flirtation—she had no cause for jealousy. Never had there been any question of courtship between them. The lemonade sank into the rug as they stared at each other.

The remainder of the house party entered the room a few minutes later. Janice drummed her fingers on the gilded chair arm. Irvine lounged against the mantel half a room away while a maid gingerly plucked pieces of glass from the rug.

"Avalon," Mrs. Jackson whispered. "I do believe Janice has gone over the line and thrown something at Mr. Irvine."

"Nonsense," Miss Bridewell mouthed back. "If she had, Mr. Irvine would not look so collected. Surely it was an accident."

"Lemonade doeth get thicky when it drieth." Maria approved the cleanup. "I hope you did not thpot your thkirt." The Banshee Brigade went into full cry.

"Glasses should be made with an edge, so they can't slip out of the fingers."

"Should clear a path so we don't trip."

"Can't use this room for cards now."

"Will it smell like lemons all day?"

"She isn't doing it right."

"Lemonade, bah. What's wrong with a good burgundy?" A headache assailed the lady of the house. Fond as she was of Janice's set, sometimes they talked altogether too much.

"How about the gallery?"

"I do hope our game will not be long postponed. I

want revenge for losing ten shillings the other day."

"Good it's not port. Port stains."

Amidst the chatter of the Banshees, the most important comment was not uttered aloud. *Thank God I moved them.* Then Dalton arrived and shooed everyone from the room so the carpet could be rolled up and the floor cleaned.

* * *

What was taking so long? A letter had been sent—there should be a reply any day. It was simple to caution oneself to patience, that the letter would be answered in good time, but Brinston was too efficient at his work. Who would think the man would be savvy enough to look behind picture frames? It was unnerving to close the door at the west end of the gallery while Brinston opened the east.

If it wasn't that bastard, it was his brother, sister, or that damn valet snooping. Or one of those twits, Martha or Vera. Morgana take the lot of them.

With all of them searching, those damn papers were moving around the house like a gamester outrunning his creditors. It was tempting to put them back in the box. At least one could remember where they were.

Hmm, that was a thought. Would they be stupid enough to not check the one place they didn't think the papers would be—where they belonged? It would negate the chance of being caught in the act; finally secrete the papers where no one would look. No. Better not chance it.

The papers couldn't be seen under Mrs. Jackson's wardrobe. They should be safe there.

While one occupant of the room ill-wished her, Martha plinked on the pianoforte.

Lord Brinston was ignoring her. Martha could come to no other conclusion. When his shining presence was added to the group in the drawing room, the ducal heir spoke a word, threw a smile, gave his attention to every person in the room but her. She bristled, condemning her brother for possessing such a haughty friend and herself for caring about him.

A flirtatious Honoria had him trapped. Lord Brinston looked bored. Served him right. Martha's fingers flew through a difficult run.

Do I love him? she wondered. *I hardly know the man. I have seen him seldom and there is no intimacy between us. He does not care for me. How could I? I can't love him. I won't!*

Ignoring the contradiction, Sir Hurst's sister played the coda and compared Squire Michael's flamboyance with both her brother and his. Hurst always was tidy, conservative, and elegant. Lord Brinston added something more, an indefinable air that called to Martha. Michael, on the other hand, seemed like a schoolboy aping his elders—too loud, too bright, too everything.

To achieve her comparison, it was necessary to look at Lord Brinston. Martha spent a considerable time doing this. She should have looked at Michael also, but somehow never did.

She surrendered the pianoforte to Charlotte and joined Vera in their corner. Soon enough, Lady Coletta was seated with the girls, interrupting Martha's inner musings. Playing with her demure string of matched pearls and grinning like a fiend, Coletta was the least imposing of the ducal progeny in attendance at the Manor of the Ashes.

"Look at Michael," she whispered. "He is about to play a trick." They watched from across the room as Squire Michael took Maria's wine glass and, creeping quietly behind his brother, dribbled sherry into a stem of claret sitting on a table. Brinston, in conversation with Honoria, reached for the glass and took a sip; a pained twisting of his lips signaled discomfort. Then he swallowed. And swallowed again, closing his eyes.

Michael and Maria rounded Brinston's back; Maria

engaged Honoria in conversation. Brinston glared and tried to take his brother's glass.

"Poor Brin," Coletta said. "Can't you just taste sherry and brandy mixed?" She shuddered.

Enjoying another's prank as well as her own, Martha mentioned, "I admire how comfortable you are with your brothers. I have tried to think how it would have been if I had been born before mine."

"Or even to have a brother rather than a sister," Vera interjected. "To meet gentlemen your brothers brought home, at holidays, for example. Janice brings them, but..." She looked distastefully toward Mr. Lacey.

"You have no control over who comes. I suffered from that also." Coletta laughed. "I remember one of Brin's friends developed a violent attraction for me—I was so absorbed with my wardrobe I failed to recognize his passion—but when my brother caught him confessing his love for me, he told him to "cut line," I was but his *sister*. My retaliation was swift. I had that boy so entranced he asked the Duke for my hand."

Vera nodded. "Janice acts like that. It is irritating to be treated like a dimwitted child."

"I was worse than my brothers, when I think back," Coletta shrugged. "I know I invariably crowed when I caught the larger fish. I doubt Michael has yet forgiven that I was better with the bow and arrow."

As two faces reflected absolute astonishment, she said, "I was raised by the Duchess more independently than is usual. I shared a tutor with my brothers. Mama also encouraged physical activity: fishing, riding and running about the estate for the health of my body. Papa taught me to shoot and fence."

"Shoot?"

"Most ladies scream when they hear a pistol, don't they? Helpless things, they don't seem capable of more than dressing and dancing."

Awed, the girls hung on her words. Lady Coletta had

seen numerous seasons, rejected more suitors than Vera or
Martha thought of meeting without a breath of scandal, and
had learned the valuable commodity of kindness. Emulation
had Vera straightening her spine.

Conversation groupings shifted. Honoria pulled on
Janice's arm. "Come here," she ordered in a low voice.

"What is it?" Janice put down the china shepherd so
its back was to the shepherdess and followed her friend to the
wall.

"You have to make him stop."

"Honoria," Janice protested.

"No, I know you think it nothing, but he gives me
the shivers. Please, just tell Mr. Irvine I have no interest in
him."

Janice shrugged. "I have. Ignore him." Their
conversation was interrupted by Maria and Charlotte.

"Janice," Charlotte cried, "tell Maria what you used to
color your shells. I particularly admired how you shaded the
roses on that picture frame." She turned to Honoria. "No less
than three shades of red; the flowers looked darling." The
female Brigade began discussing the use of Brazil-wood in
painting shells.

Mrs. Jackson threw a hand to her mouth. "Oh, I
forgot." She bustled from the room.

Michael wandered over and Vera lifted flirtatious eyes
to him as Martha excused herself. "Tell me, who was Juliet?"
Vera asked.

"From one of Shakespeare's plays," Michael said. "She
was fair as the sun; Romeo was her beloved."

"I don't know her. Is Juliet in one of the histories? Or
The Merchant of Venice?"

"The play is called *Romeo and Juliet.*"

"It must be prodigiously romantic."

"It is. They both die at the end."

Lady Coletta's laugh tinkled as Martha skirted the
room and slipped out the door. No one would pay her the

least mind. She had business to tend.

* * *

Robert Jackson noticed Lord Brinston tense as the door closed after Vera's little friend. He suppressed the unholy amusement that burbled up his throat at the look on the marquess's face. Fancy Brin muddled by a little girl.

Not so little, he acknowledged ruefully as he looked at his daughter. Both Martha and his Vera were nigh grown. Still, it looked as if Brin was past paying attention and into obsession. He hated having the girls searching for the report. His complaints grew stronger by the hour. Yes, it was most amusing.

Unaware she had drawn anyone's attention, Sir Hurst's gremlin sister was bent on mischief. Martha climbed the stairs and traversed the empty hall.

She had chosen her time well; the servants should be at their meal in the service wing and the family and guests were all in the drawing room. The tea tray would not arrive for another hour, so there was little reason to think any of the company would interrupt her.

Deserted did not begin to describe the corridor. It was dark and the ceiling felt like it was pressing down upon her. Flickering candles threw menacing shadows at paced intervals. The curtains lining embrasures gave the sense of hidden figures; their folds seemed to undulate in the dimness.

Pale busts of England's past seemed alive, following her progress with sightless eyes. Arriving in front of Dom Lacey's bedroom door, her shaking hand fumbled on the knob. Then she whisked into the unlocked room. The eerie atmosphere dissipated.

Brocade drapes were pulled for the night. Through the dimness she could see Lacey's toiletries spread on a table (cosmetic powder and a bottle of Gowland's lotion testified to his dandyism), wash basin and pitcher on a stand next to it. A gilded mirror glowed above. Martha lit a candle and placed it atop a bureau next to a small traveling case.

She flipped the box lid up; studs, tie pins, and loose change lay jumbled. Eying the dimensions of the box, she realized there was no space for a hidden compartment of any size. Dropping the lid, she turning to survey the chamber, her white dress shimmering.

A small leather-topped desk littered with papers sat at the far side of the room. Gliding over, Martha turned the papers, reading bits of them. Lacey's mother seemed his most regular correspondent; sporting papers, memorandums from a tailor regarding the cut of sleeves, and other paraphernalia of the carefree bachelor were what she found.

Where else could papers be hidden? Opening the dual doors of the rosewood wardrobe, she patted the coats hanging there. The Banshee did not have a large wardrobe, but the coats he did possess were well-made, if foppish. No crackle came from any of the pockets. She knelt and stuck her arms inside several pairs of boots. No paper.

Next, the ghostly figure flitted to the bed and lifted the mattress at the sides. Nothing along the edges. She tucked the sheets in and smoothed the coverlet. The edges of the carpet were flung back to reveal faintly dusty wood. The maids did a thorough job cleaning and no bundle lurked. She circled the room, checking where she thought paper could be hidden. Nothing.

Then she saw the umbrella leaning where the wardrobe met the wall, and her imp of mischief awoke. Returning to the desk, Martha rummaged until she found several unused sheets of paper. These she tore into tiny bits, which she dropped into the closed umbrella.

At last, she snuffed the candle, opened the door, and ran into a hard male waistcoat.

"Oh, spare me Elaine's grief," she gasped and took a smart step back.

"Done?" Lord Brinston took her upper arm in an

unbreakable clasp and without another word propelled
Martha along the hall. They turned the corner by the main
stairwell and headed into the east wing at a fast pace, never
sighting another face. Dim candles flashed by, the curtained
embrasures looked like dull spots against the wall. Holding
her arm, the marquess didn't look at her, only steered her
around sharp corners and down long halls.

He felt the flush of battle on his cheek. The blood
pulsed in his ears. Not since Lord Brinston had subdued the
smugglers at Ramsgate had he been so challenged. Her step
lagged; his hand tightened and pulled. It made him peevish,
having this girl insert herself in his business.

No, it went beyond peevish. If she wouldn't behave
like a lady, he wouldn't treat her as one. Brinston lengthened
his stride. Martha stretched her legs as far as the hem of her
dress allowed to keep up with the headlong rush. The girl was
panting for breath from skipping and running to keep up
with his stride by the time Lord Brinston flung open a door
and pushed her in, slamming the door closed. Martha was in
her own room. Where she belonged.

Brinston strode the corridor, seething, although no
agitation showed on his face. That girl was going to be the
death of him. He'd had to use a scrying spell to locate
her—never would have dreamed she would be in there.
Didn't the chit know the consequences of being caught in a
man's bedchamber?

At moments, Martha seemed a schoolgirl, giddy with
her first experiences in society. Then, remembrance came that
she was but a few months behind Maria Wentworth in
age—the same Maria that his brother intended to take to
wife—and Brinston was confused again. No, the Dunsmore
chit had not been presented at the Queen's drawing room,
but she was all woman in a girl's form. Of an age to be wed,
he reminded himself.

God help him.

* * *

Martha stared at her dressing table. *No, I do not like him, much less love him,* she scolded herself. *It was humiliating. Being towed like a—like a recalcitrant sheep returned to the flock—no—a dog escaped from the kennel. But his hand...even though he held me firmly, it did not hurt, not the slightest. Not like that vile smuggler, who tore my sleeve and left bruises ringing my arm.*

When she entered the room, Vera found her friend gazing out the window. "Did you find anything?" Vera bounced on the bed. "I did not. Maria Wentworth is untidier than any of the girls at school. I imagine her maid gave up trying to neaten up after her long ago."

"No," Martha replied. "I found nothing to cast suspicion on Mr. Lacey or explain what he was going to sell the other day. But I dislike Lord Brinston extremely." She untied the cords and twitched the curtains into place over the window.

"Martha, really. You have been mooning around forever over him. Ever since he saved you from that smuggler at Ramsgate, all I have heard is how marvelous your 'angel' is. You were in love with him; he was more handsome than any other, more the gentle knight. How did you change your mind? You didn't speak to him in the drawing room, not that I recall."

"It was not in the drawing room that I discovered my enmity. He met me as I was leaving Mr. Lacey's room, the contemptible man."

"Oh, this is disappointing. I was certain you would make a match with him and become a duchess. You kept calling him an angel and I thought— Outside Mr. Lacey's room! He knew you went in! Oh dear, I do hope he does not mention the circumstances to Papa." Vera twirled a finger around her chestnut braid. "I don't see how we could explain to Papa why you were in Mr. Lacey's bedroom. He would be as cross as Miss Kilborn after you wrote that letter to your brother. Did Lord Brinston say anything about Papa?"

"No." The answer was reluctant. Martha glared into the mirror that glittered over the dresser. "He is the most odious...Vera, promise that Lord Brinston won't intimidate you into not seeking those papers."

"He must be like Papa when in a temper. Best to stay away from him." Vera was familiar with the autocratic decrees of dominant men. Papa could be unbelievably stern. At Martha's glare, she sighed. "Yes, madam, I promise. I will keep Lord Brinston at arm's length, refusing to listen to him on any subject of any consequence, even if he threatens me with a pot of boiling oil." She bent her head to begin the self-imposed task of straightening Martha's jewelry box.

"Drat. Chains knot themselves. Did you know that, Martha?"

* * *

In the linen room, Amelia showed her guest the fine lace her grandmother had been used to creating. Coletta oohed and aahed the workmanship. "Grandmama used carved ivory bobbins," Amelia said as she explained the process. "I remember wanting to play with them, they were so pretty, but I wasn't allowed to touch."

"I wish I knew how to make this. It's exquisite. How can you bear to keep it hidden away and not use it?" Coletta fingered the fine threads. "This is silk."

"Hah. Wait till you wed, my dear. You will learn. If I laid this lace out, Robert would manage to snag his studs on it, or drop cigar ash on it, or absentmindedly wipe his nose with it. Men," she concluded.

Coletta laughed. "I think I know what you mean. Men are like cows, are they not? Heedless of their surroundings and impossible for the reasonable person to fathom. Look at my brother, Michael. He chases Maria

Wentworth all over England rather than taking his life in his hands and offering for her. Sure of her father's refusal, he dares not try. I'd elope rather than care about a father's decree."

Amelia's eyes sparkled. "Maybe he will resolve his doubts. Speaking of romance, have you noticed Brinston's behavior with Martha? I find it rather telling."

"You are incurably romantic, are you not? It would be a wonder if Brinston fell for so young a girl. She is just out of the schoolroom, after all." She changed the subject. "Amidst your dreaming, Amelia, have you noticed anything suspicious?"

The lady of the manor furrowed her brow. "Those dratted papers. No, I had my maid poke around—she found nothing except some of those horrible Gilray cartoons. Nor have I noticed anything that seems pertinent, other than Mr. Lacey's association with that vulgar man. Thank goodness he meets him away from the manor; I don't know what I should do if called upon to entertain a man of his stamp over the tea table."

"Has Mr. Jackson come to any conclusion on that?"

"Yes. He says that Mr. Lacey is following the time-honored custom of selling his valuables to cover losses at the gaming tables, most probably some snuffboxes his grandfather collected. There are hints that Maria and Charlotte Wentworth are doing the same."

"Their brother, I would assume. I have heard tales of him." They rolled the lace back in its plain linen holder so it did not crease and went to find Miss Bridewell. Agnes had a fascinating book that told how bobbin lace was made.

* * *

Damn, damn, damn. Brinston was being a little too clever, him and that pointy-eared valet of his. He would ruin everything. Something had to be done about their snooping about looking for the papers. In for a penny, in for a pound. A body can only hang once.

It was in the gardener's shed—such an innocuous package. Blue with white lettering. It was best for clearing vermin from the barns, the farmers said. But it wouldn't do to give it to the whole household. Lord no. What would he eat, but no one else? Well, except Martha Dunsmore. Wouldn't mind if she nibbled too. Irritating chit, into nooks and crannies where she hadn't any business. She was almost as bad as Brinston.

Has to be something with a strong enough taste that wouldn't be universally eaten. Brandy? No, the chit wouldn't drink it. Too bad it couldn't be something at the dining table. That would be easiest, but it wouldn't do to kill the whole house. Something would come up.

Rat poison.

Chapter Nine

A house party had certain expected entertainments. One favorite that could not be dispensed with was the picnic, to be held on a day when the weather cooperated. Food would be lugged (by servants, so it was not an onerous chore) to some bucolic site, along with tables and chairs for the comfort of the diners.

Mrs. Jackson had no intention of shirking convention. Today was designated picnic day. A sumptuous luncheon had been loaded into a wagon at the kitchen entrance and was even now wending its bulky way toward the favorite outdoor eating spot of the neighborhood, the ruined medieval pottery. Furniture had already been delivered to the site; it was shrouded by Holland covers until the party's arrival so as not to collect dew, leaves, or bugs. The stable boys, saddled with the chore of delivering and setting up the furniture, had completed their work and returned to the manor. If there was a bit of grumbling at the idiocy of it all, no ears of consequence heard.

Every vehicle was taken from the stables and horses hitched. The same stable boys who hauled furniture contrived a picturesque sight. Five conveyances stood in a row on the gravel drive at the front of the manor; seven fine horses stamped and whinnied their approval or displeasure at being hitched to the conveyances. Likewise, seven grooms held on to the horses to see that they did not leave for the picnic with vehicles unoccupied.

The only person missing was Bryce Irvine, who was to catch up with the party later, after checking that the leak in the grain barn was plugged. He had volunteered. Vicar Broom and his family, as well as two other families resident in the neighborhood, would meet the manor party at the site.

Effervescent Banshees capered. They would fill the barouches and curricle, with the excess joining Robert and Amelia Jackson in the traveling carriage. Standing on the graveled drive, heedless of stones digging through the thin leather soles of her slippers, Maria waved her handkerchief to Janice and trilled, "Thith ith the betht idea, dear Janithe."

Honoria added under her breath, "Especially if that dreadful man doesn't join us." A groom's strong hold on the curricle's pair saved them from disaster as the horses took exception to the white square waved before their eyes.

Lord Brinston consented to escort the two youngest ladies of the party, Vera and Martha, in the pony cart. In acknowledgement of the ignominy of the exalted marquess driving a lowly cart, one of the stable's finest had been hitched to the shafts. Lady Coletta, peeking to the end of the line as she mounted her carriage, smiled at her brother. He tipped his elegant gray beaver with a wink and a wry grimace.

Thankfully, it was but a short drive to the pottery. Squire Michael was bored by Colby's reminiscences of picnic delicacies past, Honoria was piqued because her salmon lutestring clashed horribly with Maria's green muslin. Janice got a cinder in her eye and cried copiously while Lacey fretted.

Silvester was in the throes of a fascination with the history of the snuffbox. Charlotte could listen endlessly to the sound of her favored suitor's voice—she didn't mind his verbal debate as to whether Bilston in the Midlands or Battersea by the Thames was the superior enameller. As host, Robert Jackson could but follow his guest's conversational lead. His patience tried to the limit, he directed a long stare at his mirthful spouse.

In the cart, Lord Brinston had one eager young lady hanging on his every word. The other young lady took exception to every other word. "You handle the reins well, my lord," Vera ended a stultifying silence as the cart swung through the gates onto the lane. "I imagine driving a pony cart is an insult to your skill."

"Never, Miss Jackson," Lord Brinston replied. "A pony cart can be a challenge—it all depends on the horseflesh. This is an excellent animal."

"Papa gave you the best horse," she confided. "We should have the pleasantest ride, even if we are relegated to this old cart."

"I aim to please."

Vera was peeking at the marquess's waistcoat. "Tell me, if you please, sir, are all the gentlemen at Camelot wearing understated clothing?"

Lord Brinston glanced at her. "Understated?"

"Yes. Dull, as your waistcoat is." Vera flushed at her daring but Lord Brinston grinned.

"Yes, my dear, unfortunately gentlemen are wearing dull colors. You would have to blame Beau Brummell for that."

"Oooh, do you know the Beau?"

Silent thus far, Martha perked up. "My brother knows Brummell," she reminded Vera.

"I must confess," Brinston said, "he is a stimulating companion."

"Hurst says Brummell is inflated with his own consequence and could fly away like one of those monstrous balloons people keep pushing into the sky. They fill them with hot air and they rise right up," Martha pronounced.

"The Beau is an arbiter of fashion, one it would behoove you to cultivate, Miss Dunsmore," Lord Brinston warned. "It would do your reputation no good to disregard his estimation."

"Pooh. I will follow my own fashion, not what is decreed by a fatuous man who has become more eminent than he deserves. I don't see what Mr. Brummell should have to say as to my wardrobe's contents."

Vera spoke up. "Surely Mr. Brummell would be

tolerant of differences in aesthetic judgment. After all, not everyone cares for the same hues nor is suited to the same cut of dress."

He looked kindly at Vera. "True, but within the latitude of what is considered smart, the Beau has the last word. If he decrees that a color is *passé,* you will not see it on anyone in the Park within two days."

"So you only wear lackluster colors because someone else insists on it." Martha put her nose in the air. "Avalon forbid you should be original and wear what pleases you, rather than what pleases Mr. Brummell."

Disparagingly, the Marquess of Brinston looked Martha up and down before he focused his eyes back on his driving. "Your dress is last year's style. A deep flounce hasn't been seen in ages and the trim is all wrong. Further, your bonnet, pleasing as it is on you, lacks dash. If you appeared in town dressed as you are, you would be written off as a dowd. This without Beau Brummell's glance falling upon you."

As Martha fumed, speechless, Vera hastily changed the subject. "And the Opera, sir. Do you attend?"

"I sometimes do, Miss Jackson, though it is not my favorite style of music. I prefer orchestral to choral music."

"You go because Mr. Brummell says you should, I suppose," Martha muttered.

He caught the sentence. "No, I do not attend the Opera because of Mr. Brummell. Rather, if the company I find myself with wishes to attend, I am willing."

Vera was becoming desperate; she rolled her eyes at the sky, searching for an inoffensive conversational gambit. "Have you been to the play often?"

"Certainly. Everyone goes to Covent Garden." Lord Brinston gritted his teeth.

Martha smiled. "Ah, still no originality. I would not have taken you for a sheep, but then, I do not know you well, do I."

"Baa," he growled.

Martha shifted on the bench. Her skirt caught in a wickedly long splinter on the edge of the wood. "It's going to rip," she muttered in dismay as she worked to remove the material.

Vera exclaimed at the disaster; Martha's eyes filled with tears. Twisting at the waist to reach, her sensitive fingers picked at the splinter, but the wood was tangling more and more in the threads of muslin. "There is going to be a gaping hole," she moaned. "Why, oh why didn't I accompany Mrs. Jackson in the carriage?"

Vera's fingers plucked at the wood around the speared material.

"Don't pull," Martha gasped. "If I nudge each bit of wood free..."

Brinston looked over Martha's shoulder. The dress would be ruined. Worse, her chocolate eyes were leaking unhappiness. He knew he shouldn't, but he did it anyway. With a wave of his fingers and a single whispered word, the material slid off the splinter without a snag.

"Thank goodness," Martha said. "I can't even see the spot." The crisis passed, her eyes cleared. She refocused her irritation on Lord Brinston.

So it went, all three miles of country lane worth. Vera tried to find a neutral topic, Lord Brinston tried to follow her lead, and Martha sniped at his replies. Oil and water, Vera decided. Her friend and her father's associate should be kept as far from each other as could be contrived. But she would have been amazed if she could have peeped into their thoughts.

Martha was intent on showing Lord Brinston that she was not to be taken for granted. He had held the reins of their association the whole time she had known him. She resented him forcing her to step as he ordered. At Ramsgate, he had been an angel. Now he emulated Mordred. *No more,* her self-esteem ordered.

Lord Brinston's arrogance at their last encounter

rankled. Who was he to haul her to her room like a dog to the kennel?

Brinston recognized the message Martha was trying to convey. His problem was he was not sure how he should answer the lady's challenge. He saw but two choices: accede gracefully, admitting the justice of her complaint, or aggressively insist that he retain the upper hand. He couldn't let go of a vision of his friend's sister on the ground in a pool of blood. People who committed espionage tended to err on the side of violence. Martha didn't have the least idea what could happen. Brinston did and he wasn't about to let her chance being hurt. Or killed.

The marquess, faced with a quandary, fell back on comfortable, familiar arrogance to carry him through the situation. It had worked for him before. Unfortunately, he had a suspicion it was not a good way to handle Martha.

When they reached the pottery, Lord Brinston swung Vera down. As she stepped back and waited for him to help Martha, he turned and strode toward the group gathered in the clearing. Being a gentleman, he did his best not to scurry. He kept his back to the girls as he merged with the Banshee Brigade. There was safety in numbers.

"Well," Martha harrumphed. "That tells you his manners." She clambered down.

Vicar Broom's brood was already cavorting around the pottery. Ladies stretched out on huge blankets, disdaining the chairs set at tables. With picnic baskets set to hand, they prepared to idle a few hours away. "Ah, we have the cold chicken and chilled bottles," Amelia commented, rooting around in a huge wicker hamper. "That outlandish curry dish of Lord Brinston's must be in another basket. Have you heard of curry, ladies? It's some heathenish spice from India, terribly strong and burning. His description was so awful, I told Cook to make just enough of the recipe for Lord Brinston. No one else would care for it."

Another lady wriggled her toes. "Are you of the same

mind as I? I plan not to move until it is time to go home."

"We can chaperone from a distance today," Anne Broom agreed. "It is not as if there were any gentlemen here who would go past the line with our girls." Her eyes followed her younger daughter, flitting around the Brigade.

Lady Coletta kept her peace and smiled. She'd seen enough intrigue between the sexes to scandalize the court for a month; her brother Michael's stuttering romance alone could support a penny-press novel. Didn't Amelia feel they needed chaperonage? Moreover, Coletta enjoyed the curried rice recipe Brinston had introduced to the Shipley family chef. But no matter. "A restful afternoon is welcome," she murmured.

"Avalon." Agnes Bridewell loosened her bonnet strings. "This group has been well-behaved from the moment they arrived at the Manor. I have not seen anything objectionable from any of the men, including that pest, Robert."

"His improprieties are carefully conducted behind closed doors," Amelia said.

Robert Jackson and several others made themselves comfortable on chairs a short distance from the recumbent ladies. A spirited discussion of plans for the harvest gala to be held that autumn gave way to desultory meanderings. Vicar Broom praised the poor box donors to the skies and his daughter quizzed the gentlemen on the hazards of hazard.

Well away from meddlesome chits, Brinston was thankful Jackson had warned him. At some time in the distant past, rites had been practiced here. Not in the pottery, but somewhere near. They hadn't been black rites, not that he could tell, but the woods around him echoed with the remains of spells. They seeped around tree roots, swirled, and crawled over his skin with ghostly tentacles.

Magic permeated the air.

Because Robert had warned him, Brinston hadn't been caught by surprise. He was able to guard himself against the aural remains. He had thought to examine some of them, perhaps analyze what the spells had been intended for, but there were too many. They were too tangled. After what must have been centuries of the broken bits floating around, they had no more meaning than random letters of the alphabet scattered over a wide beach.

All they achieved was to make him uncomfortable. Uneasy. A little distracted. Moving to stand with his back against the bole of a tree, Brinston cocked his head and stared at the sky. When Coletta tucked her hand into his, he smiled, grateful for the warmth.

"Does this place disturb you so much?" she asked.

"No," Brinston slowly answered. "It isn't disturbing. It's more diffused than that." His sister looked perplexed so he tried to explain. "Think of the fog at Camelot," he said. "It makes your skin clammy. Fog interferes with sight and muffles sound. It can't be avoided. No matter how tight your windows and doors, it worms its way into your house and hampers you. There is a physical interaction between you and the fog. This," he indicated the woods with a sweep of his hand, "is less substantial. One can sense it, but you can't see or feel it. It's more like perfume. Unmistakably there, but it only impinges on your nose. Stop up the one sense and it is impotent, harmless."

"So you are only threatened by the magic in the area in one way?"

"It's not a threat, any more than the scent of roses is a threat. It's just there."

Coletta looked relieved. "I thought, watching you, that there might be danger."

"No, There is no danger. Only irritation. As if I were in a room with fifty women, all wearing different perfumes. I am irritated by it, but if I could just dampen my senses, I could ignore it. Render it meaningless. My concern is that I cannot monitor the protective spell."

As her eyes flew to his, he shook his head. "Not to

worry, little sister. The enchantment only wavered for a short time; there is no reason to believe leaving it untended for an afternoon will be harmful."

"I saw how tired renewing the spell made you. This is perhaps the first time I am glad not to have your gifts. I don't feel anything, don't sense anything."

"You don't really wish to be a wizard or magician, sweet Letta," Brinston said softly, rubbing his thumb along hers. "Researching spells and old magic satisfies you. I've never seen you wanting to set an enchantment yourself."

She stretched up and kissed his cheek. "You know me too well, dear brother. I'm going back to the ladies. Let me know if you need me."

"If I get lost in the trees, I'll bellow my head off."

* * *

Michael kept hold of Maria's dainty hand after he helped her over a fallen log on the path. She thrilled at the touch, as did he. Voices could be heard close by, but no one was there to see him overcome by emotion.

Michael swept Maria into his arms. A sweet kiss later, he laid his forehead against her bonnet. "I don't have you to myself nearly enough, my love," he murmured. "When we are back in town, do you think it would do any good if I spoke with your father? I don't want to wait fifty years to marry you."

"Oh Michael," sighed the delicate lady. "If only you dared. But Papa ith thtill determined on a title for me. He wath rumbling about Sir Perth before we left. Ath if I could like him after knowing you."

"Then I shall be patient a while longer. But not too much longer, my little dove." He lowered his head for another kiss.

In a small clearing to the west of the pottery, Janice twirled around Dom Lacey, her ankles flashing below her outspread skirt. "Vastly fetching, my dear," Lacey grinned, admiring the ankles more than the dress Janice was touting. "But if you twirl more, you will become hopelessly dizzy."

She giggled and leaned against him. "You are right. I am dizzy already. Hold me, Dom." Janice knew what she was doing, flouting the conventions and anticipating his reaction.

"Baggage, what if someone should see?"

"They may watch *a bras ouverts.*" She lifted her glowing face to look him in the eye and pursed her lips in the enticing manner she had practiced in the mirror. Lacey had as much self control as the next man; he promptly covered the presented lips with his own. Two minutes later, his hand slid up her midriff.

Silvester glowered at the vicar's daughter as she gathered bluebells by the east wall of the ruins. Charlotte leaned over and whispered, "If you gave the tiniest little push, she would land in the bushes."

He shook his head. "Then your father, not to mention hers, would have my hide. Tale would be sure to get back to both with the speed of a prime *on dit.* What bet you I would be thrown out of the manor? Come, my goddess, can't you think of some other way to detach the tenacious Miss Broom from my side?"

Charlotte sighed. The girl was thickheaded and immune to hints. This picnic was not generating the opportunities for flirtation she had hoped for. How she longed for a kiss.

Honoria and Sir George absconded with two bottles of claret and settled in a small clearing somewhere behind the pottery, south of the elders. Sipping and listening to the wildlife, they enjoyed a companionable silence like a long-wed couple. Neither felt the need for excitement or passion. The wine was excellent.

* * *

To the north, Vera chased Martha down a path. "Got you," she panted as her hand touched Martha's back.

Martha veered toward a small clearing as she slowed her pace. Coming to a stop, both girls fought to breathe normally as they finished the lengthy game of tag.

Her chestnut curls bouncing, Vera plopped on a flat boulder. Lying on it with a hand holding her heaving chest, she rolled her head. "You will be the death of me, Martha Dunsmore," she complained. "I thought we escaped from the schoolroom and here you have me running around like a hoyden."

"Or a gremlin," Martha gasped, joining Vera on the boulder. "Remember, I have to keep in shape, else Hurst won't recognize me when he comes." She laughed aloud. "Imagine him demanding of your father, 'Where have you put my sister? All I can find is this lady.' He would be fit to murder. I don't believe he would know what to do with me."

"He would take you to Camelot and marry you off to the first gentleman who offered," Vera predicted. "Then he would be free."

Martha lay back on the sun warmed stone. "He's not like that. He would make certain the gentleman would treat me kindly first."

Fanning her heated cheeks with her hands, Vera stood. "Put you on a pedestal, you mean. How depressing. Stay here. I'm going to go snitch some of the chicken and lemonade. We can have our own private picnic here." She moved up the path.

Martha closed her eyes on the stray thought that there was nothing to stop a certain marquess from offering for her.

Lord Brinston stood unnoticed in the woods and watched Martha, thankful he had not eaten the marmalade. He was certain it held cinnamon. If he had begun itching, his defenses would be nil. He'd forget himself; he'd lose his famous control and leap on the girl. It didn't matter that deep down that was what he wanted to do. He was going to retain control if it killed him.

The faint miasma of magic, long dissipated, but lingering like strands of cobweb in the woods, strummed on his sensitive nerves, increasing his discomfort. He hadn't told Coletta all. Magicians felt more intensely than others. Much more intensely. It tended to knot their stomachs.

She stretched like a kitten in the sun, arms over her head, and closed her eyes.

Damn the girl, how dare she entice me? Brinston thought. Breasts thrust skyward, ready for a man's attentions, Martha made him want to stroke her like a tabby. She would arch her back and purr...muscles tightened. That was not fair, he then acknowledged, consciously relaxing. She was oblivious to his presence. Brinston shifted on his feet, wishing the chit would go. He wanted to be closer, much closer, but that was not wise. Not unless he was prepared to wed her. An honorable man did not seduce his friend's sister—not unless the ring was ready for her finger.

A ring. He shuddered. That decision was too important to make under the influence of desire. But curse Lancelot, what desire!

As a slight movement registered in the periphery of her vision, Martha turned her head, expecting to see a rabbit or deer. "What are you doing here?" she asked as she sat up on the stone.

The marquess lifted the corner of his mouth and ambled toward the girl. She was too innocent to know that he labored under extreme emotion, nor could Martha have guessed that that emotion was desire. "I was admiring Nature's bounty. This glade is magical; I imagine Oberon shall pass through momentarily."

"Rather, you were spying on me. Hmph." Martha turned to admire the leaves overhead. The glade was as timeless as Cadbury but lacked the unsettling green of the forest in that place. Birds sang, leaves rustled and bountiful nature ruled. The residual effect of long-dead magic imbued the site with a feeling that was irresistible. She could imagine faeries dancing in a circle, their maliciousness mellowed in an ecstasy of revel. Not that she would reveal it to him, but having Lord Brinston at her side, here in this magical place, was Avalon.

This was the most intimate she had been with her angel since that day she went shopping and was attacked by a smuggler. How was it Lord Brinston seemed more approachable standing in a patch of primroses than he did in the drawing room? His attire was as elegant as always, his carriage as erect, yet something about the marquess reminded her of his tenderness after killing the smuggler, how he had kissed her forehead.

His eyes, those changeable gray eyes... They made her shiver.

Martha longed to ask if Lord Brinston recalled meeting her in Ramsgate. Not once had he mentioned or done anything to show that he was her angel, that he had slain a dragon and kissed her in the back room of a shop. The question was on the tip of her tongue, but she didn't ask. He gave no indication of knowing her. What if he said no? So much time had passed...

"I haven't found the document," she said instead, pushing away from the large stone. "I tried to roll this boulder over to check under it, but it is too heavy. Have you come to oblige me in this?"

His growl was wondrous to hear. "You need a keeper, girl. Someone to watch and make sure you don't go over your head. You have a genius for trouble." He now stood but three feet from Martha's boulder. "Should I inform Mr. Jackson of your meddling, you would be in the basket. This is not an affair for ladies to be involved in." His hands clenched, his eyes flared.

Martha was thrilled to have discomposed him, but was astonished when he moved to stand toe to toe with her. "Excuses, my lord," she purred, concealing a spurt of...was it panic? "I believe you fear I will discover the missing papers. It would be a blow to be beaten at the game by a young woman, would it not?"

He drawled, "Not a chance. You don't have the training to lend success to your endeavors. You don't know what you are seeking."

Martha's eyes narrowed at the words and the cutting tone. Her temper rose. "Papers, my lord, papers," she spat. "I can read and so will recognize the importance of the papers. I shall be the one to return them to Mr. Jackson and you will have to acknowledge my cleverness."

Those marvelous gray eyes deepened as if clouds rolled in and lightning sparked, but Brinston's face remained calm. Martha stared, fascinated. Every time she looked in his eyes, they were different, mirroring his soul in a manner that gave her goose pimples. She was so captivated by his eyes she forgot their dispute.

Growl lowered to a whisper. "I freely admit your resourcefulness. I fear more that you will be harmed. Comely young ladies should not tangle with the ruthless characters who deal in stolen documents."

Skin tingling at his tone, Martha wrenched her eyes from him. "I can care for myself. I am not some mindless debutante—"

The words were cut off by Lord Brinston's lips landing on hers. The kiss was ferocious. Brinston put all his frustration with Martha's defiance, all his resentment with wanting to do this, all his disgruntlement at battling against love, into the melding of their lips. Her lithe, warm body squeezed into his and Brinston tried his damndest to make them one being. Lips nibbled, teeth grazed, tongue swept. His hands...his hands wandered commandingly over the girl he had captured. Brinston couldn't get enough of her. Blood roared in his veins.

Martha melted against him, helpless. She had wanted this forever. Reaching to grasp his head, she anchored herself to Brinston's chest as he shifted and deepened the kiss. Lost in the feel of his mouth on hers, Martha's hands were left to direct themselves. They clutched at hair as fine as silk threads; her fingers became addicted to mussing. All the while, lips tasted and enjoyed.

Both were immersed in the glory of love. It was too intense, too enthralling to be less. Her age meant nothing, his arrogance less. In this endeavor, they were equally inexperienced and confident.

The flat boulder made an uncomfortable bed, but neither noticed discomfort as the hard male body bore the softer female to the stone. Brinston was heavy atop and solid between her legs. Rather than being shocked, Martha wanted him closer. Her senses tumbled and like him, blood roared in her ears. A chaste kiss on the forehead in Ramsgate had made her angel unforgettable; lovemaking in the woods made him indispensable.

Their lips and tongues clung and thrust as hard as their bodies. Martha's skin clung, craving the warmth of his; Brinston's hips thrust, trying vainly to penetrate through layers of cloth. They were in a conflagration, hurled into the fire. Pent-up desire exploded.

Cheery humming came from the path. Vera was returning. Brinston untangled himself from Martha. Their eyes met for a moment, as fierce as Wellington and Bonaparte at the joust of Waterloo. Then he turned and faded back into the trees. Martha was left gasping like a landed trout on the boulder.

* * *

Lord Brinston stormed into his brother's chamber. Michael, emerged from a warm bath, stood with water droplets rolling down his back and a towel slung around his trim waist. He turned at the slamming of the door and arched a well-shaped eyebrow at the simmering man stomping across the rug.

"Lord, what a wretched picnic. Don't tell me you enjoyed yourself. Ants in the curry and she's the rudest chit I have come across in a long time," Brinston grumbled. "No matter what I said, she contradicted me."

"I presume Martha Dunsmore is the subject," Michael drawled, waving his man away.

"How can you tell?"

"When we left for the picnic, Vera Jackson, the other choice I could have made, looked happy. Martha, on the other hand, was none too pleased at sharing a vehicle with you. And *you* looked ready to spit nails at the ruins. What did she do, call your driving into question? I can see the Dunsmore chit tempting fate by banging on your skull."

"Banging wasn't the half of it. No, she had no comment to make on my skill with the reins. Pity other subjects were not out of her range. She called me a sheep and a toad-eater."

Michael grinned. "She called you a sheep? That's good. Did you baa?"

"Like a *sheep.*" Brinston slammed his palm against the wall. "Enough, brother. Just help me stay away from her. I might strangle the chit and Hurst would end up calling me out." His eyes took on a faraway look. "She's but a child, playing at finding the plans. Claims she will be successful and I will have to admit her superiority as a sleuth. I could shake her, though at times..." He turned to his brother, who was combing his hair. "Never mind. I can handle Martha. Her impertinence will roll off my shoulders like marbles down a stair. Have you checked as I asked you to?"

Michael flipped strands of hair this way and that with the comb. "Yes, Lacey is clear. Up to his eyes in debt, of course, like half the nobility. But his brother and cousin were both with Wellington—he often said he would have been there also but for his father's distress over his going. No sign of traitorous activity.

"That man he is meeting, Nehemiah Light, is a queer duck, wanting to open a museum for snuff. Wonder if anyone would ever visit it?" Michael shrugged. "Has a building hired in Broad Street—it is thought he is chasing after Lacey's grandfather's collection. The old man had a good eye for snuffboxes. The collection is comprehensive, including a good selection from the last century."

"So we can take him off the list. She wasted her time searching his room." This was said in such an odd tone, Michael turned to stare at his brother. Brinston had absently picked up a small carriage clock. Twirling the minute hand around and around the clock face with a finger, he glowered at the wall. When a tinny 'sproing' signaled that the hand had broken, he just as absentmindedly began to twirl the hour hand.

Criminey, Michael thought. *Brin can't think of anything but the chit. Has Coletta guessed?*

Chapter Ten

Robert Jackson's study was lit by a trio of candles and a small fire. It was late; Jackson and Lord Brinston had agreed to meet after the occupants of the manor retired for the night. What they discussed was not to be overheard at any cost. For the Owl, secrecy was paramount. Tipping off the thief to the efforts made to apprehend that thief would be just plain stupid.

Reporting the status of his mission to find the missing rocket troop plans took less than an hour, then Brinston accepted a bumper of brandy from his host and introduced a touchy subject. "It's a delicate matter. You may not be pleased," he admitted.

Jackson looked at his friend and colleague with amusement. "You mean to inform me about my daughter's, and her friend's, efforts to find the report."

"So you already knew. I wonder at your forbearance."

"You don't have children, Brin. Someday you may come to understand that daughters are harder to handle than the most fractious stallion. You don't yank their reins. The girls should take no harm with us to watch over them."

"I pray you are right, but I intend to discourage their activities anyway. They have no business interfering. They're getting in my way."

When Jackson laughed, the marquess rubbed the back of his neck. "You may think what she does is harmless, sir, but Martha is too bold for her own good. She is sure to come a cropper, and perhaps involve Miss Jackson."

"Then I rely on you to prevent disaster." Jackson chuckled more at Brinston's expression. Amelia's house party was offering a fount of amusement for the host. First Irvine was making a fool of himself over that Banshee chit, now Brin was tied up in knots with Vera's friend. He had lost his prospective. The girl's actions were taking over his view, becoming as important as the contest between England and France.

The marquess was fast losing patience so Robert changed the subject. "By the by, Du Lac was pleased with your dealings with the smugglers in Ramsgate. It was a brilliant move on your part to allow the gang leader to slip away; I was astonished how much of the spy network you uncovered with that inspired decision."

Brinston demurred. "I was lucky. It could have gone entirely wrong."

"But it did not. Your skill as a tactician grows. Thank Avalon the list did not get into French hands. We would have lost many of our best operatives if it had. Would have hurt badly. It amazes me that the covert activity continues though the search is over."

"If I do not manage to recover the rocket plans, we may be facing an equally bad situation," Brinston reminded his host. "The troop could be dealt a killing blow if that information becomes known by the wrong parties."

A fervent look suffused Jackson's face. "The rockets are very promising. If they can be controlled properly, the clash of the line may be a thing of the past. Just think of it; no more legions of fallen men." He took a sip from his drink and continued.

"No more killing one by one. One or two accurately placed rockets and the battle would be over. And for what? An ark so old it has lost its meaning. Like that chalice sitting in the Tower. It held its purpose centuries ago. Now it is only good for men to lust after." His glass chimed on the table. "But if our foes gain access to the plans, our work could be turned against us. That must not happen. The subtle changes proposed for Congreave's rockets must not get into the wrong hands.

"No, my boy, I have the utmost faith in the Owl. You have never failed and this situation is not the trickiest you have dealt with by far. Indeed, you have made excellent progress towards apprehending our thief."

"Never had to work around an impertinent chit," Brinston grumbled.

His valet was waiting for him when Brinston reached his room. "I thought I told you not to wait for me?" he snapped. The valet recoiled almost imperceptibly. Brinston rubbed his neck ruefully. "I'm sorry, Barnes. I'm frustrated, but I shouldn't take it out on you. Was there something you needed?"

"Yes, my lord," Barnes said. "Mr. Dalton approached me earlier with information. According to him, an interesting anomaly was observed in the French salon. The carpet was shifted, as well as the furniture, some time in the recent past."

Brinston's head snapped up. "Did Dalton find anything?"

"No, there was nothing there. But he was certain the furnishings had been disturbed. The room was cleaned shortly before the guests arrived. Then lemonade spilled, causing the maids to take up the carpet for cleaning. Dalton was positive the room had been tampered with."

"Thank you for telling me." Brinston pulled the pin out of his cravat with a savage twist.

"What does it mean?"

"You didn't guess? I am surprised. The papers were hidden there. It is no longer material. They were moved long since."

* * *

The next morning, after cutting flowers for a few vases, Vera and Martha headed up the stairs in the main hall. Janice was descending; they met in the middle of the flight. Looking down her nose, Janice brushed past Vera, knocking a glove out of Vera's hand. Then, performing a little dance, the elder sister managed to kick the glove. It ended up at the foot of the stairs.

"Janice," Vera protested, but her sister ignored her. Tripping lightly down, she stepped over the glove and went out the front door. The butler, at that moment entering the hall from the back, picked up the item. Raising his head, he spied the young ladies.

"Is this yours?"

"Yes," Vera said ruefully. She ran lightly down and retrieved the glove. "Thank you, Dalton."

"I am at your service," he intoned. "If you need—ahem—assistance, let me know." The butler looked significantly at the front door. "It would be a pleasure."

Vera smiled and joined her friend.

"She needs bringing down a peg." Martha said.

"I know," Vera said.

"That bit is the last straw. She sticks her nose in the air as if we smelt of the stables." As they turned the corner of the south corridor, Martha became more forceful. "She needs a reminder of her fallibility."

"Her friends are the only ones who don't seem to care how awful she is," Vera gloomed. "Mama looks ready to strangle her and Papa...I thought he was going to take a switch to her when Janice said knights who fail in their quests should be executed."

Martha stopped and planted her hands on her hips. "I do not hesitate to say that she is unbearable. I can't imagine what Mr. Lacey sees in her."

Vera peered down the hall. One door was open; she thought it was the empty chamber next to Lady Coletta's. To ensure she was not overheard, she lowered her voice. "It is because of their ears. If you stand directly in front of Janice or Dom, their ears cannot be seen, as if they have been pinned to their hair."

Martha's shoulders heaved as she continued the

analysis. "She has become intolerable. It worsened after her presentation two years ago. I complained once; I was told Janice had a great success amongst the nobility and her head was turned a bit. Mama swore she would settle down soon, but I have yet to see any sign of it. The Banshee Brigade does naught but encourage her haughtiness. If she would but marry and depart to her husband's estate." An immense sigh emphasized the desirability of that outcome.

Pausing to straighten a watercolor on the wall, Martha said, "Well enough a thought, but for the here and now, I think we are justified to retaliate." The picture tilted the opposite direction and Martha raised her hands to it again. "I have been mulling possibilities."

Not satisfied that the picture hung straight, Martha stood back from it and tilted her head. Vera coaxed, "Leave that. Every time a door closes along the hall, the picture rearranges itself."

"But it offends me," Martha replied absently, reaching to tip the corner a smidge. Just then, a door closed and the picture sagged to the left. "Pooh," she exclaimed.

"Is there a problem?" a deep voice enquired. Both girls swung around. Lord Brinston pulled a negligent hand from the pocket of his inexpressibles. He looked at Vera, then at Martha, and repeated his question.

"No, my lord," Vera said as Martha began, "The picture..."

He moved shoulder to shoulder with Martha and looked at the painting. "I see." He removed the picture and propped it against the wall. "That is easily remedied." Taking hold of Martha's hand, he placed her thumb just below the nail protruding from the plaster. "Lean against it hard," he said.

She leaned and he placed his hands over hers with his thumbs on the nail. He experimentally pushed, then moved behind Martha. "Can't get it straight that way," he muttered, and pushed again.

Lord Brinston murmured in her ear, "Lean harder, my girl." So Martha leaned. But he leaned also, pressing the length of his body against hers as he pushed at the nail. His hands, warm and hard, not moist in the least, surrounded hers as his form seemed to envelope her with the masculine aroma of lemon and leather. Hot lemon, hot leather. Lord Brinston was a furnace that sparked a fire in the girl.

Martha opened her mouth to protest just as he said, "There," and stepped back. "You can take your hand away now, Martha." She shifted and he hung the picture back on the hook, where it hung square.

"Just a little trick I learned. Now, if you will excuse me." With a short bow, he sauntered down the corridor. Vera and Martha watched him go, then they turned to look again at the watercolor. It hung perfectly straight.

"Well," was all Vera could think to say. "I'll tell Dalton." She grabbed Martha's unresisting hand and pulled her along. Once inside the safety of Vera's room, Martha began to recover her poise. Glowing fireflies stung where he had touched her hand. Her back also. What was happening in her stomach didn't tingle—it burned with feverish joy.

"So, what shall we do?" Vera crossed to the table and began stuffing floss willy-nilly into her embroidery bag, knots and all. Martha didn't answer; she hadn't a clue what Vera was referring to. She'd had a firm purpose that morning: avoid thinking of Lord Brinston, avoid Lord Brinston. He could have cooperated.

Why had he kissed her? Martha was afraid to know.

Vera threw the bag; it clipped Martha on the shoulder. "Wake up. I said, what shall we do to Janice?"

With an inward shake, Martha's imp pushed Lord Brinston to the back of her mind. She bent her head close to her friend's ear and began to speak. Hushed voices and muted giggles bespoke a prank in preparation.

"Mind now, this was not original to me. I heard of it happening to another." Martha would not claim the inspiration. Nor would she confide the existence of coals—red hot, incinerating coals of desire—in her stomach. Her attention was best turned on someone other than mystifying aristocrats. Someone like Janice, who needed a setdown.

"But it is perfect." Vera bounced on a seat, flouncing the forgotten embroidery bag to the floor. "When shall we act?"

"You know the old saying; 'Never put off till tomorrow what you may accomplish today.' Shall we see what we can bring about now? Then I would like to search the attic." Vera's grin faded to puzzlement.

"What is in the attic?"

"The papers, silly. They might be hidden there."

Around the corner of the hall, Lord Brinston leaned his forehead against the cool plaster wall and groaned.

* * *

That afternoon, Barnes, Lord Brinston's dedicated manservant, slumped in the most comfortable chair in the servant's hall, sipping a mug of stout and watching Miss Bridewell. Standing in for Amelia Jackson, who was occupied with Cook concocting the perfect Beef Wellington, Bridey supervised three maids in the fine sewing needed to repair some lace.

Bess and two others, eyes bleary from concentrating on needles and the finest silk, stretched their arms and backs. None of them were best pleased; why Sir George and Mr. Lacey had seen fit to use delicate lace doilies to wipe their boots was beyond the maids' understanding. Two hours they had been at it, setting the tiniest stitches in the cobwebby lace, drawing edges together and restoring the designs of the doilies.

The male servant's presence was tolerated because he gave valuable pointers on knots to anchor their darns.

Seaman's knots, if the women had only known it, but they worked on lace as well as on ship.

"Excellent work," Miss Bridewell commented. "I cannot see the tears, girls. This is ready to be laundered and put back in place." She smiled. "Mind you place the lace centered on the chairs, so it looks neat, but not so low it slides down. The aim is to protect the upholstery from the gentlemen's hair pomade. Now, if you will excuse me." She bustled out. The maids settled back in their chairs and folded the darned lace.

"I have to help Cook today," Annie grumbled. "I hate to chop veggerbles. But she is shorthanded and Dalton said I have to. They're making that Wellington beef thing. Too complicated to bother with, if you were to ask me."

"Miss Vera will want her pink muslin ironed for later," Bess mentioned.

"Don't mind fixin' lace so much. That was easier than yesterday," Kate put her pence in. "I had to turn out the linens, trying to find lace to use for what we fixed. Someone made a mess there, they did. All the ways in the back, the sheets were all jumbled. One sheet was all unfolded, rolled up and stuffed in the corner. And it was one of those sheets as we never use, lessin' we have to. Took me forever to neaten up. Who did that, I'd like to know."

Barnes slipped from the room unnoticed. Where would his lordship be? After checking that the billiards room and archery range were deserted, the valet tracked him to the stables, where Brinston and Michael were admiring the thoroughbreds. Catching his master's eye, an impromptu meeting was held under the spreading oak. The depredations on the linen closet were as significant as Barnes thought.

Brinston sighed. "At least we can assume the report is still on the premises. Our devil is moving it around enough to make it difficult to search for. Ingenuous hiding places too. Indications are it is not kept so close that discovery will point to the culprit. Smarter than I would have thought. We shall have to be more vigilant. It will take luck to find the document before our thief decides to make off with it." He clapped the valet on the back. "Good thinking, Barnes. Look for a raise in your wages, man."

"One last thing, m'lord," the servant said. Brinston lifted his brows. "Some muffins were sent to your chamber, but I could smell cinnamon, so I snuck 'em out and threw 'em in the privy. The bottoms were scorched or I would have eaten them myself. If anyone asks, you could say they were good."

"Barnes, you old scoundrel." Brinston laughed. "You amaze me. You're telling me you didn't eat those muffins?"

"I told you, sir, they were scorched."

The younger man dismissed his valet. So that's what the prickle had been. Hmm. It wouldn't do to tell Barnes that his uncharacteristic disposal of food was due to the generic protective spell. It performed just as it should for once. Subtly, danger was dispersed. Brinston and the valet had spent two agonizing hours sweating over the composition of that enchantment, checking that it covered as many variables as possible. It had been the devil of a problem since, fading in and out at the most inconvenient moments. But for now, all was well.

Barnes appreciated the labor, but not the result. No, it wouldn't do to tell him. The valet hated for magic to be used on him. To be told he had been subject to it would give him a spasm.

Then the marquess' smile faded. *Must have been more of that rat poison. The spell wouldn't have activated without it being needed. Thank Merlin it held.*

* * *

Eyes gazed at the wall with a curious lack of expression, but thoughts roiled behind them. There was a daunting agglomeration to worry about.

The report should be safe in its new hiding place. If it was found, no one would be able to point a finger. Unless someone decided the billiards room was...

If only things were in place. *Can't go haring off and expect to find a buyer just like that. Have to stick to the plan.* That letter to the Council was difficult to word; how did one couch a request for the name and direction of a leading Bonapartist sympathizer? Was clever there; Mr. Jackson's contacts would think the information was for him. Half-wits.

That bloody arrogant marquess. Tiptoeing around, shoving his nose everywhere. It was vexatious that rat poison hadn't worked. No more of that—Cook almost saw. There wasn't any way to explain one's presence in that part of the kitchen at that time. Could only pretend hunger so many times to account for one's presence there.

Brinston shouldn't be a danger now anyway. The blockhead was too busy with Martha Dunsmore, the little witch. Still, killing him off was a wise idea. Maybe a poisonous snake in his bed.

From that impulsive start, it was working out right. *Not even Jackson has a clue. They're all simpletons. Every single one of them. Can't see the trees for the forest, go bumbling along. I'm ten times smarter than they are.*

Taking the report was a felicitous caprice; it would achieve what was needful. Money was imperative—it was clearer every day that it was crucial to success. The most advantageous sale could be achieved at Camelot, no doubt. The plans must be worth piles of money to the right people. Bonapartists would pay well; the Russians if not the Prussians. The Chinese were too cheeseparing.

To finally have enough money. What would come first? A new wardrobe, perhaps. Recognition would follow. It was always the people with the most money who got the most respect and attention.

And choices.

* * *

"Of course I could do it." Vera swept into a chair to the right of the veranda doors. Banshees milled around the drawing room, conversing animatedly. Or as Papa would say, bleating like a flock of sheep to be sheared. It was teatime and Vera was thirsty, but she had forgotten that detail. She was bantering with Squire Michael. If her mother heard their conversation, Vera would be sent from the room, but she was exhilarated. *Squire Michael* was paying attention to her.

"I don't believe you can," he said.

"Nonsense. Anyone could do it."

"So do it." Michael folded his arms. *There, he had the chit,* he thought. Either she employed a cutting tongue for five full minutes or Vera would have to keep silence. A bet that she couldn't imitate a Billingsgate fishwife was inspired. With her father nagging that he watch himself around 'his baby', something had to give. Vera wanted to act out *Romeo and Juliet,* for God's sake. Especially the dying scene. That would thrill Robert Jackson for perhaps ten seconds. Then he'd be after Michael with a gun.

It should be amusing, watching this girl attempt to unsheathe claws. Not for one minute did he think she could do it. The younger Miss Jackson was too green to blast him. It took a measure of sophistication to affect a clever setdown. She'd never manage. Then she would lose the contest and have to stop nagging him about *Romeo and Juliet.*

Vera gave Michael a coy smile. That is, she probably thought it was a coy smile. His opinion was that she looked like she had taken caster oil that morning. Michael sympathized with anyone who had to ingest that medication, so he smiled back. Then he leaned forward and went for the kill.

"I understand if you feel unequal to the challenge, Miss Vera. It takes *je ne sa quoi* to beard the lion and you are a very sweet young lady." After a lifetime deviling Coletta,

Michael was an expert at teasing and he used every last ounce of his skill to bring Vera low. It was all in a good cause. "But I don't believe you can play virago even for five minutes." She lifted her chin.

"Well, if you cannot, you cannot." Michael shrugged.

"I fail to understand what Maria Wentworth finds to admire in your character," Vera blurted. "Most people object to being pushed, you know."

"So you admit you can't act the fishwife."

"I did not say that." Her eyes narrowed. "Shall we begin with your manners or your appearance? Either of those subjects should give me ample scope for complaint." She took a deep breath. "You should have asked if anyone wanted to ride this morning. My mother commented she would have liked to go also." Michael waited.

Her eyebrows lowered. "Yesterday Honoria Silvester was displeased that you won at cards. It is courteous to let the lady win."

She was failing miserably. Michael asked a leading question. "What's wrong with my appearance?" There was a long pause.

"I don't know," Vera admitted. "You dress with all evidence of style and taste. I have tried to decide where you fail, but the effect you present doesn't come up to the mark." He leaned over her in a threatening manner, but Vera continued with a sniff. "Your cravats are too tight around your neck. It appears you would benefit from purchasing extra length in the material. Or do they come in different sizes and for vanity's sake you purchase a smaller size, as ladies sometimes do with slippers?" She started in simulated surprise.

"Oh, poor Squire Michael. Are you in the position of having to obtain them ready made? I understand those unfortunates who cannot afford to have their clothing made by a *modiste*—oh, I am sorry, gentlemen use tailors, do they not? Whatever, those who must purchase already constructed

clothing often have to be satisfied with less than a perfect fit."
She made a moue. "So sad to be light of purse." She glanced
at her fingertips. "Then, your boots look nicer; they show no
evidence of lack of funds. Perhaps it is carelessness that brings
you to pay less attention to your cravats than you should."
Gauging the effect of her words, Vera rejoiced. Michael
glowered. She was besting him.

"It is confusing. Your brother and sister both look
well-turned out. I would have thought you could do the
same. Have you considered having your valet take lessons
from Lord Brinston's servant?" she asked. "If your man
improves his skill, it may offset your disadvantages. Even
cheap goods benefit from careful handling." She drew a deep
breath. "And your coats. I hesitate to say it, but you are aware
that padding is almost always obvious?"

A few minutes later, she triumphantly joined Martha
against the wall.

Once Michael stopped sputtering, he realized that
Vera had spent appreciably more than five minutes cutting
him to ribbons and not once had she yelled like a fishwife.
Damn. He'd lost the bet. How was he going to explain to Mr.
Jackson that he had to act out the love scenes in *Romeo and
Juliet* with his daughter? He'd be *persona non grata* at the
manor. Brin would have to trap the thief without his help.
Coletta would torment him. Maria would feel abandoned.

No! He'd think of some way to weasel out.

Trying to decide if he should strangle the girl or
merely hide behind Maria's skirts, Michael opened the
drawing room door in time to see the footman duck behind
the dining room door. A smothered guffaw told why he hid.

Honoria and Sir George nodded to Michael and
entered the drawing room. Irvine glumly sat on the stairs,
ledgers and papers scattered the floor and stairs. *What did I
miss?* Michael wondered.

Dalton appeared. "Aha," Michael said. "Do me a
favor. Find out what that's about, will you?"

The butler glanced at the dining room door and noted the howls of laughter. Setting his mouth, he went in. Michael leaned against the wall to listen.

Dalton was firm. "Explain yourself, Holt."

"I'm sorry, sir. I just couldn't help myself," the footman said, gasping. "But Mr. Irvine was going up, his arms full of business ledgers. He was reading something in one of them."

"That is funny?" the butler asked.

The footman's voice wavered as if he would laugh again. "No—you see, Miss Silvester was coming down. She looked a vision, all right. Transparent muslin, I think it's called. You could almost see the—ahem. It made his—Mr. Irvine's—eyes bulge. He ran up and offered an arm to her, but his eyes were glued below her neck."

"And?"

"The chawbacon, er, Mr. Irvine should have known better. He stuck out his arm, meaning to help her down the stairs, I suppose. He must have forgotten his arms were already full. The ledgers tumbled down the stairs. You should have seen the lady's nose, Mr. Dalton; it went up like...

"Well, Sir George was going through the hall. She stepping right over the ledgers and yelled, 'Yoo hoo' to him like Mr. Irvine wasn't standing right there. You should have seen his face." The footman dissolved into laughter.

* * *

Hours had passed and the occupants of the Manor of the Ashes had retired. Before leaving the hall, the ever-faithful Dalton reported the latest incident to Mr. Jackson, who thanked him gravely for the warning.

In the lavish master suite, Robert had come close to banging his head against the wall in frustration. His wife plopped him down on the rug in front of the fireplace and threw a hairbrush in his lap.

"He'll come about, my love," Amelia consoled. "When Bryce realizes that Honoria is set on Sir George, he will turn from his infatuation." She curled up in front of him.

"It's a curst nuisance. The man can't settle to anything. Moonstruck." Robert began running the brush through her hair. Admiring the glints the fire drew from it, he began to relax. "I asked him if he could locate an entry in the home farm ledger. What did he bring me? Three ledgers—investments, household and one from that estate I sold. Don't know where he dredged it from. Eh, it has to be ten years old. Now I know what he did. The pages were bent every which way, the spine on one cracked right through. Irvine didn't notice anything wrong. Smitten. Don't know if his head is ever going to come straight."

"He fails to notice Janice is ready to slip a dagger between his ribs," Amelia pointed out. "I am at a loss what to do with the girl; she is beginning to worry me. I understood the attention she received in Camelot flew to her head, but she has not steadied as I thought."

"You will rein her in, my little general. You have the knack." Robert was still thinking of his assistant. "Stupid thing for him to do, fall for a society light. Remember when he did it before, Amy?" She looked puzzled. "Ho, you can't have forgotten," he said, holding his mouth so the laugh didn't spill out. "Your niece, when your niece visited us in London."

"Oh, my yes," Amelia answered. "Jennifer. I had forgotten."

"What? The famous moment when Irvine flung his greatcoat over the puddle in her path. How mud spattered all over her gown and Jennifer cursed him. She actually said 'bloody'."

"Poor Bryce slunk away. He didn't come back for several days, did he, Robert."

"No, he didn't. Almost thought he'd given up his employ."

Lifting the curls flowing down his wife's back and breathing in the scent that clung to her, Robert forget his irritation. "Have you noticed one of those Banshees haunting the stables, Amy? Damn fool tried to pull Conqueror's tail. Hutchins thinks he means to purchase one or more of the hunters."

She turned and twined her arms around Robert's neck. Nuzzling his ear, Amelia whispered, "You refer to Sir George, my dear. Will you sell to him?"

"I suppose I must. With his reputation for horseflesh, it would be a feather in my cap if he did want mounts. Only Brinston is considered a better judge, you know. Brin's a wizard at it."

"I suppose I do know. That cultivated manner that so irritates adds to Colby's mystique." Amelia sighed. Robert was becoming impatient with his daughter's friends; he hated having them at the manor. Already he had confused the Wentworth and Silvester girls at luncheon, causing an awkward moment. Next he would begin addressing them as "You there."

* * *

The Banshee's unaccustomed air of diffidence hung over his brawny shoulders like a fur piece. Robert Jackson watched the man tiptoe (actually tiptoe!) around the chattering crowd at the tea table. If anyone other than his host had been paying attention, he would have plucked the fragile cup of tea from his fat fingers and substituted a hefty dose of brandy. The lack of alcohol had obviously addled the man's brains. As it was, only Jackson paid any heed to the man, and he had no intention of breaking out the decanters in the middle of his wife's tea time. She would have his liver and lights, having commented the night before on the prodigious amount of spirits the Banshees had consumed during their stay at the Manor of the Ashes.

The Brigade was absorbed in a debate on the merits of musicales versus rout parties during the season. Mr. Jackson's well-loved daughter Janice opined that rout parties were much to be preferred, as one could arrange to meet another so easily. Her father made a mental note to speak most sternly to the chit on the unacceptability of assignations and turned his attention back to her friend.

The cocklehead rounded the last chair between himself and his host. Giving a fleeting look to the other Banshees, he lurched as he tiptoed to Jackson's side.

"Skoal," Jackson greeted him.

"Skoal? What bloody kind of word is that?"

"Never mind," Jackson muttered. The man obviously had something of great moment to impart; an explanation of the Danish toast would muck him up. This Banshee, the only one Robert recognized with any frequency, irritated him no end. What was his name again? *Damn. Can't recall.* Well, whoever he was, the man hadn't an ounce of sense about him and was full of his own consequence. Not a pleasant combination, but the idiot was a guest of the manor so he was prepared to be polite.

The Banshee maintained an exaggerated air of secrecy that wouldn't have fooled a two-headed pig. His eyes slid around the room and he clipped words out in an undertone. "That roan you have training. Like the way he jumps. Would like to round out my stables with him. What would you take?"

"The roan? Oh, the two-year old with the white blaze." Jackson frowned and eyed his guest like a tutor examining a toad left in his desk. "You have no use for the roan, sir. He's not up to your weight."

"No, no. I can't agree with you. His withers, you know."

What did withers have to do with it? "I can't think you watched him closely enough. He does better with a light load—hesitates at the jump with a heavier man on him."

"Didn't notice that."

"You wouldn't have. I ordered the heftier grooms to stay off him. I didn't want to spoil the roan by making him bear a greater weight than he is comfortable with."

The idiot nodded his understanding. "Ah. But want one from your stables. Impressed. On the sly, you ken. Don't want Brinston butting his nose in."

Jackson bit back a smile at the transparency of the man. Now he remembered; this was Colby, Janice's idiot of the hunting circuit. The Banshee wanted a horse from the Manor's highly regarded stable, most likely to advance his reputation for a canny eye. For some ungodly reason, he had acquired a reputation.

Nobles considered Colby to be the epitome of the English squire—bluff, gruff and a bruiser on the hunt field. Jackson had seen him hunt. He did well enough. Well-lined coffers supported his reputation a bit better than his seat. Brinston, on the other hand, was the one man the upper ten thousand considered better than Sir George at picking a choice horse.

Ah well, it went both ways. If the Banshee's rep was raised by coaxing an outstanding mount from the Manor's stables, so the Manor's name would be enhanced. Society lemmings would see to that. Also, it would be prudent to acquiesce. If Colby went away unsatisfied, he might make Janice's (or even Vera's) coming season unpleasant. There wasn't much a man wouldn't do to guard his reputation, as Jackson had learned. So he ran a list of the available horses through his mind and clapped the Banshee on the shoulder.

"Tell you what I will do, Sir George," Jackson invested his own whisper with a note of conspiracy. "Seeing as you are such a friend to my daughter, I'll make special dispensation for you. There are three two-year olds in the Manor stables that would suit your string. Two of them don't get seen much, as I held them back. Thought they were special, you understand. The third was kept on the chance the

Prince would want him. I will give you first choice of the three. Only one, mind. Speak with my head trainer. You will want to go over their papers—I keep them in the top left drawer of the desk in my study. Help yourself."

The Banshee was like a child promised two Christmas's per year. He practically danced on his toes, remembering at the last second to rock instead of leap. Forgetting his wish for secrecy, George pumped Robert's hand. "You won't regret it," he boomed. "Dare say all my set will be heading here when they see the quality of the horseflesh you manage. That'll go a long way towards making the Manor of the Ashes a force to be reckoned with on the hunting circuit."

Jackson nodded and smiled. *Certainly it will. As if the Melton hunting set had never heard of the Ashes. Now to remember to tell Hutchins.* The head groom appreciated tall tales.

Turning away from the fool, he checked the room. Brinston was chatting with his sister, but his eyes focused unblinking across the room. He was acting a bit strange there. Jackson noticed he never spoke to Vera's little friend, but watched her like a suspicious Bow Street runner. Why was the man glaring so? Brinston had more on his mind than concern over Martha's interference in the matter of the report, Jackson decided.

Amelia had mentioned the possibility, wanting to know if she should write Martha's brother. Robert had cautioned his lady to silence. Watching now, he realized his wife was correct. The boy seemed at that sensitive stage. *How did I fail to notice?* he chided himself. Before he knew it, Brinston was going to be rolled up, horse and tackle. Caught tight in parson's mousetrap. Jackson laughed quietly. It couldn't happen to a better man. Or a sweeter girl.

Gracing the set of chairs by the open French windows to the veranda were the Banshee sister and brother, Honoria and Peter Silvester. Desirous of a *tête a tête,* they had isolated themselves. One didn't need words to know they were quarreling. With their backs to the veranda, they were unaware of Martha, who had taken a turn around said veranda and was reentering the room through the portal at Honoria's right.

Martha heard the words between the Silvester siblings. Her mouth formed a silent "Oh."

"Told you before, I meant to sell them to the most discerning bidder, not that nodcock of a Frenchie." Silvester's tone was sullen.

"But de Lauren is always *au curent*. He practically got down on his knees to beg for them." Honoria sounded coy. "Think of the further opportunities he would put you in the way of."

"Don't want opportunities. Just want to sell the damn things and forget about them."

"Then why not to the Comte? He offers more money, does he not?"

"He's not the most honorable choice."

"Honorable—why ever should morals be brought into the matter? If you had wanted that, you would never have got started on the business." Honoria's tone degenerated from coy to caustic. "Make up your mind, Peter. Either burn the things and have done with it or swallow your morals and sell to the highest bidder. It's not like it matters what de Lauren wants them for..."

"That is where you are wrong, Hon. What use that demned Frenchie puts them to is the whole matter. Besides, De Lauren is apt to tell half of Mayfair what I did; I should end up having to flee the country. Care to join me?"

"At least you would have the money." Honoria flounced away.

Male had put female firmly in her place. Usually the first to defend another woman against an overbearing man, Martha felt the faintest glimmer of respect for the dandified Silvester. She would never have guessed he would exhibit honor among thieves. *Good for him. It does matter who benefits from a crime and why,* Martha thought. *Favoring the French over our interests would be despicable. Imagine him realizing that.* She turned to go back outside. She had to think over this development. What to do?

Then it hit her. *Dear Lady. Peter stole the papers?*

Brinston's hand clenched as Martha flitted back to the veranda. What was the minx doing? Out—in—out. She should make up her mind. He took a half step forward, but thought better of it. Much as he would like to drag her into the room, he couldn't do it. How was he to keep an eye on Martha if she couldn't stay put in one place more than a moment?

It was more than a need to keep track of her actions. Brinston wanted to see the chit...hear her dulcet voice...smell her. None of that obnoxious heavy perfume the ladies of Camelot affected; Martha smelled sweet. Honestly sweet. He ran his hand through his hair, unmindful of the irresolute picture he presented to the company.

This indecision would be the death of him. How far was he prepared to go; was he willing to give up his freedom and wed the chit? He knew what state his heart was in. It was tangled in silk bonds, aching and bumping around his chest in an ecstasy of love, and would probably never be free. But that was no excuse for jumping impulsively into marriage.

No, long acquaintance was the ticket. Knowing her for at least a year, he wouldn't run into any nasty surprises. Like she drank. Or helped herself to people's tablespoons. Or their men. At least a year—otherwise, a man couldn't be sure. He glared at the door.

* * *

Shortly before the hordes would arrive in the drawing room, Brinston shifted the sack he held to his left hand and turned the door handle of the billiards room. The door was almost as quiet as his footsteps; he slipped into the room like a puff of smoke.

"Good evening," Martha said, looking up from a kneeling position in front of the cabinet that held the cue sticks. "Are you here to look for the papers? Be my guest." She stood and dusted off her skirt. "I haven't found them."

He thought his head was going to come off. Tension sometimes had that effect on him. "You came down early."

"I hadn't had a chance to check this room," Martha said cheerfully. "It is the last on this floor I have been through."

"Why don't you give me a list of the places you have searched so I don't duplicate your efforts?" His sack clattered against a table leg as he dropped it.

"Is that necessary?" Her chin lifted, a red flag to the bull of his writhing emotions. He stalked to the table in the center of the room and leaned against it. It was that or shake her until her head rattled. Conciliating, the chit was being conciliating. Martha gestured to a handsome painting of the manor house that hung between the windows.

"You might want to look at the back of the painting. The paper covering the frame has been torn, perhaps recently. I thought the papers may have been tucked in there, but if so, they have been removed."

Just like that, he forgot his irritation. The plucky minx. Trust her to find anything that should be found. If she were a male, she would make a decent assistant. But she was female; skirts, shawls, breasts...He stalked to the wall, bracing himself against her proximity. Shoulder to shoulder, they inspected Martha's find.

"I think you may be right," Brinston said. "There is no dust in the seam."

"Would there be dust there if it was an old tear?"

"Probably," he murmured, becoming absorbed in the examination. "Dust gets everywhere, even behind a framed painting. Oh, not as much as a tabletop or the floor, but some. I have never heard of a maid dusting behind the artwork." He ran his finger along the paper and rubbed the tip. "See, as clean as Letta's fingernails." He re-hung the painting, taking care to straighten it on the wall. "You are correct; the report was hidden here and then removed."

He turned. He was much too close; their bodies almost touched. Martha backed away. "I must be in the drawing room before anyone else comes down," she murmured. Half sheepishly, as if she realized what a coward she was being, Martha slipped out the door, her white-on-white embroidered muslin dress swishing. Brinston watched her close the door and sighed.

Martha was a problem; one he could not resolve. Imagine her daring to enter the billiards room, a room off-limits to a young lady. She needed a spanking. Someone to clamp down on her. He sighed again and retrieved the bulky sack from the floor where he had dropped it. *At least she located the spot I need to focus on.*

Using a bit of chalk, Brinston drew a circle on the uncarpeted floor in front of the manorial likeness. Standing to the side of it, he traced four figures corresponding to the points on a compass. Then he stood a measured five feet back, faced the wall, and raised his arm. "Mighty Merlin, drinker of the four waters," he intoned, following the mage's name with a mixture of Greek and Hebrew, omitting Latin. Merlin hated Romans.

Mist rose from the floor within the circle. Wreathing through the air, it snaked around the carved picture frame, illuminating spots along the gilded wood. Then, as if a puff of air had blown through the room, the smoke dispersed and the mist whirled away. A few stars tinkled in the circle and then went out, one by one.

Brinston rubbed the side of his face. *Our thief is wilier than I would have believed possible,* he thought. *Not an enchantment, but an intensity of purpose that mimics. Wasn't in existence when I arrived. We checked. Wondered why questing didn't work. Now I know.*

Moving to sit on a side chair, he sank deep in thought. A non-magical capable of generating barriers to magic. What has changed to bring it about? What brings it on? Is it anger? No, not merely anger. Rage. A consuming rage; the kind that eats a man's soul.

No, malignant feeling that intense couldn't be hidden. It would be visible to the most obtuse. Colby should even have noted it.

What else?

Insanity. *By Arthur, that's just what I need; a mad traitor running around the manor. Can't be too strong yet or I would have seen it. I hope. Maybe it's obsession or some other minor manifestation. Well, Brin, don't borrow a crutch. This isn't a surprise.* He rose to wipe the circle away with a cloth. Scrubbing to remove chalk from the cracks in the flooring, Brinston pondered his next move. *Wish I could locate the report magically, but I'm going to have to do it the hard way. And quickly. The madness is growing.*

* * *

They met in the study at midnight for the purpose of discussing the missing troop report. "She searched the billiards room." Disgust was more evident than the tinge of admiration Brinston felt for Martha's cleverness. She had managed to scrutinize that male preserve one step ahead of the Owl.

"Did she find anything; that is what we must determine." Robert Jackson was grim. Bryce Irvine listened, one hand tucked behind his back.

Brinston said, "She held nothing and her attire did not present obvious hiding places. The skirt was too diaphanous for a hidden pocket."

He was relieved at Martha's failure to discover the missing plans. To have an unfledged schoolgirl meddling in his affairs was the outside of enough. For her to succeed—an admittedly arrogant investigator like himself would never live the disgrace down at Whitehall. Wouldn't the lads crow; the Owl, who maneuvered around scores of the roughest smugglers and other criminals, outwitted by a chit barely old enough to be out in society. Her words at the picnic still burned his ears. 'It would be a blow to be beaten at the game by a woman.'

Maddeningly, the chit's assessment of Brinston's motivation was truer than she knew. Martha thought she would find the document and embarrass the expert spycatcher. He had denied it, but deep inside Brinston knew half his objection to Martha's interference in the search for the rocket troop report was vanity. The Owl would not be bested, not by a female. By Merlin, not by a female so young she didn't have permission to waltz.

He would be entombed in the crystal cave before he let anyone know it, though.

"Your daughter fared no better, Mr. Jackson," Michael added. "It took her an unconscionable period to go through the buttery." He dropped into a chair. "Are you certain she is capable of doing the deed thoroughly? I got the impression she was diverted from her mission by a knot of kittens."

"I am certain of nothing." Jackson wiped his brow with a lawn handkerchief. The prolonged search was beginning to wear on his nerves. "Of course you will search yourselves. These girls know nothing of espionage and likely would miss the most obvious hiding places. We have the advantage of experience. In their innocence, Vera and Martha could gaze straight at the document and think nothing of it."

Brinston and Michael exchanged glances. Martha innocent? Of the techniques of espionage, yes.

Chapter Eleven

The Banshee Brigade was going riding. The group, along with assorted other members of the house party, milled around the stable yard chattering as grooms saddled horses. Robert Jackson stood to the side with the ladies Amelia and Coletta, who declined the treat in favor of a morning puttering in the stillroom. Coletta was to show Amelia how to steep rose hips for a nostrum she swore helped stave off fleas. With a full pack of hunting dogs in the kennels, fleas were a seasonal problem.

Watching one of the Banshee women braid a mare's tail, Robert shook his head and grumbled under his breath. After listening for several minutes, Amelia took him to task. "Really, Robert, one would think you ungenerous. What harm from the young people riding?"

His hand cut through the air. "Don't you recall that one's skill in the saddle? What's her name, something Wellward? Since old Turtle died, I fear we haven't a mount temperate enough for her." He grumbled more under his breath and stamped his foot, as bad-tempered as an aroused stallion. "I'm returning to the house. Don't tell me what she rides." Robert strode away.

Amelia made a face and Coletta laughed. "Old Turtle?"

"That was not the horse's proper name, you understand. She was called Sylph, but her gait gained her the name Turtle. My poor husband is correct—Charlotte had difficulties with her. Hutchins will do his best, I am sure." Their attention returned to the Brigade, now mounting.

Janice wore her new habit, a pristine white velvet. It had been designed to complement her horse, the pure white mare Lake Lady. If her mother thought white velvet impractical, she admitted that Janice looked a vision. Charlotte, she of the non-existent equestrian skills, scrambled atop Homebody, who stood asleep while she arranged her high heeled boots in the stirrups.

Vera was astride her favorite, Amber Glow, and Hutchins had assigned Martha to the restive Silver Streak. The mare tossed her head as if to show off the white streak in the glossy brown mane that had named her. The girl competently calmed the fidgets.

The ladies set, the gentlemen mounted. Squire Michael delighted in his steed's appellation, Henry VIII (he had sired two fillies and a weak-kneed foal in six attempts at impregnating mares), and Lord Brinston, whom Hutchins trusted, rode the groom's cherished Morgan's Chariot.

Twelve horses paraded from the stable yard.

A mere two hundred feet down the lane, Homebody decided the clover at the edge of the ditch was to her liking and lowered her head. Martha watched Charlotte bounce forward, saving herself from a fall with hands on the horse's neck. She squealed, dropped the reins, and blurted a refined "Help."

"I dropped them," she said, as helpless as a kitten climbing in a lion's mane, as Homebody chomped another juicy bit of clover. The horse's head went down again.

To Martha's amusement, Silvester dismounted Thrumming Thunder and gathered Homebody's reins. Charlotte refused to take them. He shrugged and remounted, intending to lead the horse. That steed, no longer able to reach the clover, thought perhaps Thrumming Thunder's flank might be tasty and took a nip. Silvester was unprepared; his nether parts met the road as Thrumming Thunder thundered past the equestrians.

He stood and gingerly swiped at his rear. "A stroll is preferable to riding," Charlotte said.

Henry VIII proved true to his name as Michael and

Maria cantered down the lane. Her Slightness did not appreciate his highness' flirting and butted her head against Henry. Unfortunately, Michael's leg was in the path of the mare's head.

"I don't know why you find it so funny. Maria tried to pull her mare away," Martha said to Brinston. "Her Slightness is in a royal snit."

"I tend to laugh at incipient martyrs," he said, still chortling. "Maria's horsemanship defeated him, yet he goes back for more punishment." With Brinston cheering him on, Michael managed to halt the gamboling mare by grabbing the reins.

"I believe Her Thlightneth ith too throng for me," Maria admitted. "I juth can't hold her."

With a wry glance at his brother, Michael decreed, "We can stroll in company with Charlotte and Peter." He dismounted and almost fell.

"If the bruise on his thigh does not prove too uncomfortable," Brinston added.

Maria handed Michael Her Slightness's reins. In the handoff, the mare realized her chance; she turned and took her royal snit back to the stable.

"Oh, Arthur." Brinston howled with laughter. Martha couldn't help but join him.

The stable yard was still in full view. Hutchins watched the shenanigans with a broad grin. Then he sent a pair of grooms to retrieve the unwanted horses. The reduced company continued their ride.

Vera, Martha, and Lord Brinston enjoyed their ride. Atop good horseflesh, they had the benefit of two bruising gallops and the perfect outing. As they approached an outlying cottage, Vera said, "I believe I'll stop here."

"Would you like us to come with you?" Martha asked, feeling a disinclination.

"No." Vera pulled her horse up. "I've known Mary Green all my life. She'll be hurt if I don't visit, but it would be boring for you. Take the left fork—it's prettier that way."

Martha turned in the saddle, torn between riding with Lord Brinston and staying safely with Vera. Her mind was eased when he amicably said, "I've been that way before. The road winds down a hill and offers sweeping views. You'll enjoy them."

Silver Streak seemed to agree. She had no hesitation about following Brinston's mount. Martha took the path of least resistance. She allowed the mare to have her head and admired the scenery. Dark curls glinted in the sunlight, wide shoulders flexed under a brown tweed coat. Who noticed trees and landscape?

When they came to a stream, both dismounted to give the horses a drink. Martha gave Brinston a mischievous look and removed her footwear to dabble her feet in the brook. He looped the horses' reins to a branch.

"The water's warm," the girl commented in some surprise, as most running water was as cold as could be.

"Is it?" Brinston asked and sat at her side. "Help me remove my boots, m'girl. You're not the only one who can pamper your toes. My feet are suffering."

Martha rolled around and obligingly tugged at the fine Spanish leather boots until they popped off. Brinston scattered his stockings on the ground. When his feet plopped in the brook, the splash spattered her face.

"Aaaah!" he howled. "That water is ice!" He pulled his feet out, then plunged them back in the icy stream, mock shuddering in distress.

Martha lay back on the ground and laughed herself breathless, swinging her feet in the water the whole time. "I would never have taken you for the gullible sort, my lord," she chortled when she caught her breath.

Martha is too damned attractive, he thought. *That carefree amusement bubbling is one of the strongest lures the woman has.* Her slim legs, alternately hidden and visible with the swing of her feet in the water, drew his appreciative eye.

"Isn't every man gullible when a pretty girl speaks?" he asked, masking his captivation.

"Not in my experience. My brother has never once believed my utterances."

"So I am more gullible than Hurst. When I see him, I'll beg lessons; wouldn't want to go my whole life so constricted." Stretched out, Brinston propped up on an elbow.

"One would think you had no sisters," Martha commented, "Did Lady Coletta never tease?"

His grin was unholy. "Letta? She bullied me unmercifully. I was small as a child and she towered over me, though she was a bit younger. Took full advantage of her size, my sister. She kept it up, even when I surpassed her in growth. Guess she was too used to belittling me."

"I like her a great deal."

"That's my Letta. There is not another soul at Camelot as admired as she, 'cause she does not bully them. Only me," he sighed. Savoring the adorable, he thought how fresh she was compared to Camelot's practiced flirts. *Doesn't hardly know how to draw a man. How can this minx hold my attention so well?*

Martha sat up. Plucking a long blade of grass, she threw it in the water. "I daresay it is for your good. Squire Michael is the youngest then?"

"Yes, Baby Mickey was Letta's name for him. Until the day he left the girth on her pony's saddle loose. She mounted and began walking around the stable yard." Brinston's hands traced an arc in the air. "With each step, the saddle shifted a bit more. Letta hung on until her hair was sweeping the dust, then the groom rescued her. Her face was a picture of mortification and rage. Michael laughed himself silly and she never called him 'baby' again."

"I never would have dared such a prank with Hurst. Again, he is much my senior, so I bedeviled him in more roundabout ways."

"He has spoken of some of those ways." Brinston tugged a silken tress of her hair, relishing the softness. "We traded tales of siblings once at Oxford. He pounded all the fellows with his stories of you."

"You have known him a long time then, my lord."

"Call me Brinston, or Brin, as many of my friends do," he suggested, then stood and pulled her up beside him. "Yes, he is a good friend. Now, my feet are frozen—come, let us back away from the water." They settled in the sun on a warm patch of grass and thrust their feet in front of them to dry. Brinston wriggled his toes, trying to take his mind off seduction.

Barbed tendrils of magic tingled along his skin. Allowing Martha to talk, Brinston probed carefully for the cause. Ah, the protective spell. If it didn't hold...

* * *

Unseen, a barrel raised.

To steady the arm, lean against something solid. Better, prop the arm up, seeing as shooting a firearm took a lot of practice and the target was a distance away. Propped up and leaning, there wouldn't be any sway or shaking to spoil the shot. A scrubby pine offered support. Its lower branches lobbed off, it was deep in the woods, where the unwary would not look. Safer, but a lot more difficult.

"Hold still Brinston, for Merlin's sake. It's not easy to get an accurate shot from this distance. You don't want to be winged; a good clean shot through the heart and you won't feel any pain. I'm tired of your interference, my bloody perfect toad. If you just hold still, I'll take care of you.

"This is the easiest way. They'll think it's poachers. Poachers are convenient, don't you think?"

The tethered horse responded to the low voice with a whicker. Butting its head affectionately against the braced back, the horse knocked the sharpshooter's head hard against the pine. The figure sank to the ground. Above the ear and buried in the hair where it wouldn't be seen a painful lump formed. Ouch, that hurt.

Squinting against a throbbing headache and propped against the tree again, the gun was carefully aimed and fired. There was an uncharacteristically inaudible pop. The bullet went out the barrel and fell to the forest floor with a soft thunk.

Crystal hell. Must be something wrong with the powder.

* * *

Ah, that's all right. A pound of prevention for a ton of cure. It had better continue to be effective. Brinston turned his attention back to the pixie alit on the grass next to him.

The thought wandered again through her mind. Did he remember her? Somehow, it didn't seem to matter as much. Like now. Martha chattered about Hurst; Brinston sat back and listened. Or did an excellent imitation of listening. It was only for a minute that he seemed distracted, then he turned his head and smiled at her.

I'd like to see that smile every day, Martha thought. *He says I may call him Brin. Perhaps we shall remain friends. I'll be able to see him, talk to him occasionally.*

They fell companionably silent. Sharing details about their siblings had broken a barrier; a bond of friendship layered under the attraction both felt. The stream burbled along its frozen way, doing nothing to cool the heat that shimmered between them. Inches apart on the tickling grass, both felt the tug of fascination, the pooling of heat that signified desire.

It was another form of magic and Brinston spun a dream. He could enchant her; she would twine her arms around his neck and vow undying love. With a spell on her, Martha would mean it too.

But that would boomerang—he would never know if it was the spell or her true feelings that made her care. Wasn't right to use magic that way anyway. Magicians had to be careful about that. There weren't many of them; you were born with the skill or you weren't. If a born magician misused his power, non-magicals would rise up and put a stop to it. In a bloody way, if history was anything to go by. Socrates, Joan of Arc. Sir John Oldcastle in 1417. Above all, Mordred. Non-magicals claimed otherwise, but those, as well as others, were executed for their magician's abilities. The bloody history of magic went back a long way, back long before Merlin.

No, a spell wouldn't work. He'd have to use his charm to make Martha love him. If it could be done. If. How to tell love from desire? Brinston wasn't sure. It shimmered in the air. Maybe love, but definitely desire.

When he could stand the intimate position no longer without snatching a kiss, he urged departure. He averted his gaze as Martha donned her stockings and viciously pulled on his own, faulting himself for responding to her innocent lure. But like Galahad, who had to quest for the grail, Brinston was compelled to further their acquaintance.

Guiding their horses on a meandering route through a stand of trees on their way back to the road, he said, "You will be at Camelot next spring. You will lead Hurst a merry dance then, whether he will or not, Martha. I look forward to watching you conquer the nobles."

She swayed as, with a tug on her reins, Silver Streak skirted a depression in the path. "What is Camelot like?"

"Busy. Every kind of entertainment, from the circus to fireworks."

"Do you enjoy it?"

"No." Silence spread in rings around them, punctuated by the shuffle of the horses. Comparing the stifling activity of Camelot with the lazy airiness of the countryside, Brinston continued. "You meet the same people everywhere. They say the same things, do the same things.

Camelot is the deadliest dull party imaginable. Yet if one maintains one's perspective and accepts the shortcomings of the court, one may enjoy London a great deal."

He cantered, Martha followed suit. "I don't believe that everyone says the same things."

Brinston grinned. "The past three years, Lady Edgemere speaks of her weakened hip each time I greet her. Baron Rogers believes his gouty toe the most fascinating of topics. The elderly Miss Calverson is most original; she tells me, in detail, of her newest embroidery design. Most prolific with a needle, she is. She mapped the Giant's Dance in blackwork last year."

Martha laughed with a hidden sigh for the man who didn't enjoy the society he led. She knew from her brother that the nobility was an exacting beast, but it was a jolt to realize that those who danced the dance nightly might take no joy from it. If there was some way to lighten his burden...

Birds twittered lighthearted in the tree over her head; Martha wished to capture their simple joy and present it to the man at her side as he continued his cynical assessment.

"The Corinthians live for their horses, mills, races, and wagers. The dandies idolize their wardrobes, as well as everyone else's." He shot a glance at Martha. "The debutantes have two, no, three conversational pieces."

"And those are?" Her lashes fluttered.

"The weather is first—and safest. Then there are the events of the season: balls, gossip, and fashion. Those topics are inexhaustible."

"The third topic must be the search for the Ark of the Covenant."

"No, my dear. The third topic is gentlemen; their looks, attentions, amount of blunt they can boast of and the success or failure of their flirtations." Leaving the birds behind, they trotted through a field.

"The sky is darkening. Do you suppose it shall snow?" Martha shot him a glance pregnant with mischief..

The marquess stared at the sky. "Not a cloud to be seen. The air is warm. How do you think it may snow?" he asked in some confusion.

"Why should it not? England has had snow in the past and shall in the future."

"But not in July," Brinston objected.

"Pooh, you are too literal, sir," Martha scolded. "If I am to speak of the weather, I shall be an original." Following Brinston's stallion through a gap in a hedgerow, her nonsense continued.

"The gossip is that Sir George is dangling after Honoria Silvester. Her fashions are up to the mark, much more distinctive than his, but he seems not to mind. Honoria's *modiste* is a wonder. Though when she wears rose, it clashes with his complexion. She should choose a new beau." Martha paused, "Although, if it does snow, the match may be saved by an alteration in Sir George's skin tone."

Admiring her skin tone, he said, "With conversation like that, you *will* be put down as an original. I shall visit you in Bedlam."

"But does Sir George have enough fortune for her needs? Ah, who knows..." A lightning-blasted tree gave her an excuse to avert her gaze.

"Every dowager and mother of a marriageable chit will know the answer to that question," Brinston broke in. "They have sources that Whitehall would love to tap. My sister has told me of the conversation around the tea table when gentlemen are not present. If they are not fortune hunters, they are still man-eaters. Let a man lose at the gaming table and the ladies tote his loss up in their ledgers before rising the next day."

Martha was saddened by this further indication of his disillusionment with society, but kept up the banter. "Never mind a gentleman's pocketbook. I have no interest in that. I want to do everything," she enthused, turning to the marquess, her eyes sparkling with relish. "The Opera, balls,

Merlin's Gardens. Even with the same people and same conversations."

"Here. This is the turn back to the manor." Brinston reined in and continued the interrupted conversation. "And Almack's. If you don't displease the patronesses."

As they entered the tree-dappled lane, Martha said, "I won't. I shall be a patterncard of propriety, and speak only on approved subjects." She threw the marquess a languishing glance, determining that she would never add to his disgust of society; never would Martha Dunsmore join the fortune hunters or man-eaters. She would not wish to displease Lord Brinston. "After I dazzle the gentlemen with my conversation, nothing I do will be of moment. Besides, Lady Jersey is my godmother. If I do misbehave, she will rap my knuckles and defend me to one and all. I shall hide under her umbrella."

"Then I'll reserve a waltz, if I may." Brinston shifted in the saddle. "Bless Hutchins for giving me Morgan's Chariot; this is the best horseflesh I have ridden in some time. His gait is smoother than I have ever seen before. Wonder if Jackson would sell him?"

The stables came into sight. Martha's heart whirled from Lord Brinston's abrupt turning of the conversation. Roses bloomed in her cheeks, recalling how her eyes hadn't strayed from his long bare toes, lightly dusted with hair, waving in front of her in the grass by the stream. Gracious, she hadn't seen her brother's feet since she was in leading strings. Bare feet looked odd, as if the Lady of the Lake had played a prank on humanity. Why should the sight of Brinston's toes be so beguiling?

Beyond toes, she was to call him Brinston. Brin. Now she could do in public what she hadn't dared do in her mind. Martha had wanted to be able to look at her angel, but now her goal expanded. Someday, somehow, he was going to kiss her again. Just one more kiss. Something she could remember for the rest of her life.

Riding at her side, the magician valiantly

acknowledged to himself the irresistible urge to be the gentle knight at this girl's side as she discovered the wonders of London town. If he was stamping the seal on his fate he would not have her disappointed. Not by others, not by himself.

She would talk about snow in summer, would she?

Lent his cachet, Martha could do or say nearly anything at Camelot and the dowagers would smile. She deserved it and she would have it. The darling would not care about a man's fortune more than the man.

He dismounted and handed the reins to a waiting stable boy. "Thank you for a delightful ride," he said formally, lifting Martha from Silver Streak's back.

* * *

"Miss Vera," the butler whispered before they could turn into the drawing room. "Perhaps you and Martha would appreciate hearing the completion of the riding expedition." The trio shrank back under the shadow of the stairs.

"Where is everyone?" Vera asked.

"In the garden."

"Then we won't be interrupted. Do tell us all," she demanded with a grin.

Dalton kept his voice low. "Miss Janice took a fence—Lake Lady sailed over the top rail of the west field with inches to spare, she said, landing a respectable distance from the pond."

"The stagnant pond," Vera corrected and he nodded.

"Mr. Lacey spurred Conqueror on; that splendid steed outdid Lake Lady, landing at the edge of the pond and slipping into the water."

"Was she injured?" Martha exclaimed.

"No, neither horse nor rider suffered injury, except to their pride, I suppose. But it was a long ride back, reeking of pond scum. White velvet did not prove resistant to splashing either."

"Serves Janice right," Vera gloated.

Martha's imp knew Dalton had more to say. "What of Honoria and Sir George?"

"From what I gathered, Sir George and Miss Silvester turned aside onto a poorly marked path and ambled a great distance. They were the last to return to the stables; they became lost in the country lanes. Dancing Donkey took the bit between her teeth and bolted into a hay field. When the chestnut was coaxed to depart the field, Sir George inadvertently led the way east rather than west and thus the pair followed the wrong track.

"Hutchins was preparing to send a search party for them when they returned. Miss Silvester looks like she is seriously contemplating abandoning her efforts to attach Colby."

* * *

"Do you know any wizards?" Dom Lacey asked. "I met one once when I was little."

"A wizard!"

"You know a wizard?"

"I don't know him. My father did. He did tricks. Changed doves into turtles, magicked a seamstress into sewing leaves into a skirt. She thought it was...what'd they call it? A patchwork velvet." Lacey shaded his eyes against the late afternoon sun.

The Banshee Brigade was in the garden once more. The elder members of the party wandered the paths, enjoying a pleasant walk after tea, but the Brigade clustered about their quasi-Colonel, searching for an enlivening topic of conversation. Lacey's contribution sparked interest.

"I don't believe in magic," Janice stated. "It's something the lower orders dreamed up."

Neither Honoria nor Peter had an opinion for once,

but Maria held deep conviction about history. "What about Merlin?"

"Pure nonsense."

"That don't sound like a wizard," Colby boomed. "A dashed charlatan, that's what he was."

Charlotte, decoratively draped over a wrought iron bench, shuddered. "How dreadful for you," she murmured. "I would fear being turned into a handkerchief. Someone would blow their nose on me and the maids would launder me."

"Your father allowed this wizard near you?" Maria asked incredulous. "I cannot believe it. The danger he introduced to his beloved son; what could he have been thinking of?"

"Magic is bunk," Colby said.

Maria sat straighter on her bench in front of the hollyhock bed. "It is not. Magic is real. When I chose Hepplewhite for my sitting room, Papa said it was magic. Papa knows more than any of us. If he believes, I must. No matter how frightening."

Michael smiled at his lady. "I find you magical on all fronts."

"Maria, you are a ninny," Janice rudely said. "Your papa didn't mean there was magic, but that it was a miracle you showed good taste. It doesn't prove the existence of magic at all."

"No need to be so critical," Charlotte defended her sister.

"But there is magic," Maria cried, tears filling her eyes. "I can prove it. When—when—when I was small, I lost my favorite dolly. You remember Philomena, Charlotte. She had blonde curls and the sweetest smile. She always smiled."

"Maria."

"Oh, all right." She made a face at her sister. "As I was saying, Philomena got lost. I cried and cried, until Nurse said she would find her. And she did. When I asked her how she found my dolly, Nurse said it was magic."

Charmed by his love's tale, Michael frowned when Colby hooted. Opening his mouth to defend Maria, he was distracted by movement from the corner of his eye. Standing behind an arbor, where none of the Brigade save Michael could see him, was Brinston. A stern, implacable Most Honorable Knight and Marquess. An offended magician. Michael settled for a mild rebuke and waited to see what would happen.

"Maria is correct," Lacey announced. "There is magic in the world. I know what I saw. Don't fret my dear; these disbelievers will have their eyes opened one day."

"I am proud of your perception," Michael softly added in Maria's ear. He was rewarded with a brilliant smile. Glancing up, he received a further reward.

Brinston's hand was raised.

"I am surprised at you, Dom." Janice's voice carried beyond the arbor. "It is folly to encourage Maria in her wrong-headedness. It almost sounds as if you believe magic a force of nature rather than..." She cut off as a rhythmic drone signaled the arrival of a stream of bees.

They flew in over the flowerbed, a line of furry black and yellow insects, roly-poly. They should have been intent on the nectar to be found in the flowers. Except they ignored the flowers. Buzzing, the bees made straight for Colby. He ducked as the first of the insects looked like it would smash into his nose.

"Yikes," he sputtered as more bees followed the first. Performing a tight figure eight in flight, the bees swung around his head, flying just inches from his face. He ducked more violently, slipped on the grass, and fell. Honoria shrieked and batted at her hair as the bees diverted from her friend and wheeled around her. She crawled under a bench.

Surrounded by the buzzing symphony, Charlotte joined Janice's vocal concert with gasps and trills of horror. The secluded garden was full of flying insects and their drone.

Silvester fell over Charlotte's bench as insects

hummed past his ears. Landing on his rear, he flailed his arms, fending off a line of bumblebees that whipped around him. Janice screamed as five bees alit and crawled across the lace of her bodice. They set sail into the air and whirled around to her back, lighting one by one on the nape of her neck and then taking off again. Lacey endured a milder attack. Two bees hovered in front of his eyes and then wandered away as if he was of no interest.

The Banshee Brigade was routed. The members flew to the house, most waving their hands in the air and screeching. The bees did not follow. They reformed a line and flew out of the garden, following the path they had taken to get there.

Holding her arm to stop her from bolting, Michael and Maria were left behind. Returning to the house in the wake of their friends, he kept her to a sedate walk, though she was almost as frightened as the other ladies.

"Let them go," he said. "The bees don't seem interested in us."

"Why did they come like that?" she wondered, wild-eyed. "It was as if they wanted to fly right into Sir George. But no one was stung. I am sure no one was stung. Charlotte's hair fell down; were there bees in her hair? And Janice; I have never seen her so discomposed."

Michael wriggled his shoulders. "Who knows. Maybe it was magic."

In the drawing room, the Brigade huddled around the pianoforte. Shaken, Colby spilled the brandy as he poured a round for all. Michael delivered Maria to her sister and wandered back outside. He didn't have to go far. Brinston stood at the terrace steps, waiting for him.

Cocking a brow, the elder didn't wait for the younger. "A beeline. Interesting concept," Brinston said with a boyish wink.

"You shouldn't have done that," Michael responded.

"I know, I know. But they were trouncing your

Maria. What else could I do?"
"Turn Colby into a toadstool."
Brinston's ribs ached, he laughed so hard.

* * *

Martha and Vera were ensconced by the window,
discussing serious business. "Nothing has happened yet," Vera
grumbled. "We should throw a hint Janice's way or try
something else."
"Be patient. We don't want to spoil the prank,"
Martha pulled the ribbon in Vera's hair. "By the way, there
has been no time to tell you; I looked in Michael's room last
night while the gentlemen were at billiards. I knew I
shouldn't trust him. He has a letter...Vera, are you listening?"
Vera vigorously shook her head. "Oh no, Martha,
Squire Michael is the most satisfying flirt. He couldn't
possibly be wicked. Why, you saw how attentive he was at
tea." Vera's voice trailed off. "His aspect is so noble."
"Yes, but you did not see the letter," Martha said. "It
could have been referring to the missing papers. Vera, truly, it
sounded most suspicious."
"Whatever. He is much more handsome than his
brother. Martha," Vera smoothed a ribbon on her knee, "do
you think he might come to prefer me over Maria?"
"If he has any judgment he will. The letter said—and
I quote. That is easy, it was so short and curious—'Brooks
928 Quig. Check first.' Does that not sound strange? Like a
code or something. Vera, please pay attention. I need your
assistance."
"He is the most intriguing gentleman in the party. I
cannot be sure—are his eyes gray or blue? I always was partial
to blue."
"I don't know. Michael is too busy escorting Maria
Wentworth for me to notice."
"But he did single me out after dinner last night. Even

though I am not skilled at piquet. He was more patient than Papa."

"Yes, Vera," Martha replied obediently. "He was immensely attentive." But that letter; it was drenched in the perfume of suspicion.

Vera braided lavender, cherry and gray ribbons together. "I don't think he means anything by it, but wouldn't it be marvelous if Michael did like me?"

If he was the thief, Vera would be wounded. Martha sought a reason for her friend to disdain him. "That dandy? He likes his cravats better. Wait until we get to Camelot. There you will meet someone more interesting than a tailor's dummy."

"You don't really believe he took Papa's papers, do you?"

"I don't trust him. Michael is such a fribble."

Her friend's head wagged in despair. "Martha, you have no romance in your soul. No gentleman who looks as fine as Squire Michael could possibly be a villain. Now, Lord Brinston—he isn't as handsome—wouldn't he make a splendid traitor?"

Martha threw a comfit at Vera.

"Temper, temper," a deep voice chided. Martha turned. Vera's 'splendid traitor' leaned against the frame of the French window. Somehow, he looked lighthearted.

"You intrude on a private conversation, Lord Brinston," Martha snapped. Concern that he may have overheard Vera's taunt blinded her to the twinkle in his eye.

"Not at all," he drawled. "I was in search of rational discourse when a missile flew. Ah, there is Mr. Jackson. If you will excuse me, ladies. I prefer the cavalry to the infantry." With that setdown, he sauntered across the room.

Incensed at his inference that she was childish, Martha fished another comfit from the bowl and sent it sailing. That missile met it's mark with a satisfying thump, but Lord Brinston didn't turn his wounded head. *And to think he kissed me,* she fumed.

* * *

"Vera, don't tell me you have forgotten the *Ladie's Home Journal.*" Miss Bridewell laid her scissors on the table. "I asked particularly for that periodical—it contains a drawing of the opera cape I meant to show you. It would be delicious in blue velvet. Martha, you might see a design you would like made up as well. I do love to create with luxuriant materials." Humming and shaking out a skirt of figured muslin, Miss Bridewell smoothed the seam she had sewn. Martha leaned over, admiring the small, unpuckered stitches.

Vera had reclaimed Miss Bridewell's shawl from the parlor. "Bridey, I am sorry. I did not see the *Journal.* It wasn't on the table where you said it would be."

"Hmm, perhaps one of the servants put it in the library. Your mother keeps old copies there."

With a sigh, the girl resigned herself. "I will look. It was the last issue you wanted?"

On her reluctant way to the library, Vera's slippers clapped on the stairs. Miss Bridewell could be a martinet; one of the maids could have been sent for the periodical, but no, one was not to order servants to do everything. 'It does no harm to accommodate your elders' was one of Bridey's favorite maxims. Of course, *Bridey* was elder. *Thrice have I gone up these stairs,* Vera griped. *It is probably in her room and I am wasting my time.*

Skimming past Tom footman outside the library, Vera turned the handle and entered the room. The periodicals were kept in a basket on the lowest shelf by the first window; she pulled it out and thumped it on the table.

"Not this issue, nor that. Avalon, these are all out of date. Why does Mama keep these old things? The fashions are exploded!" The girl glanced around the room. Where could the newest issue be?

The door to Robert Jackson's study stood ajar. Seated at the desk was the Banshee regular, Sir George Colby. He leaned to the left, lifting papers out of a drawer. She peered—what was he doing? He read a paper, laid it down, and read another. Then Colby picked up a third and seemed to be comparing between the papers. Vera gasped and forgot fashions, periodicals, and Miss Bridewell. Papa's papers! Rushing to the door, she flung it wide.

"What are you doing, Sir George? That is Papa's desk," Vera demanded.

At her explosive entrance, Colby plopped his hands on top of the papers, jumbled them together, and stuffed them back in the desk drawer every which way. Guilt was ground into the pores of his face. "Ah, er, ah," he hemmed, his neck flaming red. Slamming the drawer shut, he jumped around the desk and strode to the door. "I'm just...just...lookin' for paper to write my mother," he blurted, "Can do it later." He rushed from the room.

Vera stared after him, mouth hanging open and eyes wide. If she hadn't just witnessed suspicious behavior, she would give Janice her favorite shawl. Curious as to the papers in the drawer, still Vera remembered her upbringing. Sir George's snooping didn't excuse her doing the same. She couldn't look, but Martha needed to know this development without delay.

Up the stairs for the fourth time, shuffling her slippers and musing about Sir George, Michael overtook and passed Vera. He mounted the stairs two at a time, looking in a bit of a huff, giving her the barest civility. The girl paused and watched him navigate the upper hall.

The only other person to be seen was Holt footman, carrying a heavy vase full of white roses that swayed as he minced. At least he minced until the lord met him; Michael collided with Holt, who perforce performed a neat bow to keep from sitting on the floor. Unfortunately, Holt's arms couldn't hold the laden vase straight as he bowed. Roses, water, and Holt cascaded to the floor at Michael's feet.

"Grrr," Michael apologized and sidestepping the mess, splashed his way down the hall. Vera was gratified to learn a new word from Holt. No, more than one new word. He had likely heard them in the stables. They sounded the sort that would come in handy when life became too frustrating to keep a stiff upper lip. Martha would love them.

* * *

All the words were familiar to Michael, who, while he regretted the accident, was too wrought to care. He stalked the corridor until he reached the room he sought. The door banged, shutting out the sound of Holt's swearing.

He bellowed, "Richard, what are you doing still in your room? I have been seeking you downstairs and outside the last half hour." Michael stomped across the floor. "You slipped up. That damn chit was in my quarters."

Brinston turned from the window. "Are you referring to Martha Dunsmore? When? She could not have searched your room. Between Barnes and myself, she was not unattended for a moment."

"My room has been gone over, my clothing disarranged, my bedding pawed." Michael thumped a fist on the mantel. "Flinty-eyed chit. She stewed around in my snuff jar. Intolerable. The note detailing my appointment at Brooks with Quigley on the wool investment was crumpled. She must have done it while we were in the billiards room. Spent an hour last night straightening up after her."

Brinston clapped Michael on the shoulder. "I thought I discouraged her from snooping. It seems I was not forceful enough. Don't worry, brother, I will handle it." He smiled wolfishly. Drastic reprisals were in order.

Chapter Twelve

Ladies plied needles and gentlemen lounged around the solar. Having bowed to the inevitability of inclement weather, ennui set into the house party. Such glorious weather as this corner of England had enjoyed the day before, all knew they must pay the toll of rain. While heavy drops sprayed the window glass, the company gathered in languid hope of amusement.

Maria labored over the fringe her friend had taught her to make. She had forgotten how to finish off the piece, but smiled benignly and persevered, precisely as her mama instructed her. It was the mark of a true lady in the face of adversity not to admit defeat.

Bryce Irvine leaned over Honoria's shoulder, admiring the sparkling circlet of gold-filleted crosses on the altar cloth she was stitching. He was not to know that the cloth had been conceived three years before during her first season, when the beauteous Honoria was in firm pursuit of the Bishop of Leeds' eldest son. With abysmal taste, he wed the gauche daughter of the Bishop of Camelot, at which point the cloth's completion slowed to a near halt.

Honoria dutifully took the work everywhere; the lady's industry and piety while stitching attracted more sober-minded peers than her low necklines beckoned rakes. It was a great pity Honoria preferred raffish gentlemen. She cast flirtatious glances over Irvine's shoulder at Brinston, reading the Camelot paper.

Keeping their eyes on the company, Martha and Vera again were a bit apart, whispering. "She hasn't discovered it missing yet."

"Then we shall have to be patient." They frowned at

each other. Vera's lips dipped lower, having had more practice.

"Shall we play hide and seek?" Honoria suggested, desperate to put the despised altar cloth down.

"Oh, yes."

Silvester, winding a finger around one of Charlotte's brown curls and tugging, mumbled, "Rather have a tooth drawn."

"Let's do."

"Was hopin' for a game of billiards."

"Thuch fun." Depreciating the groans of gentlemen loath to participate in a childish game, the ayes of the enthusiastic ladies won. Unlike dull men, they possessed imagination and could see themselves caught in a shadowy corner by their favored sir. What better prospect was there for a rainy day than flirtation?

"No going outside, please; you would only get wet." Mrs. Jackson's was the voice of reason and maturity.

"And do not disturb Cook. She is agonized today," Miss Bridewell added, not looking up from the intricate lace she was tatting.

"Please, allow me to sit here and rest. I am still fatigued from my journey." Lady Coletta smiled as she told the whopper of a lie. Not a chance that elegant lady was going to romp around the manor with the Banshee Brigade. She'd rather dogs licked the skin off her face.

"The ladies shall hide and the gentlemen seek," Honoria spoke before another damping suggestion could be made.

"We should omit the servants' quarters."

"House is large enough without dragging up in the attics."

"Leave plenty of time for hiding—I am not familiar enough with the house to find the ideal hiding spot immediately."

"A time limit on finding people; we must have a

limit."

"*Celui qui veut, peut,* " Janice murmured.

"Shall we draw names to decide who to seek?" Less dull than the other men, Michael had divined the possibilities. He had a definite managing streak, and an idea as to whom he should like to catch in a dim corner. Somehow he would manage to mark the correct name and find it in a hat.

"Oh, no," Janice pooh poohed that idea. "That is much too easy. What we should do is seek a hiding place that suggests our finest qualities; if a gentleman wishes to find a particular lady, he must decide what place reflects her character best." Her glare at Irvine indicated that gentle knight should beware lest his choice of prey was in error. He was eyeing his boots and failed to take the warning.

"Oooh, how clever!", "Pleathe, let uth do it that way!", and "How delicious!" in feminine voice was balanced by a chorus of masculine groans.

Of course, the nature of courtship being what it was, feminine desire was held sacred; the ladies dispersed from the solar in a whirlwind of skirts to whatever locations placed them in the most favorable light. The gentlemen followed after a semi-decent interval.

Maria, she of the piping (or would piercing be a better word?) soprano voice, whisked into the music room to hide behind the covered harp. (Michael always smiled when she played.) Lacey pulled the sleeves of his jacket over his wrists and strode to the music room, hearing again in his mind the lilting notes of the pianoforte as Janice played. Circling the room, he spied a ruffle draped around the covered instrument. He tiptoed to the front of the harp and tipped it forward. His lips puckered and found the forehead of his beloved Janice—Maria shrieked and subsided to the floor.

Janice, forgetting her clumsiness in tripping Sir Fellows in a quadrille at Almack's, slipped into the ballroom to peek from behind the window curtain. (Mr. Lacey must recall their meeting at the Duchess of Devonshire's ball.) Silvester, sure his favored lady, Charlotte, would remember the waltz they had shared at Merlin's Gardens, set off for the ballroom. He swung the door open, began humming, and danced around the room, his eyes scanning the area. With a quiet, "Aha," he waltzed to one curtained window and pulled his lady into his arms. Janice stumbled over his toes and he winced.

Charlotte darted to the library. (After all, Sir Hunnycut's opinion was that Byron could have used her as his inspiration for *The Maid of Athens.* Peter had agreed with that assessment.) Michael thought hard about Maria. That quietly accomplished lady would surely choose the library in which to hide. In the dimly lit room, where the drapes were pulled to help keep the dampness of the rain from the shelves, he spied a slender form tucked behind the statue of Athena. "My love!" he cried as he pulled on Charlotte's arm.

The beauteous Honoria stood undecided in the hall, then whisked into the dining room to partake of a small glass of sherry while she debated where to hide.

Bryce Irvine let himself into the conservatory, thinking that the sweet smelling Honoria would be found among the exotic blooms. He searched. Humidity wilted his cravat and his hair. A palm branch scratched his neck and a stray bee stung his thumb when he pushed aside a blooming bush. The only thing he discovered was Mrs. Jackson's smelling salts, which she was not aware was missing.

Colby, impatient with childish games, decided the effort of seeking Honoria would not be equal to a glass of the fine, well-aged brandy Jackson stocked. He checked the hall; even the footmen were absent for the moment. No one would see his defection from the absurd game. So Colby entered the dining room, where he knew a decanter and glasses could always be found. There he found the object of his affection, sipping a glass of fruited sherry and gazing out the window.

Martha and Vera, the quietest members of the hiding

group, mounted the stairs together. "None of the gentlemen will wish to seek us," Vera hissed.

"Perhaps not, but I do need to check Sir George's room."

"Whatever for?" Not accustomed to being an investigator, Vera had not considered the possibilities of hide and seek.

"The papers, silly. This is the perfect opportunity to search for the missing papers. Who would think to look in Sir George's room for a lady? We shall have as much time as we need."

"I wish Michael would seek me, but he was looking at Maria Wentworth in the most disgusting way. Like Beastslayer when he doesn't want to ride out in the rain. He is not worth flirting with after all." They grinned at each other, knowing Vera didn't mean a word of disparagement of her chosen knight.

In the salon, Lord Brinston folded the paper and set it on the footstool next his chair. His nose lifted as if he were following the scent of crumb cake. Coletta looked at him, eyebrow cocked, and he smiled. "Going to blow a cloud," he said, excusing himself with a lie. His sister coughed behind her hand and wondered what he was really going to do. Surely he didn't mean to play hide and seek?

Three quarters of an hour later, Martha plopped in a wing chair set to the left of the black basalt fireplace in Sir George's bedchamber. "Not the tiniest piece of dubious paper here. Shall we cease to suspect Sir George?"

Vera sank to the floor, poking a finger into the soft skin of her throat. "I don't know. I suppose he could have a hiding place outside his chamber, but that would not be as safe, would it? If you had only seen him at Papa's desk—he acted as guilty as sin."

"We shall keep our eyes upon him." Martha humphed in aggravation. She looked around the room, wondering if they had missed a hiding place. Jumping up, she

peeked behind a picture frame. No, nothing there. Her
cheeks puffed.

"We can still play a prank," she said. "I came
prepared." Vera, her eyes alight, watched as Martha opened a
drawer and carefully removed the shirts that were stacked in
it. Pulling a threaded needle from her sleeve, Martha ran it
through the shoulder of each shirt, tying a simple knot at the
end. "There. A clothesline. When his servant takes the top
shirt out of the drawer, they will all come out." Vera clapped
a hand over her mouth to stifle her giggles.

"Now to throw dust in the eyes of anyone who thinks
we may not have hidden for the game. You return to the
solar, Vera. Make sure you crow that no one found you. I
shall skip along somewhere else and hide for a few more
minutes before 'giving up'."

The girls slid around the corner of the hall and trod to
the stairs. Vera went down, Martha turned to the right,
entering the wing housing her chamber.

As she passed the first door, it opened and an arm
shot out and grasped her about the elbow. She teetered and
stumbled through the doorway. The door closed with a snap.

"Very clever, Martha." Brinston trapped her against
the closed door, his hands under her armpits, keeping her
upright. "Adroit maneuvering; you choose your distraction
well. Not quite well enough, though. Would you care to
explain what you were doing in Colby's quarters?"

Martha quivered at the closeness of that large,
masculine body, feeling hunted. Her mind quivered and
found a simile. Poor rabbits; they got chased all over by dogs
and men with guns, trying to cower in holes, their little fluffy
tails quivering. Was this how they felt? Hunted. Trapped. A
fricassee would never taste the same. In the meantime, why
not try denying it all?

"In Sir George's room?" Martha sputtered. "How dare
you accuse me of something so improper. No lady would
enter a gentleman's bedchamber." His body leaned against

hers.

On second thought, perhaps attack would work better. "I could scream, my lord. How would you explain bringing me here?" An arm waved around his side at the bedchamber, although Martha's eyes couldn't see around the solid body crowding her against the wood molding of the door. The body leaned harder. Martha felt squashed and strange feelings skittered around her stomach. For Avalon's sake, enough. She wanted Brinston to kiss her, not scold.

The final resort always must be honesty. "I didn't find anything, if that is what you want to know," she muttered. It worked. The body stopped leaning and stepped back.

Lord Brinston surveyed the girl he had coerced into honesty. Martha leaned against the door as if she needed a prop. A young miss's white muslin dress clung to her lithe figure, deepest black hair curled around her ears and forehead, slipping from the confinement of pins. Her face was pale and her eyes glinted mute distress.

Oh, by the idiocy of Accolon, he had scared her too much. He kept forgetting how young she was. Thus, he spoke in a moderate tone. "It would be better for you to cease your attempts to find Mr. Jackson's document. Leave the business to me. I am trained for this, you are not, nor do you have the experience that allows you to anticipate the villain."

Unwisely, the Owl turned his back, thus missing the pleasure of the sight of an eruption brewing as he continued. "This is not a pursuit suitable for tender feminine sensibilities. Endeavors such as this are best left to men. I have it in hand." Brinston's voice droned on in the classic, dominant male litany. "I am sure Sir Hurst would agree that you would be better occupied with maidenly subjects. I have noticed a lamentable lack of effort on your part in those activities acceptable for your sex."

The volcano gathered strength as a hot wind blew through Martha's head. Brinston continued. "It is all a piece with your deplorable tendency to pull pranks on people. But the person who took the report is too dangerous for pranks, my dear. If you had any sense, you would realize you are playing with nettles." The marquess looked out the window. "For the sake of your safety and decorum, you must cease your search. What if you were caught? People would think you a thief, if not worse. Your reputation would be in tatters."

Lava flowed through Martha's veins on hearing 'deplorable tendency'. It picked up speed, racing through her arteries at the twin concepts of 'safety and decorum'. The pompous voice strengthened as the marquess explored his theme. "Perhaps you left the schoolroom too early. A proper education would have turned your thoughts to a more decorous demeanor. Music and stitchery would be more appropriate occupations for you than skullduggery. I have noticed that your performance at the pianoforte wants polishing."

Criticism of her activities was bad enough, but the dreadful man cast a slur on her musicianship. A wholly feminine rage melted her 'decorum' and erupted from Martha, spewing forth as a volcano, uncontrolled and lava hot. 'Safety' was forgotten as another of her 'deplorable' tendencies erupted.

"Oooh, I will show you—music and *stitchery!*" She slammed the door on her exit and stalked down the hall, plotting death.

Brinston grinned lopsidedly and slapped his thigh in glee. That paid her back for snooping in Michael's room. If he couldn't stop her spying, he could devil her. Gads, it was fun. Teasing that little spitfire was more fun than pulling the wool over Banshees.

It was what she deserved; his scrying abilities were overworked, keeping track of the pixie.

* * *

I will draw on every bit of my puka heritage—I'll beat

him at his own game. Martha was going to show that arrogant Brinston, come what may. She gnawed her knuckle, contemplating possibilities. At long last, she uttered a satisfied sigh. She knew what she would do. Not the most inventive plan, but sometimes simplicity was best. It would gall the marquess no end if she succeeded; if her scheme failed, no harm would be done.

* * *

When Vera appeared in her doorway the next morning, pulling on gloves, Martha urged her friend to go on to the village without her; she was going to laze in her room.

"We were so busy yesterday, I have the urge to be quiet now. If you would, bring me a length of ribbon to go with my pink muslin, please," the devious girl begged. "But don't tell anyone I am not going—I would hate to have Mrs. Jackson worry that I am ill, when I am merely feeling lazy." Vera, being a simpler soul and having no idea that Martha was bent on a wicked plan of revenge, went off.

Next, Martha rang for the maid. Bess, a simpler soul than Vera, was thrilled at the thought of aiding the fine lady and agreed she could do as asked with no difficulty. Her plan set in motion, Sir Hurst's little gremlin was positioned at her window, which overlooked the paths to the stables and gardens. The sun beckoned; she almost regretted staying inside. But 'the desire accomplished is sweet to the soul' the Bible says, and Martha's desire was strong indeed.

Her patient outlook was rewarded; Michael and Brinston strode the path to the stables, swinging crops. Both looked exceptional in dress and form; did Camelot contain any finer gentlemen? One was more pleasing to the eye, yet her attention was glued wistfully to the other. Not for the title, mind, but for the inexplicable tug she felt in her heart.

How was it she could tell his thoughts when his face showed no emotion? When he looked at her and Martha knew Brinston wanted to be with her, no one else noticed. When his slate eyes turned smoky and tender... She shook off the distraction, refusing to delve into her soul. The two gentlemen would be some time if they were to ride.

Bess returned, reporting success. Martha strode down the corridor, shortening her steps on the muffling carpet as she approached the room she sought. A quick glance around, then she turned the handle and entered.

She hadn't believed that she could get in. The valet was not an idler who tarried in the village taproom; he spent most of his time within this suite of chambers, and its occupant supported the servant in this aim. Thank goodness Bess had managed to draw him away.

Martha looked around the sitting room—it was neat as a pin with few of its occupant's belongings lying around. The walls were a soothing green and as in her room, touches of yellow enlivened. Papers were in neat stacks on the wide refectory desk, an unusual item of furniture to find in a sitting room. The occupant had no aversion to the large table—it was obvious it was in regular use. The impression given was of a controlled business-like environment.

Not all was business. A book sat on a mahogany table next to the stuffed leather chair at the fireside. Again, by custom, the chair would be found in a library, but its comfort was evident. Martha supposed Mrs. Jackson had the furniture placed so for this particular person's pleasure. She wandered over and glanced at the tome on the table.

Surprise, surprise, it was Mrs. Maria Edgeworth's newest *Tales of Fashionable Life,* the book Vera scrambled (and failed) to smuggle into the manor. Mrs. Jackson wanted to read it first to be certain it was suitable for young ladies. She, unlike Martha's Aunt Pemberton, had no prejudice against novels, at least those she did not deem too fast. Vera was told to be patient; after the house party ended, her mother would have leisure to peruse the volumes. Then, if she found it fitting, the girls would have their turn with the *Tales.*

Martha pinched herself. This was not the time to woolgather. She picked up the tome; the page had been marked in the enticing account of *Vivian.* She transferred the marker to a page further along in the story and set it down precisely as it was before. Then she turned her attention to the desk. What would be least obvious?

Writing implements lay in a bluish pearlware tray of the type made popular by the Spode factories—the pen wanted mending. Martha took up the knife beside it and gave it an incisive point. Hurst liked the nibs she put on pens. She swept the bits into the bin next to the desk and set her sights on other matters.

The next room Martha hesitated to enter. It was one thing to enter a sitting room—the bedchamber was another matter. The invasion of privacy... Determined to do a thorough job of it, she took the handle of the door in hand. Martha's eyes swiveled, looking for opportunities. Noticing tapestried slippers under the bed, she knelt and moved them over a short ways, firmly suppressing the memory of bare toes digging into the grass, a lazy grin making her feel special. Desired. She told her mind to be quiet and looked around.

The traveling box on the dresser took more thought; gremlinish fingers touched a fine sapphire pin. A memory drifted through Martha's mind. She could almost hear smugglers cursing. After deep deliberation, the sapphire was moved to the next cubby of the box, where it nestled with an emerald pin.

That should do. One did not wish to be overly zealous.

Martha let herself out of the room. With a jaunty step she walked the passages back to her own, where she settled with a worn copy of household receipts, her soul as content as the Bible promised.

She forgot about 'eye for an eye'.

While Martha reread cures for freckles, another person was busy. Action suited thought, though neither was acceptable drawing room behavior. A rose from the vase in the hall was shredded and the petals ground between vindictive fingers. *Where to put it? Not in another bedroom, not with that nosy hussy sneaking around. The attic? No, footsteps up there might cause someone to raise the alarm.*

Mind games aren't child's play; it takes too much ingenuity to think of safe hiding places for the report. Gave one a headache. Perhaps stealing it wasn't the best idea, but returning it now was impossible. Better to forge on with the plan.

Once the timing was right, the plans could be sold; Camelot was the best place to do that. Just think of all the money to be made from them. *Why shouldn't I profit rather than Robert Jackson? He doesn't need the boost like I do.* The money would make it all worthwhile. The money would make all things possible.

The cellars. No one to hear anything with the door in the hall, a good ten feet from the kitchen. Wait until the servants were occupied elsewhere, then go down. But not the wine cellar, where Dalton may come upon them. Somewhere else down there. That should be a safe hiding place.

* * *

Brinston and Michael strolled to the house in the wake of the Banshee Brigade, back from gathering strawberries. None of that group had the least hint of a stain or smudge about their persons. All were bandbox clean and their berry baskets were empty.

"Fine horses in these stables," Michael mentioned. "Wish Jackson would sell me the chestnut, but he flat refused. I can understand why."

"Morgan's Chariot is a wonder also. If you ask nicely enough, Jackson may agree to sell you a colt from the chestnut sometime."

"P'rhaps I will. If the bloodlines ran true, would be a

horse to treasure."

For a moment, the entire party was in the hall. A blood-curdling scream came from the rear of the house. Gentlemen bolted down the hall, racing to save someone from dire death. At the doorway leading to the kitchen, the sudden press of bodies kept them from getting through. Brinston elbowed Colby out of the way and darted down the hall. The rest of the men streamed behind.

Ladies followed, secure in the knowledge that those same gentlemen would keep them from harm, but curious to know what dire emergency brought on the scream.

In the kitchen, Mrs. Forge, the cook, stood on a chair, bellowing incoherent orders and pleas. Maids waved their arms and screeched, except the weeping scullery maid, who had taken up residence upon the counter by the sink. Various men servants stood around, looking stunned or amused. A shattered china platter of fragrant beef reposed on the floor upside down, with juices from perfectly roasted meat creating streams. Next to it stood a kitchen maid, eyes screwed shut, mouth open, emitting blood-curdling screams.

Under the influence of the men of the house party, chaos transformed into an orderly silence, except for the meat maid, who, slapped out of her blood curdling screams, moaned and sobbed.

"Whatever is the meaning of this?" Lord Brinston, being the most competent person in the kitchen, took charge.

Tears dripping off her chin, the maid sobbed, "A rat. I saw a rat. It run over me foot. I'm gonna die if'n it bit me."

"I saw it too," the boot boy piped up. "It run down the cellar. Must 'ave rats, the cellar."

The butler took charge at that. Pulling the scullery maid from the counter, Dalton scolded, "You'd think the French were invading. Tomorrow I will send men from the stables to clean out the storage cellar. That will flush any rats." He directed a scathing glance at Cook, who climbed down from the chair with dignity.

Calm was restored. In groups of two or three, the quality departed the kitchen, imaginings of dire death unsatisfied. Rats, though noisome, were not uncommon, especially in cellars. Nothing to get excited about.

The men took the stairs more rapidly than the ladies and parted in the hall, headed for their rooms, where they would wash and change their attire. Brinston, entering his chambers, found his valet laying out a change of clothes.

"All well, Barnes?" he asked as he unbuttoned his riding jacket.

The rotund valet turned and smiled. "Everything is shipshape, my lord. This is a pleasant estate to visit, everything just so, yet relaxed."

"Good, good." Brinston pulled on a clean pair of inexpressibles. "Glad to hear you think the staff is relaxed." His mouth curved. Shipshape. It wasn't his place to tell the valet what had just happened. Let Barnes figure it out for himself.

With a casual air, he mentioned, "Had a thought. Tonight, after the house settles, I want to look through the cellars. Black shirts for both of us, Barnes." The marquess finished tying his cravat. "I'll be playing billiards with the men if you need me for anything. Michael has laid another wager with Lacey and I am appointed monitor. You are free until I have to dress for dinner."

Pausing as he left, Brinston added, "Get some more chalk if you can. I'm going to try questing again. I tire of this game and nothing else has worked."

When the marquess left, the valet rolled his rotundity into the comfortable leather chair. He picked up a book, careful not to dislodge his lordship's page marker, and began to read.

* * *

Mrs. Jackson closed the door. At the sound, Lord

Brinston looked up from the map of the estate he was studying. "Madame," he rumbled in his pleasant bass voice, "I didn't expect to see you. Didn't everyone go visiting?"

She wandered over near him. "Yes, they did, but I begged off, saying I had household duties to attend. Agnes and Robert will entertain the group sufficiently well." Peering at the map he had laid out on the table, Amelia pointed a finger at one particular spot. "You know there is an old wizard's lair there, don't you?" Her worried eyes searched his face.

"Yes, Mr. Jackson mentioned it."

"You don't suppose..." she began.

"You think wizards could be behind the theft?"

She glanced over her shoulder to the window before continuing. "It is something they would do, isn't it? Cause trouble, I mean."

"Yes, it is something wizards are capable of. But, Madame, if magic was at work here, we would have seen signs."

"Have you seen any signs? Anything that would point to a wizard stealing Robert's papers?"

"No, I haven't. I checked the wizard's clearing myself; it is as overgrown and desolate as any abandoned site. Not only that, I haven't seen the faintest glimmer of magic dust, not even at Camelot when fireworks were shot off last season. Wizards can't resist fireworks. If there were any around, they would have been there. There hasn't been a sign of magic in England, or in Europe, from what I have heard, for over five years."

"That's good. No one wants sorcery; certainly I don't."

"Their mischief got to be too much, didn't it?"

"Oh, yes. Poor King Louis. They went after him with a vengeance. When it was said Marie Antoinette said the commoners should eat cake, people should have begun to suspect. But they didn't and magicians brought him down. I thought the government should have pointed that out, but they never did."

"Personally, I thought wizards meddled in the revolution." Brinston shook his head. "But that is ancient history, Mrs. Jackson." He gave her a shrewd glance. "Tempting as it is to blame magic, I'm afraid the theft of your husband's papers must be laid to human deviltry."

She sagged into a chair. "I know. But why?"

"That I can't tell you. The reason must be convoluted." He hunkered down at her side. "This bothers you a great deal, doesn't it?"

"Oh, yes. The theft strikes at Robert so directly. He is dreadfully upset, though he doesn't show it. Stealing the plans... Is it hatred? I can't help thinking that we are harboring a deceitful, malicious person. He doesn't deserve that. Robert deserves much better than that from people he takes into his home."

"He is a fine man."

"More than fine." Her eyes remained shadowed. "I think he is as great as the Iron Duke."

"He's easier to like than Wellington. Robert deserves much more than he has been handed. You are absolutely correct. But don't assume it is hatred, ma'am. We don't know yet. We won't know until the culprit is confronted. Perhaps even then, we won't understand the reasons behind the theft." He patted her hand and stood. With a grim set to his face, he added, "The Owl won't let the thief get away with this."

Mrs. Jackson took his hand and squeezed it. "That's my comfort, Lord Brinston. My silliness here didn't mean that I thought the Owl was faithless. You have never failed Robert; you won't do so now. I do take comfort from that. But Robert is horribly hurt over this; more than I think you realize. Protect him. Please."

Chapter Thirteen

Richard, Marquess of Brinston, stalked into the drawing room, emanating intense rage. Mrs. Jackson, who happened to be closest to the door, thought to herself, *The poor man is become deranged. Is it something to do with Robert's document?* As he made straight for his target, she amended her thought. *Ah, as I suspected. There is something between those two. The best kind of derangement.* With a complacent smile, she moved closer, the better to overhear the confrontation that looked to be brewing.

She was in the same corner she often occupied, talking to her friend. The animation in Martha's face drew Brinston like a homing pigeon. None of the signs of worldly boredom the town beauties affected about the minx—her eyes waltzed and a dimple sank and rose in her cheek with the ebb and flow of her smile. If he hadn't intended taking her over his knee, he would have wanted to kiss her. But it was going to end—here and now. She wasn't going to disregard his wishes. Not after he got through with her.

Honoria, attempting to attract the eligible gentleman, dropped her fan in his path. A crunch heralded the death of the silk and silver trifle as he forged past. The marquess was unaware of his *faux pas*. Affronted, Honoria muttered an unkind word beneath her breath and turned her shoulder with a flounce.

"If I asked..." Vera stopped short as the marquess presented himself in front of them.

"Martha," he bit out between gritted teeth, "may I speak to you privately?"

A sapphire pin glowed in his spotless cravat. His question that was not a question received no reply as he took

Martha's arm and dragged her to the veranda. He banged the door, clipped the girl's shoulder on the doorframe, and hauled her to the left, out of sight of the interested Mrs. Jackson.

Now he had her. Brinston would exert his authority. The little pixie was going to cave in to his wishes. Or else.

"Why?" was his question. As Brinston was still gritting his teeth, it came out more like "Whrry," and Martha stepped back, setting her frame against the carved stone railing.

She pulled her head back, better to see the empurpled face hovering above her. "You will be heartened to know I have agreed to play the pianoforte after dinner. I have been practicing assiduously, *as you suggested,* so I hope you will be pleased," she said rapturously.

He absently rubbed her shoulder where it had connected with the door frame. In the light of that sweet smile, his anger was fading, but Brinston had no intention of allowing Martha to escape her doom. "What have your musical talents to do with this? I refer to your flagrant disregard for my wishes."

"Your wishes? Would that not be better phrased 'commands'?" Gooseflesh ran down her arms. "I have a brother; he is a high stickler where his sister is concerned. If I step beyond the line, Hurst is quite capable of chastising me." In contrast to her flippant words, Martha's hand went to Brinston's sleeve as if to maintain his touch.

The light pressure on his forearm combined with the silken skin under his hand muddled Brinston's head. His irritation dropped away. His voice came out low and pulsating. "Vivian had just met Miss Selina Sidney—suddenly they become engaged. My pen is perfection but my slippers are not to be found. I do approve your choice in jewels." His voice became lower and graveled as he spoke until he sounded like nothing so much as a dog growling at an intruder. "You searched my room, you little minx."

He towered over the petite girl. "This will stop now, if I have to lock you in your chamber, if I have to dog your every footstep...if I have to..." The man was floundering. His voice petered out as his hand slid from Martha's shoulder to her softly rounded chin. Skin dragged on skin so neither could ignore the sensation. Both felt the heat. Both shivered in the blast. A thumb grazed her lower lip and his eyes turned misty. As his head lowered, the girl watched his eyes; the gray area fogged and the black enlarged in the most fascinating manner. *Kiss me,* Martha begged with her eyes. *Please.*

Brinston examined the planes of Martha's face. His hands followed his eyes, feather light as they traveled fine bones and petal soft skin. They crept from her forehead, traced over the lightly arched brows, smoothing the hairs that needed no smoothing. The chocolate eyes fixed on his face received a light brushing over the long lashes, blinked, and closed, allowing the questing fingertips to brush over the lids with a stroke like angel wings. From there, Brinston's hand crept down the straight line of Martha's nose, pushed the tip up, and then swirled over her cheeks. Martha's cheekbones were caressed with velvet fingertips, the profile of her jaw outlined with the side of loving thumbs. The admiring fingers came to rest on her slightly parted lips. There they pressed and slid along the length of her mouth, which heedlessly formed a kiss.

When she kissed his fingertips, the marquess shuddered, firming muscles that tensed to pull the girl into his arms. He resisted, pulling his fingers away and stepping back. How he had lost his anger Brinston didn't know. He only knew that the anger had flown as surely as the French had fled the jousting fields of Waterloo. In its place he felt...Merlin. He didn't dare name the feeling.

Worse, he wasn't sure that he hadn't sifted some magic onto her face. It had felt like that, drifting his fingers over her skin. Like magic flowed between them. But he hadn't set a spell. He knew he hadn't set a spell, hadn't even thought of one.

Martha looked as if he had kissed her into incoherence. She leaned forward, unconsciously offering more than Brinston had taken. Supremely satisfied at her capitulation, magic or no magic, the marquess took the girl's arm and ushered her back to the drawing room.

* * *

"I don't know why this has to be done here," Barnes grumbled. "Upstairs, it'd be cleaner. And drier. And a lot less dark."

Brinston was plotting a chalk circle. "You have an aversion to cellars?"

"Ain't just cellars, my lord. This one's creepy." Barnes dragged the collar of his black coat up around his black cravat. Then he pulled at the sleeves of his coat to cover his black shirt. "I'd like it fine if you were to want to do this upstairs. The linen closet would be a good place. Too small for anyone to surprise us there." He peered around. "It'd be dark too."

"Yes," Brinston answered. "Creepy. The cellar has picked up atmosphere from one of its denizens. That's why we are here, old fellow, not in the linen closet."

"You mean that thief? He's been down here?"

"Who else?"

"The thief has been down here?" A shudder swung the lantern. "Skulking and making a pact with the devil, I don't doubt. My lord, after you do the questing spell, we are going to search for the report? Somewhere else than down here?"

"Precisely."

"Then, after we do that, we can go back upstairs and go to bed like decent Englishmen?"

The magician adjusted eight stones along an imaginary line outside where he planned to draw the chalk circle. "You can if you want, Barnes. But no, I don't plan to go to bed like a decent Englishman. I'm going to stay up all night, poking my way through all the rooms of this manor, looking for Robert Jackson's document. Once I find it, I'll pull on my bat wings and fly to Camelot."

Barnes almost dropped the lantern. "You can't fly. I know you can't, my lord. Men don't fly, not even wizards who can make honey bees do what they want."

Brinston smiled and set a shallow silver bowl in the center of the unmade circle.

The valet shifted from foot to foot and blurted, "This doesn't feel right." Drawing a clean circle on the flagstones of the cellar floor, the magician didn't answer.

Barnes shivered. With the circle complete, he could feel the power pouring into the bowl; it made the skin on the back of his hands crawl. The cellar beyond the reach of the lantern light seemed to crouch in the dark, the sundry whisperings of mice were swallowed by the darkness. That his master might fly did not seem so implausible. If he could overcome this atmosphere and successfully quest, Barnes would admit that Brinston was the better magician.

"Silence now," Brinston cautioned. He stood straight, arms outstretched, his dull metal colored eyes fastened on the silver of the bowl. Gathering his purpose and determination, the magician spoke. Sharp words, words that sliced through the dark. Foreign twisted sounding words gathered in the lantern light and focused a beam in the center of the circle, in the center of the bowl. Silver shimmered as if surrounded by heat and then began to absorb the light.

Barnes backed up, holding the now dead lantern. Brinston moved forward, stepping on two of the stones bordering the chalk, and peered into the bowl. Light swirled on the smooth surface of the silver, flashing into patterns. It shifted from simple etchings of lines to designs as intricate as snowflakes. He followed the designs, stepping on each stone in turn around the circle, until he had revolved the entire circumference.

This was the dangerous part, Barnes knew. He held his breath as the magician stepped off the stones, planting his feet within the circle, almost touching the silver bowl. Brinston's hair rose off his brow, pushed as if by wind, and the final glowing design etched a shadow on his forehead.

With no warning, the light came out of the bowl, shooting like a fountain straight up in the air. Brinston received the full force of it on his forehead. He reeled back and crashed into the cellar wall. "My lord," Barnes shrieked, running over to his master. "My lord, are you all right?"

Brinston shook his head like a wooly sheep and stared blankly at him.

"Dear God above, tell me you are all right," Barnes prayed aloud. Tears running down his cheeks like puppies scrambling to the food bowl, he began smoothing his hands over the magician's coat, which was black spotted gray. Gray dust. Lord Brinston was covered with a fine layer of gray dust.

"Barnes," he grated, "will you lay off? You knew before we started I would get dirty."

"I can't help it," Barnes sobbed, batting at Brinston's shoulders. "Cleaning this coat is going to take me all tomorrow, my lord."

"Hell's bells, man, get off me before you do worse damage," the magician roared. "Don't need to ruin a perfectly good coat as well as waste my time. I'm not in the mood to pander to your tender sensibilities now." He slapped the wall. "There are more important things here than a misbegotten bit of tailoring. I didn't find out a cursed thing—bloody waste of time—the blasted spell blew up in my face."

"My lord," Barnes squeaked, affronted.

"Your precious coat got dirtied for nothing. Confounded spell didn't show me anything useful. I want to find the report, Barnes, not watch that benighted girl paw through the attics."

Barnes trotted alongside as a livid Lord Brinston began striding towards the wine cellar. "You saw Miss

Dunsmore? In the bowl?"

"Didn't I say so? Throwing things every which way out of trunks in the attic. I'm going to strangle the chit." He stomped around a corner. "Damn good-for-nothing spell. Take it out of my repertoire, Barnes. Who needs the infernal thing. Oh, and there is a snake to be removed from my bedchamber. Get two lads from the stable to handle it, won't you? Warn them—it's poisonous. If they feed it a mouse or two, it'll be lethargic enough to dispose of safely."

* * *

Distantly, the clock in the hallway struck three times. The hands trembled, then firmed to their chore. It was nerve-wracking, this hiding of the rocket troop report. It was all *his* fault. If it weren't for Brinston, the selling of the report would be a simple matter easily concluded.

Damn that man. How satisfying it would be to put a hole in his head. His interference has to stop. Put him in the ground so he can't climb out. That's what should be, what will be, if the plan comes out right. With God on my side, what should be will change to what is. Then Brinston will be seen for what he is: an arrogant, posturing ass. Then he will die.

Almost stepped on him in the cellar. Him and his man wearing black and skulking around, looking for it. They made enough noise to wake the dead. Turned the corner from the wine cellars and there they were, swearing like jockeys at a fixed horse race. Too close. They almost had me. If I hadn't slid behind the stack of crates, they would have seen me.

Inspired. My reaction was inspired. I'm invincible.

That confounded marquess should go back to London—stick his nose into someone else's business. Bastard came too close this time; better make the arrangements without delay before he queers the deal. The buyer is eager enough, thank Merlin. It's about time. Getting a contact name was harder than expected. But the Russians are interested, definitely interested.

God is working for me—never expected they would offer so much. A massive bank account. My dream come true.

Blue silk thread, cut into long strands, tied around the sheaf of paper, rolling it into a tight tube. The silk secured, the report was placed where the knot used to be, down in the empty space hollowed from the oak by rot. One of these years, the tree would decay to the core and have to come down, but not yet. Only the gardeners knew of the growing emptiness in the heart of the oak, only the gardeners and one other.

* * *

Lady Coletta strolled down the hall with her hostess. "It was so kind of you to invite me, Mrs. Jackson. I was at a loss as to where to go for the month. Brinston had no plans to visit anywhere and town was deadly dull. I cannot account for it, but I did not wish to retire to Brinston Castle."

Mrs. Jackson patted her hand in a motherly fashion. "Camelot is empty of company now, I know, my dear. It is wonderful to have you; lends precisely the right touch to the gathering." She lowered her voice. "I hope you have no objection to my contrivances to further the girls' education in societal mores. Your manners and air are precisely what I would have Vera and Martha emulate. There is nothing better than seeing it in context."

"I am charmed, Madame," Coletta's laugh was almost a giggle, "and flattered you hold that opinion. A small gathering for dancing is an excellent thought. I look forward to it."

"It's a shame the county is so thin of society at the moment. I fear you will find our little gathering dull. If more families were in residence we could have enjoyed a much larger party. A number of our locals are most pleasant, equal to any companions to be found at Camelot."

"This is ideal," Coletta objected. "I recall my first

dance; I was overwhelmed by strangers. Vera and Martha will be more settled with familiar gentlemen requesting dances. Let them dip their toes in the pool before they jump into the waters."

"The idea has merit, my dear Lady Coletta. Perhaps you are right. I had not thought of it that way. I meant only for them to view your exquisite manners in company. But you are correct; the party is numerous enough with Janice's friends, your brothers and yourself, and the Broom family in attendance to offer a full evening of dancing without tiring of any one partner. Mr. Broom's daughters are a bit young for evening affairs, but I enjoy their company. You may recall them from the picnic. Pleasant girls with amusing conversation. The vicar's son shall be our star in the firmament. He is with the Horse Guards." She paused in front of a table to realign a trio of miniatures.

"I don't call to mind anyone in regimentals."

"No, he wasn't at the picnic. Addington has just returned for a visit. He is a handsome devil too. His time with the army has improved him, which I would not have thought possible. He is handsome in the way of Byron. With the advantage of a romantic uniform he may well pull my young ladies' heart strings. I daresay he may even cast your brothers into the shade. Addington is a good lad also, so I fear no damage to Martha or Vera from his attentions."

"The young ladies stand no chance. I will steal his attention. I always liked a soldier, from my youngest years," Coletta warned.

"Where is it?" The wail ran down the corridor. "I need it with this gown. No other will do. So where is it?" Both ladies cringed. Glancing shamefaced at each other, they turned at the corner of the hall to find a service staircase.

"All things must pass," Amelia muttered.

"In good time," Coletta consoled.

Vera and Martha paused in the hall, not having seen the elder ladies. Both were dressed in charming debutante white muslin for dinner and the promised evening of dancing to come. Martha's dress had a Venetian blue tulle overskirt that swirled when she swayed. Vera's, deceptively plainer, featured a delicate tracery of silver embroidered vines that flashed in the light. Bless Bridey's heart, she had burned several candles late at night to stitch the vine, which raised the dress from the mundane to luxurious.

Through a closed door, Janice's strident voice could be heard. "If I do not have it, I may as well remain in my room." Murmurs from a hard-pressed maid rose and fell. Then the door was flung open and Janice hurtled into the corridor. Stopping dead at the sight of Vera and Martha, the older girl pushed tight fists into her hips. "I might have known. What did you two hooligans do with my nacre pansy?"

Vera began a pious monologue on the values of keeping one's belongings in their proper places but Janice would have none of that. "I know you took it. You have been the plague of my life forever and this is just what you would do to make me miserable." She stamped a foot clad in a white silk stocking on the floor. "You get my pansy before I go to Mama."

"Mama doesn't want to hear about your pansy," Vera said. "She went downstairs long before us to handle one of Cook's crises. She will not be pleased if you fail to show your face downstairs before the final dinner bell, either." She swept along the hall, towing Martha with her.

"At long last," Vera crowed. "I despaired of Janice ever missing that pin."

"Now we have to wait until she finds it." They pondered the progress of the prank. Martha asked, "Why is the cook upset?"

"She can't get the pots off the stove again." At Martha's bemused glance, Vera explained, "Papa had the newest stove model installed after he saw it in London this past spring. Cook is scared to death of it and daren't go near it half the time. She calls Dalton or a footman to take the pots off when they are hot."

Descending the stairs, Martha verified that no one was in listening distance. "Vera, you checked the upstairs sitting rooms?"

"Yes, but I found nothing."

"The stables are clear also. I must say, the head groom thought I was eccentric, wanting to see the tack room."

"Don't worry about Hutchins. He's a dear. Even if he thinks you are up to your ears in mischief, he won't go to Papa."

The two young ladies eased into the drawing room, where assembled family and guests awaited dinner. They had no desire to bring attention to themselves. Robert Jackson, at the end of the room, noted their entrance and returned his attention to the Marquess of Brinston.

Interesting to see Brin's eyes sharpen when the girls entered, Jackson thought. He had about made up his mind that his associate, unlikely as it seemed, had fallen in love with Vera's friend. *Strange, he dallies with innumerable lights of society, but has never shown the slightest hint of seriousness. Now Martha has him on his head.*

Who would have thought the mighty marquess would fall off a cliff into the arms of an almost schoolgirl? At least he isn't mooncalfing around like Irvine. Not much.

Indeed, Brinston did seem distracted. Once Martha was in the room, it appeared he couldn't follow the conversation. Lady Coletta frowned and poked him in the ribs twice to gain his attention.

Two Banshees were flirting while another pair traded *on dits* that had been already spoken at least once. (Repetition was not as much a *faux pas* as not knowing every detail of the latest scandal. Banshees were more scrupulous than many in this regard.) Tinkling laughter rang out; more Banshees joined the conversation. The Brigade was at rest, awaiting its leader.

Unaware they held the attention of Lord Brinston, Vera and Martha found side chairs and settled in. Martha twirled her fan as she watched Honoria Silvester shoot coy glances at Brinston. That gentleman seemed not to notice. Was Honoria interested in the marquess? The thought of those grey eyes belonging to a Banshee made Martha feel a bit low. Lord Brinston's attentions to herself faded when she compared her meager attributes to the beauteous Honoria's charms.

The next to enter the room was Mrs. Jackson. Looking pleased with herself, she flashed a brilliant smile at her husband but took a seat with the girls. "My dears," Mrs. Jackson said. "I require compliments, please."

Vera laughed. "On what cause, Mama, should we compliment you? You look quite superior tonight, is that it?"

Martha chimed in. "Cook burned the roast and you solved the disastrous dilemma with more than your usual aplomb?"

"No," the lady admitted, leaning closer. "I lost my slippers and found them without having to call for assistance."

"Mama," Vera protested.

"No, my dear, you don't understand. You have been at school and have not been privy to my difficulties." Mrs. Jackson turned to Martha. "You have your aunt to advise you, I know, Martha, but perhaps she is more reticent than I. I have come to believe ladies should be more aware of what the future holds." Martha basked in the maternal attitude. Vera, however, was embarrassed by her mother's frankness.

"Don't look at me in that fashion, daughter," Mrs. Jackson scolded. "Since you have been at school, my absentmindedness has grown to an alarming degree. I cannot find my embroidery scissors in front of my face, I have forgotten where things are kept, and I find it impossible to control these episodes. It is harrowing. My nerves are unsettled as I continue to be afflicted."

"Where were your slippers, Mama?" Vera tried to
stem her mother's candor.

"I removed them to adjust my stockings. Then I
could not find them anywhere." Mrs. Jackson sounded
truculent. "I searched high and low; would you believe they
were neatly on the bed pane. I looked right at them and did
not see them." Martha bit back a smile. Vera's mama looked
much as her daughter did in a pet.

Mrs. Jackson gave her daughter a disgusted look.
"Wait until you are my age, my girl. I have confirmed with a
few of my friends that my affliction is not unusual. Many
ladies of my general situation have similar difficulties, if not
worse."

"I don't understand." Martha tried to divert Vera
from the diatribe she looked to be preparing. "How could
absentmindedness have anything to do with your age?"

"They call it the change of life, my dear," Mrs.
Jackson spoke in hushed tones, "when one's monthly courses
slow and eventually halt. There are other unpleasant
symptoms. Mrs. Farley becomes so terribly warm that she
must use a handkerchief on her forehead. Another lady bursts
into floods of tears at the most trifling matter. She was never a
watering pot until now. She has withdrawn from society,
embarrassed by her intemperance."

Vera huffed. "Mama, please. Can you not discuss this
in private?"

"Do not censure my behavior, young lady," Mrs.
Jackson said in a seldom heard stern tone. "I do as I wish and
do not appreciate criticism from my daughter. When you
reach my age, you will be glad I spoke of this to you." She
nodded to Martha and stalked over to Mr. Jackson.

"Really," Vera sputtered. "Mama is impossible."

Martha said, "I find it charming that she is relaxed in
her views. Aunt Pemberton is so strict, she would never speak
of the matter at all. I like your mother, Vera." If Martha was
jealous of anyone or anything, she was jealous of Vera's

mother. She wanted Mrs. Jackson for her own.

Chapter Fourteen

Janice floated into the room. "Ta la," the delicate lady fluted and the Banshee Brigade came to heel.

"My vision of Avalon, thou celestial being of light."

"The sun has returned to earth. Let us bask in her reflected beauty."

"Such a cunning sash."

"'tis not the sun, but the moon with her mysterious shadows and silvery gleam." Irvine had studied to attain the distinction of Banshee. His words were spoken to Janice, but his eyes darted to Miss Silvester. That lady was not known for her perspicacity; Honoria watched Lord Brinston.

"Behold the glory of Guinevere come among us."

"How I envy you the dath." The Banshee Brigade commenced maneuvers. In the corner, Miss Bridewell watched the movements with a touch of disdain, shaking her head at an immodest bray of laughter.

Lady Coletta spoke in an undertone. "Peter Silvester was banned from the Jersey presence after he seduced Lady Jersey's maid. His reputation has not tarnished because Silence was rendered speechless. She was livid and will not forget her anger; she had been carrying on a flirtation with Silvester herself and cannot comprehend how he could prefer the maid over her." She turned her eyes from Brinston's face. "I believe he is unsteady enough to follow so great a miscalculation with a greater dishonor."

Her brother eyed that gentleman, resplendent in puce, charming Charlotte with sham magic tricks. Silvester, pulling a coin from her ear, snagged a lock of hair, tumbling her pile of hair off center. She squealed and her sister helped her to tuck it up.

An argument broke out between Squire Michael and Colby. "Dash it, know which foot," Sir George blustered.

"You got it wrong. 'tis his left, I tell you."

"Remember distinctly—he was going into Tatt's—I was behind him."

Janice joined the discussion. "Whose foot is what?"

For once Colby was not solicitous. "Byron. His right foot is the crippled one."

"He leads with his right foot at Jackson's. Would be a disadvantage t'were it crippled. It's the left." Michael was obdurate.

"Stupid thing to get wrong. How'd he mount like that? I've seen him top a horse any number of times—Byron does it just like anyone. Left foot in the stirrup, then hoist up. Can't stick a cripple foot in the stirrup and lift yourself so easy."

The Misses Wentworth joined the fray and before anyone could prevent it, the Banshee Brigade was in full cry. "I never notithe hith limp. He ith tho dreamy." Maria's studied intellectualism shone.

"I read *Childe Harold's Parsonage.* Couldn't put it down," Charlotte chimed in.

"Doesn't ever lean to the right. Must be his right foot."

"Shot the tops off his soda bottles—most daring."

"Lady Gwen, Sir Byron's half sister's friend, said he blamed his mother's tight..." Janice trailed to a halt, belatedly remembering that 'corset' was not said in the drawing room.

Irvine muttered, *"Oh never talk again to me...Of northern climes and British ladies."*

"Had his carriage made after Boney's."

"It's *Pilgrimage,* nodcock, not parsonage."

"Know it's his left."

"Lady Caroline Lamb thinkth he ith wonderful."

"He uses Hoby for boots."

"C'est tout dire."

"Don't his appearance and manner convey the idea of a fiend incarnate?"

"He makes me shiver."

"He said he searches for 'an ideal and perfection that do not exist in the world of reality.' I say, what does that mean? Curst rum touch."

Dalton ushered in the vicar, Mr. Broom, his wife and children, invited for the meal and an invigorating evening of dancing. His daughters glanced around the room with bashful airs, as young ladies barely of an age to be out in society were wont to do.

The pride of the vicar's house, Mr. Addington Broom, resplendent in scarlet regimentals, made a beeline for the group he perceived as the most attractive and approachable. He pulled closer the chair Mrs. Jackson had vacated. "I say, this evening promises to be jolly," Addington's eyes were glued to Martha. "Mama said we were to have dancing. Vera, introduce me." In the next breath, he said, "Miss Dunsmore, would you honor me with the first set?"

"Addington, this is not a ball, but a dance. No dance cards nor promising of dances ahead of time." Vera was caustic. "If you want to dance with my friend, ask her nicely after dinner, when we are in the drawing room."

Again Lord Brinston ignored Martha's presence. He never approached, never spoke to her. A pang assailed at the thought. She was but a schoolgirl, capable only of attracting younger gentlemen. Martha yearned for a smile to work its way into a pair of gray eyes. Of course, the smile should be directed at herself, not at the likes of Honoria Silvester. She did not know his thoughts.

Lord Brinston, standing across the room, frowned into his immaculate neckcloth and swore to himself, *I will not dance with her. If I go near her I will do one of two things; either I will throttle the little minx or I will throw her over my shoulder and leave. I will not dance with her. I dare not.* But he could look, and look he did. She seemed content with that young pup, Addington Broom. *His uniform resembles a footman's,* Brinston thought disparagingly.

Dragging his attention away, he probed. *Have to come to some resolution soon.* He didn't sense anything new; if anything it was worse. The thought brought a frown to his eyes.

The company complete, they went to the dining room and enjoyed a most splendid repast, punctuated at intervals by comments about the scandalous and fascinating Lord Byron.

* * *

Footmen had cleared the center of the drawing room of furniture and rug during dinner; the space was ready for dancing. Mrs. Broom agreed to provide music on the pianoforte. Martha was grateful that the younger Mr. Broom solicited her hand for *The Bishop* since Brinston seemed unlikely to approach.

Addington's masculine form and fine cut jaw were pleasing enough, but it was his attire, the dashing uniform of the Guards, that caused her heart to stutter. The young lady could resist the romanticism of a military figure no more than others. Addington's conversation, centered as it was on the design of the perfect dairy barn, brought Martha's heart back to earth with a thump.

"Once I sell out, will settle on my little farm, y' know. The hardest question to answer is how many stalls to build. Will my herd grow appreciably over time? Or shall I decide to concentrate my efforts elsewhere?" Addington puffed as he swung Martha through the figure of the dance. "Cows are the coming thing for the county. Guernseys have proven profitable. Or I may dabble in mangel wurzels. Interesting crop, mangel wurzels."

Vera squeezed Martha's hand as they passed in the

figure and gave a luminous smile. The marquess danced effortlessly and Vera floated as light as air in his company. Martha envied her friend the distinction of so polished a partner as Mr. Broom's toe caught the edge of her foot and pinched.

Promising herself she would not be jealous of her friend, Martha said, "Mr. Broom, I know nothing of mangel wurzels. Pray what are they?" That simple question occupied her partner for the remainder of the dance and left the girl free to mull over her own thoughts.

The set ended. Martha settled on a straight chair against the wall to catch her breath and Addington wandered away to solicit another lady's hand.

"Nicely done, my dear," Miss Bridewell said from the adjoining chair. "I watched you trip down the line. Mr. Broom, for all his good looks, can try the patience of the most knowing deb—you sailed through your set with him quite nicely. I noticed only the most fleeting wince. What did he speak of that held you so spellbound?"

"Cows and mangel wurzels."

"Not so bad, dear. Janice told me he spent a dance detailing the contents of his accounting book. I should think cows would be a trifle more interesting; tails and such things."

Taking advantage of their clasped hands at the end of *Draper's Garden,* Michael whisked Maria into an embrace behind the window curtain. There he coaxed a kiss. A tie pin caught in Brussels lace; a delicious moment ensued as he brushed his hands along her front, disentangling himself.

"Michael," she whispered, "I love you." Maria emerged from the alcove pink and breathing hard from the ardent kiss that followed her declaration. An observant Robert Jackson thought she may have danced the *Half Hannikin* a bit too strenuously.

A draft wafted from the French windows. "My shawl." Mrs. Jackson's tone was panicky. "Where has it gone?" She ran her hand along the seat of her chair. "I had it right here..."

Robert leaned over the back of his wife's chair. "Don't fret, my love, here it is, spread artfully on the chair back."

"Avalon," Amelia gasped. "I thought I did it again." Vera turned her back in disgust.

The Banshee Brigade paired off in anticipation of the next dance, announced as a waltz. Next to Janice, Honoria sparkled, in her element with Bryce Irvine and Sir George glaring at each other over her head. "This reminds me of the Cowper's ball," Honoria trilled. "Poor Emily isn't up to throwing a decent do any longer. At her age, you know..."

"I danced with the duke that night," Janice said. "Often older people cannot tolerate a crush; he did rather badly. If it weren't for the title, I would have cut him dead. Isn't that the same gown you wore that evening, my dear?"

"No, I never wear the same twice." Honoria's dress was a dream of silver lace caught up over winter white satin. Satin rosebuds lined the bodice and echoed in the hem of the sweeping skirt. The maid had performed wonders with her hair, producing an intricate arrangement of braids, curls and more rosebuds.

Mrs. Broom thought the one damsel looked like a trellis in the rose garden and the other would be improved with soap washing out her mouth.

A determined Colby attempted to elbow the obdurate Irvine from Miss Silvester's side; Irvine retaliated by stepping on Colby's instep with an unobtrusive grinding movement. Which beau would dance next with their mutual heart's desire?

Robert Jackson bowed before Honoria. "May I have the honor?" he asked. She laid an elegant hand on his arm.

"Couldn't be his right foot. The man fences. How could he present arms?"

"His right is misshapen, I am certain." Michael threw that remark over his shoulder as he escorted Vera past Mrs. Jackson.

As the opening notes of *The Duke of Kent's Waltz* sounded from the pianoforte, Janice gave Irvine a melting smile and bestowed her hand on the lurking figure of Colby.

With uneven numbers amongst the company, one lady perforce must sit out each dance. Despite this mischance, the men performed wonders, honoring each female with a dance. Miss Bridewell often graced a chair, although Mr. Jackson, the vicar, and Lord Brinston each took her to the floor. There they discovered, if they had not already known it, that Agnes was an accomplished dancer, light on her feet and responsive to her partner.

Mrs. Jackson vocalized her gratitude of the masculine sensitivity to uneven numbers, lamenting the shortage of congenial company in the neighborhood. "Aren't the gentlemen marvelous? If only the Pabodies and Mr. and Mrs. Watson had not gone to Brighton after the season, we should have been a much larger company. Betwixt the two households, we could have added a round dozen to the floor," Mrs. Jackson assured Lady Coletta. "Both families are amiable—indeed Rex Watson is highly sought. He is one of the gentlemen researching that Rosetta stone they hauled back from India."

"Egypt, my love; the Rosetta stone is from Egypt," Robert whispered.

"Oh, yes. My error, Robert. I keep thinking about the unusual robes ladies wear in India and Egypt and get confused. Mr. Watson was telling me of the Egyptian ladies—they wear dots on their foreheads. Most peculiar."

No one sensed it. There was no outward sign of the violence being contemplated nor of the animosity roiling in one breast. Hatred of the Marquess of Brinston and other members of the party should have cast a dark pall over the evening. It should have spilled over the waxed wood floor, staining it black for all to see and guard against. Instead, the thoughts coiled in one mind, twining and seething like a mad python.

A knife slid into the ribs would be easy, but not here, not in front of these fools. By Mordred, no. Here, everyone would know instantly who had done it. That wouldn't suit. Have to be able to get away with the report.

There is that old knife in the attic. Looks to be from Italy with all the intaglio. Anyone could have found it. No one will—not with the papers wrapped around it. Almost think it's enchanted, that report. Every place it's hidden, it is safe just long enough to be moved again.

Nice, strong blade on that dagger, not rusty and sufficiently keen. Even with the silver unpolished, it is a lovely thing. Excellent balance; feels good in the hand. It would feel better buried in one of their backs.

Which one? Brinston? The girl? She's a nuisance, rummaging the house. Came close the one time, if she put some thought into it. She didn't find the hidden compartment in the cupboard, though. Don't know who made it or what it was for, but it has to be one of the most clever hiding places ever. That valet was just lucky he stumbled on it. No, the malevolent one decided, *the chit isn't worth the risk.*

Brinston. No risk eliminating him. Would be worse letting him live. He has too much experience. He'd almost won a number of times. Luck on my side. Luck or divine intervention, the thief thought. *Yes, it must be Merlin helping me. My cause is just.*

Later, some time later. The knife would slide in, as easily as into a haunch of beef.

Across the room, two figures swayed in the dance like mirrored reeds. "I never guessed it was you," Vera breathed, splaying her hand along his shoulder. "Papa didn't give a hint, but he has told thrilling tales of your daring exploits." Her eyes fixed on the majestic face of her dancing partner in awe.

Squire Michael tried to look modest. Under the worshiping gaze of his partner, his toe pointed and his ego expanded. "I've been doing it a few years. Be useful, don't you know. They need something delivered and I oblige."

"Isn't it terribly dangerous?"

His shrug was eloquent. "When the matter is vital, who counts the cost? Danger is nothing." They circled, elbows twined, then stepped back the two steps the dance demanded, her skirts skimming over the toes of his dancing slippers.

"You mustn't be modest, Michael," Vera chided. "Papa told me about the time the bad man shot a hole in the boat and you had to swim to shore with papers clutched between your teeth. They had difficulty deciphering the message because you bit off one edge. Something about the number of shields that nasty Napoleon had. He was so pressed to read around the teeth marks that Papa showed it to Mama and me to get our opinion if one number was a three or an eight. Such bad luck that the part you ate was the most crucial section."

As Michael alternately paled and flushed, Vera enthused, "It is thanks to your ingenuity that they now use such a heavy weight of paper. The chances of a disaster of that ilk occurring again are greatly reduced." The dance separated them, but the girl's glowing face did not dim. Vera was delighted to be dancing with a hero of the search effort. As they came back together, she burbled, "Papa calls you 'the Ship' because you are faithful in delivering important documents. That is a clever play on your name—Shipley and Ship."

"I cannot lie; that is the name I am called by. Vera," Michael peered down with a shred of anxiety. "You do understand this is confidential information, do you not? It wouldn't do for society to know this about me. My usefulness would be at an end."

"I wouldn't tell a soul. I don't tell secrets. Papa has impressed upon me since an early age that there are times when one just cannot reveal one's knowledge." As he glanced toward Mr. Jackson, Vera admired his chiseled profile. Squire

Michael made a most satisfactory hero. If he would only indicate a preference for her over giddy Maria Wentworth, then Janice would be served a heaping portion of humble pie. Vera had waited years for an opportunity to show Janice up; she couldn't let this pass.

Irvine tried to coax Honoria into the alcove previously occupied by Michael. She batted his hand from her arm and in a cross voice inquired, "Whatever do you want with me? It is not *comme il faut* to pester me." To the accompaniment of the turned heads of Mrs. Broom and Mr. Jackson, Irvine, his lips in a stern line, flourished a courtly bow to Miss Bridewell and took that happy lady into the dance.

Jackson wondered how long it would be before Irvine surfaced from his infatuation. He hoped it was soon; the assistant's work suffered as he chased after the indifferent skirts of the visiting lady. If he would only start to think straight, maybe Irvine would realize where he had gone wrong and amend his behavior before it was too late.

"Byron swims, you know. Quite good, what?" echoed through the room.

"His billiards work don't compare."

"He is a Whig but hardly stays to vote..."

The notable exception to the symmetry in the selection of partners was the Marquess of Brinston, who made a concerted effort to avoid Martha. It is doubtful anyone else noticed his slight unless they had paper to keep score on. Often standing next to Martha, he appeared to accord her the grace of his charm, but the ducal heir adroitly managed to seize a dance with every lady at least twice and not once with her. Now, unless an earthquake parted the floor, it was Martha's turn to twirl about the room with him.

Brinston stood at her side, sipping a glass of wine. He was under great duress. Sometime soon, he was going to have to work on that spell. It just wasn't behaving right. Not only was the prickle of magic running up and down his arms, he knew he shouldn't have eaten any of that fig compote. It must have had cinnamon in it. He surreptitiously scratched but welcomed the discomfort. It helped to keep his mind off her. The magician's hazy eyes flickered in her direction but instead of inviting Martha to dance, Brinston set his wine glass on a side table, crossed behind her and bowed before Charlotte.

It didn't matter that he wanted to dance with her in the worst way; Brinston had ordered himself away from Martha. The Wentworth would serve as punishment for his sins.

At Lord Brinston's slight, red raced from Martha's bodice into her hairline. She fumed at the cut. If others noticed the marquess' neglect of her, awkward questions could arise. Why did he not wish to dance with her? There was no reason for the vexatious man to avoid her. Pique coalesced into determination.

Moving to the door, she slid unobtrusively through the opening. Now was as good a time as any to check Peter Silvester's room. Anything was better than staying to be slighted further by ramshackle manners. The dancing might continue long enough to run through Charlotte Wentworth's belongings also.

Blue tulle shimmered in the candlelight thrown from wall sconces as the lithe figure floated up and down hallways. Someone must have Mr. Jackson's papers. She was determined to triumph over the overbearing Marquess of Brinston—she would find the missing papers before he could.

The upper hall was deserted. With the gaiety of the dance, the staff not attendant in the drawing room congregated in the servant's hall. Unseen, Martha slipped into Peter Silvester's room and lighting a candle from the mantel, began patting the clothing hanging in the wardrobe. He owned a prodigious number of coats and an amazing number of pockets in those coats. Feeling nothing bulky enough to be stolen papers, she set the lit candle on the desk by the window and began examining the papers scattered over the mahogany surface.

Gracious Avalon, there was a sheaf of paper inserted into the middle of one of the magazines. Excited, she snatched up the papers and turned them toward the candle flame. When a hand reached around her, Martha gasped and jumped.

"What did you find, hmm?" Brinston trapped her between the desk and his powerful body. Martha could not move sideways or forward. She could have gone backward, but that would have fetched her tight up against the wall of his body. She was not going to do that.

"Let me go," she panted, kicking back at the long legs behind hers. But leather soled satin dancing slippers don't bite; Brinston chuckled and squeezed with his arms. Martha was drawn back into his chest. A tantalizing aroma of lemon, leather, and something unidentifiable enveloped her.

"If you dare to enter a man's rooms, you must pay the forfeit," he breathed in her ear. "I warned you to stop searching. Now hold still and let us see what these papers are." He moved a tiny bit nearer, surrounding her with his heat.

The close embrace kept the sheaf of papers in front of her. She looked at them, excitement at possibly having discovered the missing papers resurfacing and damping the indignation she felt toward Brinston. As her captor flipped pages, her eyes widened. The top two pages appeared to be an unfinished letter, but the three following contained sketches. She had never seen such lewd drawings. A man and a woman on a bed, arms and legs entwined. A woman curled around a man driving a curricle, her legs and skirt drawn up. The third, most explicit, showed an unclothed couple on a garden bench. The figures smiled vacuously.

"Ohh," Martha moaned, her cheeks burning.

"Is that what you expected to find?" Brinston drawled, shuffling the papers into the periodical and tossing it on the desk. His arms continued to hold fast around the discomforted girl's waist. "Not what I thought you were seeking, Martha. I must confess I am surprised."

She was so angry, spots flew before her eyes. Twisting to escape the marquess's arms, Martha managed only to turn to face him. The sapphire cravat pin danced before her eyes, the warmth of his body beckoned.

"You despicable cad, let me go!"

Brinston chuckled. "Let you go," he echoed in a mocking tone. "Go where? Back to the dancing? On to search another room? I warned you to cease your efforts, now you must pay the forfeit." He took a tiny step forward, pressing against Martha's front.

"You go beyond what is p-pleasing," she stuttered, lifting her chin and furious eyes to his face. "I do not acknowledge you a forfeit. Nor do I have to obey your commands, Brinston."

The arrogant peer scanned the girl's face. "You like to play with fire...I'll give you some." A curious glimmer appeared in his eye. Languidly, his head dipped until his mouth hovered above Martha's. Then, in clamoring silence, their lips met.

Martha had not anticipated his lips coming to hers, nor the slow, sinuous press and slide, so different than the touch he had surprised her with before. A movement of her head caused nothing more than a shifting of lips that fit marvelously well.

A groan wrenched from him and Martha watched his eyes drift closed as Brinston's arms wrapped more securely about her waist. That movement sent the most enticing flicker of nerves along her torso. The feel of him dragged an exhalation through her lips; they parted and she relaxed in his arms, her own eyes fluttering shut.

Brinston took advantage of her surrender; his tongue swept into Martha's mouth to create havoc in her heart. The two bodies bowed, seeking to nestle together.

The kiss went on and on. He had intended a brief

grazing of the girl's mouth to quiet her. She would ignore his wishes, would she? Instead, the sweet clinging of Martha's lips set his heart pounding; the limber warmth of her body urged him to closer contact. His head swam. Never had he felt so powerful and instantaneous an attraction to a female. He had to get closer, ease the ache that built so explosively.

The pull of the magic between them was so intense the Owl failed to note the tingle of his protective spell intensifying. Martha was pressed against the desk and bent back by Brinston's body. With the tilt of her head, she seemed to be lying on the wood surface. Brinston pulled her tighter in his arms, shifting his leg between her thighs and drawing her ever closer to the heat of his need. Sensation prickled along her body, escalating as their bodies fused and rubbed.

All conscious thought erased, Martha kissed him back, twining her hands in the lapels of Brinston's jacket. Equally mindless, his lordship reacted by lowering one of his arms along the swell of her buttocks, lifting her hips, shifting her between his legs. A sizzle of feeling shot up her stomach as something hard pressed at the apex of her legs. The girl drew in a deep breath and squirmed instinctively.

Wonder of wonders, he squirmed back. It felt so good to both that they kept it up for some minutes, rubbing against each other, faster and harder, until Martha thought she was going to explode. She convulsed under the barrage of feeling, breaking Brinston's concentration.

My God, what have I done? he thought, appalled at his loss of control. *Sink me if it isn't the unthinkable.* Like Lancelot, he was afire.

With a curse, he dropped Martha onto the desk and pulled his body away from her. She gave a low cry and arched upwards. He froze. She lay, flushed and trembling, staring at him with dazed eyes. Delectable lips, swollen and red, further proclaimed Brinston's loss of control. He stepped back with a jerk, locking his knees against the pulsing need to return to those delicious lips and the spot between her legs. He wanted that more.

Martha's hands fell to her sides, unresponsive fingers curling over the paper on the desk. She looked well-loved, but the man hadn't found ease; he ached, how he ached, to complete the deed. "Bloody crystal hell," he grated.

Martha's eyes sparked back to life though her body, replete with something she did not understand, draped over the desk. With a grimace of distaste at his own lechery, Brinston barked out, "You're good," glaring up and down her form. "How much practice have you had?"

The girl stared dumbly back, not understanding the insult. "Get up. You look like a doxy pleasuring a regiment." Brinston reached for her hands, jerking her to a sitting position. "Silvester or his valet could enter at any moment. It's time to go." He pulled her to her feet, ruthlessly tugging the wrinkled muslin and tulle skirts, and turned Martha toward the door. She, still struck dumb, stared.

Brinston did it again. He grabbed and hauled the bewildered and dazed girl through the halls. Martha bounced off two walls and almost capsized around one turn, being saved by an iron arm tightening around her waist. Finally, he opened a door and thrust her in. Slamming it shut, his footsteps stormed along the corridor. Martha was back in her room.

His emotions roiled. *For Arthur's sake, what do you think you are doing?* he scolded himself. *Are you that angry at her searching yet another bedroom that you have to maul the girl?*

Brinston stopped in the middle of the corridor and banged his shoulder against the wall. Shock rocked through him. No, he wasn't angry at Martha for searching Silvester's room. That wasn't it at all. Probing his feelings, it was just what it had seemed. Desire and anger at himself for acting on the desire had prompted him. Defensive, he crossed his arms.

May the Lady of the Lake save him, Brinston hadn't minded Martha's amateur sleuthing. When he entered the room and saw her holding a sheaf of paper, his instinct had been admiration. *Can't be,* he argued. *She's female. Barring Letta and Mama, I never met a competent female.*

Except for Martha, his conscience roared. *Why don't you admit it? The girl has everything. Honor, brains. Even the wit to mount a competent search for the report.*

NO! Brinston slapped his hand against the wall.

* * *

Malevolence rolled down the hall. Silvester's door had been open a crack. *Anyone walking along the corridor could have seen. Would serve the cursed marquess right to have to marry Martha, grinding himself against her like that. They looked like they were doing it right there on the desk. Disgusting display. She'd climaxed.*

His back—it would have been so easy to stab him in the back while he pleasured himself. Brinston was dead to the world, satisfying his animal urges. Could have crept up without being heard, they were breathing so hard. The knife would have gone in clean. But she would have seen. Too risky. Might not be able to silence her before her screeches attracted attention.

Those shameless... Like Lancelot and Guinevere, their rutting would arouse a saint. It started the blood flowing; certain portions of the anatomy were throbbing uncomfortably from watching. *Would have to see about getting some relief before stalking Brinston.*

The knife shoved into its sheathe and stuffed into a pocket. One of these times, he'd be alone and defenseless.

Chapter Fifteen

Coletta carried the folded paper down the hall and knocked on her brother's door. Admitted, her voice whispered in the hall. "I heard from Collie, Brin." The sound was cut off by the door's closing.

In the room, Coletta waved her letter at Brinston's back. "I have uncovered the rumor, brother dear," she announced. "I told you if you were patient, my friends would dig up the information you required. Collie has done just that."

He turned from the mirror where he had been finalizing the drape of his cravat. "And that is?" he inquired, eyebrow quirked. Nodding dismissal to the valet, Brinston turned back to the mirror.

His sister was so intent on her errand, she failed to notice how distracted he was. Indeed, Brinston looked as if he had not slept for rabbits nibbling at his toes.

Instead of looking at him, Coletta focused on the letter. "Colleen Devlin writes that Silvester dabbles in oils and has been seeking a purchaser for a set of four paintings. The Comte de Lauren is said to be interested; he wants them to grace the dining room of his gambling hell. The art is, well, rather skillfully wrought, but not of the sort to showcase in the family home."

"Ah, that is indeed the confirmation I wanted." Brinston crossed to his sister and kissed her on the forehead. "Thank you, sweet Letta. Your network of letter writers should be conscripted by the Council of the Round Table; it would save them much time and angst." He returned to the mirror with a laugh. "If de Lauren wants the pictures, they wouldn't be suitable to hang in your hall. He has libidinous tastes."

"I can understand secrecy," she mulled. "Mrs. Silvester the elder is a tartar who keeps the entire family under her thumb. If she knew what he is doing, Mrs. S. would lock him up." Coletta shrugged. "Beyond the danger of arousing his grandmother, Peter could be accused of entering trade. You know how some view those who have the gall to earn money by the labor of their hands. It could be the death of his aspirations at court."

Brinston slid a pin into his cravat. "I imagine it would be better to be accused of treason than trade," he added dryly.

"Ah, but you keep treason quiet in your ranks," Coletta riposted, "and trade is ferreted out so religiously." She slipped out of the room.

"Yes," he answered his departing sister. "Treason is kept quiet because letting it out just causes more trouble. I wish this were such a simple matter, sister mine, but it isn't. This is insidious, more dangerous than most. Your average traitor has nothing over a madman. I must bring a stop to it soon. If I can."

Barnes came back in the room. "My lord, if this is going to continue," he said. "I ask that you bring a stable boy in at night to check the bed. I don't want to have to do it again."

"What, there is something you are not up to?"

"Yes."

Brinston threw an arm over the valet's shoulder. "We knew the spell wasn't perfect. Snakes are just snakes. The magic didn't recognize that it was being used in a lethal manner."

Barnes sighed. "I understand that. As you say, snakes are snakes. But the only thing that would be worse would be a spider. A really big one, like that tarantula spider your friend brought back from Africa."

"Better, we should amend the spell, try to work in protection against natural dangers. If our thief is clever enough to throw a snake between my sheets, Merlin only knows what he will think of next."

"Tonight?"

"Tonight. And I'll check the bed from now on."

"Yes, my lord."

* * *

Martha slowed as she spied the tall man guarding the juncture of the upstairs halls. Chin tilted, he examined the landscape hung on the wall with smoky eyes that could soften Nimue's stony heart. Martha was reminded of her valiant angel. His ability to focus on a subject intrigued, especially when it was she he was concentrating on. Jealousy of a landscape ran through her veins.

Admiring his elegant pose, she was still hesitant to approach. The previous evening's events had rattled her more than she cared to admit. What was that explosion of feeling? Besides being beyond delicious, she didn't understand it. It had been earth shattering, but he had not felt the same, not if one judged by his reaction. Rather, he had been disgusted.

There was no putting off the meeting. She squared her shoulders and walked up behind him. "Standing around corridors with nothing to do. Humph. You dally too long, Lord Brinston. Mr. Jackson looks more worried every day. Cannot your vast experience find the papers? They must be found soon, I am sure." He turned and she quaked, taking a step back. A metallic sheen hid his emotions.

"Good morning, my dear," he said.

Avalon, with one glance, he made her want to repeat the encounter in Silvester's room. She wanted his lips on hers again. Brinston's kisses were irresistible. She wanted his weight pressed against her length. It was addictive. She wanted to explore the feelings the investigator roused with a touch. But Martha had lost her self assurance somewhere in the night.

Brinston held out his arm. "Would you perambulate with me in the gallery? We can continue this fascinating dialogue while admiring the Jackson ancestors." She shrugged and accepted his escort.

Entering the long, sunlit gallery, lined with portraits and landscapes of the countryside surrounding the Manor of the Ashes, the young lady prepared to go on the offensive. "I saw no other ladies out of their chambers yet," Brinston mentioned as she opened her mouth to speak. "They must be taking an extra measure of rest to recover from the exertions last night."

"The dancing was agreeable." *Did he do that with other ladies, even the Banshee Honoria Silvester? Rub against them? Or more?* She shivered. That would destroy her, Martha knew, for Brinston to do that with others. She could almost feel his body on hers now, heavy and tempestuously warm.

Brinston ignored her involuntary shiver. He stopped in front of a portrait. Rather crudely executed, the paint was thickly streaked behind the subject. "This is one of the men who saw the manor burn in the 1500's," he said as Martha again opened her mouth to speak. "Mr. Jackson told me there is some question of his culpability in the deed. Seems he entered into a large wager and seeing the house go up in flames saved his bacon."

Anyone peeking into the gallery would have seen the agreeable scene of a graceful lady and stalwart gentle knight inspecting the late sixteenth century portrait of a ginger-haired man in an unfortunate shade of green. The painted image's protruding teeth were exposed in a wooden smile and his lack of clothing sense echoed his lack of looks. The living lady smiled no less woodenly than the Jackson cavalier. This was not a Gainsborough masterpiece, but another satiric etching by Gilray. On guard against the emotions buffeting her, Martha didn't know what to make of this meeting.

Not for years had Brinston felt so unsure. Never had he done what he contemplated now. To be honest, never had he done what he had done the night before, not with a well-bred virgin. Not with the untouchable, off-limits sister of his friend. So discomposed was the Owl that he mouthed inanities, babbling about a mansion's history he knew little of and cared less for.

He opened his mouth and closed it. Lord, he was about to tell her. *Keep your head, man. You don't dare reveal your magic. She has enough of a hold over you as it is.*

He monitored his words. "Men down the ages have been known to make gaffes," he said. "I must apologize for my own last night, my dear. I can make no excuse for my behavior. One is not supposed to maul a lady and I don't think there is any other word for what I did to you." His gray eyes, warm as sunlight sparkling on a lake, fixed gravely on the woman before him. "I can't say I regret it happened. It was merely the wrong venue." Did she know he never apologized? Not to anyone. Not for anything.

No she didn't know. She had been wondering if she dared to place her arms around his neck. The suddenness of his confession threw Martha off her guard. She threw him a glance from under her lashes. He looked like he meant it. Now, was he sorry for mauling her? Or for kissing her? She hoped it was for the latter; she had loved every moment of his loving. Flustered and unable to think, she murmured, "Accepted. It is best forgotten."

Brinston was too experienced not to hide his amusement. He understood Martha's confusion; she was an open book to him, one of the most delightful books he had ever encountered. She wanted him to kiss her and he was more than willing to obey her wishes. This lady was pluck to the backbone. No matter what he threw at her, she rose to meet it, be it unsanctified loving or awkward apology. She made him love her, God help him.

It was then he made his decision. Sometime soon, by this time next year at the latest, Richard, Marquess of Brinston, was going to stand at the altar with this blithe spirit.

Not for mauling her the night before, which he assuredly had, but for wanting to. When he promised to love and care for her, he would mean every syllable.

He couldn't wait. He wanted to do it now, today, so he would have the right to be with Martha every second of every day. Most of all, he wanted to kiss her again and finish what he had begun in Silvester's room. Then he wanted to do it all again.

The rightness of his decision caused Brinston to offer a concession. Martha could not know how great this indulgence was, that he never discussed his investigations with anyone other than his superiors in the Council. "I have completed my inquiry," Brinston said. At her inquiring look he added, "I have solved the riddle."

The change of subject threw her unease away. Her eyes rounded. "Who is the culprit? Have you the papers?"

"No, our villain is still in possession of the document. As to the identity of the thief, I am forbidden to tell you that, although Mr. Jackson is aware of my conclusions. Martha, this farce rapidly comes to its end. So...you must cease investigating, sweetling. If you happen into the *dénouement,* you could be in danger. Our villain grows desperate, you see, and if cornered may well be unpredictable as Mordred."

"Then he may make a mistake. I could be of assistance."

His eyes softened, flecking the pewter depths with flashes of silver. A valiant heart in a delectable shell, Martha Dunsmore would be a fitting consort for a king. His hand smoothed over her cheek. Martha stilled like a rabbit scenting danger. But the danger was to her own heart, which was hammering in her breast.

"I cannot put you in the way of harm. I should be too worried about you to work effectively. Please, my sweet, honor me with your trust."

She licked suddenly dry lips with an unsteady tongue. "I should so like to help you, but I will defer to your wishes.

You will tell me when all is done, will you not?" *And kiss me again,* she added, silently and more fervently.

"With a glad heart." Brinston's smile bathed Martha like a waterfall. His hand touched the gleaming curls that lay beside her ears. "Such wondrous hair," he murmured, "like ostrich feathers. I could run my hands through it forever." A finger wound around a curl and pulled, tugging Martha toward his strong form. "I could touch..." Their lips met in a fleeting caress. "I wish to touch..." His words ceased, replaced by action. Lips clashed, arms wound bodies together, and two souls became one.

When the glorious kiss ended, Martha gazed worshipfully into Brinston's silvery eyes. Magic dust sparkled there, she could have sworn. Her angel had stolen some magic dust.

* * *

Miss Bridewell stepped jauntily into the solar. Mrs. Jackson was before her, perched on a chair set before the window, peering at her embroidery silks. A small fire glowed in the grate, enough to take off the dampness from the air. "Ah, Agnes, you come in good time." Amelia smiled at her companion. "My, you look to be in a sunny mood."

"I am, Amelia, I am." Miss Bridewell swung her workbag. "Mrs. Forge has promised apple scones for tea."

"How agreeable a treat. I believe apple is your favorite, too." Amelia dug into her workbag, scattering more skeins of silk on the floor and her skirt. "Do tell, Agnes, do you see those strands of blue I saved to shade the *fleur de lis* with? I cannot find them anywhere."

Miss Bridewell leaned over and began turning skeins this way and that. "You put them in your bag the other day, Amelia. They must be here somewhere."

Amelia sighed. "I know. I twisted them with the white. But they are not here."

All the silks were soon spread over laps and cushions. Miss Bridewell, kneeling at Mrs. Jackson's feet, shook her head. "No, dear, they are not here." She thought for a moment. "Did you give them to Janice?"

"No," she replied, mournful. "Janice has had her needlework out a grand total of once since she arrived home. So busy with all her friends, you know." She began stuffing skeins in the workbag. "I daresay if I ask the servants to find the blue, it will somehow have been tucked in Robert's humidor with his cigars. Then it shall smell and I won't enjoy working with it at all."

"How unlikely," Agnes chortled.

"Be a dear and ring for Dalton. I might as well admit defeat and ask him to find it."

Dalton's trained footmen and maids conducted a protracted search for a missing skein of blue silk, precisely the shade of the shadow under the hawthorn hedge, but finally admitted defeat. During the search, Janice, tailed by the Misses Wentworth and Honoria Silvester, surprised the older ladies by wandering in equipped with various pieces of fancy work.

Following them, Martha's wary silence ushered herself and Vera into the solar almost unnoticed. It was love. It was love for both of them, she was certain. One part of Martha wished to soar into the clouds, felt capable of dancing over the pond without wetting her feet, and knew all dragons were conquerable. She had found the one man fashioned to love her unreservedly and he was deserving of her devotion. It was a miracle.

The other side of Martha's soul was mired in fear. It had been too easy. She had stumbled upon her love. There had been no great barriers to overcome before achieving happiness. Vera's novels indicated the path to true love was full of angst; why was Martha's romance so uneventful? What would go wrong?

Miss Bridewell directed a keen look at smudged eyes

and patted the seat next to her. "Come join me here on this comfortable couch." Martha lowered herself on the settee next to the older woman. "You look tired, my dear," Bridey began.

The girl nodded but did not reply as Maria opened a conversation. "Lady Jackthon, do allow me to thank you for the thumptuouth party latht evening. I had thuch a good time." A feminine chorus echoed her sentiments and a minute by minute dissection of the evening began. Amid piping comments like, "he dances divinely," and "most amusing conversationalist," not to mention delicately phrased inquiries into the status of various flirtations, the butler, chagrined at his first rummaging failure, drooped his shoulders and reported the disappointment to Mrs. Jackson.

"The embroidery silk is nowhere to be found," Dalton mournfully said. "We did discover your missing flagon of perfume in the drawer where the decks of playing cards are stored. Only about one third of the scent spilled."

Vera's thoughts were her own. It was he that foiled the plan to steal the Prince's snuffbox. He that delivered the stolen papers to the Manor. *Papa trusts Michael completely, even though he is a member of the Banshee Brigade. Appearances are deceiving,* the girl decided. Could any other members of the Brigade have redeeming value? She was quiet, contemplating Squire Michael's clique, and failed to notice her friend's distraction. If she had paid attention, Vera would not have deciphered Martha's mood.

Martha did not understand it herself. He had kissed her again. Oh, glory.

Miss Bridewell unrolled her tapestry work, the complex heraldic shield in shades of gold on black meant for an armchair. With the seat finished and the back partially completed, Bridey was pleased with the pieces. As the center came into view, she was astonished to see a pin embedded in the right quadrant of the motif. "What is this?" she wondered aloud.

Mrs. Jackson peered over. "What is what, Agnes?"

A diminution in twittering signaled that they had caught the attention of the ladies. "How did this bauble come to be pinned to my work?" Bridey held up the canvas.

"How pretty," and "Doeth it belong there?" were overshadowed by Janice's enraged, "My nacre pansy!"

Before anyone could move, Janice snatched the needlework piece from Miss Bridewell's hands and stomping over to the chair across from Charlotte, waved it in Vera's face. "You snake. Here is where you hid it. Jealous, I suppose, you cat." Janice's face was gaining color. "Jealous of my belongings. I should pull your fingernails out one by one."

"That will be quite enough." Mrs. Jackson's voice seldom sounded so stern. Janice was startled into silence, though she still glared at her younger sister. Consternation hung over the room. Everyone could see maternal anger at the daughter's passionate outburst.

"You will apologize to your sister for your unreasonable words, Janice," Mrs. Jackson decreed, "and to the remainder of the group for your intemperate behavior."

The successful debutante had not been so scolded in a number of years. She wasn't going to knuckle under now; Janice's response to her mother's chastisement was swift and irrefutable. She flung the canvas, nacre pansy and all, on the fire and stormed out of the room.

* * *

The men of the house party gathered in the library, where another warming fire burned in the grate. The late night and excessive exercise of dancing and playing gallant had left them unambitious; like the ladies, they thought to spend a quiet morning. Only Lord Brinston had taken a scant half hour ride. A large breakfast added to the general lethargy.

Bryce Irvine had pulled out a racing periodical, Peter Silvester was poking a toe at the fire, and Dom Lacey was doing his best to figure out how to open the humidor, having obtained permission to light a cigar. The humidor, with its clasp chased in silver, seemed determined to keep the air pristine; Lacey had not found the trick of opening the lid.

"Shall we turn our hand to cards?" Robert Jackson asked.

"What say, jolly good idea," Colby seconded Jackson semi-enthusiastically. "Gives me a chance to take back what I lost to Brinston at billiards t'other day."

"Or add to the total," Brinston softly stated. His brother glanced at him, narrowed eyes acknowledging the hit. Colby missed the murmur.

"Decks are in the drawer over there." Jackson waved his hand towards a small side table against the wall. "They should all be complete. Ship, help me pull the table closer to the fire. Bit damp for my old bones, don't you know." Colby opened the drawer and pulled out a sealed deck of cards. Wrinkling his nose, he whooshed out a big breath. Then, remembering his manners, he stomped over to the games table and threw the deck down.

An invisible cloud of attar of roses scented the air. Brinston jerked, Michael suffered a coughing fit, and Jackson laughed so hard his chair fell over backward, landing him on the rug. "Smells like my good lady has been here," Jackson snorted out. "Gads, I should keep her under lock and key."

* * *

One person's noxious thoughts went unnoticed by all in the house. *There must be a way to kill him. Never would have thought it so difficult a task. Look at all the people that die every day. Nothing worked, not rat poison, not shooting, not the knife. Well, the knife didn't work because it was sure to bring blood into it. Don't like blood.*

How else can one kill a man? Drop a chandelier on him? A falcon could attack. Crystal hell, bring back those rats and have one bite him. Give the bastard the plague. He's the greatest threat to the plan, he has to go. Everything else is in place. He definitely has to go.

Fingers drummed a table nervously. *Can't tie a string across the staircase to trip him—there isn't anywhere to tie it on the one side. Besides, who is foolish enough to miss seeing a string?*

He's never alone; it is hard to plan something where there won't be witnesses. Accolon knows it is hard enough to kill one man. Has to be more than doubly hard to kill two. So there can't be a witness around.

The report is safe. At least that is accomplished. Never in a dozen years will anyone find it. Selling it, bless the Lord, is going to do everything. Money in the funds will turn the trick.

Running out of time, fool. Got to kill Brinston before he catches you.

* * *

Martha skipped as she went through the hall. Hours spent mulling Brinston's behavior had resurrected her confidence. He had kissed her. No matter she didn't understand the rest of his behavior, everything must be all right. He had kissed her.

In the drawing room, she stopped dead. Brinston, standing by the French doors, turned, looked, and looked again. A slow smile stretched across his mouth. "Very nice," he said. "I especially like the..."

Martha blushed. And twirled.

With an intense look, Brinston prowled across the room and placed himself in front of his pixie. Wearing that gown, she was *his*, no one else's, ever. He laid a hand on her shoulder, fingering transparent muslin. Climbing from the bodice, that muslin covered, but didn't cover, the flawless expanse of Martha's skin.

His hand smoothed over the material, running from her shoulder down her bare arm, and back up. From her shoulder his fingers slid to her throat. He wanted to move them down over the enticing mounds the gauzy stuff failed to hide, but he restrained himself and reached past Martha's throat to grasp her chin.

"Hurst bought me the gown in Paris. Do you really like it?" she asked, anxious for his approval.

"Like doesn't come close to describing my feelings," he rumbled. "How did you talk your brother into in?"

"I didn't. It was a surprise." Martha stepped a bit closer to him. "You see, I am a dreadful card player. Hurst said that this gown would give me an edge, that I might win if I wore it when I played whist with a gentle knight."

"You win by default," Brinston said and set his lips to hers. The kiss was sweet. Fighting to keep his raging feelings from overwhelming his innocent temptress, Brinston drank, sweeping her mouth with his tongue. In return, Martha sipped from him, inexpertly dipping her tongue into his mouth. Then they tangled, two lovers wrestling. She moaned—he moaned—someone moaned.

Her head was whirling. Had Brinston kissed her before? Not like this he hadn't, not even when they were in Silvester's room. There, the overwhelming sensations had been below her waist. Now, the feeling was flowing down from her head, into her heart, sinking all the way down her body to her toes, which curled. Someone moaned again and Martha tucked herself tighter into his body. Against his chest, against him everywhere. She was starting to feel that lost feeling, the one she had felt the night before. Like magic was sparking in her blood.

Before it got too heated, before Brinston could lose his head and strip the outrageous gown from Martha, he broke the kiss. Running his hands over her hair, he cupped Martha's head. Her eyes were closed and she was breathing quickly. She had been as powerfully affected by that kiss as he had.

Steps could be heard in the hall. Someone was

coming. Brinston set Martha away from him and turned her
to face the window. His pixie needed a few more seconds to
recover her aplomb. He opened the French door to usher
Martha out to the terrace. He laid his hand flat on the door
and said a few garbled words. *There, no one would come
through.*

Have to stop doing that, Brinston scolded himself.
Magic is potent stuff. Shouldn't use it to ease her way. Still, he
left the spell in place. One never knew, not with a madman
loose. He stepped over the threshold and closed the door.

The working of the door hinge had pulled a string.
Overhead, the string tugged a heavy bucket off center on the
exposed ceiling beam. The bucket scraped along the rough
hewn wood, caught on a ridge and teetered. As the door
closed, the bucket overbalanced, tipped, and spewed a stream
of lye on the carpet in front of the door. A moment later, the
bucket bounced off a glass pane of the door and fell into the
lye, splashing more burning droplets through the air. As the
lye ate through the carpet to the floor, paint blistered on the
door and woodwork. Wallpaper dissolved.

* * *

The evening raised spirits. Ladies reposed on couches
and chairs, the gentlemen decorated the walls and two
hassocks. The party was gathered in the blue salon. Most had
dressed informally, but Mrs. Jackson, on a whim, wore a
splendid brocade robe her brother had sent from China. She
looked exotic, like a figure painted on Chinese wallpaper.

Robert Jackson strode in, nodding to the company.
"Amelia, why are we in here? The drawing room would be
more comfortable."

"I know," his wife answered in a mournful voice.
"The drawing room must be redone."

"Redone? Do you mean redecorated? New
paint—new furniture?" At her nod, Robert forgot he had an

audience and roared. "Amy, have you lost your mind? You took that room down to the plaster just last year. Had the painters in. Got paper, a new rug. Every stitch in that room is new."

She made a helpless gesture. "There was a—an—accident." Her face brightened. "This time I am going to purchase a Wilton carpet."

Robert sputtered, but Maria Wentworth was already speaking. "Wilton. That is a wise choice, Lady Jackson. They have become very popular in town."

Janice chimed in with "I would prefer Wilton. Brussels is so *bourgeois*. The Cheleavs removed the Wilton from their drawing room in Kay Square and put in Brussels."

The Banshee Brigade was bent on gossip and from lack of initiative, the remainder of the group acquiesced. The Brigade knew many in the nobility and those people were not around to refute anything said, so it was something of a free for all.

"She can't see a foot without spectacles. Of course, she would not be caught dead in them, so when she turned to enter the room, she walked straight into the wall."

"Is that why she squints so. I thought she was sneering."

"The dimwitted lady thought it was a new fashion and wore the dress to Haversham's ball. When she raised her arm in the dance, the whole sleeve parted from the bodice. Now Sir Denison is rattling around town alone as Lady Denison has retired to their estate. It will be long before she dares show her face in company again."

Perched on a substantial chair at the back of the room, Martha hadn't contributed to the conversation. Instead, she marveled. He roosted on the arm of her chair. When he came in the room, he had glanced around, sauntered to the windows. After gazing at darkness for a few minutes, he wandered. Picked up a decorative box and studied the heraldic pattern, set a porcelain shepherdess to kiss her shepherd. Then smoothly, so smoothly, he hitched up his trousers at the knee and perched on the wide rolled arm of her chair. It was done casually, but he was tense.

Martha's angel was so close she could feel his every breath. On edge. "What's wrong?" she whispered.

Brinston gave her a confused glance.

"Something disturbs you."

Brinston was startled. Yes, something disturbed him. That damned cake had cinnamon in it. What self-respecting cook would combine strawberries and cinnamon? How had she known? He hadn't scratched once.

"It's nothing," he growled. "Pay attention; you don't want Honoria to think you are snubbing her."

Martha sniffed. The chatter around the room hadn't paused.

"Speaking of *modistes,* heard Miss Templeton ran off with hers. Her papa has scratched her out of the family Bible."

"Lady Caro has a ring from him. It's the prettiest trifle—two clasped hands that can be shifted apart. I always did say Byron has the most romantic heart in the upper ten thousand."

Brinston whispered in such a low voice that his words reached no one but Martha, "Lady Caroline Lamb does not have any jewelry from George, though she would like to. He has been running from her persistent chase."

Martha shivered. The baritone rumble dragged along her nerves. There *was* something wrong, but if Brinston wouldn't admit it, she could ignore it.

"He was sneaking a cigar on the veranda. Y'know how the countess dislikes that habit. When she smelled smoke, she set up a screech that stopped the company dead..."

The marquess' deep whisper corrected. "The Earl of Blakesley does not smoke. It was her sister with the cigar.

"The drapes caught fire and he just stood there. She sent him to stay at his club until he promises to stop smoking."

The deep voice said, "And her sister has gone to Glastonbury."

Martha swallowed a giggle.

"Did you hear the latest about the prince? An accounting of the additions and remodeling at the old Deputy Ranger's Lodge was presented to the Treasury by Colonel Bloomfield. The project has cost 52,000 pounds."

Amid the gasps, Martha caught, "That's the only true thing we have heard. If there is something expensive to delve into, trust Prinny to find it."

"Why, he could have torn the place down and begun anew for that price."

"The south façade was extended from sixty to one hundred seventy feet. There is also a new Eating Room added in the center of the south front and a new entrance."

"Lavish. I would love to see it."

The marquess grinned and contributed a bit of gossip to the room. "I have heard a highly placed gentleman, one who has been impervious to the dart of Cupid, has finally succumbed." To Janice's demand to know the name of the gentleman, he replied, "Oh, but it would be more entertaining for you to guess, my dear Miss Jackson." His enigmatic eyes were on Martha as he spoke.

"Sir Obaldstone."

"It couldn't be him, thilly. He ith nearly thixty. Who would have him?"

"That Italian count has been seen with Lavenby's chit. Could he be the man?"

"*Entre nous,* it must be Paxton."

"Or has Sarah Carpenter caught Brown-Inkering?"

Lady Coletta sat by Robert Jackson on the settee. At her brother's inscrutable announcement, her eyes flew to his face and lingered. A moment later, Brinston glanced at her. To her quizzical look he raised an eyebrow and bent his head. Coletta settled more comfortably on the seat. *Mama will be pleased,* she reflected.

Martha faced forward, wondering to whom Brinston was referring. Then she forgot about love and lovers as she realized what was wrong with the man. *Oh, for Avalon's sake,* she thought. *Doesn't he know about bog rhubarb? It will clear those spots right up.* Reassured, she concentrated on the swirling conversation.

The hubbub continued. It seemed the Brigade would prefer to throw names around indiscriminately than pin the marquess down to the truth of the love-struck member of the nobility. At one point, Mrs. Jackson depressed Mr. Lacey's guess that it was Sir Perth Sullivan taken with a certain opera dancer; her sharp "Can we remain within sight of the bounds of good taste, please," shut several mouths at once.

Martha pivoted on the chair arm. "Of whom did you speak, my lord?" A slight smile was her only answer. "Ah, I have found you out," she said in an admiring tone. "That some gentleman has fallen in love is a false tale, is it not? You wanted to stir the group up, you dirty dish. If we pressed, you would cry out the first gentleman's name you can recall. But the Banshee Brigade will spend the rest of the night speculating. That will provide you with ample amusement."

Brinston broke down and laughed. Shoulders shaking, he whispered once more in Martha's ear, "You are too sharp by half, brat. Now sit back and enjoy the farce." Hidden by her back, he tugged on a black curl.

Martha kept her poise; the fingers that had entwined themselves in her hair now played up and down her spine, stroking. It was simply delightful. Because she had her back turned, Martha did not see the man's firm lips tighten, nor did she hear his sotto voce "He has been caught tight."

He doesn't act like a hero, Vera thought. *Look at him, mooning over Maria like a chawbacon. I almost expect him to drool and start rolling his eyes. How is it Papa trusts him to deliver important papers? Look at the Banshee Brigade.* Sir George's hair had slipped onto his forehead, exposing a broad expanse of shiny pate. The man couldn't help that he was balding, but he was culpable for surreptitiously wetting his finger in his cup, dabbing droplets of tea on his head and plastering the hair back in place.

Honoria gave Bryce Irvine the cut infernal, gazing at the floor when the poor man directed a remark to her. *That was rude,* Vera thought. So typical. What happened to the idea one is known by the company one keeps? *Papa detests the Banshee Brigade for their utter uselessness and inanity, but uses the 'Ship' to make his deliveries. I can't reconcile it.*

Dalton brought the tea tray, complete with apple scones and tarts. Janice poured and Vera handed cups around. Michael did not eat—his attention was so focused on Maria the entire evening, he seemed in a daze. When the last tart reposed on the plate in solitary splendor, he grabbed it and handed it to her. Vera watched from the corner of her eye as Maria slipped a finger into the jam atop the tart and made a moue. Quick as a flash, Squire Michael dived for a cloth and wiped her finger clean.

Vera almost gagged. He may have been a hero, but Michael was never a St. George.

The group broke up at an early hour. Mrs. Jackson led the way to the door. Suddenly, she stopped and moaned.

"My dear?" Her husband was at her side in an instant.

"Oh, Robert—" Amelia grabbed his hand. "I lost them." The company gazed at the lady of the house uncertainly. What had she lost now? A few of the men glanced around to the sofa she had occupied and could see nothing left behind that would cause her such distress.

"Mama?" Janice asked. "What have you lost?"

Amelia turned her head blankly toward her elder daughter. "Go away, Janice. Your father will assist me. Please, everyone, go upstairs. It is nothing." People began drifting out, looking at each other in confusion. When Dalton closed the door behind Peter Silvester, emptying the room, Robert turned to his wife.

"What did you lose, Amy?"

"My stays. The blessed things are down to my knees."

* * *

Obeying the light knock, Barnes opened the sitting room door.

"This is for Lord Brinston," Martha said, thrusting a tea cup into the valet's hand. "Tell him to drink every drop and he will be more comfortable by morning." With an airy "Goodnight," she drifted down the hall.

Barnes closed the door, looking at the cup thoughtfully. "My lord," he called into the bedroom. "Can you take herbal tea?"

"No," Brinston replied. "It interferes with my concentration. Not a good idea when I am maintaining spells."

Setting the cup on a table, the valet continued with his self-imposed task of dusting the sitting room. His mind likewise dusted the facts and impressions it had collected over the last several days. *He's far gone, he is. Head over heels for that girl, but won't admit it. The family should be pleased. She's got empathy. Knowing Lord Brinston, he wouldn't ever admit he gets those itchy spots, not to her. But she guessed. That's a sign she matches him. Wonder if she has picked up about the magic?*

If his lordship is going to marry with her, he should tell her. Barnes' shoulders rolled. *What am I saying? He'll never tell a blessed soul.*

From the bedroom, the marquess called, "Who was at the door?"

Barnes smiled and called back, "Miss Dunsmore."

His employer's head popped around the door frame with satisfying quickness. "Martha? What did she want?"

"She brought you some herbal tea for your hives." Barnes paused. "My lord, have you told her you're a magician?" His response was the closing of the door.

Chapter Sixteen

Martha balanced on the edge of the bed, fiddling with an amber-topped riding crop. She hadn't changed. Instead, fully clothed, she wondered at the odd tension she had sensed in the drawing room. He had acted normally, laughing and chatting with the Brigade, but behind his smiles had been something. What had it been?

The girl shrugged her shoulders and went to stand before her window. It was a cool night; the moon, a full circle, ran in and out of menacing clouds. Shadows danced where the trees and bushes swayed with a gusting breeze. It was an eerie night, when superstitious folk would say wizards were abroad, doing evil. Nothing else moved, but Martha was still uneasy. It felt as if something important was about to happen.

She made up her mind. Staring out the window would not make the feeling go away. Better to look around, see if there was anything amiss. If there was trouble, she would honor her promise to the marquess and withdraw. Martha grabbed a heavy cloak from the cupboard in case she went outside. No sense catching a chill.

On the main stair, she paused, listening. Nothing stirred. The servants, guests, and family had retired. No lights shone. She padded down the remainder of the stairs and stood on the cool floor of the hall.

I should go to bed. The girl tried to convince herself that she was merely being fanciful. What was she imagining? "No, I shall check outside first." Her murmur did not lift the heavy silence she felt like a hand against her neck.

The front door was in front of her, but Martha turned and went along the passage, past the dim stairway, past the dark cavern of the library. Finally she came to the side door that everyone took when headed for the stables. It gave out into a serene green courtyard protected from the weather by high ivy-covered stone walls. A gate let one out of the courtyard; diverging paths led thence to the gardens and the stables.

The door was locked. Her forehead cooled against the mellow wood as the girl contemplated the bolt thrust into the iron ring on the door frame. No one had used this door. Perhaps nothing was happening. But stubbornness made her drag the heavy cloak over her shoulders and pull the bolt back. There were other exits.

The courtyard was, of course, empty. The cloudy sky allowed only a few stars to twinkle. Martha wandered from the enclosed area and stopped in front of the paths; one to the stable, one to the gardens. If someone was bent on mischief, they would probably go to the stables. But something, some looming sense, made Martha turn toward the gardens. She walked, straining to hear in the silence of the scene.

An owl hooted once insistently. She turned her head toward the sound, startled by the haunting command in the shriek, but perceived nothing.

Reaching the corner where the path branched again, she turned and surveyed the house. Martha had walked far enough to see along the whole wing—no light shone in the windows, only the moon, flirting with racing clouds, glinted off glass. She took a side path, one that wound through the perfumed rose garden and on into the wood. Then she saw him striding with a long step toward her.

"Sir," Martha called. "Whatever are you doing out here?"

He had on a dark overcoat and tall beaver hat, dressed as if for travel. His gloved left hand held something – something whitish that crackled as he tightened fingers around it. Martha's eyes focused on that something until the shape made sense. A rolled packet of papers. Her eyes widened and swung to the man's face.

"Martha," he sketched a bow. "I'm taking a breath of air. What do *you* do here?" His voice sounded tight, strained.

"I couldn't sleep." He tilted his head and continued looking at her. After a long pause, Martha started. It wouldn't do to stand here all night staring at the man. She had to get back to the house; Brinston would have her hide.

"Well," she said brightly, "I should return to my room. It must be quite late. Would you care to escort me?" She turned and began walking nonchalantly so as not to arouse his suspicion. Two steps later she stopped. Not because she wanted to, but because his hand was tightening around her arm. He was not moving.

"Now what do I do with you?" His question seemed not to require an answer, but she tried.

"Take me back to the house." She spoke calmly, trying to still her galloping heart.

"No." His hand and the papers were over her mouth. Martha screamed, but the sound deadened in leather and parchment. He pulled her down the path. When Martha did not walk, but dug her toes into the dirt, he jerked her up.

Terrifying minutes later, a dark shape loomed in front of them. Martha shuddered at the sight of the building they were approaching. What was he going to do to her? He pushed her into the dark building and slammed the door closed. Reeling from the push, Martha put her hands out in the dark. They hit a wall; it was a tiny building, more a hut or shed.

Where was she? She groped her way back to the door, stumbling over things. What things? "At least he isn't in here with me," Martha muttered. "I thought he was going to murder me. Now, how do I get out? Where is that stupid door?"

Talking to herself seemed to help, at least until her hand hit the door handle and tingled from the blow. She pushed, but the door did not move. "Oh, he locked it." The mutters were louder now. "How am I going to get out of here?" Martha pushed and banged on the door again and again. It shook, but did not open. Then she heard it—a horse led over the grass so as not to make a clatter. She banged both fists hard against the door.

"Let me out," she called, but the horse did not pause. The hooves clop-clopped a steady beat across the grass and faded away. A huge sigh burst from her lips. "He will have my hide."

Her eyes flared and shifted in the dark. They glowed with a deep blue light as Martha began rooting in the building's contents, looking for something to help her open the door. Not thinking that it was dark and she shouldn't be able to see the cobwebs dripping from the rafters of the open ceiling, she realized where she was. This was a tool shed, tucked into the trees away from the path. It held hoes, shovels and other tools for the gardeners. A heavy shovel fell on Martha's toe. Once she could walk again, it might help open the door.

Then a footstep ground in the gravel of the path.

"Let me out," Martha called, leaning against and banging on the door. "Help!" The door swung, tumbling Martha into strong arms. She looked up, eyes fading, and suppressed a sigh. "It's about time. He is getting away."

Brinston laughed. "Whatever happened to you, sweetheart?" He guffawed again and began flicking a hand over her cloak. "You're filthy."

"Mr. Irvine happened. He has the papers..." Martha grabbed his hand, which was brushing down her front in the most intimate manner. "Never mind the dirt, Brinston. He took a horse. We have to catch him." She started toward the stables, only to be stopped again by a hand on her arm.

"We catch him?" the marquess echoed. "Who is 'we,' sweetheart?"

"Why, us," Martha swung toward the tall man, "You and I. Who else?"

"I shall go after Irvine. You are going back to bed."

"What?! I can ride as well as any man! I want to help catch the monster!"

"No, you are not going after Bryce Irvine."

"You can't stop me." Yes, he could—and he did. Brinston whirled Martha around. When her body stopped twirling, she was standing inside the doorway of the shed.

"I am sorry for this, sweetheart, but you did promise. No time to stand around arguing," the marquess gently said and swung the door closed in Martha's astonished face. As the bar fell into place locking the door, Brinston raised his voice. "Someone will be along soon, my love, and let you out." He stepped away but turned back to the door.

"Stay at the Manor until I return, Martha," he ordered. His footsteps faded away.

All Martha's efforts to escape the shed only gouged the door. Hoes and other garden implements bent under the force of her attack on the door. When it refused to give way, Martha decided to dig her way out. She did make something of a hole in the dirt fronting the door, but the stone threshold kept her from using the shovel effectively in her bid for freedom. It couldn't get far enough under the stone to start a tunnel.

The girl finally gave up, swiping a dirty hand over her forehead and pushing hair from her eyes. The bitter taste of fruitless endeavors stung her tongue.

"Stuck," she growled, "while that dirty dish runs away with Mr. Jackson's papers and Brinston catches him. Ooooh, if only I'd had a gun." Martha failed to specify who she would shoot; Bryce Irvine, for stealing Mr. Jackson's secret plans for a rocket troop and locking her in the shed, or Richard, Marquess of Brinston, for not letting her have the fun of catching the thief and locking her in the shed.

Resignation brought a bedraggled Martha to sit on the dirt floor, her cloak wrapped about her for warmth. Leaning back against the wall, she philosophically decided she would have to wait till morn, when the gardeners would come along and let her out. When she met Brinston again, she would beat him with the dratted shovel.

It began to rain.

Chapter Seventeen

Amelia shoved open the door to her husband's private study and tottered in. Looking dazed, she plopped herself into the comfortable wing chair before the desk and covered her eyes with her hands. Robert, much alarmed at this behavior, abandoned his solitary breakfast of eggs and toast, shot to his feet and rounded the desk. He knelt in front of the stricken woman.

"What is it, my love? What's wrong?" He pried one hand from her face and held it in his own large paw. "Come, sweet Amy, tell me."

"Oh Robert," Amelia wailed, her other hand coming away from her face and clutching at him. "It is too dreadful." Her eyes were wild; the poor lady looked as if she had seen the evil Morgan le Fey.

"What is so dreadful, my love?" His even voice settled Amelia enough to speak.

"Oh, Robert," she repeated. "You will have to send me to Bedlam. It has all gone beyond the pale—I am appalled at myself."

"Nonsense. Whatever is the matter, I will right the problem."

"You can't," she sobbed. Robert enfolded his distraught wife in his arms and began rocking her like a baby. What had gone wrong? It must be dreadful to put his even tempered wife in such a taking. After soothing her for several minutes, she hiccupped and the storm diminished.

"Now, my love, take hold of yourself." Robert's hands rubbed and squeezed. "Tell me what is wrong."

"It's too terrible," she groaned, comforted enough to speak clearly. "I have lost her. How I did it, I do not know, but I have lost Martha. What will her brother say? What can anyone say? She was put in my charge and now she has come to some harm." A heartfelt sigh broke out of the unhappy woman. "You will have to put me in Bedlam, my dear, no question about it. Else Sir Hurst will call you out and shoot you. I will end my days stark raving mad. Please put me where I can no longer lose things, please."

Robert sat back on his heels, a frown creasing his forehead. "You have lost Martha?" he queried. "What do you mean? She is in her bed."

"No, she is not, Robert. Bess went in with her water and came to alert me on the instant. She is not in her bed; indeed, she is not in her rooms. Nor is she with Vera, or in the dining room, the solar, the conservatory, the hall, the sewing room..." Amelia stopped, frantic to catch her breath. "I can't find her anywhere within the Manor. It is raining, so one would not think she went for a walk or a ride. I have lost her."

A scant hour later, even the phlegmatic Robert Jackson was beginning to wonder if his wife had spirited Martha away in some fashion. She was not within the walls of the Manor. Her bed was not slept in, her room was undisturbed. The whole house was undisturbed.

With the exception of the missing Bryce Irvine and Lord Brinston, of which matter Mr. Jackson was wholly conversant, though he deplored it, nothing else was amiss. So where was Martha?

* * *

Vera woke and rose to the demands of the crisis. She held a bottle of hartshorn in one hand, vinaigrette in the other, hovering over her stricken mother, who could not stop crying. Agnes Bridewell had the honor of burning a feather periodically when Mrs. Jackson fell into a swoon. (Vera originally was the keeper of the feathers, but the small matter of a bed curtain becoming entangled in a burning feather switched Bridey and Vera's roles.)

Robert Jackson stood in the front hall, deep in discussion with Dalton and Hutchins, the head groom. Dalton had lost his look of imperturbability, while Hutchins was soaked to the skin from the rain. The groom's grizzled gray hair hung in strings around his worried face, dripped onto his shoulders and added to the puddle under his waterlogged boots. No one seemed concerned about the damage caused to the Aubusson rug that was collecting the rainwater. Everyone knew Martha was missing; no one admitted to any knowledge of her whereabouts.

"Thee ith not in my chamber. I checked the wardrobe and under the bed," Maria announced, almost the last of the Banshee Brigade to return to the hall. She joined the ladies lined up along the stair and patted her disordered hair in place.

Sir George and Honoria had investigated the dining room; brandy fumes circled their heads. Lacey one upped them by demanding the keys to the wine cellar of Dalton; a dusty bottle cradled in his arms, he protested that someone had to search the cellars and he was not afraid of the dark or rats.

Janice disdained looking for her sister's wayward friend, going so far as to comment, "I don't know what the fuss is about. Martha shall return soon. She probably went into the village for ribbons or lace." She earned a reproving stare from her father; he thought his eldest daughter would be improved by a forced stint with his aunt in Cornwall. Maybe the wilds of nowhere would settle the chit.

Returning to the pressing subject of lost sheep, Jackson dismissed Janice from his mind. "She is not in the house," he said to the assembly, running his hand through his hair. "Martha must have gone out. Have you seen any sign, Hutchins?"

"Martha is not in the kitchens," Charlotte breezily

uttered, sweeping into the hall with a warm bit of fluff in her arms. "But Cook is keeping the darlingest kittens warm by the fire. See?" She waved the mewling baby under Lacey's nose. "Precisely the shade of my new muff. I wish to keep it."

The groom spoke as if not interrupted. "Nay, m'lord. Tain't hide nor hair o' anyone out there. 'Cepting Mr. Irvine and Lord Brinston gone who knows where, there's no sign o' nothin'. Did one o' them take her, ye ken?"

"Brinston would not have. Irvine? Who knows; I would not have thought it of him, though it is beginning to sound like a possibility." Jackson sighed. "In light of his behavior *vis a vis* the papers, Irvine has darker depths than I dreamed. Ship, do you have any ideas?"

Squire Michael stepped out of the background, where the men of the house party had gathered, awaiting events. "You have searched the grounds, sir?"

"Not everywhere; the rain and gloom hamper us. But where would she have gone?"

"The pottery? Martha may have thought to go there." Michael shook his head as he said the words.

Jackson shrugged his shoulders. "As well try there as anywhere. Hutchins, send three men over to the ruins. Tell them to search the woods around the pottery. If she went there, she may have a twisted ankle and be unable to navigate."

As ideas were tossed out, someone went to check. The vicar's manse, the church, the village, even the road towards London was searched. Honoria's comment that the hoyden may have run to Gretna Green with the missing Mr. Irvine was ignored. The Banshee Brigade began assessing the options, for once keeping their voices low.

No one found Martha.

The day and the rain wore on. Mrs. Jackson was a limp rag on her bed. Nothing convinced her that she was not the cause of Martha's disappearance. She refused to sleep—she was adamant that she could not rest until the poor girl had been found safe. Amelia stared at the canopy of her bed, periodically cried, and castigated herself for not taking better care of the girl. Vera huddled in a chair in the corner of her mother's room. She was frightened for her friend—Martha would not have left the Manor without telling her what was happening.

"Where can she be?" Vera wailed again and again.

Miss Bridewell's face sagged as she kept close watch out the window as if she could conjure the missing girl out of nowhere. A deep line scored her brow. *Did this unhappy event have anything to do with Martha's upset after the dance? Should I consult with Mr. Jackson about my suspicions of a budding relationship between Martha and Lord Brinston? After all, Lord Brinston is missing also. Mr. Jackson is aware of his and Mr. Irvine's departures—at least he was not surprised. Are the three together somewhere?* The thoughts went in circles around her head. Miss Bridewell could come to no conclusion.

Robert Jackson and Michael paced. Both knew about Brinston and Irvine—they could only wish the marquess good fortune. A private discussion had them agreeing that Brinston would never have taken Martha with him as he hunted Bryce Irvine. It would be too dangerous.

Whether Irvine had taken Martha hostage or harmed her in some way if she had interfered with him, they did not know, but concern for the girl overtook the men. It was their deepest fear—Martha may have gone missing because Irvine had done something to her. A full search would have to wait till morn; darkness and pelting rain hampered all efforts.

The Banshee Brigade was silenced. Silvester and Charlotte, Lacey and Janice played a morose game of loo in the solar, jumping at the sound of their cards shuffling and discussing the game in undertones. Colby and Honoria shared a divan and a decanter which steadily emptied.

Colby stared at a cupboard against the far wall, then strode over to it and swung the lower door open. He returned to the decanter mumbling, "Not there." Maria burrowed in a corner chair, wringing her hands for a full two hours, and watched Michael pace the room.

The outdoor staff collected in the stable where a rousing game of dice was instituted. The weather did not allow work on the grounds and the distraction of their superiors worked in favor of eager gamblers. As one or another was ordered out into the cold rain to search somewhere, another would take his place in the gaming circle.

The men did not allow a witless gentry mort to interfere much with their unscheduled holiday. Not until Silver Streak stretched her long neck over the stall gate and lipped one of the solitary pair of dice out of the air did the game halt.

Lady Coletta was in the kitchens, trying to impress some sense into the hysterical cook, who alternately demanded the return of a kitten belonging to her granddaughter and the finding of senseless young ladies. When a maid threw a bowl of peas at the scullion, Coletta lost her temper and ordered servants hither and yon. The implacable voice of authority calmed the staff, though Cook threw her apron over her head, undone.

"Magic," she moaned. "By Nimue, I've heard stories about it. Poor girl must have been taken by magic."

Dinner was served on trays in the drawing room, prepared by the kitchen maids while Cook sat in a rocker and moaned. Not much was eaten of the simple fare; much was drunk.

All the searchers reported nothing. A scan of the gardens from upper windows showed no sign of Martha. No footsteps were found in the mud around the pottery. No one had seen any ladies out on a rainy day. As the evening dragged, people began drifting to their rooms, shrugging into nightwear and collapsing into bed.

Cook, Amelia, Vera, and Agnes were put to bed with laudanum. Lady Coletta tucked each of them in, offering soothing words of hope, then went in search of her couch, worn out by her unvoiced fears for Martha.

"Richard said I didn't want to be a wizard," Coletta muttered as she turned her bedcovers down. "He was right, except..." Her weary body slid into bed. "If I had powers," she told the bedpost, "perhaps Martha would be safe in her own room."

The outdoor staff tumbled into their cots at a late hour, still brangling over the odds of Silver Streak eating the second die if given the chance. The rumor had penetrated the stables, but their collective masculine arrogance kept fear away. "There ain't no more magic," one hand insisted, glancing uneasily over his shoulder. The others were quick to agree.

The Banshee Brigade pulled nightcaps over their heads and lay in bed, most sleeping, one snoring, and one worrying and wondering. Jackson sent Dalton off to his room at midnight. The poor old butler's hands were shaking. The owner of the Manor of the Ashes remained in his study, swirling brandy in a snifter and puzzling over Martha's disappearance.

A groom, the unsung winner of the dicing game, had been sent galloping to Devon, where it was presumed Sir Hurst was to be found. Nothing more could be done till the new day began.

"Magic" was the general explanation for the girl's disappearance.

Chapter Eighteen

The next morning, the rain finally stopped. The sun rose and shone over the Manor and that particular corner of merry England. With a glistening new day, the servants began their routines. The disappearance of one of the Manor guests was upsetting of course, but life had to go on unless they wanted to receive final wages, a half-hearted letter of recommendation, and a boot out the door.

Cook, heavy-eyed and cross from the sleeping draught she had taken, busied herself at her worktable, avoiding the cursed stove and cuffing the scullion for carelessness. Maids and footmen carried hot wash water in graceful jugs, laid fires to chase away the damp of the morn, and cleaned chamber pots. The boot boy grumbled over all the mud on the gentlemen's boots and the grooms and gardeners gathered in the servant's hall for breakfast.

"Wot's to do t'day, Bill?" Chancy forked a pile of eggs and kippers into his mouth and chewed. Chancy was second assistant to the head gardener and was working his fingernails to the quick to become first assistant.

Bill wiped ale off his mouth with the back of his hand. "Gots to snip dead roses, m'lad. Jake and Matt'll do cleanin' up from the rain, you and me'll start back on the reg'lar chores. You git the snips from the shed. Me, I gots to find more string fer the arbor. Rain knocked some of the roses off the trellis."

Chancy grunted agreement and clomped out the door in his heavy work boots. As he passed Cook, the gardener snatched a crispy strip of bacon off the platter; she whipped his back with a towel. As he chortled and banged his way out the door into the kitchen garden, Mrs. Jackson was sleeping flat on her back, not having moved a muscle since swigging down a hefty dose of laudanum the night before.

Vera was curled on the chair by her window, worrying and yawning, trying to throw off the lethargy left by her dose of laudanum. Agnes Bridewell was tossing in her sleep, dreaming the nightmare of the chaperone. She had lost her charge at the ball and was searching for her. Bridey ran down dark garden paths and through conservatories, spying two shadowy figures repeatedly but was horrifyingly unable to reach them. Tangling bedclothes hampered her quest.

Michael was dressing in riding clothes. He planned to search for Martha. Robert Jackson was poring over a map of the estate, wondering what hiding place could have trapped one small dark-haired sprite and praying she was on the estate. The Banshee Brigade to a man and a woman slept the sleep of the just. Just not too bright.

Chancy stretched and took a deep breath of clean, rain washed air. Drops of water sparkled on the grass, bushes, and trees; it was a fine morning. He liked snipping dead flowers off the rose bushes. It was an easy chore, not hard on the back like digging, not tedious like planting. So he whistled as he unbarred the shed door, stepped over the threshold and into a hole. As he fell flat on his face, Martha woke up.

"Ooomph," Chancy said inelegantly as he ground his face into the foot stretched in his path. That is how Martha got blood on her slipper—the gardener's nose hit her foot hard.

Martha woke. She blinked up at the ceiling, trying to focus bleary eyes. Thin beams supported rough pieces of wood overhead. Where was she? Tattered cobwebs, accented by a shaft of sunlight, draped from a beam to the door frame. A few gardening tools hung drunkenly from nails in the unpainted plank walls. Oh, yes, the shed.

Sitting up, her head swam. Her stomach was queasy, her mouth dry, and her left foot throbbed from the shovel hitting it. Her right foot featured a new ache. The big toe felt like someone had smashed it. Then she heard a sob.

Avalon, how had she missed him? A man rolled back and forth on the dirt floor, clutching his nose. Blood spattered his face and the ground. "Are you well?" seemed inadequate, but it produced a response. He groaned between two more sobs. His noises made her flesh creep. Who knew what he intended? She had to get away from him.

Keeping both hands against the wall since she felt distinctly unsteady, Martha rose to her feet. Stepping over the man, who blocked the doorway, she began limping to the house.

Martha bounced off a tree trunk. One hand to her head, she stopped for a moment to get her bearings. She was dizzy; that was how she had veered off the path. It was over there, past the privet hedge. She stumbled back and weaved up the path to the nearest door (the same door she had exited thirty-one hours before). Once in the house she headed straight for Mr. Jackson's private study, sliding along the wall when her balance proved insufficient to hold her upright. Her sore toe hit a table leg.

Bouncing off a footman told her she had reached the library. Ignoring his distressed cry, she grated, "Is he there?" Her throat hurt; her voice quavered like an old woman's.

Not waiting for an answer, Martha lurched the length of the library until she reached the study. She burst through the door, hopped around the desk and fell into the safety of Mr. Jackson's arms. He caught her and gave a mighty hug before setting Martha at arm's length and looking her over with a keen eye.

"By Mordred, girl, where have you been? Are you well?" Jackson caught Martha again and began rocking her back and forth. The girl squeaked, protesting for her bruises, and he plopped her on the desk. "You are injured. Where, my dear? If that contemptible Irvine hurt you, he may dread facing me more than the Council Secretary."

"N-no, Mr. Jackson. Not Mr. Irvine, b-but the gardener, I think." Martha tried to clear her throat.

"The gardener; how dare he. Tell me which and I will string him from an oak."

Eventually, Martha was able to tell her story. When his hands stopped shaking, Jackson even listened. Then, recollecting she had eaten nothing, he slid her off the desk and into his chair. "Eat this," he ordered and yelled, "Holt." The footman, who obviously had been just outside the study door, came in immediately. "Send word upstairs that the missing lamb has returned to the fold."

Martha had attacked his breakfast of eggs and ham. Plucking a cobweb from her hair and wiping it on the rug, he poured a full mug of ale from a small pitcher and slid it by the plate. Lifting it with shaking hands, Martha drank half of it before picking up the fork again. Jackson pushed a plate of toast closer and hovered.

Once she had eaten, he laid a hand on her shoulder. "You were foolish to take on Irvine yourself, my dear," he said, "yet I applaud your bravery. To bring you up to date, Lord Brinston is after him—when and where they meet, I cannot tell, but meet they shall. Brinston will not allow him to slip away. We will have to wait to see what transpires. The marquess will keep me informed." He gave the slim shoulder under his hand a final squeeze and paused.

"Oh, by the way, I forgot until this moment. You should expect your brother sometime, Martha. I sent a groom with a message to him last night."

* * *

The marquess rode Morgan's Chariot at a steady gait through the rain. The London road was dark, deserted, and slick. Brinston had no proof that Irvine had taken this route, only well-honed intuition. After all, where else would the man take the report? Only at Camelot could an amateur spy find the connections to sell military secrets, only at that cosmopolitan castle could an idiot like Irvine hook up with the real enemies of England, the people who would commit mayhem to get their hands on the plans for a rocket brigade. While he rode, he mentally revised the Nimuian holding spell. It was simply done. Simple was usually most effective.

By Merlin, the man was inept. He stole the rocket troop report on a whim, never thinking that an expert would cull his name from the mismatched inhabitants of the manor in less than a second. Who else had the motive, opportunity, and stupidity to remove state secrets from a dispatch box left in his keeping?

As soon as the document went missing, Robert Jackson had known Irvine had to be the culprit. No one else at the Manor of the Ashes had any conceivable interest in the plans; Squire Michael was the only other person who knew the report existed. Considering Michael's pristine record—his ready access to secrets that remained safe, that the 'Ship' delivered the box from Camelot knowing its contents—only Irvine was suspect. Jackson had known that Irvine was the thief. He hadn't liked it, but he had known.

A gust of wind blew rain in Brinston's face. Plucking sodden leaves off his thighs, the marquess mulled the possible repercussions of the situation. Irvine was some sort of cousin to Sir Hertford. With the intimacy between Hertford's lady and the Prince, a closeness which showed no sign of slackening, Irvine's idiocy could create a tidal wave of political problems. The gossip that would go around—Prinny's Mistress' Cousin Caught—Lord, the newspapers would make hay of the scandal. The Prince might never recover from it.

Brinston kept Morgan's Chariot to a steady trot. No need to risk the horse's legs on the slick road. He would catch that chawbacon soon enough. Thoughts of his darling Martha, left languishing in a tool shed by Irvine, honed Brinston's knife of retribution. That he had been forced to do the same added a sharp point.

Magic shimmered in the air, stirred by the magician's anger.

Robert Jackson's assistant revealed the depth of his inanity at every step. Knowing the Owl was arriving soon, he should have cleared out. Knowing the consequences of his actions toward Brinston's pixie, Irvine should have fled to Argentina, China, or the Antipodes. Only in one of those places would he have been safe from reprisals. If the fool had known the ruthlessness of the sort he would have to deal with to sell the report, he would have never taken the bloody thing in the first place, rather than going off half-cocked, the loose fish.

If Jackson had elected to deal with Irvine himself, the assistant may have squeaked by with a lost career. He would have been out on his ear, sweeping street corners for pennies. Instead, his brazenness led Jackson to bring in a higher authority; the Owl.

A protective spell had kept Irvine from harming anyone. No one at the Manor had felt it or seen it; a complex series of magical commands had ensured that nobody would be hurt while the spell held sway. Brinston had fashioned it after one in an arcane book the Duke had purchased in Greece. Mixed Latin, Greek, and Hebrew made the spell wildly potent. He was proud of that spell. His composition had been inspired, his invocation masterful. The spell stymied the pygmy-brained Irvine.

Brinston smiled grimly, offering soft words of praise to Morgan's Chariot. That steed was worth his weight in consols. Surefooted and calm, the stallion passed over the sea of mud as if it were nothing. *Too bad Jackson will not sell him.* He set his mind back on his task.

With the Owl on the scene, current events were inevitable. Brinston shook his head, releasing an accumulation of rain from the brim of his hat onto his shoulders. The only thing Irvine had done right was hiding the document, moving the document, finding clever places to conceal it. With that darling little minx sniffing around, not to mention himself, Michael, Robert, Amelia and Coletta, Vera, Dalton and Barnes, Irvine must have suffered the trials of Pellam hiding the plans, the worm.

But now the nodcock had done himself in. He was stupid enough to pick a miserable night to take French leave, which annoyed the Owl. He was maggoty enough to do it with his own stallion, Beastslayer, killing any chance of eluding capture. That horse was entirely too memorable. Hell's teeth, the man was queer in the attic.

But Bryce Irvine had laid unfriendly hands on Brinston's little darling, on the Owl's fey sweetheart. He had frightened Martha and locked her in a shed. No way was the Owl, sixth magician of the realm, The Most Honorable Knight, The Marquess of Brinston and future Duke of Haverhorn, going to let the man get away with doing that.

The hell with the report, Irvine was going to die for daring to treat Martha with less than perfect respect. Brinston's hands tightened on the reins. *The spell should have caught him by now. Wonder how much further I'll have to go?*

Morgan's Chariot rounded a sharp corner in the road. Layers of mud, ever-widening puddles, and loose stone made the going tricky on this poorly maintained stretch; Brinston eased up on the reins, allowing the stallion to set his own pace. The rain intensified, dropping water from the skies like sand from a bucket. Trees failed to deflect the torrent from the travelers; man and horse were soaked. The Owl's consolation was that Irvine was equally wet, however far ahead he may be.

The stallion picked the way through a mucky spot. He slowed to a walk, which Brinston allowed. *A good horse,* Brinston mused, *is worth more than its weight in consols—it's worth a thriving estate. Would Jackson accept the Castle in exchange?*

No, Robert Jackson was not likely to give up Morgan's Chariot for anything less than Faust's trade.

Brinston shrugged. His soul was not his to barter—it was in the hands of a pixie and he would have it no other way. No matter the steed's ownership, bless Morgan's Chariot as a treasure; it was equal to or greater than his namesake's. They rounded another curve.

Ahhh, it was about time. Brinston smiled, not grimly, but ferociously. There, sitting in the middle of a puddle, bedraggled and shouting curses to the weeping sky, was his mangy fox, run into a hole and awaiting punishment.

Actually, it was an amusing sight and his lips quirked. Bryce Irvine crouched cross-legged in the water, covered with muck to the eyebrows, cursing and shaking a fist at the dejected stallion, Beastslayer, which swayed out of his reach. Irvine's face, where it was not streaked with black, was red with fury.

"You miserable beast!" Irvine shouted. "Afraid of a bit of mud, are you? I'll sell you to the knackery if you don't let me up on your back." A colorful string of oaths emphasized his intent. He tried to stand in the shifting muck, only to lose his balance half way up and sit back with a splat. Muddy water sprayed the horse, which shied. Irvine swore harder.

Brinston sat undetected atop valiant Morgan's Chariot, enjoying the show. Beastslayer danced away from Irvine's questing hand. Well-mannered the stallion may have been, it did not like mud. Nostrils flaring, head tossing, the horse shied away from every attempt of its master to capture the trailing reins with dripping hands.

The holding spell was indeed simple and effective. Irvine, unable to rise from the muddy puddle without assistance, cajoled his steed. "Whoa, Beastslayer. That's right, come over next to me and let me grasp... Damn your hide. Can't you hold still?" the mud-covered man howled.

"Now, Beastie," Irvine tempered the tone of his voice, "come stand next to me. That's right, let us try again. This slippery slope is nothing for you, stout heart that you are. Move a bit closer...let me grab the rein...come back here, you sorry excuse for a horse. I can't get up, can't you see? Every time I start, my feet come from under me. This damn puddle is a wretched concealed valley in the road. I can't crawl up, can't stand up. How else do you think to do the thing? Shall I fly out of here?"

Beastslayer was having none of man or mud. He sidled out of reach, then stood, glistening black nose hanging in the torrential downpour. Brinston had seen more than enough. He lifted his head and laughed, allowing the rain to wash over his face. The bellow brought Irvine twisting around, eyes rolling with fury, while Beastslayer shied once more at the geyser erupting from the puddle.

Irvine shouted, Irvine screamed, Irvine swore. Nothing helped. There he was, trapped in a hole in the middle of the road when he needed to be on his horse. The damnable marquess sat his own horse and laughed at him. How dare he laugh? There went his horse, tail streaming like a pennant, as Beastslayer hied off to London. Irvine had finally been too vociferous for the stallion's great heart.

"Blessings, Merlin," the Owl murmured thanks for a holding spell cleanly executed.

"Now, what shall we do about you?" Brinston growled to the thief. "You sad excuse for a traitor. Incompetent, didn't you know?" He brought Morgan's Chariot a few feet closer. "Can't do anything right, Irvine, can't even hold your temper. Your own fault Beastslayer has taken off. Tsk, tsk."

Irvine howled while Brinston hauled him out of the sloppy depression in the road. "Now, thanks to your witlessness, you have a long walk to Camelot," the Owl stated. "But first, a bit of business." The marquess's hard fist bit into the skin on Irvine's nose. The hapless man slid back into his puddle, splashing water and muck in every direction, including onto Brinston and Morgan's Chariot, who whickered.

"That was for Martha." Brinston hauled him out of

the puddle again. His fist at the ready, he growled, "Now, hand over the report, sapscull, else I shall send you to Mordred on your own account."

Blood dripped from his nose, rain pounded his bare head, and the idiot's hands shook, but he still had an iota of spirit left. "To Mordred with you, Brinston," he shouted, shaking his arm so vigorously he slid closer to his muddy valley, "and may he take that little witch of yours also."

The Owl shrugged and gleefully avenged his beloved Martha's name, although he ended almost as mucky as Irvine. A few well placed fists and the treasonous Bryce, eye swelling closed, bloody nose running with the rain down the coat front that covered his cracked rib, and head ringing from the pounding he took, admitted defeat.

"I only wanted Miss Silvester to notice me," the filthy villain yelled from his ignominious position on the ground. "I wanted to sell the report, damn and blast it. Then I'd have the money—the money I never had—the money to attract her." His voice died to a whisper. "The money to make her love me." Irvine's hand shook harder than ever as he took a mangled mass of paper from the pocket of his coat and shoved it in Brinston's direction.

"Here, take the bloody thing," he mumbled. "Wish I'd never heard of Robert Jackson." A stringy bit of silk, spotted dark but still showing blue in places, snaked out of Irvine's pocket.

As the precious document hit Brinston's hand in two parts, bits of the pulpy mass fell off the whole and plopped into Irvine's puddle. Other bits remained stuck to the filthy assistant's fingers. Those parts Brinston managed to catch squelched as his hand closed around them. Paper can only absorb so much water, after all.

* * *

"The plans are safe. They did not get into the hands

of England's enemies. My work is done. I have no intention of remaining," Lord Brinston stated coldly.

Here in this office, buried deep in the House of the Round Table, Lord Du Lac presided. Only privileged members of the Inner Circle met here. Decisions that could not wait on the convenience of the Round Table were debated and decided. The operators of the secret groups that worked to keep the country safe from espionage received their orders from this office.

On the wall was a map, ancient and tattered along the edges. This map had been drawn by Baudwin, governor of Britain when Arthur fought against the Romans on the continent. After surviving the Battle of Camlann, Baudwin had become a hermit and devoted his years to the quest of locating the treasures of the world. It was his wisdom that helped Percevel bring the holy Grail to Britain. The precious cup was in the Tower, where it's undiminished power threw a mantle of protection over England's heart.

With Percevel's glorious deed to inspire them, countless knights over the ages had sought the Ark of the Covenant. When Richard the Lionhearted led the Crusades to Jerusalem, he believed the Ark to be secreted in the cave that had shielded Jesus's slain body. But the Ark eluded Richard. It eluded Edward II, who decided the Ark was housed in a remote church in La Réole. He had failed to find the casket, but sparked the conflicts that became the Hundred Years War.

Baudwin's map showed the location he had decided held the Ark of the Covenant. Wellington himself won the map with his brilliant logistics on the jousting field of Waterloo. Cleverly pitting England's knights against the French Royal Guard, Wellington won joust after joust, until the tournament belonged to England. And he won the map from Napoleon.

Rather than broadcast the stunning win to the world, the map was kept hidden. Baudwin's conclusion had been faulty, but his map might still hold clues to the location of the Ark. At this moment, standing in profile to the historic map, the head of England's Privy Council and the sixth magician of the realm locked horns.

Brinston slapped a fist into his palm. "I have obligations to meet. Personally overseeing the disposal of Bryce Irvine is not something I am prepared to do."

"Tyler can't handle this, m'lad," Du Lac twirled a paper knife between his hands. "He has fallen apart already. A good man with routine, he cannot tolerate messiness. Since the matter is connected through both Robert Jackson and Irvine's uncle to the Council and the throne, this matter must be treated delicately else it could end up a royal mess. I leave tomorrow for Vienna; who else am I to rely on?"

Brinston's sigh startled an aide in the antechamber. "Can't one of the undersecretaries take over?" he pleaded. "Failing that, Sir Adrian Hughes is a good man."

"Hughes is promised elsewhere. No, Brin, if this matter is to be kept quiet, I cannot bring more people in. Already the Manor house party is aware of events—if word of Irvine's culpability gets around, it could be an embarrassment. That is not something we dare hazard. You will remain in town and deal with it, *if you please.*"

Those iron words were Brinston's downfall. No, he did not please, but when the Councilor said 'if you please' in *that* tone, the request was elevated to a command. So in London the marquess remained, negotiating with Sir Hertford and the Irvine family and depressing the rumors that began flying around town.

Kowtowing to Hertford left a metallic taste in the Owl's mouth, but the sense of precious time ticking away at the Manor of the Ashes was worse.

* * *

At that self same manor, two young ladies were

resting after their harrowing experiences. Though Martha was the one assaulted, Vera's emotional storms had been more draining. Miss Jackson had learned a valuable lesson; it is harder to be the one who sits and waits than to be the one to march to war. Martha hadn't learned anything new. She had prior awareness of how much she cared for a certain peer of the realm, drat the man for staying away.

"I am relieved you are safe," Vera said. "My eyes are still sore from the crying I did for you." They sat in the arbor, scattering petals of the last roses over the ground. "Half the staff was convinced magic had taken you."

"If only Lord Brinston allowed me to chase after Mr. Irvine," Martha complained. "Not that I wished to be in danger. When Mr. Irvine locked me in the shed, I thought my heart would stop beating. But both he and Lord Brinston relegated me to the role of helpless female, which I am not. I should dearly love to take a switch to that man." As she did not specify which man required a beating, Vera was not to know that Martha was unsure whom she wished to lay hands to—Bryce Irvine or Lord Brinston. Vera thought Irvine was the switchee.

"I don't think the Council will wait for you to get to Camelot with a switch, Martha." Vera was not laughing. "The government will most likely hang him for a traitor. After all, he did steal Papa's papers."

"How sad that is. I wonder why Mr. Irvine did such a vile deed?" Martha's question was destined to remain unanswered for a time. Looking up, she spied a man striding through the garden, making a beeline for the arbor. "Hurst, oh, Hurst!" she squealed and ran to meet him.

He was thin, not in an unpleasing way, with a hawkish nose and higher cheekbones than Martha could boast. His dark eyes, so dark as to appear black, could look as soft as a raisin or as hard as coal, depending upon his mood. This beloved brother, who had given a young orphaned sister his love and attention as unremittingly as a father, wrapped wiry arms around the girl and lifted her clear off the ground.

Vera watched the two heads meet in a long, affectionate embrace. Their hair mingled and it was impossible to know which tress went to which head, so similar was the black. Sir Hurst's hand touched Martha's face in a caress, flashing a heavy gold signet ring.

"Hurst, I am so glad you have come," Martha sighed as he released her.

"A little bird told me you were skating on thin ice. Have you been up to your tricks?"

"Not really." Her brother sounded so severe, but she knew the depth of his love and was not frightened at all.

"Miss Jackson," Sir Hurst greeted Vera. "You look as blooming as these roses."

Amid Vera's blushes (though she never felt the least *tendre* for her friend's brother, she was not immune to Sir Hurst's charm), Martha's joy, and Hurst's aplomb, the three spent a merry hour in the arbor. The last few weeks of the school term were rehashed and the house party at the Manor of the Ashes detailed. Martha and Vera steered the talk away from governmental papers, spying, and other such topics. Despite their tact, Hurst brought the conversation around to the event that had hastened him from Devon.

"Miss Jackson, I hope you will agree to my being private with my sister at this time." Obedient to the iron command behind the request, Vera flashed an apprehensive glance at her friend, then left brother and sister alone in the arbor.

Hurst cleared his throat. "So, Martha, my dear, I should like to hear what you have been doing, and most specifically, where you disappeared to that Mr. Jackson had to send a groom hot-foot to fetch me." He folded his arms across his chest and managed to look magisterial.

The dark-haired girl ran her tongue over lips gone dry. Censure was coming, she knew. Nevertheless, she answered her brother bravely. "It was not as serious as you imagine. I was never in danger, only locked in a shed." The story came tumbling out.

Martha had the gift of relating a tale concisely, so Sir Hurst Dunsmore, Knight of the Golden Fleece, quickly discerned what led to his sister being incarcerated in a tool shed for more than a day. Not that comprehension was followed by understanding.

Hurst blasted his sister for her foolishness in meddling in Mr. Jackson's affairs. "You have a better head on your shoulders than that," he said, concluding his fifteen minute lecture. "If I recall correctly, you told me you would rein in the propensity for pranks—you were afraid others would take a dim view of them. Can't you control your puka side?"

"The Jacksons like me. They laugh at my pranks. Hurst, for the first time in a very long time, I felt puka wasn't bad." Her head hung and he sighed.

"Puka isn't bad." Hurst echoed her disbelievingly and threw his hands in the air. "For Arthur's sake, girl, puka means nothing. It's an excuse for you to act like a gremlin. You don't get away with it—not with me. In consequence of your foolishness, you shall return to Uncle Pemberton's care. Aunt is feeling well at long last and when you are in her company, you behave."

"No, Hurst." Martha was aghast. "I cannot leave yet." Her hands grasped his as a rosy blush covered her cheeks. "Think how Mr. and Mrs. Jackson would react. They would be positive that you blamed them for my poor judgment. Never would you convince them otherwise. And Vera—Vera would be devastated if I left before the time agreed. Please, my dear brother, do not make me leave. Can you not remain with me? I promise most faithfully to behave as a perfect lady if I may remain."

"Cut line." The knight's voice was stern. "All your arguments have merit, yet there is something else. Tell me all or we leave as soon as possible."

Martha's cheeks were berry red and her eyes lowered

to the ground. "Lord Brinston ordered me to remain at the Manor of the Ashes until he returns from Camelot. I dare not leave until I have seen him."

"Lord Brinston ordered you..." Hurst stopped, his brow furrowing in thought. After a time, he said, "Then we shall stay a while, provided Mr. Jackson agrees. If Brinston wants to speak with you further, it would be discourteous to leave. But I will tolerate no more pranks from you, do you understand? No more hoydenish tricks or I'll take a strap to you."

"Thank you, Hurst. I promise I shall be all you would wish." Very quietly, so he wouldn't hear, she added, "Puka is too something."

* * *

The men were established in deep leather chairs in the library. The remainder of the household had retired; only these two kept from their beds. Candles guttered, but the fire burned brightly, throwing sufficient light for conversation.

"I don't suppose it will do harm to tell you." Robert Jackson stretched his arms forward to work a kink out of his shoulder. "Irvine was overset at Honoria Silvester snubbing his courtship. Got some thought in his mind that he would sell the report for a fortune and win that fickle lady's hand. Bah, and I thought my assistant had more in his brainbox than porridge. He's not so much villain as fool."

He leaned over and refilled his snifter from the decanter that sat on the table between the two. "When the Knights of the Round Table convene, Irvine will stand trial and likely be hung as a traitor. A pity—I don't think that's the truth of the tale, but the Council will see it that way. Though it's no more than he deserves, becoming enamored of that Banshee. Poor taste there. I'd have more sympathy for Irvine if he had fallen for your sister.

"Martha is a charming young lady, most charming.

Admire her initiative and bottom; not much she is not up to. Have the notion 'twas what caught Brinston's eye. Impeccable taste, unlike my former assistant. I agree, you see, there must have been something between your sister and the marquess The behavior you describe confirms my suspicions. And he sent that note to her from Camelot. You have no objection, surely."

"None. It would please me immensely to have Martha wed to my old friend," Hurst said. His snifter swirled and brandy coated the edges of the crystal. "But a polite note informing Martha of the disposition of her attacker isn't a declaration. I have been here a fortnight already and Brinston does not return. We cannot impose on your wife indefinitely, cordial as she has been. The remainder of your guests left days ago."

"No problem as far as I see, my lad. Stay as long as you like."

"That won't do. I have business in Devon and Martha should return to the Pemberton's care. What keeps the man from the Manor?"

"I imagine the Council has laid claim to him. At times in the past they have placed all their trust in the marquess—Tyler for one cannot handle a sensitive matter without Brinston to hold his hand. Du Lac thinks the world of him."

"I shall give it a few more days, with your permission. But if Brinston cannot tear himself away, my sister and I might as well leave."

Jackson laughed. "At any rate, you cannot go until your hat reappears. How my good lady could lose something she shouldn't have touched in the first place..."

Chapter Nineteen

Martha slapped the slippers onto the bed. "Vera, he is a worm, a cad, the worst sort of rake. He told me not to leave until he returned—you know how long it has been. It was a lie. All Brinston did was send an oh-so-polite note telling me that Mr. Irvine will be 'taken care of.' It took perhaps five minutes of effort and told me nothing. I had to find out the end of the mystery from your father. *My* mystery!"

"How can you say so? It was ordained, I am sure. After we heard his name from Lady Coletta, I knew it was meant to be. His name is Richard," Vera whispered. "Not a name to repel one. If he had been called Mortimer or...what was that other name?"

"Alphonse, though he would never have been given such a piddling name. Aunt Pemberton's chef is Alphonse. He is French and has whiskers sticking out of his nose."

"There you have it. And he earned his honors doing a quest. So much more honorable than merely inheriting a title. It was written in the stars that you meet and fall in love." Vera fell back on the bed with a romantic sigh. Bess folded the last glove into a trunk and retrieved the slippers from the bed, wagging her head.

"Then the stars were wrong. He was trifling with me. I never want to see his face again." Martha was adamant. She put her blue redingote over her arm. "Vera, I am so sorry to leave, but Hurst says he needs to tend some business and won't stay another day. We shall meet soon."

Tearful goodbyes were said in the bedchamber so that later, in the hall, both could keep countenance. It would not do to discompose their elders. Fathers and brothers were notoriously intolerant of feminine megrims.

The family was gathered to see Martha and Sir Hurst off. Despite her resolve and earlier tears, Martha felt a tightness in her throat as she said her farewells. Miss Bridewell urged Martha to write often, advising what fashions she would most like made up for the season. Bridey was going to have shopping trips planned to the instant.

Mr. Jackson bestowed upon her a hug no different than he would have given either of his own daughters with a harrumph that resounded through the hall. The imperturbable Dalton abandoned his impassivity long enough to wish the young lady a comfortable journey. His bow was deeper than Martha's consequence permitted.

"It will be but a few months, my dear," Mrs. Jackson enfolded Martha into a warm embrace, "then we shall meet up with you in town. Miss Bridewell is captivated at the thought of outfitting two winsome young ladies for the season. I shall busy myself garnering introductions and invitations. Oh, I wish you could stay," she finished, her hug tightening. "You are a delight to have around the manor. I do not know what we shall all do without you." Her questioning glance at Sir Hurst received a polite negative.

"I am sorry, Madame, but Mrs. Pemberton is anxious to have our girl back." Hurst was gentle but adamant.

"Then we shall await you in town," Amelia acquiesced.

"If she does not misplace the townhouse," Jackson gave the aside to Hurst. The carriage was ready, loaded with trunks. They climbed aboard and it pulled away from the manor. Martha poked her head out the window, waving. When a bend in the gravel took the house from her sight, she pulled her head back in, sighing.

* * *

Martha tucked herself on the tree limb. If she was quiet, no one should find her for some time and she needed to think. Months had passed. Now it was February and Aunt Pemberton was bustling around, arranging their departure for London. How she dreaded it.

Aunt Pemberton was ever intent on being the proper everything, including substitute mother. Her love for Martha could not be doubted. She treated her as the daughter the Pemberton's had not borne themselves. The Pemberton boys, both older and now at Oxford, needed little attention from their mother, so Aunt had ample time to devote to her orphaned niece. Since Martha's visit to the Manor of the Ashes ended, she had been making endless lists pertaining to a debutante's introduction and giving them to Martha to be studied.

Martha loved the Pembertons and appreciated the care she received in their household, but Aunt's rigid insistence on propriety chafed. Restrictions would be imposed on every aspect of her visit to Camelot, from clothing to behavior to activities. Martha's nature had always been restive; now she felt she might suffocate.

She wound her skirts around her ankles. Though the day was warmer, there was a damp chill in the air. Winter had not yet given up to spring. But the serenity of the oak she climbed was more important than warmth. Martha needed solitude to contemplate her options, limited as they were. She could either go to Camelot, be presented and see the Marquess of Brinston, or she could stay away from town. Camelot seemed more impossible every day.

Dear Uncle Pemberton immersed himself for long periods in his library, searching out obscure references to the knights of the ancient and weaving a comprehensive history of the Round Table. Kindly but vague, Uncle seemed to forget Martha's very existence now that he was trying to fit Owein's story into North Rheged's history. He left the running of the family and the household to Aunt Pemberton and rambled around mumbling about the sequence of events surrounding a magical fountain. His fond niece knew he would not provide a buffer against the vicissitudes of court. Aunt Pemberton would insist on full participation.

Fluffy clouds dotted the blue sky as she thought, *What am I to do?* The closer the date came for her departure, the less Martha desired to go. The thought of meeting gentlemen was insufferable. (One particular gentle knight could not be faced, she acknowledged to herself.) A new wardrobe did not entice. (If he did not want to speak to her, what good would a new gown do?) One could not enjoy a decent ride; walking one's horse in the park was mandatory. (Avalon forbid she see him in the park. She'd push him into the Serpentine.) Nothing about attending the season drew Martha's imagination or induced anticipation. The notion of an introduction was tainted by the probability of meeting him. He himself said one encountered the same people everywhere.

There was nothing else to be done, Martha concluded. The sooner she wrote, the quicker it would be done.

* * *

My dearest Hurst,

All goes well here. Aunt Pemberton is fully recovered from the Ailment she took last year. Her cheeks are filling out more than before and she is chock full of enthusiasm. She sends her love and a request for a few jars of the quince jelly your kitchen makes so ably.

Uncle wrings his hands about Owein. Something about the Forest of Broceliande and a lady named Laudine. He thinks it changes the time of the Battle of Argoed Llwyfain. Perhaps you could explain it to me, as Uncle's words sound a Banbury tale. He is incensed, saying Owein could not have saved a lion when he was about to be killed by a serpent because of the dates of the battle. I do not know who these people are, other than Owein. I am almost sure he was one of King Arthur's Knights.

My cousin Justin was sent down from Oxford for some reason connected to his finding of a five-legged dog. I do not know what he did with it, but the don was not pleased. He returns to university soon—I shall miss his company. He taught me to play Faro—a most amusing pastime, although I had to write my vowels to him. Please, could you send that billiard stick Justin liked for him, then my debt will be paid. I do not think I should continue with faro—I do much better with whist. My cousin honored me with a gallop on his stallion in payment of his obligation. It was exhilarating and no, I did not come a cropper.

The milliner had the prettiest silks so I am working up a new pair of slippers for you. Do not change your foot size, if you please. The design is exactly as you would like—I found a drawing of the Prince and copied his face. It is a challenge to my skill to produce a good likeness. You see I have not forgotten your desire to humble his highness at your feet after his horse beat yours at Derby. You shall do so, even if you do not dare to tell him of it.

Dear brother, I know you will be peeved, but I have come to the decision that I do not wish to go to Camelot this spring. I would lief you took me to see this new place of yours in Devon. Please do not be cross with me—this conclusion has been wrenching. I have not discussed this with Aunt yet, I await your reply.

Your devoted and loving sister
Martha Ann Dunsmore

* * *

"Why are you so interested in Whole Place? Thought you would have wanted to go to Havenhurst. You have not been to Peterborough in several years. Last long break you were begging to return home," Hurst grumbled. "I think you are being hen-hearted. Never would have thought it of you."

The trees were beginning to leaf out; the pale green intensified against the gray sky. She hated the hue; it recalled his eyes.

"Thought Aunt Pemberton would have an apoplexy. Poor Uncle Pemberton had to leave his study when she exploded. I wager that is the first time that has happened since Matthew was born. He looked bewildered at the commotion; I felt sorry for the man. If he is distracted and loses his reasoning about Esglad, it will take some doing to remove you from his black books."

Martha let her brother's disgruntlement wash over her and watched out the carriage window. The roads were poor but passable, the spring thaw having occurred a fortnight before. The damp earth beneath the carriage wheels looked as black as a knight's battle armor. Or his hair...

"...the season. You have been nattering on about your introduction for two years. Why should you change your mind? You planned your ball five ways and sent me countless letters with directions for decoration of the drawing room. Pink and gray silk, hah. Your little friend, Miss Jackson, is bound to be disappointed.

"Waltzing! You couldn't wait for Lady Jersey to approve you for the waltz. Ain't no dancing in Devon. Don't think I am going to get up a house party to amuse you either. Stubborn chit."

Martha fought back tears. Vera *would* be distressed at her friend's defection. But it was impossible to show one's face in town. *He* would be there. Why was she so disappointed? Brinston had done just as her brother would have; he had kept Martha out of danger. Why did she fear seeing him?

"...thought you outgrew these changeable moods. Merlin knows Aunt Pemberton would tame a griffin, not to mention a stupid chit like you. It's not as if you were in leading strings, should have developed a more demure manner by now. Aunt should have beaten you. Contrariness is not becoming, whatever people mumble about ladies...I shan't talk to you."

She was not going to think about him. Not about his broad shoulders, or that devilish grin, or his kisses... Stupid man.

"...approached Lady Jersey about vouchers. She was so excited at seeing you. Nattered on about how you resemble Mama and what a *succès fou* you will have. Had all sorts of plans for introducing you to court. Now she will blackball you from Almack's, not that you wouldn't deserve..."

Her eyes closed. Despite the tall figure dancing behind her lids, she was going to go to sleep. Devon and Whole Place would be that much closer if she slept.

Sir Hurst's indignation ran down. He looked at his sleeping sister, at the changes winter had wrought. Martha was pale, and he would swear she had lost a stone. The way she had been eating her meals explained the looseness of her gowns; Martha picked at the food on her plate, taking the choicest bits, and rejecting the remainder. Aunt Pemberton said she traced the border of the plate with the tine of her fork fifteen times one breakfast without tasting a morsel. The girl claimed a lack of hunger.

The downturn to her mouth when she thought no one was looking was distressing enough, but the false cheer she put on in public was worse. She smiled and laughed, chattered and charmed, all without an iota of animation. What could a mere brother do to right the devastation of his sister's heart? If she was determined to avoid town, he would not complain.

Damn Brinston.

Chapter Twenty

"I am tired of your Friday face, miss," Hurst yelled.

"Gammon, I have been more cheerful than you. Moping around in a fit of the spirits because you want to go to Camelot and flirt," his sister yelled back.

"I would never have thought my sister such a gudgeon. You should be in town yourself, finding a husband so I can get you out of my hair."

"Then I will return to Uncle Pemberton. At least he does not bellow like a peacock."

"Peahen. The Pembertons are at Camelot."

"Loose fish. I shall stay here and not speak to you." Irene Stratmoor rushed to the library, banging the door against the wall in her hurry; a bit of plaster fell to the floor. A distant cousin, widowed in the joust against Napoleon and left with a smallish jointure, she was invited to stay at Whole Place as chaperone for Martha. If she had known how volatile the relationship was between brother and sister, she would have declined.

Sir Hurst made the commission sound simple; provide companionship for his darling Martha until she made her introduction. He failed to mention the argle-bargles these two got into.

"Enough," Irene's soft voice was not above that of the brangling siblings, but Hurst's ears had sensitized to the sound.

He turned, shamefaced. "I am sorry, Cousin Irene." He *was* sorry. Hurst had promised himself to cease haranguing his sister and here he was, at it full tilt.

Martha flounced around to face the window. "I am not. Hurst is a beast. Cousin Irene, he called me the nastiest names."

"All deserved, if you are to be immoderate in speaking to your elders." Irene uttered the reproof as gently as before. "I wish you would at least try to get along better with your brother," she complained. "My heart cannot stand the clamor of your clashes. Most ungenteel. Whole Place is appealing, but the tranquil atmosphere is destroyed by your quarreling. A lady does never raise her voice to that level."

Hurst ran his fingers through his dark hair. Yes, he was wrong to argue, but somehow having this cousin with her ever soft voice chide Martha made him yearn to wring Irene's neck. The atmosphere at Whole Place was not serene. Mrs. Stratmoor was correct that he should deal better with his sister and she with him. But did not the lady see that her constant corrections of Martha's behavior put everyone on edge? How could he forget how the argument started—he had tried once more to make Martha agree to go to Camelot. She was an immoveable rock, the stubborn chit.

Martha stared stonily at her cousin. True, she should not have been speaking so loudly, but Hurst was as guilty as she. He started it with his demands that she do this, do that. Why was Hurst never the target of Irene's scolds? Her heart bumped and began aching. She had not meant to be combative, but Hurst had again broached the question of her introduction. Did he not see she could not go to Camelot? He was obstinate. Impossible. Almost as stupid as Brinston, the clod.

"I shall return to the linen closet now," Irene murmured. "The mingle-mangle there is beginning to sort out. The pillow cases were jumbled with the sheets." She shook her head and directed a reproachful look at Martha. "It is disgraceful, the condition of the household. If you would spend your time in housewifery, your disposition would take a turn for the better, I troth. I expect you to make amends to your brother, my dear. Then, to atone for your lapse, you may ply your needle until teatime."

The door closed so gently the click of the latch could not be heard. Martha glared at her brother, who paced around the room. When she did not speak, he did.

"Troth? What does she mean by that?" He slapped his thigh in irritation. "She makes less sense than the geese on the pond." A shriek reverberated through the hearty wood door of the library. "Must have seen a mouse," Hurst grumbled and deliberately sat on a chair.

"Aren't you going to go see?" Martha busied herself rearranging a vase of tulips that had looked just fine a moment ago.

"I'll go if you go." That settled that.

* * *

Much later, Hurst tracked his sister to the butler's pantry where she was hiding from Irene. She rubbed a cloth across a silver platter while she and Thompson discussed the health of the latest batch of kittens in the barn. "Their ma up and left 'em," the footman was saying. "They's so little, I guess they ain't all gonna make it. Pity, but so the good Lord o'dains. I do the best I can."

"Warmth is the greatest need next to feeding, is it not?" Martha concentrated on a tarnished teapot handle. "If you kept them in a warm place, that should help."

"Mrs. Stratmoor don' want 'em in the house, Missy," Thompson gloomily stated.

"Nonsense! We must do all we can to help the tiny things along. Besides, if Sir Hurst allows it, Mrs. Stratmoor's objections can be of no moment. Bring them in, Thompson." The old man left, a gleam of hope in his eye. Hurst entered right after him.

"What do I allow?" he asked, hoping, futilely he knew, that it would be nothing to upset the household.

"Good afternoon, Hurst." Martha kissed his cheek. He repeated his question. "Oh, Thompson is worried about a litter of kittens. I told him he could bring them into the house to keep them warm. Irene objects, but they are too small to stay in the barn at present."

Hurst nodded. "Then if Cousin Irene mentions the matter, I expect *you* to deal with it, my dear. I am going to London in the morn. Business, don't you know. Should be gone a week more or less. Try not to irritate Irene too much while I'm gone, hmmm? She might take it into her head to lay an egg."

"Isn't that like you, run out and leave me with the problem you created. We both know she will object to the kittens if she sees them. Her hysterics when she saw the ants... They came in after the crumbs *you* left in the solar. Remember, brother, you brought her here, not I. If anyone has to deal with goose eggs, it should be you."

"Are you saying I am a coward?" Hurst bowed, mocking himself. "Probably so; I don't like goose eggs." He squeezed Martha's hand. "Try to get along until I return, won't you?"

Her eyes flashed. "I will not promise anything where she is concerned, other than that I will attempt not to poison her." She turned back to the teapot with a careless shrug. "You should hurry back. The longer you are gone, the more likely I am to search out something noxious to slip into the tea."

* * *

Hurst sank into the overstuffed chair in the corner of White's back room and picked up the paper. News of Napoleon's return from exile covered the front page and he closed it again. Jousts he did not need. What, or rather whom, he did need, he had been unable to find. Well, tomorrow was another day. He closed his eyes, blocking out the myriad of gentlemen who would have approached; the weary knight did not desire a game, dinner, drinking companions, nor any invitations, whether they be to royal events or otherwise.

Across the room, two exalted members of the Privy Council played a quiet game of whist. Others read, drank and ate. Old Sir Symordon snored and a waiter nudged him on the shoulder. This, the back room of White's Club, was meant for those in search of quiet. Even Old Sy wasn't permitted to disturb the peace. Where else could lords of the realm be assured a quiet hour? Certainly not at home, where wives, daughters, aunts and mothers nagged. Sisters too.

Despite the discomfort of a too tight cravat, the low voices in the room lulled Hurst toward sleep. Drowsing, his head dropped back on the comfortable leather club chair. It was so good not to hear a soft voice insinuating Martha's sins, nor a sharp response from the sister who had too much to bear.

In that half state between wake and sleep, where cares smooth away and dreams replace them, he heard her again. *Never can make out the words,* his drowsy mind mulled, but someday he would. Then he would understand the quest. A nudge on his shoulder jolted the man awake. He blinked, expecting some waiter to be shushing his snores; demned if he hadn't nodded right off. The nudge came again and he looked up.

Ahhh, success. "Been lookin' for you," he drawled sleepily. "Plant yourself. Wanted to know, am I callin' you out or not?"

"If you wish; I am at your service. But don't believe it necessary." Brinston dropped into the chair across from his friend. "Where the devil have you been? I have been patiently waiting for you and Martha to appear in town."

"Devon," Hurst replied, relaxing the tight gut he had hardly been aware of. "Watching the birds fly around and the grass grow. Recommend it—lends an appreciation of one's blessings and the joys of town."

"Waiter, a bottle." Brinston raised his hand. "You are

dry, *mon ami*. Allerton told me you were seeking my company; that is the reason for my entering this benighted club. Did you know they have been permitting Crowley to dice here? Standards. Slipping. No excuse for it."

"Then don't sit at a table with the man." The waiter set a bottle of fine brandy on the table between the two, complete with sparkling clean snifters. Thus settled, Hurst prepared for an awkward interview by tugging at the too tight cravat and sighing. "I must ask your intentions, my lord. Else we may still meet at dawn."

Brinston stiffened and tugged at his cravat in turn. "Damnation, I have every intention. If she were here as you intended, I would be courting her properly. Satisfy the wags, don't you know. But no, you have to stay buried in the country where I have no access. What did you expect me to do?" He sighed. Heavily. "That's not all of it, Hurst. I'm doomed. Dead." Martha's brother froze, expecting to hear the worst...at the very least something dire.

"I was in Bond Street...saw a fan. It was perfect for her, so I bought it. Pretty thing, with lace on the edge and bees painted on it."

"So?" Hurst asked.

"A brooch at Rundell and Bridge. And a bracelet...no two bracelets. Earrings."

"Shouldn't do that. She's not married to you."

"Necklaces too. Bridge nearly cried, he was so happy. I can't go near the Arcade. Got parasols, handkerchiefs. A clock that chimes every fifteen minutes. It's driving me mad, that clock."

"She's not yours, Brin."

"Took Letta to the modiste. Madame Clothilde had a bolt of silk. It was just the color of her eyes..."

Hurst growled and Brinston defiantly said, "I had it made up." The marquess shot his friend an evil look. "Fifteen ball gowns. Cloaks, slippers, everything. A full wardrobe.

"Then I realized I hadn't armoires enough, so I went

to the furniture shops. Got four; they match. The bed and other pieces too." Brinston dropped his head in his hands. "A caricature from Mrs. Humphrey's. It's of Peter Silvester chasing some chit around Almack's. Thought Martha might get a laugh from it."

Hurst's voice was tight. "So you purchased a wardrobe for my sister?"

"Didn't have anywhere to put a set of furniture," Brinston mumbled. "Or the damned clock. Oh, I forgot the sofa and chairs."

"Don't tell me you bought a house."

"In Leicester Square. And Brighton."

"Two houses?" Hurst roared.

"Sussex also. That's a full estate. Spent a month there. Had to repaint." Hurst's jaw dropped. Brinston looked up, his eyes a bit wild.

"I'm dead, Hurst, dead and buried. I'm in parson's trap, leg shackled already and I don't have a wife. Where the crystal hell is Martha?"

"You bought all these things for my sister?"

Brinston nodded. "Especially the estate. She'll like the gardens. That's why I bought it...the gardens are pretty."

"So you do want her."

"It's beyond want, Hurst. If I don't have Martha, I don't know what I'll do. I...I missed the magician's meeting, you know." Hurst nodded. "Was at Waring & Gillow picking out china."

Hurst ran his fingers through his hair. "I thought..." So why haven't you contacted her?"

"I sent Martha a note."

"I saw it. A single sheet of paper. Took you what, five minutes, to write it?"

"Three hours. That note took the better part of an afternoon to write. I used up all the paper in the house, trying to get it right. Couldn't decide what I should say." Brinston gulped an entire snifter of brandy and glared while Hurst laughed and laughed. He finally dug out his handkerchief and threw it at his friend. Hurst used it to swipe at the tears that streamed from his eyes.

"So here is what happens next."

Two heads bent together. After two drinks, both cravats loosened. At one point, a head jerked back with an oath. "God's name, man, she will skin me alive." The other murmured. With the typical arrogance of the aristocratic male animal, they settled the thing.

* * *

Martha strode with a jerky step into the stable yard, the one place on the estate that Irene Stratmoor would not grace with her presence. Mice, ants and miscellaneous other vermin ran free. Worse, the denizens neglected to wash as often as the chaperone could wish. The one time Cousin Irene entered the stable yard, she had demanded that the horses be bathed —at the head groom's blank stare, Irene sniffed and quitted the field of battle, defeated. If only Martha had the same knack with her eyes as the groom.

She was going to kill her. No matter what Hurst said, no matter what the magistrate would say, Martha was going to kill her. She was going to trample Cousin Irene with the dogs from the kennel. She was going to push her down the front steps and into the fountain where the chaperone would drown.

How dare that woman! Treat her as a schoolroom chit. Speak to her so. Not once, *once,* since Hurst left for London, had Cousin Irene spoken a kind word. No, it was all do this, don't do that, a proper lady would never think of the other, all the while bemoaning the absence of her deified Sir Hurst. Today's outburst had been frightening. The woman was touched in her upper works. Face powder (with just a hint of rouge for color) had seeped into her brain.

She was going to leave every kitten and cat from the

whole county of Dorset in Irene's room and let the woman expire from an apoplexy. Martha wandered along the stalls, rubbing her sore cheek and concentrating on the horseflesh.

The groom would have her head if she upset the cattle; Martha moderated her step and willed her soul to calm. She would stay in the stables until Hurst returned—then she would give him what for. Leaving her with that harridan; wasn't it like a man to run away. It was all his fault. He brought the woman here and when she proved impossible, he disappeared. The least Hurst could have done was told the chaperone that Martha was released from the schoolroom and Irene was to cease *instructing* her.

Lock her in with the Banshee Brigade. They would send her over the edge.

The young lady in deceptive sunny saffron muslin stopped in front of the last stall. "Good morn, Beauty Mine," she crooned to the chestnut hanging his head over the rail. The stallion received a soothing pat on the velvet of his nose. Then Martha picked up the kitten that wandered around the horse's hoofs and snuggled it.

The insidious thought intruded; would her brother see him in town? They were friends, after all. A cloud of depression settled over her head. Martha shook herself hard. "None of that," she scolded. "You aren't going to think about that stupid man."

Perversely, she was unable to think of anything else. Or anyone else. Why had she been so determined to finish it, to help catch Mr. Irvine and retrieve the papers? Martha sighed and leaned her forehead against the stall door. It was perversity, sheer perversity. Lord Brinston had said she couldn't do it and Martha had thought, "I can too." Worse, she had acted on her thoughts and bedeviled him. She had been locked in the shed for her faults.

No wonder he didn't come back to the Manor of the Ashes. I disgusted him with my obstinate refusal to obey. Hurst is annoyed with me for the same reason. But, she wailed inwardly, *everyone has their faults. Are mine so unacceptable that he couldn't love me? I thought he cared.*

He should have cared. There wasn't any reason why he shouldn't. I am worthy of love; more worthy than Honoria Silvester. More worthy than Janice Jackson by a stone's throw. Lord Brinston is a poop if he doesn't recognize that I, Martha Ann Dunsmore, am the perfect wife for him. She stomped her foot. *Stupid man. Stupid.*

It was too late now to try to do anything about it. It was too painful to remember. Lord Brinston had gone on with his life and she had no choice but to do the same. Martha wielded her anger against Irene to stave off despair.

Stake her out in the sun, covered with honey, and let the ants at her. Which would be Irene's end, ants? Or the emergence of freckles on that sniffing nose?

It started in such a silly way. Thompson, the sweet old footman, was polishing the hall mirror. He was doing a tidy job; the glass sparkled and the frame was spotless. He crooned as he labored, a tuneless low song that reminded Martha of the chanting one heard in cathedrals. Age quavered his voice, but the kitten tucked in his vest seemed not to mind.

An orange tabby, striped with white along its chin. It was a tiny little thing, poking its head out of Thompson's coat, batting miniscule orange paws at the rag as it fluttered around the mirror. When it failed to catch the cloth, the kitten turned its face up and rasped a tiny tongue along Thompson's vest.

The love shown by the kitten made Martha smile, standing in the doorway of the breakfast room. This was one of Thompson's wards, its eyes new opened and in the best place it could be, nestled near the beating heart of its substitute mother.

Irene came down the stairs, clutching a paper, probably a list of Martha's duties for the day. The chaperone had devised that irritation the day after Hurst left for London—Irene wrote endless chores she deemed it imperative for Martha to perform and harangued the young lady at her failure to heed the lists.

Her inflexible mind, intent on lecturing her charge, could not appreciate that Martha had no intention of overseeing the maids' turnout of the third bedchamber, nor was she going to stitch new hangings for the dining room. Martha found no fault with the drapes; it was Irene who felt bilious about maroon velvet. They were nearly new, flattered the room, and in any event, Martha had no interest in sewing when the days were so bright, even if her brother had authorized the change, which he hadn't.

The chaperone just couldn't understand that with all the will in the world, neither she nor Martha had the authority to make changes at Whole Place. It was Sir Hurst's home, not theirs.

When Irene saw the footman, she nodded, pleased at the quality of his work. Then she spied the kitten and a screech emitted from her mouth. Thompson dropped the polishing cloth.

"Aaaarrrgh! Get it out, get it out!" Irene screamed again and again. Servant and young lady stared in amazement at the chaperone. "Now. Get rid of the vermin!" Irene was turning red. She darted forward and slapped at the kitten, missing it and striking Thompson in the chest. "Vermin."

Martha darted forward and grabbed her arm. "What are you doing, Cousin Irene?"

The chaperone's response was to twist out of Martha's grip and claw at Thompson's front. "Vermin," she hissed. "I won't have vermin in the house!" Thompson backed away as the kitten disappeared into the safety of his linen vest. His eyes rolled at Martha—no understanding of the chaperone's behavior glimmered in his lined face.

The young lady, not understanding much more than the footman the violence of the chaperone's attack, attempted to grasp Irene once more. Her reward for her effort was a stinging slap across the cheek.

As she reeled back, Irene yelled at the top of her voice, "Damn you, you spoiled little chit. How dare you lay a hand on me. I will not have vermin in the house, do you hear! Get it out *now!*" Irene's arms flailed in the air.

The butler, stately Hawley, ran into the hall from the back of the house. Taking in the scene in a glance, he insinuated himself between Irene and Martha, bravely placing himself in the line of fire.

"I ain't vermin," Thompson said in his quavery voice. "Vermin is foxes and rats. I ain't that." His bewilderment was ludicrous, though Martha couldn't find a well of laughter. Her cheek stung.

"Vermin! That nasty cat! Remove it or I shall destroy it!"

Martha aimed Thompson toward the kitchen and gave him a little push. "Go," she ordered. "Take the kitten to the barn or your room. Wherever, get it away from Mrs. Stratmoor before she loses her reason completely."

With the kitten gone, Irene calmed a bit. Her voice was still strident, however, as she railed. "I will not tolerate vermin. He must go." Swinging to Hawley, Irene continued. "I want him out of the house by this evening, the footman and his vermin."

Martha shook her head. "You cannot let Thompson go, Cousin Irene," she warned. "Hurst likes the man. Neither you nor I have such authority at Whole Place in any event."

"No! You cannot tell me what I cannot do! Pernicious chit, I shall lock you in your chamber and you shall have nothing but plain bread and water!" As the abuse flowed from Irene's mouth, most directed at Martha but including kittens, footmen, and vermin in general, Hawley herded Mrs. Stratmoor up the stairs, down the hall, and into her chamber, where he closed and locked the door.

Martha was stunned at the vituperation thrown at her. When the butler returned to the hall, she flicked her eyes at him. "That was worse than when the fox ran across the drive. I shall be in the stables if you need, Hawley." She slipped out the front door, not bothering to fetch a bonnet.

Cuddling a kitten in the stable, Martha made her decision. She was going to have to brave town. Ride in the park, dance at Almack's. And when she saw him, she would stomp on his toes. Even if she had to do it in front of Lady Jersey. That would teach the supercilious cad of a marquess to trifle with her. But first, she had a dragon to slay.

Dribble brandy in her tea and introduce her to Lady Jersey. That would kill the woman.

.

Chapter Twenty-one

Hurst returned to a house of strife. Irene was not speaking, she alternately secluded herself in her room and stomped around the garden kicking the flowers. Martha rejoiced in freedom from persecution. Hawley tiptoed, belatedly fretting that locking the chaperone in her room was beyond the pale. Thompson, the only member of the household unaffected by the contretemps, followed his usual routine, toting a bit of orange fluff that squeaked, growled, and purred in a most vermin-like manner.

It's nice to keep her about, Hurst thought as Martha flew into his arms in welcome. *Can't be selfish,* he reminded himself, giving his sister an exuberant hug. She was still suffering; that was clear to anyone who cared to look. Dull eyes, pasty smile, and a nasty bruise on her cheek. Oh, crystal hell.

He was covered with dust, his carriage was covered with dust, and his horses' coats could not be discerned. Summer had arrived, and in its wake dragged a hot sun, cloudless skies, and a lack of rain that turned the roads to...what else but dust? He ran his tongue along gritty teeth and Martha, the discerning creature, steered him into the drawing room and presented him with a glass of something wet. It was red, cool, and thick.

"Bah, what is this?" Hurst spit it back into the glass, where it globbed and burbled.

"Raspberry juice, an experiment with your chef. Do you like it?" Martha asked. She was not about to tell her brother that at her direction the chef had strained out one decanter's worth of the liquid and all who tasted it declared the results vile. Water and spices had been mixed in, but that improved the mixture but a tad. In revenge for the sullying of his culinary reputation, the chef had the decanter of juice placed in Martha's reach each day, vowing to continue until she drank the stuff.

It daily became thicker and more venomous. Soon it would turn and be discarded. Until then, the chef was adamant. He never dreamed Martha would palm it off on the head of the household.

She took the glass from her brother's hand and replaced it with one of lemonade, tart and chilled, the way she liked it. Hurst grimaced and drained the glass. Couldn't tell the chit that he detested lemonade—at least she had cups of sugar poured in to make it less sour. She looked more cheerful now. That was worth any amount of lemonade. But where had that bruise on her cheek come from?

"Let me bathe and change, my dear, and rejoin you. This dust has gotten into every last inch of skin. Ain't comfortable at all." That would give him time to discover the latest brouhaha from Hawley.

Later, briefed by his butler, who had the gift of relating a chilling tale, Sir Hurst took his new leather inexpressibles downstairs. He was in them, clean and girded for battle in case Hawley was wrong and Irene had come in from the garden. No, it was safe. He could see her through the window, decapitating a bed of daisies.

Slinking into the drawing room, ashamed to have gone to town and left his Martha exposed to abuse, Hurst asked his sister, "How did you keep during my absence?" She didn't even squirm, the minx, while she spun him a tale of vermin.

"Cousin Irene keeps to her room and the kitten is coming along nicely, after a shaky beginning. Thompson was afraid he would lose her as he did the rest of the litter. I can't say the garden is flourishing. It seems not to be producing blooms," Martha concluded cheerfully.

"The household's a bit shaken itself," Hurst

commented. "I did assure Hawley that his position is still secure. Might even up his wage if he has to keep taking on further duties."

Martha looked a question and Hurst said succinctly, "Knight errantry." She had the grace to blush, so he let her off the hook. "Might as well unpin it completely. What do you say to a house party," his hand went to her cheek, "as soon as that bruise fades."

Martha's eyes sparked with pleasure. "Oh, yes," she chortled. "I love Whole Place, but it has been too quiet with only Cousin Irene to talk to."

"Good. I would like to invite the Earl and Countess of Shelton; Katherine grew up here and Alexander has not had the opportunity to see Whole Place restored. Pipsqueak will enjoy showing him the place. Would like to have Perth and his lady also. Shall we invite the Jacksons? You have not seen your friend and I always enjoy Mr. and Mrs. Jackson's company."

Sweet little kittens, bruises, and unpleasantness were forgot as Martha busied herself planning the perfect house party. Then the thought intruded. *Had Hurst seen him?*

* * *

Lady Shelton was so much fun. Hurst called her "Pipsqueak" and ordered her to see to the household—the tiny featherlight woman stood tall (almost to the height of Hurst's cravat pin) and snapped back, "If I am to do that, I wish a raise in my wage." Hurst roared with laughter and Katherine's husband, the intriguing Earl of Shelton, raised a brow and inquired if indenture papers were required.

"After all, if I am to hand my wife over to you, Hurst," he drawled, "I should make some profit off the transaction. Enough to afford more nannies for the tot this minx has foisted on me."

It was a cheery dinner, with Lady Shelton waving a

fork at the room and informing her earl what had been done to make over the space. "It was dilapidated, in so sorry a state we despaired of making anything of it," she announced. "It wasn't until Hurst brought in the ceiling painters that one could see any promise in this room. The delicate tones they used on the arches gave me the palette for the walls. It is curious that I lived here for so long and never noticed the fineness of the carvings. Hurst saw them at a glance."

Shelton's brow lowered in a frown. His countess, undaunted by that glowering face, beamed. Leaning closer, she said, "I am so glad Hurst has my old home. He loves it as I do. I truly enjoyed bringing the house back to what it should be, you know." Shelton's face softened as he looked into her bright eyes.

It was then that Martha recalled the little her brother had told her of his assumption of Whole Place's ownership. Lady Shelton lived much of her childhood in the house; her uncle and guardian lost the place at the gaming table to Martha's brother. However it had occurred, Lady Shelton had restored the interior of Whole Place for Hurst.

"You did a marvelous job making the rooms flow," Martha complimented Lady Shelton. "I particularly like the pale jasper of the hall."

"Thank you, my dear," Katherine replied. "Though I do not deserve the praise. The shade is as I recall it when I first lived here. Upstairs is where my imagination created chaos."

Martha gazed around the richly appointed dining room. The party was exuberant, attacking the food as soon as it hit their plates. Those plates reflected the richness of the drapery with a wide maroon border edged in gold. Hurst and the Sheltons were talking at high speed. Everyone looked to be having a lovely dinner; everyone except Irene.

She fumed at the high spirits of the party. At that instant, she spoke her first words since sitting to the table. "The draperies should be replaced," Irene said. "Maroon is not a proper shade for the dining hall, nor is the style suitable. They should be more ornate, with tassels and fringe."

The conversation stopped dead for a moment. Hurst had lifted a bit of bread to his mouth; butter dripped.

"Harding took over his uncle's stud," Lord Shelton said into the echoing silence. "Do you recall his theory of naming horses, Hurst? Well, he's stuck to it. Raced My Son John against Alvanley's gray."

Cousin Irene did not say another word. Hawley removed her maroon-bordered plate with the chef's spiced mushroom ragout untouched. No one paid attention to the thunderstorm at the table.

If only Martha could find a man who would dote on her as the earl did Lady Shelton. She pushed away the memory of stormy gray eyes and concentrated on the lighthearted banter around the table. The aroma of fresh steamed sole wafted as fish, cooked to perfection, flaked onto the fork, jolting her memory back to a long-eaten dinner at the Manor of the Ashes. Her memory stirring, Martha faded out of the conversation. He had looked so striking, debating fishing lures with Mr. Jackson and ignoring the ladies' curve of the table.

"Perth arrives tomorrow, Pipsqueak," Hurst informed Lady Katherine, whose own fork had stilled while she watched Martha's distraction with a line of concern between her eyes. "But you have only to tolerate him. His lady is unable to come—seems she is in an interesting condition and Perth is wrapping her in clouds of solicitude."

"How does Clarissa feel?" Katherine asked. "I hope she is not suffering. Presenting her cavalier with a token of her affection is bound to be wearying."

"Hah. She glistened like an amethyst. Perth seems to have polished her hard edges," Shelton put his bit into the conversation, "so much so that Clarissa no longer heeds the clock. Rumpole ran into her on Bond Street. She was positively cordial —and dressed in morning attire at five in the afternoon."

"Perth has made inroads on her demeanor, then." A spate of laughter woke Martha from her dreams. She focused on Lord Shelton.

"They were two hours late to dinner at Devonshire House. I heard the duchess did not wait a minute, but sat to table precisely on time. Clarissa and Perth showed up as the sweet was being passed and were pleased as punch. 'The sweet is the best part of the meal,' she averred. The duchess seemed accustomed to her—never blinked an eye."

Through Lady Shelton's giggles she choked out, "Perth still maintains his aversion to timepieces?"

Hurst sipped his wine. "Worse than ever. None of the clocks in their townhouse are wound, visitors to tea are amazed to find that supper is served because Perth is hungry, and her *modiste* insists on visiting the house rather than having Clarissa come to the shop for fittings. *On dit* is that Madame Claudette was interrupted from a fitting with the Princess Amelia by Clarissa, who wandered into the shop at the wrong time on the wrong day for *her* scheduled fitting. The princess had an attack of nerves and Clarissa floated through the whole, oblivious to her error, only informing Princess Amelia that her dress was of an unfortunate cut and most unbecoming. At that, the princess exchanged her nerves for a full case of the vapors. She crumpled into a chair – you know the way she has—and the legs gave out. She ended up on the floor, wailing."

While everyone laughed, Lord Shelton turned to Martha. "You will see, my dear," he concluded with a benevolent nod. "Sir Perth Sullivan; although the most delightful of companions, is decidedly mad."

* * *

Shelton was right. Sir Perth was decidedly mad and the insanity was contagious.

Hurst kept everyone on the alert. Martha and the Sheltons had to remain in the drawing room, ready to greet the newest guest. Lady Katherine, keeping an eye out the window, at long last leapt for the door. "He's here," she called as she ran outside.

Martha arrived at the portico as the curricle drew up with a flourish. She couldn't get a good impression of the man until he ran up the steps of Whole Place, shouting at the top of his lungs, "Kate!" Lady Shelton, smiling broadly, opened her arms to welcome him. Instead of greeting the countess properly, Perth grabbed her around the waist, swung her into the air, and twirled in a mad waltz. Then he plopped her on her feet, turned to Lord Shelton, and wagged a long finger in that man's face.

"You done it again, fox. I felt her waist. Now she won't be in town for the little season." Lord Shelton beamed. Perth punched him in the shoulder. "Selfish. That's what I call it. Thought when you regularized things with this angel you meant to share."

"He will share," Katherine said. "As soon as the child becomes unmanageable, he will be packed off to you."

A babble followed Hawley's progression to the drawing room, where the poor butler tried to do the house proud and hand around refreshments in the proper manner. The silver tray of gleaming glasses and a choice of three wines was ignored in favor of shouts of laughter, rapid fire talk, and other accoutrements of a boisterous rout.

Martha watched wide-eyed as her brother and his friends broke nearly every rule of proper drawing room behavior Aunt Pemberton had drummed into her head. Lady Katherine indiscriminately kissed all three men. Her demonstrativeness was followed by raised voices, interrupted speeches, and milling forms. Hurst complained, "You didn't tell me."

Perth shot back with "You could have guessed, couldn't you?" and Lord Shelton grinned ear to ear and tried to explain something no one paid heed to.

"Miss Kate!" Thompson appeared in the doorway, tears in his eyes, and was enfolded in Lady Shelton's arms for a long moment. "I brung him to meet you," He showed her the orange tabby kitten, grown more robust and active from its time spent in the footman's care.

"Oh, mercy," Katherine laughed as the kitten escaped, using her skirt as a tree trunk. It ran about the room, finally climbing Hurst to perch on his shoulder. It was pandemonium, even with only a few persons participating.

Irene Stratmoor, lips in a thin, tight line, tapped her toe under the tea table. The group unwound and began settling, though they still did not do it right. Hurst sat on a table, kitten cradled in his hand, purring and kneading his thumb. "Calm yourself, children," he scolded.

"Yes, Papa." Katherine folded into a chair and Lord Shelton propped his broad shoulders against his wife's leg as he arranged himself on the floor in front of her.

Sir Perth stalked to face the young lady he did not know. "Who's this?" he called over his shoulder. "Can't be a Dunsmore, much too pretty for that family." He stopped a few feet from Martha. Her eyes widened when, with a wink, his back turned on her and gangly arms set akimbo on his hips.

"Hurst, you dog, where do you find them; the incomparables, the loveliest visions in the isle? The ladies who break my heart because I am shackled and out of the running."

Martha's opinion was decided when the knight did the kindest thing. Swinging back to take her hand, he laid a kiss on her knuckles and whispered, "Greetings, my bewitching Miss Dunsmore. You know who I am and I know you. It has been too long before this meeting, little friend."

Speechless. She was speechless. This madcap man, who swirled in, creating the greatest ruckus and turning even Hurst into a madcap, had in a twinkling changed into the most mannerly gentleman she had ever beheld. She smiled. Indeed, Sir Perth was mad, most deliciously mad.

He nestled her hand into his arm and escorted Martha to the prime seat in the room, the wing chair to the left of the fireplace. For the remainder of the afternoon, Sir Perth lavished Martha with the most unexceptional conversation and attention, showing not a hint of unsteadiness. She loved him. Who could not?

* * *

"The Jackson family arrives today," Hurst announced at the breakfast table, "so our little party will be complete. Let the revels begin."

Perth, wandering in late, sauntered to a chair next to Lady Shelton with an overflowing plate. Eggs piled atop a slab of sirloin, kippers swam in marmalade. "I met Miss Vera Jackson at Lady Crowe's musicale. Seemed to have Scoville on a string," he said, smiling at Lady Shelton. "You may have another wedding to attend soon, m'girl."

"I say, tie him up tight, that's the way." Hurst put his oar in.

Martha objected. "Vera would not entrap anyone. She is the most amiable creature and would attract admiration wherever she goes."

"She certainly attracted Scoville. He mooned around the edge of the room. Only perked up when Miss Jackson played the pianoforte. Made me lose m' concentration. Clapped smack in the middle of this long run. Clarissa boxed m' ears right in front of Crowe." Sir Perth cut into his meat. "I say, this is perfect. Can I steal your cook?"

"I would rejoice if your friend married my cousin." Lady Katherine smiled at Martha. "When I met Baron Scoville, I was impressed. I admire a calm man, even if he has the misfortune to be related by marriage to Shelton. It must be arduous for him to have to acknowledge such a connection." As the earl pretended to bristle, Katherine twinkled at Martha. "Miss Jackson would be fortunate to attach him. The baron's manners are much better than any the gentlemen present can boast and he is attractive. I do wish I had met him earlier. It feels rewarding to have upright relations."

"He is the best of either of our families, my love." Lord Shelton poked his wife with the handle of his knife, exhibiting the manners Lady Shelton deplored.

"Alex—what would your mother say?!" This comment almost had Sir Perth falling from his chair, his hilarity was so intense. Martha wondered what Lord Shelton's mama was like. Considering the affability of the son, she must be a darling. What made them laugh so?

The knight dabbed marmalade off his chin. "Reminds me of Rovleston and his daughter. She wanted to go to Brighton. The Baroness wanted to go to Bath. Rovleston sent the chit to Bath and his wife to Brighton. Stayed at the club a few months. Drank a lot of port."

When peace was restored, Hurst warned his friend, "The vicar wants to hold a special service tomorrow. I would appreciate your attendance. Remember, the dowager will not be there." He turned to the company at large. "We all should attend—as the holder of Whole Place, I have some standing in the neighborhood; wouldn't want to blot my name with Mr. Willmore."

More marmalade came off Perth's cheek. "Bah to churches. Always make me feel like m'mother is goin' to box m' ears. Too bad Clarissa has taken the habit."

No one seemed surprised or curious. "What is the service for?" Martha asked. "I have heard nothing. There are visitors in the area—the inn in the village is full, Thompson said."

"The service is by way of a dedication," Hurst replied. "It's likely Vicar Willmore imported all these visitors to fill the coffers for his latest pet charity. Tell you what, Martha.

Day after the morrow we will make a progression through Shapwick and see who all these strangers are. Show off Alex's manners to the children."

Approval rippled around the table, then ideas for amusing the party on this bright day were broached. Whole Place's visitors were pleased with whatever was proposed; they made organizing the house party simple for an inexperienced young lady. Martha appreciated their collective ease. She smiled more than she had in months. It was almost a relief, having to concentrate on guests, forced to smile and be gay. If only—

Projecting a picnic on the lawn of Whole Place that was wholeheartedly approved, her heart soared. With regal trees shading the house, the open area was inviting and she could handle a picnic with her eyes closed. The chef would be amenable, especially since she had apologized for the raspberry punch, and croquet could be set up for a game or two.

"Watch your balls," Shelton threatened. "The croquet I play is not for the fainthearted." Eyebrows wraggled to match his evil grin.

"We will be home when the Jacksons arrive," Martha mentioned. Her heart did a little skip. It would be grand to see Vera again and find out in person how her Camelot season had gone. Letters did not suffice to give Martha the details she longed to hear.

Had Vera met him? She took a few moments to compose herself. If only her feelings would calm down. It had been months since she had last seen the man; there was no call to continue thinking about him.

* * *

Shelton's Croquet technique consisted of slamming Hurst's and Perth's balls into the distance and nudging Katherine's and Martha's closer to the wickets. Martha aimed and with a crack, Lord Shelton's ball rolled into a flower bed.

"Can I whack the flowers?" he asked as they sought sight of the ball. It was buried in shiny pinks and trefoil. Columbine stalks were snapped, fading blooms hung upside down. The ball hadn't done the damage; Mrs. Stratmoor's rampages through the garden had been extensive.

At Martha's reproachful look, Lord Shelton sighed and tiptoeing amongst the plants so as to crush as few as possible, gently nudged the ball with his mallet. It went to the edge of the bed, almost but not quite escaping the flowers.

"I win!" Katherine crowed, jumping up and down.

"I place second." Martha echoed her jubilation. Croquet humbled the men; Hurst grumbled about treachery and lost friendships. After placing ahead of would-be Corinthians in the croquet game, the ladies sat on blankets in the shade and basked in the attention. The food was sumptuous and the air balmy. Lady Shelton was kind—not once did she condescend towards a young woman who had not been presented at court.

Cousin Irene had caused a straight chair to be brought from the house. Her megrims did not dampen the company; Martha ignored her, scattered polite sentences were thrown her way.

"Tell me more of Harding's stud," Hurst demanded.

Shelton laid his head in Katherine's lap. "I presume you want the names."

"What else?"

"Let's see. They've all been renamed. There's Crooked Stile, Unicorn, The Baker's Son, and Peter. Mother Hubbard has been entered at Epsom. Prinny has gotten into the spirit. He swears to beat Harding with his entry, renamed Old Cupboard for the event."

"The Four-in-Hand Club is up in arms."

Katherine leaned over and whispered, "Sir Harding had complained vociferously at his uncle's expenditures to no avail. The former Sir Harding nearly beggared the estate providing for the stables. Shelton says that while he would just as soon sell the stud, now that he has stepped into the knight's shoes, he has decided to keep the winners and recoup some of the lost funds through racing. But Sir Harding is doing it with his usual flair."

"Nursery rhymes," Martha whispered back.

"Precisely."

Thompson, having borne away the dishes from the delicious meal of cold chicken and all the accoutrements expected at a picnic, returned with his aged arms full of fluff. The footman's thin legs wobbled as he navigated to the edge of the blanket the ladies sat on. "They's but five weeks, Miss Kate," he quavered, laying a small kitten on her lap.

As he distributed babies among the group, he continued. "The ma's not goin' ta make it, she bled too much bringin' 'em out. But she's held on to give 'em the start they need. Jest in time fer me little orange baby to be set right." He winked at Martha, who grinned back.

"The orange tabby, Thompson's last, has returned to the barn, where it made friends with Hurst's stallion. The grooms are not pleased. The horse, a huge chestnut, has taken to kicking walls whenever his little Tabby wanders away," she confided.

The chaperone, sitting on her chair at the rear of the group, made a strangled noise and jumped to her feet. Only Hurst noticed her movement; his bland stare made Irene close her mouth.

Martha cuddled a white button-eyed kitten in her lap. The baby mewed, nudging her with a tiny wet nose and rubbing its head along her hand. She ran a finger over the tuft between its eyes and watched Cousin Irene stalk to the house—thank goodness she had not gone into a rage as she had before when a kitten was introduced to her presence. What held her tongue?

Lady Shelton held a ball of gray and white fur so fuzzy it looked like a barrel with pipe stem legs. "Oh Thompson, bless you. I have missed your kittens more than anything. Hurst—thank you for allowing Thompson to take in fondlings. It's a project we undertook together when I was young."

Her baby crawled up the lacy bodice of Katherine's gown only to fall into the depression it found at the top edge of the material. It righted itself with a tiny bleat and continued its climb, needle claws trying to find purchase on the countess's skin. She squealed and used her palm as a platform for the kitten, who accomplished the climb with a minimum of effort. Under Katherine's chin, it curled up on her palm and licked a dainty paw.

The gentlemen, who also held kittens, played. When babies began to yawn, they piled them in Martha's lap, where they staggered over each other and curled up for a nap.

Imitating kittens, Lord Shelton closed his eyes, his head still pillowed on his wife's lap. Perth wandered toward the gardens. "All creatures find you comfortable," Hurst whispered to his sister. "Why cannot Irene find peace?"

She rose to his bait, quieting when the kittens were disturbed. Before Martha could defend herself more moderately from her brother's teasing, the sound of coach wheels and horses signaled the arrival of more guests.

"Vera!" The name tumbled out of her mouth. "She has arrived! Oh Hurst, get me up so I may go to her." She ran to the drive. Hurst following, juggling kittens.

Chapter Twenty-two

Martha was so eager to speak with her friend that she dragged her to a bedroom before the girl had a chance to take a breath.

"Tell me all," she begged. "I want to hear everything about your season, Vera."

"You should have been there," Vera remonstrated, shaking out the skirt of a modish twill traveling outfit. "I wanted you with me so many times. I vow you would have enjoyed it tremendously. I did."

"I want to hear details."

"Baron Harris." Vera sighed. "The fuss of the season was worth it to meet him. Camelot is not all fun, you know, once the newness wears off. I don't understand Janice's fascination with society."

Martha tweaked her hair and she grinned. "He is tall, with curly blonde hair that he brushes into a windswept. His eyes are blue, and he has the curliest, longest eyelashes. Why wasn't I born with those lashes?"

When Martha threatened her hair again, Vera continued. "I met him at Gunter's when he spilled his ice on my skirt. Oh, Martha, I think I am in love." Her hands clasped, Vera treated Martha to a detailed description of the Baron Harris's person, detailed descriptions of their every dance together, and detailed descriptions of the Baron's mama, who was the fly in the ointment.

"She wants him to snatch up a heiress," Vera gloomed, "or one of the incomparables. But he is resisting her blandishments." She perked up. "Like in one of the novels we read—he is staunch in the face of adversity."

"But what of your aversion to love?" Martha asked.

"You said often enough that you preferred a comfortable arrangement, not a grand passion."

"I changed my mind. As long as I do not suffer kidnapping, love is satisfactory."

"But you still read romances?"

"Always. You shall see when you come to London. The bookstores are a marvel. Especially Hatchard's. They have every novel ever printed, Martha."

"Tell me more."

"I saw the grail at the Tower. Ate ices at Gunter's. Danced at Almack's. We even went to Merlin's Gardens by boat," Vera said. "Baron Harris was most attentive to me. Miss Sandringham nearly became ill from the movement of the water, but she recovered amazingly after we arrived—she insisted on dancing in the pavilion. Can you imagine, waltzing in the moonlight. It was perfect. Lord Brinston obtained one of the premier boxes for our supper—he was the most gracious host."

"You saw the marquess?" Martha queried faintly, wondering that she didn't sink through the floor at the mention of *his* name. "You never mentioned him in letters."

"It was only the one time. He didn't appear at any balls or routs that I recall. Lord Brinston invited us to Merlin for Papa's sake, I believe."

"Did he escort Miss Sandringham?"

Vera's eyes rolled. "No, she was attended by Mr. Longley. Lord Brinston was with one of those incomparables Baron Harris' mama wants him to attract. Lady Mary Swift. Her father is high up in the Council; Papa knows them well." She leaned forward and lowered her voice.

"Martha, that lady is determined to catch Brinston. You should have seen her hanging all over him, laughing at every comment with an annoying little titter. She hadn't a moment to be civil to the ladies, she was so busy with the marquess. I would never act so."

"Did Brinston like her? It seems to me if he did not

wish her attention, he would know how to stop her."

"I couldn't tell. It's well you no longer care for him—Brinston was fawned upon by all the ladies. Anyway, Merlin's Gardens was so much fun. We ate ham sliced as thin as paper and drank a punch that made me feel warm and silly—the fireworks were amazing. They set them off at the end of the evening. I have never seen such a sight. Sparkling color bursts in the sky. You should have been there."

No, I should not have been there, Martha thought. *Everyone fawns on him. All I want to do is hit him over the head.* She sighed.

Later, after tales of balls and the Opera, not to mention the shopping in Bond Street that Vera's avaricious soul enjoyed, Martha thought to ask of Janice Jackson and the Banshee Brigade. "Did you see any of them in town?"

Vera laughed. "Do you know what Papa did? He gave the chatelaine at the manor a quarter's holiday to spend with her family and installed Janice in her place. I heard the row all the way up the stairs from the library when she was informed of her disgrace and punishment. Papa was disgusted with my sister's behavior during the house party and determined to discipline her. He gave Janice a choice—go to Cornwall to my great-aunt's or stay at the manor and practice her housekeeping skills."

"She must have been ecstatic."

"Oh, my yes. She was screaming at Papa, which of course made him more dictatorial. That is when he decided to make Janice act as chatelaine, not just manage the house. So she is there now, and Papa says that if she does not perform her duties adequately, he will banish her to Cornwall for an entire year. Dalton is to keep an eye on her. You cannot know how relieved I was that she was not at Camelot for my introduction. I dreaded her condescending to me before all her acquaintance."

At a knock upon the door, Martha jumped. The maid who came in carried a large parcel. "It's from his lordship, my lady," the maid informed her. "He asks that you wear it to church tomorrow."

Martha was perplexed by her friend's excited, "Oh, the secret is out!" until Vera explained.

"Mama had it made for you at Sir Hurst's request. It is from the best *modiste* in London. Do open it, so we can see." As Martha began tearing the paper away, Vera said, "I have not seen it, but Mama told me your brother has exquisite taste."

Martha pulled a gown from the box. No, not only a gown, but positively the most tantalizing thing ever. It was winter white, woven through with pink, silver and gold bits of thread that made it shimmer as the silk slid and caught the light. Cut on simple lines, the dress had no trim other than a pattern of black pearls beading the bodice and sleeves. She could have been knocked over with a feather. Hurst had this made for her?

"Martha," Vera said reverently, "I have never seen a gown to equal it, not on any of the incomparables. Not even Lady Diana, who is the toast of town, has worn anything to equal it. You will look like a fairy princess."

Martha looked at her friend, then, laying the dress on the bed, she ran out of the room, straight down the stairs and into the library, where she threw herself into her brother's arms. Shelton and Perth, who had been idling in the chairs before the hearth, unobtrusively left. Martha clung to Hurst, too overcome to speak.

"I take it you like the gown, then, my dear," Hurst whispered in her ear. Martha gazed at him with her heart in her eyes. "It's a bit grand for our little church, but I would like you to wear it to the service tomorrow. Did you see the bonnet to go with it?" Hurst's Adam's apple bobbed behind his cravat as he swallowed hard.

"Dear Hurst. Oh, thank you."

* * *

Mr. Willmore's church service bred anticipation in Lady Shelton. Hidden behind the closed door of their bedchamber, Katherine whirled around her husband, chortling, and exclaiming. "It is so right. I feared Hurst had overstepped himself, but it will be perfect. Oh, my dear, it will be a resounding success."

Lord Shelton, accustomed to being made dizzy by his wife's enthusiasms, reached out a hand and gathered the ecstatic dervish into his arms. "Are you so certain now, love?" he asked, nibbling on her ear.

"Yes," Katherine affirmed. "Did you not note the air of sadness that hovers like a miasma around that poor girl? It couldn't be more right. You have my permission to tell Hurst that I approve. What shall I wear?" She skipped from her husband's arms and darted to the wardrobe. "Something romantic..."

"The pink frilly thing with lace on the edges. I like that on you." Shelton leaned against the wall and watched his wife with enjoyment.

"This is the most romantic thing, Alex. I can hardly wait."

Hurst was in the library, his haven from the outside world, lifting a bumper with Sir Perth. His anticipation of the following day did not match Katherine's; Hurst's stomach was in a hard knot and he was willing to wait forever. "What if I am wrong?" he asked.

Perth, relaxed in a deep leather chair, lifted his glass. "Nothin' to worry about, dear boy. You can always flee to the continent."

It was difficult to rub the back of his neck under the layers of neckcloth, but Hurst managed. "You have always been a comfort. I should not have done this," he decided. "It will never work."

"Bit late to decide that," Perth said. "Best go through with it. I'll be noble and throw myself between you and

Martha if she attacks. Worst she can do is bite. But," he took an appreciative sip of brandy, "if it makes you feel better, think you're right. Girl looks pulled. If she were m'sister, would worry about her going into a decline."

Mrs. Jackson was certain she had forgotten to pack the parcel. Turning layers of tissue onto the floor from the small trunk she forbade the maids to unpack, she tumbled out her jewel box. Robert swooped and rescued the walnut case before it fell to the floor.

"Careful Amy, I don't enjoy picking your tiny bits of jewelry from the floor."

Bypassing her husband's disparaging remark, Amelia dug deeper in the trunk and unearthed a miniscule satin-covered box. "Here it is, Robert. Oh, thank goodness I did not forget it after all. It was under my jewel case."

"Of course you did not forget to pack it, my love. I put the parcel in myself."

"She will like it, don't you think?"

His mouth quirked. "It's just the thing, Amy, just the thing."

"I cannot wait till morn. This is the best thing Hurst could have done." Hands on hips, Amelia's mood changed in an instant. "What do you mean, you packed it? I told you, didn't I tell you, I am not going to forget anything. Did you think I would neglect the most important item to be packed?"

Robert winced and she deflated. "I did forget, didn't I?"

"No, you remembered this." He flourished the box. "Like a good general, you know when to rely on your faithful aide, but the strategy is all yours, my love. Masterful choice, you know. It's perfect."

Vera knew nothing. Her fond papa swore she could not keep the secret. Undoubtedly he was wrong; Vera was accustomed to hiding many things, including her unofficial betrothal and an understanding that her friend played pranks because she was puka. Vera hid that secret so well, she'd never told Martha that she had figured it out that last term at school.

She prepared for bed as she always did, kissing her secret miniature of Baron Harris and tumbling under the covers. Oh, if only his mama had not been so difficult, their betrothal would not be a secret. What should she and Martha do tomorrow? Oh yes, Sir Hurst had mentioned a church service. Vera decided to wear her favorite Camelot frock, the one that Baron Harris said made her look like Guinevere. Her smartest dress, the blue crape would show well next to the dress Martha had received from her brother.

Irene Stratmoor knew less than nothing. She performed her nightly ritual, pouring water from the pitcher into the tins under the legs of the bed.

"Every morning that huffy maid removes my tins," she grumbled to herself. "She lines them up on the mantelpiece and mops up the water she spills. Then every night I have to put them back. What a disagreeable house this is." She checked the water level in the last tin. No way were vermin going to climb into bed with her.

Martha was also ignorant. She went to bed in the same manner she had for the last endless months. Tonight it was worse than usual. He was escorting an Incomparable about. Slipping under the covers, she pulled a pillow over her head and cried herself to sleep.

* * *

"Can he not hurry? Everyone else has left. We shall be late and Mr. Willmore will never forgive us for arriving after he begins the service. He insisted we have to attend this church service—now he makes us late," Martha grumbled to the newel post. The wood stood stalwart, rebuking her impatience.

She tapped her toe. "Everyone else left ages ago, but Hurst insists I wait for him. Brothers." The newel, being but a wooden post, didn't answer her disgusted monologue, which made her more cross. "He will ruin his reputation with the vicar. Beyond Mr. Willmore's opinion, how malapropos it is to be behind our guests."

Hurst finally appeared at the top of the stairs and Martha gazed at him with an appreciative eye. Her brother had a fine figure; any lady would be aware of his appeal. Taking the steps one by one, he strutted, aware she watched and putting on a show.

"I see no flaws; may we leave now?" she demanded. Hurst's clothing was immaculate—dark blue coat, white inexpressibles, and an intricately tied cravat. His dark hair was brushed in the most becoming windswept he had achieved in years. The waistcoat—why, that waistcoat was the epitome of a waistcoat—rich brocade, with black pearl buttons like those on her dress.

"Patience, patience. We'll be in time."

"We are late now." Her brother only looked at her; a typical infuriating brother.

"I have not seen that vest before," she relented. "Isn't it grand for Shapwick, Hurst?"

Her brother smoothed a hand over the winter white brocade. "Thought I should match you, little sister," he replied, enjoying in his turn the picture Martha made. "You deserve that your escort match your splendor, Princess."

Martha twirled, her irritation with Hurst's delay evaporating. "Do you like it? It makes me feel like a princess." The silk dress, its white relieved by black pearls gleaming along the neckline and sleeves in an elaborate design that reminded Martha of heraldic devices, had an elegant simplicity that did indeed echo the princess of folk tales. Woven with iridescence, the silk shimmered like a fall of water in the dawn. The maid had swept her hair into a careless knot at the back of her head, with dark tendrils curling down to mingle with the pearls. The effect was one of picturesque romanticism.

"Put a circlet on your head and you'd outshine anyone at Court." Hurst was pleased to note that the air of sadness his sister had worn for so long was eased by enjoyment of the distinctive gown. If only for that, he had to be glad he had done it. Extending his arm, he asked, "Shall we go?"

The ride to the church was accomplished in the curricle, at a gentle pace so as not to disturb Martha's glorious hair. The pace likewise kept dust down; the winter white skirt survived the short journey with nary a speck of dirt. Not a cloud was in the sky and birds chirped in celebration of a perfect summer's day. His sister fretted that they were late, but Hurst enjoyed the tête a tête and prolonged it as long as he dared. Too soon Martha would move on with her life, leaving him a little more alone.

In the village, a cluster of vehicles indicated the church held a large congregation, though few people were to be seen on the street. "Are we late?" Martha wondered. "The vicar will be immeasurably displeased with us if we are."

Hurst consulted his timepiece and shook his head as he opened the church door. "We are in good time, my sweet." In the small vestibule, her dress scintillating in the sunlight streaming from outside, he put his hand out and stopped Martha. The door closed out the distracting light and Hurst adjusted her bonnet, smoothing the hairs disturbed by his action.

"I love you dearly, you know," he said in a whimsical voice. "When Papa and Mama died and I took charge of you, I determined to always act in your best interest. I hope you realize I only do my best. You are the most important person in my life."

His earnestness touched her heart. Martha leaned forward and kissed his cheek. "I love you also." Hurst held out his arm formally. Opening the age-darkened door to the church proper, he began walking her up the aisle. The congregation, standing and facing the nave, turned as one to see who had entered. Martha smiled at a few people, locals of Shapwick she had met during her stay at Whole Place, wondering at the twitters and sighs that ran through the people.

There, crowded into one pew were Sir Perth and Lord and Lady Shelton, Katherine with an odd smile on her face.

A few steps further and she espied the Jackson family gathered in a row. Vera, face aglow, beamed at Martha. At her side, Mrs. Jackson was searching for something.

"Robert, quickly now, help me find it. Martha must carry it, you understand. It shall be something old and borrowed. I pressed forget-me-nots inside for the blue."

"Here it is, my love, tucked in your reticule."

"Bless you, Robert." Mrs. Jackson paused Martha with a hand on her arm. "Here, dear, carry my prayer book." She pressed it into the young lady's hand and kissed her cheek. "With all our love and wishes."

"Thank you." Martha accepted the little book and continued up the aisle on her brother's arm at an absurdly slow pace. Then she turned her head and looked back. "Miss Bridewell is wearing her beaver bonnet—what is she doing here? Bridey stayed at the Manor of the Ashes to chaperone Janice."

She faced forward, puzzled. "Aunt and Uncle Pemberton." Aunt held a handkerchief to her eyes but smiled at her niece, Uncle seemed solemn, stern. Martha's steps faltered and stopped, but her eyes kept moving.

Mr. Willmore, the vicar of Shapwick, stood before the altar, smiling for all he was worth. Standing by him, turned facing her, wearing the most elegant blue jacket and winter white brocade waistcoat, was he. There was no smile on his face; instead he looked anxious, even slightly green. Martha focused on the waistcoat, a twin to her brother's, then raised her eyes back to his face.

He looked so apprehensive, standing there with white roses at his back and Squire Michael at his side. Michael grinned, looking as if he were enjoying every second of the event. Michael's waistcoat was the same as Hurst's and *his*. Confounded, she looked at her brother. Hurst had stopped when she had. Martha could swear he was shifting back and forth on his feet like a small boy caught in an indiscretion.

"You didn't."

"You are to be married today," he bravely replied without a stutter.

Martha stared at him, then turned and stared at Lord Brinston, wearing that wonderful winter white on his waistcoat and green on his face. Ignoring the surge of whispers from the pews, she searched the face of the man she had been missing for close to a year. No emotion was to be seen until one looked at his eyes. Those gray eyes that reflected his soul were stormy, dark, and frightened.

Why was he frightened? She had never seen fear on his face before, not even when he left the manor to chase Mr. Irvine.

Vera called, "This is so romantic, Martha, like a novel. What are you waiting for?"

Mrs. Jackson quavered, "Oh, my dear, perhaps your brother should have explained first."

"Nonsense," Mr. Jackson's voice resounded. "This is quite appropriate. He disappeared. Now he reappears just as mysteriously. Seems right to me, if a tad tardy."

Other voices chorused, offering opinions and advice. "He is such a handsome figure of a man."

"That gown came from Madame Celeste. I am positive of it. No one else would think to use black pearls to pick out the Haverhorn devices."

Martha thought it was Sir Perth who boomed, "What, she made it on time without a timepiece to muddle her mind. Nowhere else to go, nothing to do. The chit has the rest of the day to make him wait, if you ask my opinion. If the meat for the wedding supper is ruined, I'll just eat more of the sweet."

"Oh dear, you don't suppose she is going to leave him at the altar."

"If she does, we will be able to eat out on the tale for years."

In the front pew, Aunt Pemberton was beckoning Martha to continue up the aisle. Opposite her stood a man almost as tall as Brinston, with hair gone gray to match his eyes. He wore the same winter white brocade waistcoat, the same black pearl buttons. Next to him, his hand resting possessively on her shoulder, was a an older version of Lady Coletta, dressed in the height of fashion but holding a prayer book as if a barricade. A rope of black pearls gleamed down her front. Martha's eyes focused on this lady.

The man said, "Don't worry, Miss Dunsmore, the scallywag is not going to disappear again. I rely on you to make him toe the line, but the ceremony should come first."

A spasm flitted across the lady's face. "That will not occur if Miss Dunsmore does not wish it, your grace. As I have told you time out of mind, your opinion is not always dominant. It is up to her if she wishes to marry our son."

"Most irregular," the man rumbled, much as Brinston rumbled. "Can't think why she has come this far only to stop. I told her Brinston will behave. What more can she be waiting on?" Lady Coletta peeked around his shoulder and winked at Martha.

The besieged girl turned to her brother and breathed, "You dastard," took his arm and marched up the aisle. When they stood adjacent to Lord Brinston, she faced him and scanned his face, unaware that the entire congregation held its breath. Brinston gulped and touched Martha's cheekbone, an agitated butterfly caress she felt to the bottom of her feet.

He still looked frightened and Martha did not like that. Her eyes narrowed. *Green is not his best shade*, she thought, looking at his cheeks. Like a dream, echoes of the words he'd said ages ago in the portrait gallery at the Manor of the Ashes ran through her mind. *'Honor me with your trust.'*

Humph. She glanced at the vicar, who seemed to await a signal.

The congregation held its breath.

Brinston looked at the mulish scowl on his pixie's face and knew he had to do something. With an apologetic glance at his sister, he waved his hand and said in a tangle of ancient languages, "Sacred Lady, I call upon she whose waters encircle Avalon and harbor the secrets of Arthur. Take pity on mortal man and his beloved. By the authority of the great Merlin, as you quench the destructive power of fire, halt the ebb of time in this place for the spectators."

Silence fell. Magic shimmered the air like a heat wave as people ceased moving. Coletta's frozen face looked pained. Behind her, another girl unblinkingly ogled Michael, whose arm was stilled reaching into his pocket. The church settled like dust floating to the floor, with time halted.

Nearly halted.

Brinston turned to his pixie. Martha stood with her mouth agape. She looked at him, shook her head.

"You're a wizard?"

"Well, yes and no," he modestly replied. "A magician."

"What did you do?"

"Merely slowed things down. Hope Coletta forgives me; enchanting her gives her a ferocious headache. Martha, I need to talk to you."

Her voice rose. "You couldn't tell me you're a magician? I worried about you, you know."

"I was going to..."

"When you left to catch Mr. Irvine, I *worried.* Then..." Brinston waited. It took his perceptive pixie a moment of sputtering. Little spitfire.

She turned away from him. "If you're a magician, you could have found those papers by magic. You were just toying with me. Merlin, save me from stupid men." She took a step, a step away from him.

Grabbing her hand, Brinston almost hissed in pain. "No! Martha, no." Her eyes were pools of tears.

He pulled her against him, so he wouldn't have to watch the crystal drops rain down her face. "We were all searching. Michael, Coletta, the Jacksons, me and you. Every place you looked, I knew I didn't have to. I trusted your searching to be thorough. You *were* a help. And no, I couldn't find the report using magic."

He took a deep breath and shook her. Her hair brushed his chin like fairy wings on a dewed flower. "It's not easy being a magician. Those who know about it expect me to do everything by magic. It doesn't work like that. It *can't* work like that." His face nuzzled in her hair, pushing the bonnet back on her head so it almost fell off. "I've told only two outside my family, outside the Council of Mages." She stilled, her body relaxing into his. Brinston was afraid to look at her face, but he knew this was his chance to make his pixie understand. He searched for and found the words.

His voice slowed and fell to a whisper. "I was going to tell you. The moment I dropped down on my knees to ask you to marry me, that was when I was going to tell."

"But you didn't come back to me. It was a lie."

"No," he said firmly. "I was unable to come back—Hurst assured me you knew I was held there by Du Lac. And I sent you a note. You were supposed to come to town. What, I was supposed to invite myself to Whole Place?"

Martha stared at the floor, her body turning to ice. He was right. It was the prime rule of society, the glue that kept people from each other's throats. No one invited themselves. They had to wait for an invitation. One she had not extended. Why, oh why hadn't she thought it through?

When she looked up again, ready to grovel, understanding was written on his face. Loving, forgiving, understanding. Her heart swelled. Then a tiny star lit on his nose and she gently brushed it away. His wonderful pewter eyes gleamed like silver.

"Magicians have a betrothal procedure." He lowered to the floor, balancing on one knee, sliding Martha's hands into his. "They get down on their knees..." Martha watched his every move.

He took a deep breath. "They say 'I am a magician' to their beloved." Brinston fastened his eyes on her, compelling his pixie to look at him. Their eyes met. The crystal drops hadn't fallen; they hovered on Martha's lashes. *That's my brave girl.*

The heat wave seemed to coalesce, settling around the two. Time, already slowed near to a stop, seemed to hold its breath. Solemnly, Brinston whispered, "My magic is yours." Then he stood. Tiny stars twinkled in the unfelt heat, leaping around them. They twinkled, then they began to go out, one by one.

Martha glanced at Mr. Willmore, who cleared his throat. The congregation shifted in their seats, murmuring. Someone coughed. The cleric began speaking the timeless words. "We are gathered here today..." Martha paid him little heed, being preoccupied reading the gray eyes turned to her. In their depths, the sturdy truthfulness, the honor that was Brinston's dominant trait, lay like a Roman road, immutable, enlivened by magic dust.

His magic was hers? A tickle ran up her spine. Brinston was a magician, yet he'd given his magic to her. The meaning of it escaped her, but not the feeling.

He'd never done anything to harm her. Not unless she counted the shed, and, to be fair, Brinston locking her in the shed was her own fault. She shouldn't have insisted on capturing Mr. Irvine. Only once Martha had believed she had cause not to trust him. When he left her at the manor and didn't return, she had been sure he was trifling with her. Again, she was at fault for going out of his reach. Maybe she'd been wrong. Always he had sought to protect her, to cherish her. Besides, he gave her his magic. What more could a lady ask?

She softened, remembering all the reasons she did have to trust the man standing before her. It was simple. She would honor him with her trust. Sir Hurst's little gremlin knew that life would be worth nothing without this man at her side. She belonged to him, magic or no magic. And he belonged to her. Tugging his lapel, she turned Brinston to face her.

"What do you mean, 'my magic is yours'?"

"Exactly what I said. It is now your magic, not mine. You will do with it as you please. I am but your vessel."

"You cannot—do as you please?" With his head shake, the meaning of his gift came to her. Magicians held great power, more power than any other person on Earth. Unmagicked, a woman was helpless against a magician. It was a frightening situation to be in. One wrong word, one off look, as often happened between married couples, could mean death, or worse than death, with a magical husband.

But he had given his power, his magic to her. She was in control of his use of magic. Brinston could no longer use magic on her without permission? *Dear Avalon, how much he must trust me to do that.*

She knew he felt her reaction. The fear in the pewter depths diminished, replaced by glowing confidence, until his dearly beloved eyes took on the sheen of silver. She could swear magic dust sparkled in the gray depths, an echo of the stars that had danced for them. That was much better. Let him fear her *after* the ring was on her finger, not before.

The vicar was droning. "Brinston," Martha whispered.

The serenity of a mountain pond reflected in his eyes. "Yes?"

"I have a confession to make." Her toe scuffed the floor. He eyed her quizzically. Behind them, members of the congregation craned necks, curious as to the delay in the service.

Martha darted her eyes over the pews, then turned toward Brinston. "I'm puka," she mumbled.

She really didn't speak clearly. Brinston frowned. "You're what? I couldn't hear you."

"I'm puka," she whispered again, flushing.

"Of course you are." He patted her hand.

"Did you hear me, Brinston? Don't wheedle," Martha stomped her foot. "I told you I am puka. You don't just brush it off." Part of her tirade was lost due to her low voice, but her magician was unfazed.

His voice, as low as hers, held a note that grated her nerves. How else could she explain the chills that ran down her spine and the urge to lean against him? "I don't wheedle. You are Hurst's sister. He's puka. What else would you be?"

"You mean you knew?" Her voice carried clearly throughout the church.

"I have always known. My puka blood comes from my mother."

She was speechless. With nothing left to say, Martha took Brinston's sleeve and twitched, turning him to face the vicar. The congregation let out an audible sigh.

* * *

They lived happily ever after, as Vera's novels always promised; Brinston under the cat's paw, having given his trust and magic to her, and Martha firmly under his thumb, held there by that same trust and the knowledge that she controlled his magic.

"Martha," Brinston bellowed. "What do you mean by reading this book?" He shook a musty old tome in her face. "You know this is my most valuable encyclopedia; you promised to leave it alone. But it was on your desk."

"I did. I mean, I didn't." She looked up from her embroidery frame indignantly.

"Make up your mind, woman."

"I did promise not to read it, Richard."

"You most certainly did. And rather than practicing the pianoforte as you should, you go sneaking into my books."

Martha's nose went into the air. "You deliberately misunderstand. I did promise not to read that book. But I did."

"There. Just like I said, you read my book after you promised not to. Should be clearing out the linen closet or making up nostrums, not disobeying me. One of the maids is going to get the toothache and you won't have anything to give her."

"Nostrums! Oh, Richard, you goose. Don't you recall?" Shooting up, Martha stamped her foot. "You asked me not to read the book and then you requested that I make a fair copy of it so you could put it away safely. And I did."

"I did? You did?"

"Yes, you did and I did. And if you want me to make a nostrum, I'll read it again. Somewhere in there was a receipt for turning toads into stones."

Brinston grabbed Martha by the waist and buried his nose in her hair to hide his grin. "I'm too busy. That's the problem. I forgot." A chortle leaked out. It was such fun to tease his little spitfire.

~The End~

About the Author

A longtime fan of Regency romance novels, Ann Tracy Marr spends her time dreaming of the perfect world—England's Regency era interwoven with the best of King Arthur's Camelot and Merlin's magic. Marr is a wife, mother, and computer consultant, fixing the stubborn beasts and teaching people how to tame them. Her background includes a college major in English and secretarial work, which she thankfully escaped. *Round Table Magician* is her first Regency to be offered with Awe-Struck/Earthling Press. She hopes for more to come.